S0-AVQ-815

THE WARSAW ANAGRAMS

BY THE SAME AUTHOR

The Seventh Gate
The Search for Sana
Guardian of the Dawn
Hunting Midnight
The Angelic Darkness
The Last Kabbalist of Lisbon
Unholy Ghosts

THE
WARSAW
ANAGRAMS

A NOVEL

Richard Zimler

THE OVERLOOK PRESS
NEW YORK

This edition first published in paperback in the United States in 2012 by
The Overlook Press, Peter Mayer Publishers, Inc.

141 Wooster Street
New York, NY 10012
www.overlookpress.com

For bulk and special sales, please contact sales@overlookny.com

First published in Great Britain in 2011 by Constable & Robinson, Ltd.

Copyright © Richard Zimler, 2009

This is a work of fiction. Names, characters, places, and incidents
are either the product of the author's imagination or are used
fictitiously, and any resemblance to actual persons, living
or dead, or to actual events or locales is entirely coincidental.

All rights reserved. No part of this publication may be reproduced or
transmitted in any form or by any means, electronic or mechanical,
including photocopy, recording, or any information storage and
retrieval system now known or to be invented, without permission
in writing from the publisher, except by a reviewer who wishes
to quote brief passages in connection with a review written
for inclusion in a magazine, newspaper, or broadcast.

Library of Congress Cataloging-in-Publication Data

Zimler, Richard.
The Warsaw anagrams : a novel / by Richard Zimler.
p. cm.
ISBN 978-1-59020-088-9
1. World War, 1939-1945–Jews–Poland–Warsaw–Fiction. 2. Jews–Crimes against–
Poland–Warsaw–Fiction. 3. Warsaw (Poland)–History–Fiction. I. Title.
PS3576.I464W37 2011   813'.54–dc22   2011020042

Manufactured in the United States of America
ISBN 978-1-59020-847-2 (pb)
2 4 6 8 10 9 7 5 3 1

DEDICATION AND ACKNOWLEDGEMENTS

For all the members of the Zimler, Gutkind, Kalish and Rosencrantz families – my many granduncles, aunts and cousins – who perished in the ghettos and camps of Poland. And for Helena Zymler, who survived.

I am greatly indebted to Andreas Campomar and Cynthia Cannell for their unwavering support. I also want to thank Nicole Witt, Anna Jarota and Gloria Gutierrez for helping my books find homes in many different countries.

I am particularly grateful to Alexandre Quintanilha, Erika Abrams and Isabel Silva for reading the manuscript of this novel and giving me their invaluable comments. Many thanks, as well, to Thane L. Weiss and Shlomo Greschem.

A number of excellent books about the Jewish ghettos of Poland helped me in my research. Prominent among them are *The Diary of Mary Berg* and Emmanuel Ringelblum's *Notes from the Warsaw Ghetto*.

PUBLISHER'S NOTE

Erik Cohen's original text for *The Warsaw Anagrams* was written in Yiddish, though he occasionally made use of Polish, German and English words. We have maintained a few foreign terms and expressions in this edition, where we believe that they help evoke the flavour of the original or clarify meaning. A glossary is included at the end of the book.

Cohen's manuscript of *The Warsaw Anagrams* was discovered in 2008, under the floorboards of a small apartment in the Muranów district of Warsaw that had belonged to a survivor of the Jewish ghetto named Heniek Corben. According to neighbours, he had passed away in 1963 and left no descendants.

We owe uniqueness to our dead at the very least.

Erik Cohen

PREFACE

I've had a map of Warsaw in the soles of my feet since I was a young boy, so I made it nearly all the way home without any confusion or struggle.

Then I spotted the high brick wall around our island. My heart leapt in my chest, and impossible hope sent my thoughts scattering – though I knew that Stefa and Adam would not be home to welcome me.

A fat German guard munching on a steaming potato stood by the gate at Świętojerska Street. As soon as I slipped inside, a young man wearing a tweed cap drawn low over his forehead raced past me. The flour sack he'd hoisted over his shoulder dripped dots and dashes of liquid on his coat – Morse code in chicken blood, I guessed.

Men and women lumbered through the frigid streets, cracking the crusted ice with their worn-out shoes, their hands tucked deep inside their coat pockets, vapour bursts puffing from their mouths.

In my disquiet, I nearly stumbled over an old man who had frozen to death outside a small grocery. He wore only a soiled undershirt, and his bare knees – badly swollen – were drawn in protectively to his chest. His blood-crusted lips were bluish-grey, but his eyes were rimmed red, which gave me the impression that the last of his senses to depart our world had been his vision.

In the hallway of Stefa's building, the olive-green wallpaper had peeled away from the plaster and was falling in sheets, revealing blotches of black mould. The flat itself was ice-cold; not a crumb of food in sight.

Underwear and shirts were scattered around the sitting room. They belonged to a man. I had the feeling that Bina and her mother were long gone.

Stefa's sofa, dining table and piano had vanished – probably sold or broken up for kindling. Etched on the door to her bedroom were the pencil marks she and I had made to record Adam's height every month. I eased my fingertip towards the highest one, from 15 February 1941, but I lost my courage at the very last second – I didn't want to risk touching all that might have been.

Whoever slept now in my niece's bed was a reader; my Polish translation of *A Midsummer Night's Dream* was splayed open on the ground by the headboard. Next to the book was an empty tin cup that had been filled with ghetto water; on evaporating, the ochre crust I remembered well had been left behind.

Searching the apartment rekindled my sense of purpose, and I hoped that the world would touch me back now, but when I tried to open the door to Stefa's wardrobe, my fingers eased into the dark wood as though into dense cold clay.

What did it mean to be nine years old and trapped on our forgotten island? A clue: Adam would wake with a start over our first weeks together, catapulted from night-terrors, and lean over me to reach for the glass of water I kept on my side table. Stirred by his wriggling, I'd lift the rim to his lips, but at first I resented his intrusions into my sleep. It was only after nearly a month together that I began to treasure the squirming feel of him and his breathless gulps, and how, on lying back down, he'd pull my arm around him. The gentle rise and fall of his slender chest would make me think of all I still had to be grateful for.

Lying in bed with my grandnephew, I used to force myself to stay awake because it didn't seem fair how such a simple act as drawing in air could keep the boy in our world, and I needed to watch him closely, to lay my hand over his skullcap of blond hair and press my protection into him. I wanted staying alive to involve a much more complex process. For him – and for me, too. Then dying would be so much harder for us both.

Nearly all of my books were gone from the wooden shelves I'd built – burned for heating, no doubt. But Freud's *The Interpretation of Dreams* and some of my other psychiatry texts were still there. Whoever was living here now had likely discovered that most of them were first editions and might fetch a good price outside the ghetto.

I spotted the German medical treatise into which I'd slipped two emergency matzos, but I made no attempt to retrieve them; although hunger still clawed at my belly, I no longer needed sustenance of that kind.

Eager for the comfort of a far-off horizon, I took the apartment-house stairs up to the roof and stepped gingerly on to the wooden platform the Tarnowskis – our neighbours – had built for stargazing. Around me, the city rose in fairytale spires, turrets and domes – a child's fantasy come to life. As I turned in a circle, tenderness surged through me. Can one caress a city? To be the Vistula River and embrace Warsaw must be its own reward at times.

And yet Stefa's neighbourhood seemed more dismal than I remembered it – the tenements further mired in shaggy decay and filth despite all our wire and glue.

A voice cut the air with a raucous shout, dispelling my daydreams. Across the street, leaning out a fourth-floor window, a shrivelled man in a tattered coat was waving at me frantically. His temples were sunken and his stubble was white.

'Hey!' he shouted. 'You there, you're going to fall and break your neck!'

I saw a reflection of myself in his shrunken shoulders and panicked gaze. I held up my hand to have him wait where he was, clambered off the roof and down the stairs, then padded across the street.

Up in his apartment, the man recognized that I wasn't like him right away. He opened his bloodshot eyes wide with astonishment and took a step back. 'Hello there,' he said warily.

'So . . . so you can really see me?' I stammered.

His face relaxed. 'Absolutely. Though your edges . . .' He jiggled his hand and tilted his head critically. 'They're not so good – a bit indistinct.'

'And aren't you scared of me?' I asked.

'Nah, I've had visions before. And besides, you speak Yiddish. Why would a Jewish *ibbur* do me any harm?'

'An *ibbur*?'

'A being like you – who's come back from beyond the edge of the world.'

He had a poetic way with words, which pleased me. I smiled with relief; he could really see and hear me. And it eased my worries to have a name for what I was.

'I'm Heniek Corben,' he told me.

'Erik Benjamin Cohen,' I replied, introducing myself as I had as a schoolboy.

'Are you from Warsaw?' he asked.

'Yes, I grew up near the centre of town, on Bednarska Street.'

Puckering his lips comically, he gave a low whistle. 'Nice neighbourhood!' he enthused, but when he flashed a grin I saw that his mouth was a ruin of rotted teeth.

Interpreting my grimace as a sign of physical pain, he came closer. 'Sit, sit, *Reb Yid*,' he told me in a concerned voice, pulling out a chair for me at his kitchen table.

Formality seemed a little absurd after all that we Jews had suffered. 'Please just call me Erik,' I told him.

I lowered myself in slow motion, fearing that I'd fail to find a solid seat, but the wood of his chair welcomed my bony bottom generously – proof that I was getting the knack of this new life.

Heniek looked me up and down, and his expression grew serious.

4

'What?' I asked.

'You faded away for a moment. I think maybe—' Ending his sentence abruptly, he held his gnarled hand above my head and blessed me in Hebrew. 'With any luck, that should do the trick,' he told me cheerfully.

Realizing he was probably religious, I said, 'I haven't seen any sign of God, or anything resembling an angel or demon. No ghosts, no ghouls, no vampires – nothing.' I didn't want him to think I could answer any of his metaphysical questions.

He waved off my concern. 'So what can I get you? How about some nettle tea?'

'Thank you, but I've discovered I don't need to drink any more.'

'Mind if I make some for myself?'

'Be my guest.'

While he boiled water, I asked him questions about what had happened since I'd left Warsaw the previous March.

Sighing, he replied, '*Ech*, mostly the same old misery. The big excitement was during the summer – the Russians bombed us. Unfortunately, the numbskull pilots missed Gestapo headquarters, but I've heard that Theatre Square was turned to rubble.' He lowered his voice and leaned towards me. 'The good news is the Americans have entered the war. The Japanese bombed them a week ago according to the BBC – I've a friend with a hidden radio.'

'Why are you whispering?'

He pointed up to heaven. 'I don't want to sound optimistic – God might pull some more pranks on us if He thinks I'm being arrogant.'

Heniek's superstitiousness would have provoked a sarcastic remark from me in times past, but I'd evidently become more patient in death. 'So where do you work?' I asked.

'A clandestine soap factory.'

'And you have the day off?'

'Yes, I woke up this morning with a slight fever.'

'What's the date?'

'The sixteenth of December 1941.'

It was seven days since I'd walked out of the Lublin labour camp where I'd been a prisoner, but by my count I'd taken only five days to reach home, so I'd lost forty-eight hours somewhere under my steps. Maybe time passed differently for the likes of me.

Heniek told me he'd been a printer before moving into the ghetto. His wife and daughter had died of tuberculosis a year earlier.

'I could live with the loneliness,' he said, gazing downward to hide his troubled eyes, 'but the rest, it's . . . it's just too much.'

I knew from experience that *the rest* meant guilt, as well as more subtle and confusing emotions for which we had no adequate name.

He dropped his nettle leaves into the white ceramic flowerpot he used for a teapot. Then, looking up with renewed vigour, he asked after my family, and I told him that my daughter Liesel was in Izmir. 'She was working at an archaeological site when the war broke out, so she stayed there.'

'Have you been to see her yet?'

'No, I had to come here first. But she's safe. Unless . . .' I jumped up, panicked. 'Turkey hasn't entered the war, has it?'

'No, no, it's still neutral territory. Don't worry.'

He poured boiling water over his nettle leaves in a slow and perfect circle, and his exactitude charmed me. I sat back down.

'Excuse my curiosity, Erik, but why have you come back to us?' he asked.

'I'm not sure. And I think that any answer I might be able to give you wouldn't make much sense unless I told you about what happened to me in the ghetto – about my nephew most of all.'

'So, what's stopping you? We could spend all day together, if you like.'

A mischievous glint appeared in Heniek's eyes. Despite his grief and loneliness, he seemed to be eager for a new adventure.

'I'll tell you a little later,' I replied. 'Being able to talk with you . . . it's unnerved me.'

Heniek nodded his understanding. After he'd had his tea, he suggested we go for a walk. He carried a bag of potatoes to his sister, who shared a two-bedroom flat with six other tenants near the Great Synagogue, then, together, we listened to Noel Anbaum singing outside the Nowy Azazel Theatre. His accordion made the most brilliant red and gold butterfly-shapes flutter across my eyes – a glorious and strange sensation, but one I've gotten used to of late; my senses often run together now, like glazes overflowing their borders. In the end, might they merge completely? Will I fall inside too great a landscape of sound, sight and touch, and be unable to grope my way back to myself? Maybe that will be the way death finally takes me.

Heniek, when I hear the patient hum of the carbide lamp that sits between us, and watch the quivering dance of its blue flame, the gratitude I feel embraces me as Adam did when I told him we would visit New York together. And my gladness at being able to talk to you whispers in my ear: *despite all the Germans' attempts to remake the world, the natural laws still exist.*

So I must tell my story to you in its proper order or I will become as lost as Hansel and Gretel. And unlike those Christian children, I have no breadcrumbs to mark my way back home. Because I have no home. That is what being back in the city of my birth has taught me.

First we will talk of how Adam vanished and returned to us in a different form. And then I will tell you how Stefa made me believe in miracles.

PART I

CHAPTER 1

On the last Saturday of September 1940, I hired a horse-cart, a driver and two day labourers to move me from my riverside apartment into my niece's one-bedroom flat inside the city's old Jewish quarter. I'd decided to leave home before the official establishment of a ghetto because much of Warsaw had already been declared off-limits to us, and I hardly needed a crystal ball to know what was coming next. I wanted to go into exile on my own terms – and to be able to choose who would take over my apartment. A Christian neighbour's university-age daughter and her barrister husband had already moved in.

In my best woollen suit, I walked closely behind the horse-cart, making sure that nothing slipped off into the mud. My oldest friend, Izzy Nowak, joined me, hoping to escape his dispiriting home for a little while; his wife Róża had suffered a stroke earlier in the month and could no longer recognize him. Róża's younger sister had moved in to help take care of her.

While Izzy stooped down to collect leaves painted red and yellow by autumn, he kept me talking so that I wouldn't seize up with despair. I've always lost my voice at the worst of times, however, so after only a block, I had to simply wave him off. Still, my feet kept going – a minor triumph – and after a time, as if through the rhythm of walking itself, an ethereal calm spread through me. As we passed the bomb-destroyed tower of the Royal Castle, though, a group of youths looking for a fight began calling us names. To foil their effort to provoke us, Izzy began singing a popular French song in his wobbly baritone; he and I have protected ourselves with the sound of our own voices since we were schoolboys teased by Christian classmates.

Jews from where we come from learn defensive strategies early, of course.

Along Freta Street, we joined a queue of refugees in our own city. Who knew so many of us had samovars, wicker furniture and bad landscape paintings? Or that a young mother with her small daughter clinging to the fringe of her dress would think of carrying a toilet into exile?

I looked at the faces around me, grimy with dust and sweat, and etched with panic. Sensing that the direction of my thoughts was straight down, Izzy hooked his arm in mine and pulled me forward. On reaching the door to Stefa's apartment house, he took me aside and said, 'Heaven, Erik, is where the most soft-spoken people win all the arguments.'

Izzy and I often try to surprise each other with one-line poems – *gedichtele*, we say in Yiddish, a language in which motherly affection embraces the tiny and insignificant.

'But what becomes of the quiet people in hell?' I asked, meaning here and now.

'Who can say?' he replied, but as we climbed the stairs, each of us lugging a suitcase, he stopped me. Laughing in a joyful burst, he announced, 'Erik, there are no quiet people in hell!'

Stefa intended for Adam to share her bed so that I could have my privacy in her sitting room, but the boy stamped around the kitchen on my arrival and shouted that he was too old to sleep with her. Izzy – the traitor – handed Adam his colourful autumn leaves as a present and fled for home. I sat by my bloated suitcases as though beside two cadavers, soaked with sweat and humiliation.

My niece marched over to me as I fought for calming breaths. Knowing what she was about to demand of me, I threw up my hand to draw a last line she dare not cross. 'It's out of the question!' I bellowed.

Believing that my bluster might trump her son's desperation was the error of a man who had given over the raising of his daughter to his wife. Soon, I'd put Adam and Stefa in tears, and the Tarnowskis had come over to see what all the shouting was about. It was a Rossini opera performed in a grotesque mishmash of Yiddish and Polish. And I was the outmatched villain with his head in his trembling hands.

Sooner or later, you'll make Uncle Erik feel better about everything if you behave like an angel, I heard Stefa whisper to Adam that night while tucking him in, but making the boy responsible for easing me into a life I never wanted only made me embrace my anger more tightly. The irony was that Adam and I had been friends before my move. On weekends, we'd launch paper sailboats at the lake in Łazienki Park, and he'd gabble on about what it was like to be growing up in an era of Hollywood stars, neon lights and automobiles. Smaller than most boys his age, he'd found success as a darter, the incarnation of a little silver fish. I'd given him his nickname, *Piskorz*.

Yet over those first wretched weeks as roommates, even Adam's soft breathing kept me up. I'd sit under a blanket by the window, smoking my pipe and gazing up at the stars, an ache of dislocation in my belly. For how long would I be a refugee in my own city? Strangely it seemed, my thoughts often turned to how Papa would carry a folding chair and a novel to Saski Square when I'd fly my kite. Always that same kindly image of him watching over me would steal into my mind – like a silent film stuck on a single frame. One morning at dawn it occurred to me why: his fatherly caring and gentlemanly manners were representative of a way of life that the Nazis were murdering.

Though that turned out to be only one of the reasons why Papa had come to me . . .

★

One night during my second week in the ghetto, Adam burst up out of a nightmare and began sniffling into his pillow. At length, he crept to me wearing just his pyjama top, shivering, his arms out for balance – an elfin dancer teetering in the moonlight.

He must have kicked off his pyjama bottoms during the night because he had never let me or his mother see him naked of late; his best friend Wolfi had stupidly told him that his knees were knobbly and that the birthmarks on his ankle were funny looking.

When I asked the boy what was wrong, he gazed down and whispered that I didn't like him any more.

What courage it must have taken for him to step within range of the Big Bad Wolf!

I longed to throw my arms around him and press my lips to his silken hair, but I restrained myself. It was a moment of sinister triumph over what I knew was right.

Undone by my silence, he began to weep. 'You hate me, Uncle Erik,' he blurted out.

At the time I was pleased to see his tears and hear the misery in his voice. You see, Heniek, someone had to be punished for our imprisonment, and I was powerless to act against the real villains in our opera.

'Go back to sleep,' I told him gruffly.

How easy it is to lose a hold of love! A lesson that I've learned and forgotten half a dozen times over the course of my life. Still, if you believe I wanted to hurt only Adam, you'd be wrong. And I got my wish, since the chilling shame of that night still clings to me.

Stefa would walk her son to his clandestine school on Karmelicka Street every morning at 8.30, on the way to the factory where she sewed German army uniforms ten hours a day. I'd accompany him home in the early afternoon, since my work at the Yiddish Lending Library ended at one, but he refused to put his hand in mine and would dash ahead of me. At home, he'd slump lifeless into his chair at the kitchen table – the posture of an unhappy combatant in an undeclared war.

I'd make him lunch, which was usually cheese on bread and onion or turnip soup – recipes from my days as a student in Vienna. We still had pepper then. Adam would grind away like a demon, flecking the soup's steaming surface black, then lift the bowl to his mouth with both hands and savour its fire. In fact, he transformed into a fiend around anything spicy, and I once even caught him eating spoonfuls of horseradish straight from the jar, though Stefa would have spanked him if she'd found out.

In the afternoons, he'd play with his neighbourhood gang. His mother had made him swear to stay on our street, since Nazi guards had already shot several children suspected of being black-market couriers, but we now lived on an island of urban caverns and mazes awaiting his exploration, and she had little hope of him sticking to his promise. In truth, he and his friends wandered all over the ghetto.

On stormy afternoons, when he was forbidden to leave the apartment, Adam would sit cross-legged on our bed drawing pictures of animals or practicing his loopy penmanship. Owing to the influence of his Uncle Izzy and his musical mother, he'd often sing to himself, as well. Stefa had begun giving Adam music lessons when he was four or five and had first picked out melodies on her yellowing Bluthner keyboard, which meant that he now had a song catalogue in his head that extended from Zionist anthems like the 'Hatikvah' all the way across the Atlantic to Irving Berlin, though his pronunciation of English was nearly unrecognizable and often unintentionally comic.

On those occasions when I demanded absolute quiet, he'd sit dutifully on our bed and do his beloved mathematics calculations, seeking silent comfort in his own love of precision and detail. I can see now that he tried to tiptoe through those first weeks with me.

Maybe he had faith that I would eventually hear what he couldn't say.

On Saturday, 12 October, the inevitable came, and the Nazis ordered all Warsaw Jews inside the ghetto. The caravan of despair along Franciszka ska Street started at dawn. In the late afternoon, while I was watching from the window in Stefa's room, a Gestapo officer ordered a group of bearded Orthodox grandfathers to remove their prayer shawls and clothes, and do squat thrusts on the street.

'Bastards!' my niece mumbled to herself, but just a few minutes later she assured me we were better off this way.

'You must be joking!' I told her.

'Not at all!' she declared. 'Now we know we can depend on no one but ourselves.'

Heroic words they were, but I could see nothing positive in the panting desperation of those naked old men, much less in my humiliation for not running out to defend them.

Our spirits began to flag badly, so to cheer us up, Stefa invited some new friends of hers over for Sabbath dinner on 25 October: Ewa Gradman, a shy young widow who worked at the bakery in our courtyard; Ewa's seven-year-old daughter, Helena, a watchful little girl whose diabetes had left her with the gaunt cheeks and light-filled eyes of a saint in a Russian icon; and Ziv Levi, a saturnine, pimply seventeen-year-old orphan from Łodź whom Ewa and Stefa had adopted as their pet project. He had just begun an apprenticeship at the bakery and had moved his cot into one of the storerooms.

Ewa baked a sweet-smelling kugelhopf for our party, and Ziv brought along four fresh eggs and a single red rose. The young man presented his gifts to Stefa with such chivalrous formality that Adam started to giggle and I had to chase him out of the room.

As always, our building manager Professor Engal, rapped three times on our door at sundown to indicate the start of the Sabbath.

After our banquet of carp and kasha, Stefa dug a straw hat out of her wardrobe, tilted it at a jaunty angle on her son's head, and whispered in his ear. He grimaced and squeezed out a hesitant *No*, but she replied *For me, baby* in a pleading tone, sat down at her piano and eased into the sugary opening bars of Maurice Chevalier's 'Valentine'.

Cowed by his mother's insistent glare, Adam began to sing. Unfortunately, he was too nervous to find his true voice, which was unstudied but beautiful.

The boy loved music but was terrified of performing; he only felt comfortable revealing his inner life – and his gifts – to those he loved. Stefa sometimes forgot that he wasn't a secret cabaret star like her.

I saw in my nephew's eyes that he was barely treading water, so, after the first verse, I jumped up and shushed him with whirling hands. '*Piskorz*, it's way past your bedtime,' I told him, adding to our guests that we ought to call it a night.

Stefa, furious, looked back and forth between her wristwatch and me. Faking a laugh, she said, 'But you can't be serious – it's only nine!'

'The boy needs his sleep,' I told her. 'And in point of fact, so do I.'

Adam looked at me with a face compressed by fear, his straw hat in his hands.

Stefa jumped up, glaring. 'If you don't mind, Uncle Erik, I'll make the rules in my own home! Especially when it comes to my son.'

'Very well, make all the rules you want – but without me!' I snapped back, and I took a first step towards the coat rack, intending to walk off my anger, but Adam burst into tears and bolted into his mother's room.

I rushed to him, but when I caressed his cheek he turned away from me. I assured him that I didn't want an angel for a nephew. 'Especially since I'm an atheist, and I have no intention of going to heaven,' I joked.

Pity an old man with little experience of children; my attempt at levity only made him cry harder. While I was apologizing to him, Stefa appeared in the doorway, her hands on her hips. 'Now you've done it!' she began. 'As if the boy didn't have—'

'He shouldn't have to sing for me or anyone else!' I cut in. 'You know he doesn't like it.' Hoping to ease the tension between us with a little humour, I added, 'Besides, I think we can do without him singing *chansons d'amour* in Yiddish-accented French, at least till we get a bit more desperate for entertainment.'

'All you do is bully him!' Stefa yelled vengefully. 'You scare him half to death!'

She was right, of course. 'All that ends now,' I told her, and I surprised myself by adding, 'I'm through punishing him.'

Tears welled in my niece's eyes.

'I'm sorry I've been difficult, *Katshkele*,' I told her, using the pet name everyone in the family had for her.

She nodded her acceptance of my apology, unable to speak. I took Adam in my arms and kissed his brow. Stefa eased the door closed on the way out.

Adam and I talked together in whispers, since it made our friendship more intimate. I dried his eyes and spoke to him of the journeys I'd take him on when we got out of the ghetto. New York was the city that crowned his dreams, and he stood on his toes when we talked of riding up to the top of the Empire State Building, showing me how he'd look out across the widest horizon in the world.

Lying with my arm around Adam that night, I saw that my father had been haunting my mind to remind me I was failing his great-grandson. And myself, of course.

CHAPTER 2

I'd come to the ghetto planning to read all of Freud one more time, and eager to write up several case studies, but within two months I'd given all that up. It was strangely easy. As if all I had to do was hop on a tram headed into the countryside instead of the city centre.

One minute, a man can think of nothing but leaving behind seminal works that will be read in London and Vienna for decades, the next he is waiting outside a soot-covered grammar school for his nephew, examining a ripped seam on one of his two pairs of trousers and wondering if he still knows how to use a needle and thread.

Now that Adam and I were friends again, he'd tell me about his day as we walked home from school. He'd start in a cautious monotone, testing my interest, but each of my questions would encourage him to pick up his rhythm, so that his account would soon be zooming downhill at top speed. Sometimes he'd launch himself across a bridge of thought where I didn't know how to follow. His words would whizz past me like honeybees.

To have a buzzing little nephew telling me stories that I didn't have to understand or interpret was to be in a state of grace.

Adam and I soon got into the habit of visiting Izzy after school and having lunch with him. My old friend had had his elegant clock shop in New Town closed by the Nazis and was repairing watches in a dank, dungeon-like workshop at the front of a stationery warehouse on Zamenhof Street. What Adam loved most about our afternoons there was watching Izzy perform lengthy surgery on a watch or clock. The boy would kneel on his chair and lean across the worktable, his chin propped on his fists, entranced by how his uncle-by-affection could tweezer even the most microscopic gears, cogs and springs into place. And bring what was dead to life.

In a way, Izzy became the wizard in the story of Adam's life inside the ghetto. Just as Ziv was soon to become the awkward genius . . .

One Saturday evening in early November, the baker's apprentice stopped by with an alabaster chessboard under his arm and challenged me to a game. As if he was a schoolboy unable to dress without his mother's help, the tail of his white shirt was sticking out and one of his shoelaces was undone. His stiff ginger hair fell sloppily over his ears.

I thought I might have a chance against such an oddball, but within twenty minutes he had taken my queen, both bishops and a rook. Worse, the upstart had chosen his moves with lightning speed, making it nearly always my turn. A few minutes later, he had my king cornered.

When Adam asked how he could play so quickly, Ziv replied, 'I've always been able to think many moves ahead – up to ten or twelve, of late.'

After that, my nephew began to look at the older boy with eager curiosity, and late that night, he trudged over to me from out of his sleep, while I was lighting my pipe at our window, and asked if I thought that Ziv was smarter than other people.

'Maybe, though there are different ways of being smart,' I told him.

'Is that why he's always quiet, and so . . . so strange?'

Sighing, I took his shoulder. 'Wait till you're seventeen, young man, and you'll see it isn't an easy age.'

While he was humiliating me at chess, Ziv had mentioned that

Ewa's paediatrician father had started giving medical check-ups to children in an inter-school chorus. An opportunity for Adam? The boy enjoyed singing as long as no spotlight was on him, and when I asked him the next morning if he'd permit me to talk to the music director, he eagerly agreed.

That afternoon, I found out his name – Rowan Klaus – and paid a call on him at his small office in Adam's school. An earnest young man in his early twenties, he had olive skin and intelligent black eyes – handsome in a mysterious, Sephardic way.

Rowy – as he preferred to be called – told me he'd studied violin at the Vienna Conservatory until the Nazis added Austria to their bag of goodies. He wore a homemade splint on his right index finger, and when I asked him about it, he replied that he'd just returned from a labour camp where the Germans had forced him and twenty other Jewish men to dig ditches along the Vistula. 'The goons knew I was a violinist, so when they decided I wasn't digging fast enough, they held me down and broke it with a hammer.'

Now, he was terrified he'd fall victim to another labour round-up. 'I pay regular bribes, but they don't give out guarantees,' he told me morosely.

Over the next half-hour, Rowy spoke of music as a noble pursuit, emphasizing his opinions with German slang and exuberant hand gestures. Adam would be charmed by him, so I signed the boy up for an immediate tryout, and later that afternoon he successfully warbled his way up and down his solfeggio exam.

He would still have to pass the medical check-up, however.

Dr Mikael Tengmann, Ewa's father, was a cheerful, duck-footed Charlie Chaplin look-alike. In his fifties, the lucky physician still had a crest of wild black hair and a youthful glimmer in his deep brown eyes. He and Ewa lived above a broom-maker's workshop on Wałowa Street, and they'd converted one of the bedrooms into his medical office and the dining area into a waiting room.

The next morning, he weighed Adam and jotted down his height, poked and prodded him in various sensitive places, and listened to his chest with a stethoscope. While he noted down Adam's measurements, I studied the pictures of the Alps on his walls; the deep shadows and surges of sunlit stone made the mountains look like entwined torsos. All but one bore the physician's signature; a small photograph of a white-glowing Matterhorn had been signed, 'To Mikael from Rolf.'

When I asked about it, the doctor replied that he and a university friend had shared what he called 'an interest in how and why we seek out the human form in nature'.

An answer that pleased me. And to my relief, Mikael soon concluded that Adam was healthy – though too skinny – with no sign of scabies, tuberculosis or any other disease he might spread to the other miniature Carusos. Before we left, he went to his kitchen and offered Adam a big jar of horseradish as a present, since the little traitor had told him that he'd eaten the last of our supply weeks earlier and that it was the bland food we forced on him that had sent his appetite packing. Electric with excitement, the boy grabbed the jar and hopped around the room like a kangaroo.

I decided it was time for my nephew to learn English as well, especially since Polish and German no longer seemed to have a future tense for Jews. We started with the lyrics of Cole Porter's 'Don't Fence Me In' and it became the anthem he and I would sing every Sabbath. But they did fence us in, of course, and on Saturday, 16 November, we were sealed inside our Jewish prison. Our universe was reduced to little more than one square mile.

Right away, residents began hoarding flour, butter, rice and other essentials. I bought half a dozen black ribbons for my Mała typewriter just in case I got the urge to put some thoughts down on paper. Prices rose so high that Stefa would sneer at the absurdity of buying potatoes at 95 złoty a kilo or asparagus one stalk at a time for 1 złoty each. And the queues – wrapping around entire city blocks – were worthy of a biblical census day. To buy new shoes for Adam, I waited two and a half hours in one of those dismal Warsaw drizzles that always made my father promise to move us to the desert.

Over that first week, we all came out into the street as though shipwrecked, gazing at the perimeter of brick and barbed wire shutting us in as if someone had written us into a Kafka short story. We had become four hundred thousand outcasts corralled in our own city.

How is it possible? A question that makes no sense now that we know what we know, but at the time astonishment – and unspoken dread – widened nearly everyone's eyes, even the old Hasidic rabbis, who were used to seeing strange and impossible visions descending upon them from out of the firmament of their prayers.

Thankfully, Christians could still come inside with authorization, and Jaśmin Makinska, a former patient of mine, brought us fresh fruit and vegetables – as well as delicacies like coffee and jam – a couple of times a week. She was in her early sixties and worked nearby, at an art gallery just off Market Square. She brushed her hair into an aristocratic crest of white and wore exuberantly feathered hats, which both awed and amused Adam.

Jaśmin visited us for the last time at the end of November. When I opened the door to her, she fell into my arms. Her cheeks and hair were streaked with mud, and her tweed coat was ripped at the collar. Her ostrich-feather hat was in her hand – and ruined.

'My God, what's happened?' I asked, steering her to the sofa.

Jaśmin told us that German guards had discovered half a dozen bars of Stefa's favourite lavender soap in her handbag and had confiscated them. When she'd protested, one of the Nazis grabbed her, threw her down and dragged her into the guardhouse. Adam wasn't in the room, but the terror-stricken woman wouldn't tell us exactly what had happened next.

I went to the kitchen for vodka and came back to find Stefa whispering to Jaśmin while cleaning her cheeks with a towel. When my niece looked up, her eyes were darkly hooded, and I realized then what should have been obvious: the German guard had raped her.

Without Jaśmin's supplies, we would need a good deal of cash to bolster our rations of coarse black bread and potatoes, and I decided to look into the possibility of selling off some of the jewellery and silverware I'd brought with me into the ghetto. Through Jewish smugglers who ventured regularly into what we had begun to call *Sitra Ahra* – the Other Side – I was able to make enquiries at the antique shops and galleries along Nowy Świat in early December. Unfortunately, the owners – friends, I'd once believed – offered only a small fraction of what my treasures were worth. So I held on tight for the time being.

Shortly after that, Adam began foraging with the other members of his gang for chestnuts, dandelion leaves and nettles in the bombed-out lots and abandoned fields throughout the ghetto, turning their afternoons into urban safaris. He usually spent the tiny allowance I gave him on the molasses gloop that passed for candy in our ramshackle Never-Never-Land, though he managed to come home once with half a chocolate cake, earned, he beamed, by teaching a new friend in the chorus to ride a bicycle.

Adam rehearsed with Rowy and the other singers two afternoons a week. Just before Christmas, he also started taking chess lessons from Ziv in the young man's room at the bakery.

The weather had turned bitter cold by then, and it became common to see shivering beggars and even stone-frozen corpses on the street. The German guards must have hated being so far from home throughout the winter, and they started beating Jews at random to keep themselves entertained. In consequence, Adam's extensive wanderings left Stefa in a state of nervous exhaustion. She scolded him often, but he'd simply disappear with Wolfi, Feivel, Sarah and his other friends whenever we left him on his own. By this time, he and his playmates had demonstrated that they were able to avoid the Gestapo and the Jewish police far better than any adult, so after a while Stefa and I stopped worrying ourselves sick.

Still, I began to suspect that he and his friends might be up to no good – maybe even smuggling – when Adam came home late one afternoon smelling like manure.

'Wolfi pushed me into a rubbish heap!' he told me.

By then I'd heard of kids crawling through sewage tunnels to reach Christian territory and offered him a sceptical look.

'It's true!' he insisted. 'You know Wolfi is *meshugene*! And he's getting worse!'

'All right, I believe you,' I told him, since Wolfi was indeed a handful. I took him by the hand. 'Anyway, let's get you clean before your mother comes home or we'll have no peace tonight.'

Mail was still being delivered, though we had to pay weekly bribes to the postman, and a first letter from Liesel reached me in early January. The photograph she sent showed off what she called her 'Mediterranean tan'. Her new friend Petrina had short needles of black hair and watery eyes. Her arm was draped over my daughter's shoulder in a comradely manner, but I could see from the solemn way Liesel looked at her that she had fallen in love.

Liesel had posed that way to tell me what she didn't dare write.

My daughter asked what we needed, so I scribbled a long list beginning with pipe tobacco for me, pepper for Adam and bitter chocolate for Stefa.

Keeping secrets between us seemed pointless now. 'May you and Petrina enjoy a happy life together in the land of Homer,' I ended my letter. 'Inside this envelope is a kiss from your silly old father, who hopes you forgive him.'

For years, I had feared giving up my expectations for my

daughter, but when I posted that letter I felt a lightness of spirit that left me giddy – as if I'd repaired what had been broken. When I later told Izzy about what I'd written to Liesel, he congratulated me – which I knew he would – and I surprised myself by confessing to him that I was only now becoming the father I'd always hoped to be.

That evening, after supper, my nephew and I went for a long happy walk. Our last.

Know this: Adam was a child born under the signs of both the sun and moon. When he was sad, his unhappiness swept over Stefa and me like a desolate wind, turning our spirits to dust. But when he was happy – dancing by himself to a tango on the Victrola, or stretching his little fingers across Bach arpeggios on his mother's piano, or just sitting at my feet multiplying numbers – we were certain we would be able to outlast the Nazis.

CHAPTER 3

Adam carried Gloria home inside a shoebox during the third week of January of 1941, and the lesson I wish she hadn't taught us was that even fairy-light creatures can tilt the balance of several lives.

On lifting the lid off his box, my nephew told his mother and me that the manager of the Roth's Pet Shop had given him the budgerigar free of charge. As to the reason, all the boy had to do was point; Gloria's left foot was a lumpy grey mass hanging by a thread – a textbook illustration of the ravages of cancer.

'God in heaven,' lamented Stefa as she stared at the poor creature, 'what the hell are we going to do with a crippled budgie?'

Gloria limped into the far corner of the box, gamely trying to put some distance between herself and my niece. The bird was pale blue, with a bright yellow beak and slender black and white wings. She'd have been pretty, but her breast was gouged with raw-looking empty patches.

'She can't fly,' Adam informed us glumly. 'One of her wings doesn't work. So I've adopted her.'

'She's going to leave droppings everywhere!' Stefa declared, her hands on her hips.

'She can't leave anything if we don't feed her,' I joked.

The boy glared as if I was a traitor, then stuck out his tongue at me.

I stuck out my tongue back, then tried to pinch his ear, but he ducked away.

'Adam, my darling,' Stefa snapped, and her *darling* was a clue that he'd better run for cover, 'this poor bird is undoubtedly crawling with lice and is going to spread disease, and I want you to get rid of it this minute and then scrub your hands!'

My niece had begun to rely on run-on sentences to outduel her son. Hoping to broker a truce, I said, 'I'll build her a cage.'

'Oh, like you built those lopsided bookcases of yours!' Stefa observed, pointing to my rickety constructions. She showed me that sneer of hers that was like a boot on your chest.

'We'll *buy* a cage,' Adam interjected, and the little imp produced two złoty from his pocket with a cheeky smile.

'Where'd you get those?' his mother demanded, certain he'd become a criminal.

'Gambling on horses!' he shouted. His true wish, perhaps.

'How really?' I asked.

'I do maths homework for Feivel, Wolfi and some of the other kids.'

A few days later, Gloria moved into a conical cage that Izzy made for us out of a wood base and wire spokes. He soldered a swastika to the finial, since provoking Stefa was the key to the vaudeville routine they'd developed over the years.

'Izzy, that's not funny at all!' she told him, which made him grin in triumph.

'What you don't understand, Stefa my sweetheart,' he told her, 'is that madness and magic are inseparable. The swastika will prevent the Nazis from confiscating Gloria when they pass a law against Jewish pets.'

By then, Adam was in love. Gloria's repertoire was limited to eating, chirping, defecating and tearing out her breast feathers in a neurotic frenzy, but my nephew would put her on his shoulder and carry her around as if she were the bewitched form of a princess. When Stefa wasn't home, he'd even sit her on his head. Gloria seemed to enjoy riding on a bouncy perch made of blond hair and smelling of our last bar of lavender soap, but does anyone know what a budgie is really thinking in between meal times?

For Adam, joy had feathers. And after a while, I realized there was something affecting and encouraging about Gloria – maybe because her total, irremediable uselessness was proof that we could still afford at least one luxury.

Adam's chorus gave its first concert on 28 January, at Weisman's dancing school on Pańska Street. A water pipe had burst that morning, and despite some frantic mopping by the organizers, puddles were still scattered around the room.

In the audience were a few friends and acquaintances, including the renowned jazz pianist Noel Anbaum, and Ewa, whom Stefa – ever the matchmaker – had hooked up with Rowy after sizing up the young man at a chorus rehearsal. According to my niece, the two had already had three *extremely successful* dates, and the knowing look she gave me as she pronounced her assessment made it clear just how far they'd already journeyed together.

Soon, the lights flickered for the audience to take its seats. Eight girls and four boys filed up the stairs at the side to the stage, fidgeting and pushing, which made me fear a descent into musical hell. Under Rowy's raised baton, however, the children's faces grew serious, and they harmonized their Bach chorales like brothers and sisters. Closing my eyes, I felt as if I'd stopped hurtling through my own displacement for the first time in months; I was just where I wanted to be. I'd landed.

The first encore was Rowy's own solemn arrangement of '*El Male Rachamim*', which left the more religious among the audience in tears. The second was 'Don't Fence Me In' – Adam's suggestion.

As he took his bows, my nephew looked at me with such adult earnestness that I was overwhelmed with admiration. For the first time, I had the feeling he'd accomplish magnificent things in his life, and I knew then that protecting him was the most important job I could have been given for my time in the ghetto.

The next day, a blistering cold front swept over the city. Adam stumbled around stiff-armed inside two sweaters and his fur-lined coat – a full-fledged member of a corps of Jewish penguins marching through the ghetto to their secret schools. I purchased two stoves powered by sawdust; by now, coal had vanished – hoarded by the Germans. The new stoves proved criminally inefficient, however, and for several nights in a row the temperature in our apartment rose to only seven degrees.

By now, some insidious avian disease had turned Gloria's left eye milky white, and Adam was sure that the cold front was at fault. He moped around whenever he thought of her being summoned to budgie heaven, and nothing we could do could cheer him up.

I started going to bed with a scarf wound around my head into a *Thousand-and-One-Nights* turban. The sheets were ice caves, so to warm them up for my nephew I'd lie on his side of the bed for fifteen minutes, then slide over and summon him under the covers. He'd rush into my arms with his teeth chattering. I held him close all night.

The seventeenth of February 1941, was a Monday. The morning was bitter cold – 14 degrees below zero. Stefa had a sore throat and fever, and she'd developed an acne-like rash on her chest. She finally agreed that Adam could stay home from school. Not that she would join us in taking the day off. She drank down some aspirin and, despite my threats to tie her to her bed, pushed past me to work.

I bundled Adam under a mountain of blankets and, on his insistence, moved Gloria's cage closer to the heater at the foot of our bed. After the cabbage soup I made for lunch, which he and I ate with our gloves on, Adam put on the Indian headdress his mother had made for him out of chicken feathers and announced he was going out.

'The hell you are!' I countered.

'But I'm bored!'

'With only a crippled budgie and a whining nine-year-old as company, you think I'm not?'

He gave me his devil's squint.

'Nice try, Winnetou,' I told him, using his Indian name, 'but the Cohen evil eye doesn't work on other members of the tribe. Go read.'

'I'm sick of reading!' Tears of blackmail appeared in his eyes.

'Look, Adam,' I said more gently, 'when we manage to find some coal, you can go out again.' Enticingly, I added, 'I'll start teaching you algebra today, if you want.'

'Algebra is for stupid people!'

'Then go feed Gloria. She looked hungry last time I looked. And I'm sure she's even more bored than you.'

In point of fact, Gloria looked like she needed a hot bath followed by a couple of shots of Scotch whisky, but then so did nearly everyone I knew.

He sneered at me and started away, so I grabbed him. When he squirmed free, rage surged through me like molten metal and I smacked him on the bottom, harder than I'd intended, knocking him into the cabinets. His headdress tumbled off and lost a feather in front. We looked at each other, stunned, as if a meteor had fallen between us. I slumped down to the floor. My tears frightened him. He wriggled his way on to my lap and told me he was sorry. I whispered that he wasn't responsible, then picked up his headdress. I told him he could go out and play if he dressed as warmly as possible. When he fetched his woollen hat and asked me to put it on him, I made him promise not to leave our street even if Martians landed on the Great Synagogue and asked by name to meet up with him to negotiate a peace treaty.

★

After I realized that the sun had set, I put down my book and looked at my watch: 4.27 exactly. I'll never forget that time.

Adam had been gone more than two hours. I left a note for Stefa on her bed saying I was out looking for him and tacked another note to the front door, telling Adam to fetch the spare key from Ewa at the bakery if he got home before me.

Adam wasn't on our street, and I couldn't find him in any of the weedy lots he usually played in, so I went to Wolfi's parents' apartment, but my knocks went unanswered. I managed to locate Feivel and two of Adam's other friends, but they hadn't seen him. The local shopkeepers all shook their heads at me.

On the way home, I pictured how I'd find Adam warming his hands by our heater, with Gloria crowning his head. I'd tell him I'd never let him out of my sight again, which was the moral to this story as far as I was concerned.

But the apartment was empty. To calm myself, I took the last of my supply of Veronal. I'd have kept trying Wolfi's parents, but the Nazis had turned off our telephones by then.

When Stefa arrived, she was furious with me for letting her son leave the apartment. Despite her fever and my pleading, she marched out to find him.

Adam's clothes were always strewn about our room, so I gathered them up. As I was folding his pyjamas, I held the flannel top over my face and breathed in the lavender scent of him. The panic that gripped me was like drowning.

I put his clothes away in his chest of drawers, then made onion soup for supper. When the meal was prepared and the table set, I sat with his sketchbook and traced my fingers over his drawings of Gloria till my fingertips were smudged blue and yellow.

In one of his sketches, he'd drawn Gloria with a long brown pipe in her beak and a scruffy grey tuft of feathers on her head. I stared at the page, trying in vain to dispel the nightmares my mind was scripting: Adam beaten by a Nazi guard, run down by a horse-cart . . .

Stefa came home alone shortly after midnight. Her eyes were ringed by pouches of worry. 'He's vanished,' she told me, dropping down next to me on my bed. Panic hovered around her like a cold mist.

I rubbed warmth into her hands. 'Listen, Katshkele, did you speak to Wolfi?'

'Yes, but he doesn't know anything.'

'Adam probably snuck out to Christian Warsaw and couldn't make it back tonight.'

'Has he been smuggling?'

'I don't know for sure, but I've heard that many kids his age are. He probably lost track of the time, and it gets dark so early now. He must be in hiding till morning. You'll see, he'll turn up here first thing tomorrow. He's smart – and resourceful.'

I'd practised that little speech until I believed it. And by promising to go out again and look for Adam, I was able to get Stefa to eat some hot soup.

A man clomps through empty streets as if through his own childhood fears, searching across curtained windows and mounds of snow for a way to travel back in time. *Take me instead.* The words whispered by all the parents of missing children. And even by granduncles, I was learning.

A Jewish policeman whose breath smelled of mints stopped me on Nalewki Street. When I explained why I was breaking the curfew, he said matter-of-factly, 'Kids go missing every day. Just go home and wait till morning.'

'I can't,' I told him.

He told me that I'd be arrested by the German guards if they spotted me. I walked away from him before he could finish his warning.

I thought it was just possible that Wolfi had lied to Stefa to protect Adam, so I headed to his apartment again. A stinking smell was now coming from the courtyard, and I traced it to a pushcart stored there for the night that must have been loaded with rotting fish during the day. Two bony, desperate-looking cats were tied to one of the wheels, and they stared up at me suspiciously from what looked like a mush of entrails and rice. One of them hissed. I guessed that they were there to keep away rats.

Wolfi's father answered my knocks in his bare feet and pyjamas, but wearing a woollen coat. Mr Loos was a carpenter from Minsk with coarse, powerful hands, each finger as thick as a cigar. When I told him Adam was missing, he embraced me. For just an instant I went limp in his arms, as if I were a child myself.

After stealing into Wolfi's bedroom, he carried the boy out to me still asleep, setting him down gently in an armchair of faded brocade. Mrs Loos kissed him awake. The boy gazed up at me with drowsy, blinking eyes. I kneeled to be less threatening.

'Adam's gone missing,' I told him softly. 'So even if he made you promise not to say a word to anyone, you have to tell me if you saw him yesterday.'

'Just . . . just for a minute,' he stammered. 'Outside your apartment house.'

'Thank God. What time?'

'I'm not sure. Maybe one-thirty or two.'

Mr Loos brought me a chair. I sat down and leaned towards the boy. 'What did he tell you, Wolfi?'

'That he was going to buy some coal. And not . . . not to let you or his mother know.'

'What else did he say?'

'That Gloria was freezing to death.'

I hung my head; I should have known that Adam would act recklessly to save her. 'Do you know where he was going to buy the coal?' I asked.

'No, I'm sorry.'

'Listen, son, I'm not angry. But you must tell me if you have any idea where he might have gone.'

'Just one.'

CHAPTER 4

Wolfi explained to me that the apartment house at 1 Leszno Street shared a cellar with a building on Rymarska Street, in Christian Warsaw. Passage across the clandestine border cost five złoty, payable to a guard. Poles carrying goods into the ghetto put on the Jewish armbands with the Star of David that we were forced to wear. Jews heading the other way removed theirs.

Adam had crossed the cellar only once that Wolfi knew about. He'd been paid ten złoty to smuggle out an ermine jacket and bring back a mahogany jewellery box from an antique dealer living near the university. He'd told Wolfi that he had been chosen because of his blond, Aryan looks, which made him less likely to be arrested. That had been about a month before. Wolfi didn't know who'd hired Adam or the identity of the dealer. But he added that my nephew had been given half a chocolate cake as a reward for executing his mission so quickly.

It had begun to snow – big soft flakes falling atop the wild panic throbbing inside my head. At 1 Leszno Street, I rapped at the front door until the light went on in the caretaker's apartment.

'Stop that goddamned banging!' he hissed.

He opened the front door a crack. 'What's the problem, old man?' he demanded. A blanket was drawn across his shoulders and he carried a candle in his fist. As he moved the flame towards me, to better see my face, his shadow seemed to fold around us.

36

I recognized him: Abramek Piotrowicz, the attorney; his daughter Halina had been a high-school friend of Liesel's.

'It's me, Erik Cohen,' I told him.

'Erik? My God, I wouldn't have recognized you! But you look pretty good,' he rushed to add, so as not to offend me.

When we shook hands, Abram tugged me inside and said, 'Get out of that damn wind!' He shut the door and scoffed. 'This weather . . . I'm going to Palestine as soon as we get out. And I'm never coming back!'

I explained the reason for my visit and described Adam, but Abram told me he hadn't seen any boy fitting his description.

'In that case,' I said, 'I'll need to question the guard who was on duty yesterday afternoon.'

'His name is Grylek Baer,' Abram replied, adding that he'd be back only at 1 p.m. 'But I'll get word to him at dawn. Leave it to me. Let's speak in the morning.'

I found Stefa still up when I returned home, seated in the kitchen over half a bowl of cold soup. It was 1.40 a.m.

Two condemned prisoners wait for sunrise. The man slumps into his chair by the window, where he can watch a dark street emptied of life. Later, when the sky clears, he steals glances up at a dome of stars that seems too distant to provide any orientation to him or anyone else.

Our exile will never end he thinks. He lets his pipe go out and his feet grow numb.

The woman sits on her bed, one hand on a homemade birdcage she hates, staring into the milky eye of all she has ever feared.

At dawn, Stefa disregarded my pleading and headed for Leszno Street. I waited at home in case Adam made it back to us. Just before eight, three sharp knocks on the front door made me drop the book I'd forgotten I was holding.

Two men stood on the landing, the shorter one in the black

uniform and cap of Pinkiert's, the ghetto funeral service. The other, tall and distinguished-looking, held his hat in his hands.

'My nephew . . . have you found him?' I asked in a rush. Inside my voice was our future – Adam's and mine.

'Are you Dr Erik Cohen?' the Pinkiert's man questioned.

'Yes.'

'We found your nephew's body at dawn. I'm sorry.'

I don't remember anything else from our conversation. Maybe it was as we walked down the stairs to the street that the men told me how Adam had been identified by a secretary in the Jewish Council who was an acquaintance of Stefa's. Or maybe they told me that only later. My next memory is of standing outside our apartment house. The Pinkiert's cart – wooden, drawn by a brown mare – was shrouded in shadow. The undertaker – a slender man with a pinched face – spoke to me in a kind voice about catching a chill and did up the buttons on my coat. But I wasn't cold. I didn't feel anything but the sense that I'd been tugged far out to sea and would make it all the way back to land.

A single trauma can cripple a person for ever, and when I saw Adam lying in the back of the cart, I knew my life was over.

A coarse blanket covered his body but left his face exposed. It was turned to the side, as if he'd heard someone call out from the left just before death. His eyes were closed and his hair was mussed. His skin was pasty and yellowish.

Was it then that the Pinkiert's man told me how he had been found?

I climbed into the cart and kneeled by my nephew. The dark gravity of all that had gone wrong drew my lips to his. The stiff chill of our kiss made me shudder.

I took out my handkerchief and started wiping the grime off his face. I whispered, *You're home now*, as if he could hear me – and as if that news would comfort him.

Whatever made Adam Adam is gone, I thought.

Six small words, but they couldn't fit inside my head. They spilled out of me inside a hopelessness so deep and wide that it might have been everything I'd ever felt or thought.

As my craving for him to wake up dripped down my cheeks, I apologized to him. I didn't want him to think he'd done anything wrong; a child shouldn't meet death with guilt in his heart.

I intended to embrace the boy and carry him upstairs, but when I lifted his blanket away, I gasped; he was naked, and his right leg had been cut off from the knee down.

CHAPTER 5

The universe was turning around Adam's missing leg, and I was freefalling through a life that seemed impossible. Do you know what it's like to see a mutilated nine-year-old? You realize that anything can happen: the sun may blacken and die before your eyes; a crack may open in the earth and swallow the street . . . Each heartbeat seems proof that all you see and feel is too improbable to be anything but a dream.

A mad revelation: Adam's death and the fate of the Jews were linked. I stitched that conclusion together out of my panic, wondering how many months were left to us.

I looked frantically around the cart for what had been cut from Adam, as if my heart were on fire. 'What have you done to my nephew?' I demanded of the undertaker.

Talking to you, Heniek, helps me recall details I'd long forgotten. I see now how the tall man who'd knocked on our door stepped in front of the undertaker to answer my question. In his white scarf and black trilby, he looked like the ghetto's answer to Al Capone. He introduced himself as Benjamin Schrei and he told me he was a representative of the Jewish Council. 'Why don't we go up to your apartment, where we can talk calmly,' he suggested.

'Calmly?' I bellowed. 'Do you really think I can talk *calmly* at a moment like this?'

I tugged my arm from his grasp. He showed me a hard look, as though he'd already concluded I was going to be difficult. Leaning close to me, he whispered, 'The Jewish police found Adam in the barbed wire by the Chłodna Street crossing. The Germans must have discarded him there in the night. We cut him free. We need to talk.'

I assumed the police had been unable to extract Adam from the greedy metal coils without cutting off his leg. Of course, snipping the barbed wire would have been easier and quicker, but any Jew who attempted that would have been executed by the Nazis for tampering with our border.

Maybe I flinched on picturing what had happened, because Schrei's face softened and he said, 'I'm sorry to have to talk of such matters.'

Was his sympathy genuine? In those first few hours after Adam's death, everyone seemed to be reading lines in a play.

'Give me five minutes and then I'll talk with you,' I told him.

Heniek, could you have left Adam lying next to you without touching what had been done to him? You look away, as though to say I've no right to ask you, but all I mean to say is that I had to know the shape and scope of what had happened.

I reached slowly under the blanket. His skin was hard, like rawhide, and when a sharp edge jabbed into my palm – bone – I jerked my hand back. Sickness lodged in my gut, then rose into my chest, and I leaned over the side of the cart. Afterwards, I drank water out of a tin cup handed up to me by a neighbour.

Looking around at familiar faces in the gathering crowd, I wanted to vanish, but I also wanted to stay in the cart for ever, so that I wouldn't have to rejoin my life.

Each passing day would now lead me further away from my nephew. I didn't think I'd survive the growing distance between us.

I'll never measure Adam's height again.

So many *nevers* came to me that first day, but I remember that one most of all.

Adam's right arm was scratched from the sharp metal and twisted at nearly a right angle, the way it must have dangled when he was discarded. His left knee and foot were bent to the outside. His hands had formed fists, but when I tried to uncurl one of them, I heard a crack and stopped tugging.

He must have fought back. I imagined him punching and kicking, and shouting my name.

The death of a child is a single event, but the memory of it expands to cover a lifetime. Nothing I'd ever done – not even as a young man – was free of his loss: not my schooldays with Izzy, not my marriage, not Liesel's birth.

Ewa appeared out of nowhere. Later, she told me she rushed out to the street when she heard a shriek, but I don't remember any shouting. Nearly everyone on our block had known Adam since he was a baby; one of them must have let out a cry on seeing him.

Ewa began to wail. Women neighbours rushed to her. I must have entered their group at some point or summoned her to me. I must have asked her to find Stefa and told her where she had gone, but I don't recall any of that.

Had I thought of our exile into the ghetto as a dream and interpreted it correctly, I'd have lived more cautiously, since I'd have known they moved us on to an island to make it easier to steal our future – and to keep the rest of the world from knowing. I ought to have been among the first to understand!

And I should have guessed that Adam would race across all the forbidden bridges in the world to save Gloria.

I will have to warn Stefa not to lift his blanket or she will be as damned as I am.

When I saw my niece running towards me, I put my hand atop Adam's head, because his hair was the only part of him that was still soft, and I was terrified I'd forget its silken feel, and I knew I'd have to give up possession of him to his mother now.

Stefa crept forward, hugging her arms around her chest. She looked at her son and then at me with a puzzled expression, as though asking me to explain a great mystery. She didn't cry. She was enveloped by a dark spell of silence. Her nose was running and her eyes were red. She was panting.

Ewa helped her up into the cart. Stefa kissed my brow and squeezed my hand. It was unlike her to express her affection so openly, but I didn't think of that till later.

Taking off her mittens, my niece brought Adam's hand to her cheek, then put it over her mouth and pressed her lips to his palm. She stepped his fingertips over her closed eyelids, and that's when her first tears came, along with a choking sound.

'Stefa . . .' I began, but my niece's moans covered my words.

When she embraced Adam, his blanket slid down to his waist. I had to tell her now not to look any lower, but my voice had been swallowed by the terrible strangeness of this moment – the sense that the entire future of the earth and heaven was turning around what was taking place here.

Stefa rocked Adam back and forth as if he were a baby. When she reached down to lift the blanket over his chest again, she saw what had been cut from him and began to howl. The sound was like an animal having its womb cut out.

CHAPTER 6

I'd put Stefa's woollen hat back on her head, but she was still shivering as though she'd fallen through the ice of a winter lake. She agreed to talk with Mr Schrei, the Jewish Council's representative, on the condition that her son remain covered and guarded until we'd agreed on funeral plans. Ewa helped me prop up my niece as we trudged upstairs. On our landing, she began coughing as if her lungs were packed with grit.

Behind our closed door, I sat my niece on the bed and smoothed a shawl over her legs, then brought her a cup of the coffee I'd made earlier, lacing it with a little vodka, but she kept her hands knitted together and refused to touch her drink. She bent her head over her lap like an old widow curled around her loneliness, protecting herself from a world where she no longer had a home.

I think she had already vowed that her thoughts would never leave her son again – and was on strike against a world where a child could be murdered.

I took Adam's Indian headdress off our faded leather armchair – I'd been planning to sew on the fallen feather – and invited Mr Schrei, who'd been standing by the door, to sit. Ewa brought him coffee. Taking a first sip, he leaned back with a long sigh, hoping, I think, to convince us of his exhaustion, which irritated me until I realized how awkward this must have been for him. I sat up as straight as I could to fight the urge to hide, and I tried to fill my pipe, but my hands proved too clumsy. Ewa leaned back against the windowsill, watching Stefa with motherly concern. She kept

44

the loop of her amber beads in her mouth. When our eyes met, she shook her head as if to say, *I'll never believe it.*

Mr Schrei told us that Adam must have been grabbed by the Nazis outside the ghetto and executed. 'They tossed him into the barbed wire because they intended for us to find him,' he said authoritatively. 'I expect his death was a message.'

'A message about what?' I asked.

He leaned forward, his hands propped on his knees. 'As a reminder of what's in store for kids caught smuggling – a deterrent, if you will. The Germans have recently begun exercising pressure on the council to curtail illegal commerce. I believe that's why they . . . why they cut off Adam's leg – to frighten us into passive acceptance of our fate.'

'But I thought that was the only way the Jewish policemen could free Adam from the barbed wire.'

'I'm sorry if I gave you that impression. In point of fact, Adam was found that way.'

I looked at Stefa. Her lips and eyes were shut tight, and she was swaying gently from side to side, as if imagining Adam in her arms. I wanted to be alone with her, and for night to fall quickly. In the darkness, floating free of all our previous expectations, my niece and I just might find a way to talk to each other that could be meaningful. Maybe she, at least, could find a way forward.

Ewa's hesitant voice broke the silence. 'Mr Schrei, how . . . how did the Germans execute him?'

'I'm not certain,' he replied. 'There are no other injuries that our doctor could see.'

'We'll have to find out,' I told him.

'Why?' Stefa asked, opening her eyes.

'I think we ought to know what the Germans did to him,' I told her.

'It makes no difference now,' she observed. Gazing down, she added, 'I don't want anyone but me to touch Adam.'

I knelt by her. 'No one will touch him,' I assured her, but I already knew I was lying, and I silently asked for her forgiveness.

My niece pressed her hand to my cheek by way of thanks, then took off her muffler and placed it neatly on the bed behind her. Her gestures – overly precise – gave me gooseflesh.

Perspiration had glued her hair to her neck. I reached up to remove her hat, but she stilled my hand. 'No! I have to keep my thoughts inside!' she said sharply. Anxious to flee from my intrusion, she got to her feet and took a deep breath. I stood up beside her but didn't dare touch her. 'I need to boil some water,' she said. With a quick look at Ewa, then at Mr Schrei, she added, 'Please excuse me.'

After a first step, her eyes rolled back in her head and she crumpled. I caught her, and Ewa helped me lay her on the bed.

I pressed a cold compress to Stefa's brow and called her name softly. As she came round, Mr Schrei fetched a glass of water, and Ewa held it to her lips. My niece drank in tiny sips, gazing around the room, surprised to find herself at home.

Ewa helped her sit up. 'Come, I'll put you to bed now,' she said.

'No, please,' Stefa pleaded, her brow ribbed with worry. 'Take me to the kitchen.'

'She needs air,' I observed. 'Sit by the window, Stefa. I'll open it a crack. You need to sit quietly for a few minutes.'

'No, I need two towels – one small, one large. Uncle Erik, bring them to me from my wardrobe . . . the bottom shelf.' She pointed to her room.

I understood what she intended, but Ewa must have showed her a puzzled look; Stefa took her hand and whispered, 'I need to wash my son and make him ready for . . . for . . .'

She stopped there, unable to say the word *burial*.

While Ewa led my niece into the kitchen, Mr Schrei stood up. Stepping to the mirror by my desk, he put on his hat and tilted it at a stylish angle. I could see he was proud of being handsome, and

I imagined it would be difficult for him to grow old. Like me, in other words, though I'd been vain without the benefit of good looks. Turning to me, he said, 'Please accept my condolences and those of the council.' At the door, he added, 'Just one more thing. We would be most appreciative if you were to refrain from speaking to anyone about your nephew's missing leg. It could create problems. Please tell your niece and the other woman. I'm sorry, I don't know her name.'

'Ewa. What kind of problems?' I started filling the bowl of my pipe again; I was desperate to smoke.

'You know how superstitious some of the rural Jews are, about burying a body that's incomplete . . . forced to walk the earth as disembodied spirits and all that rubbish.' He rolled his eyes at the very notion. 'Spreading news of what's happened could cause panic. And since this is an isolated case, it's best if we just . . . well, I think you know what I mean.'

'No, actually I don't,' I told him.

'A little discretion will go a long way in keeping things under control,' he observed.

When he shook my hand to take his leave, I snarled, 'Do you really believe that *keeping things under control* is of any importance to me now?'

Outside, the undertaker, whose name was Schmul, told me that I would need to go to Pinkiert's headquarters to pre-pay the funeral. And that he really ought to get going. I gave him five złoty to have him stay with us until Stefa had had a chance to wash her son. He helped me carry Adam into the courtyard. Then I took a couple of swigs from the vodka bottle I'd carried downstairs, put on my reading glasses, kneeled beside my nephew and adjusted the blanket so that it concealed only his face. You see, Heniek, I had only one purpose left.

CHAPTER 7

Adam was badly scratched from the barbed wire, particularly on his belly and chest, which was where he must have been gripped by the coils. But none of the scratches were bloody, which seemed to indicate that he'd been dead for an hour or so – with his veins and arteries dry – before being discarded.

I was unable to find any bullet hole or puncture wound, but button-sized, reddish-brown bruises marked the skin over his ribs, all of them between the sleek rise of his right hip and his sternum: a handprint.

I conjectured that the largest corresponded to where a thumb had pressed down, and I tried to match my fingertips to the marks but couldn't quite spread my hand far enough. Whoever had severed Adam's leg had been almost certainly a man, and probably larger than I was.

The killer – or his accomplice – must have used his left hand for leverage while he sawed with his right. To have made such deep bruises, he'd have to have pressed down hard on the boy's chest.

When I imitated what I imagined he'd done, a small shift inside Adam, like a latch opening, made my heart tumble. Leaning down and pressing again, I heard a click – a rib was broken.

I closed my eyes to keep from being sick again. I realized that whoever took Adam's leg must have leaned over the boy hard enough to crack bone. Why the need to apply so much force? Perhaps his saw had been dulled by age or overuse, and he'd required leverage to cut through bone. Or maybe he had worked in feverish haste and had been careless – either because he risked being spotted or disliked what he was doing.

Had a Nazi ordered a Polish Christian or even a Jew to mutilate Adam?

Anguished by the sweaty confinement of my clothing, I wriggled out of my coat and threw down my hat. Knowing what I had to do next, I gulped down the rest of my vodka.

Peeling the blanket off Adam's face, I discovered a tiny cut on his bottom lip. A scrape from the barbed wire? With the tip of my finger, I touched it, then gently prised his lips apart. The end of a white string was caught between his teeth. Holding my breath, I pulled at it but it wouldn't budge.

I couldn't risk breaking his jaw or scarring his lips. I covered Adam's face and asked Schmul how long it would take for the boy's body to become malleable again.

'Up to three days,' he replied.

Stefa was more religious than I was and would never wait that long to bury Adam, which created a dilemma. 'I need for you to get a message to a friend right away,' I told the undertaker, handing him all the złoty I had left in my pocket, which he refused, saying I'd given him enough. I told him where to find Izzy and what to say to him.

Stefa might appear at any moment, so as Schmul headed off, I turned my attention back to Adam. I could find no bloodstains on his belly, chest, or behind, which was another indication that whoever disfigured him had let the boy's blood coagulate before starting his work. Yet the murderer or his assistant hadn't waited very long, for if he had, the capillaries on Adam's chest wouldn't have released any blood at all on being pressed and no bruises would have been visible.

Of course, it was possible that Adam had been mutilated right after being killed and had bled profusely but had been carefully washed afterwards. Yet it seemed unlikely that anyone would spend so much time cleaning a Jewish boy soon to be discarded.

A right-handed man – larger than me – who worked as fast as possible because he disliked what he had been made to do or feared being caught.

By now, the vodka was starting to turn my thoughts to mist, so I eased my head back on to the flagstones. And amidst the ceaseless flow of clouds, I saw that Adam's murder had taken away my terror of death; nothing worse could ever happen to me.

Izzy and Schmul helped me up when they arrived.

'Any sign of Stefa?' I asked.

'None,' Izzy replied. 'You want me to check on her?'

'No, don't go. If she hasn't come down yet, it's because Ewa managed to convince her to try to get some sleep.'

When I told Izzy what I wanted him to do, he shook his head and held up a hand between us like a shield. 'I'm sorry, Erik, I can't – it's impossible.'

'Please, look at what they've done to Adam. We need to find out what happened.'

After I pulled the blanket off the boy, Izzy reached behind him for the stability of a wall that wasn't there and nearly tumbled over. We looked at each other across fifty years of friendship; two old men realizing there were no words in any language to describe a loss – and crime – like this.

I held him while he cried. The way he shook pushed me deeply into the past.

He brought me into the present again by standing back from me and wiping his eyes. 'Erik, I don't think I can touch him,' he told me.

'Please, Izzy, it has to be someone who loved him. I can't let anyone else do this.'

He lifted his hands to explain himself, then lowered them, hopeless.

'No one else will be as careful as you,' I told him. 'I need you more than I've ever needed anyone.'

Sitting on the ground, he took a tiny pair of tweezers from the small leather case he'd brought with him, then turned to me. 'For pity's sake, Erik, don't watch me.'

Schmul and I waited in the hallway of Stefa's building. Izzy soon came to us with a two-inch length of white string pinched in his fingers. It bore no traces of blood.

'Any idea where it's from?' he asked, dropping it into my palm. 'None.'

'How do you suppose it ended up in Adam's mouth?'

'Maybe whoever killed him put it there to tell us something about himself,' I theorized. 'A kind of calling card.'

'You think a Nazi is challenging us to find him?'

'Maybe. Though it's just possible that Adam managed to secretly put the string in his mouth – knowing it could somehow identify who did this. He was a smart boy.'

Schmul had overheard us. 'But Dr Cohen,' he said, 'what about his leg? What does that mean?'

'That? That means whoever did this is not like you or me,' I replied, 'or anyone we've ever met.'

Stefa and Ewa came to the courtyard a few minutes later, carrying towels, soap and a bucket of hot water. My niece's eyes were so red that they might have been bleeding.

'I'll go to Pinkiert's and organize everything,' I assured her. 'But first tell me if you were able to find out anything at 1 Leszno Street.'

'I don't understand,' she replied.

'At the place where Adam may have crossed over. Had anyone seen him?'

'No.'

I left for Pinkiert's headquarters, which were next to the Jewish Council building on Grzybowska Street, and scheduled a funeral for the next morning at 11 a.m. At 1 Leszno Street, Abram

Piotrowicz invited me into his apartment and repeated to me what he'd told Stefa at dawn: the guard, Grylek Baer, hadn't seen Adam the day before.

'Then I'll need a list of secret border crossings,' I told Abram.

'Grylek will help. I'll have someone bring the list to you this afternoon.'

'And ask him if he knows who hired Adam to smuggle out an ermine jacket.'

I managed to speak to all of Adam's neighbourhood friends that afternoon. Wolfi swore that he knew of only the Leszno Street crossing, but Sarah, Felicia and Feivel were able to give me the locations of four other places where my nephew might have snuck out. The little mop-haired boy wrung his hands like an adult when we spoke, and through his tears of misery, he bravely confessed that Adam had twice accompanied him 'overseas', which made me realize that my nephew had led a double life. Speaking to me with his stunned mother standing behind him, Feivel explained that they'd wanted to steal food, but their nerve abandoned them at the last minute and all they managed to get were handouts of bread and jam from shopkeepers. I kissed the top of his head to reassure him that I wasn't angry. Still, the mind can be cruel; I wished that he'd died instead of my nephew.

I showed a photograph of Adam to the guard on Krochmalna Street where he and Feivel had passed through to the Other Side, and though he remembered my nephew, he hadn't seen him in weeks. At the other crossings, no one recognized the boy. I received only one lead: at the last place I tried, the cellar of a dingy restaurant, a tough-looking teenaged smuggler named Marcel suggested I make enquiries at a warehouse on Ogrodowa Street where a tunnel leading to the sewer system had been dug. 'The passageway is so cramped that only kids can squeeze through,' he noted. 'Try to speak to the owner, Sándor Góra.'

I remembered the time Adam came home stinking and thought I now knew why.

As I neared my destination, four youths standing on the roof of an apartment house on the Christian side of the ghetto wall began calling me names and throwing stones at me. Only a moment after I started to run, I took a blow on my shoulder that brought me down to one knee.

The hooligans shouted – laughing – that I made too easy a target. Luckily, nothing seemed to be broken, and my anger gave me strength. Getting to my feet, I rushed on with my coat shielding my head until a woman coming the other way was hit. Shrieking, she toppled sideways, crashing on the pavement.

'Die, Jew-bitch!' one of the louts yelled at her in Polish.

Kneeling, I took out my handkerchief and staunched the blood spilling from a deep gash below her ear. A fist-sized chunk of cement lay beside her. She was dazed from the impact. Getting her breath, moaning, she said, 'I think my collar bone is broken.'

Polish meteorites continued crashing around us. I held my coat over the woman's face. 'Can you stand?' I asked, wanting to lead her closer to the wall, where we couldn't be hit.

'No.'

'I'll get you to a doctor,' I assured her, and to test her mind, I asked her what year it was.

'I should care about the date with my bones broken by *Goyim*?' she shot back.

I grinned at her outrage. So did she, then she groaned and bit her lip from the pain.

A tall young man appeared beside me from out of nowhere. Cradling the woman in his arms, he lumbered off. We found safety in an optometrist's waiting room.

A half-hour later, after the hoodlums had grown tired of target practice, I got on my way, and I soon reached Góra's office. He was a paunchy man in too tight a suit, with a polka-dot tie and a pink carnation in his lapel. He made his living these days managing an *import-export* business, he told me with a big noisy laugh. I thought he looked like a circus barker. He reeked of musky-scented cologne.

After I explained my purpose, I handed him my photograph of Adam. As he studied it, he picked his front teeth with the mandarin fingernail on his little finger. Handing the picture back to me, he said, 'Sorry, never seen him. But there are other tunnels leading into the sewer system. He must have gone through one of them.' Anticipating my next question, he added, 'No, I don't know where any of them are.'

Back at home, I found a stout, pale-skinned young man standing beside the armchair in my room, a hostile look in his small dark eyes. His hands were locked behind his back, and the smoke from his hidden cigarette was ribboning up into the harsh yellow light of the ceiling lamp, where moths had piled up in the cup of glass below the bulb. His camel-hair overcoat was threadbare and the collar of his white shirt was stained. His thick brown hair was chopped short – it looked like porcupine needles. He was good-looking in a hard, Slavic way.

'You must be Dr Cohen,' he began, speaking Polish.

'That's right.'

'I'm Grylek Baer.' He spoke gruffly, as if I'd offended him.

'Ah, so you're the guard at Leszno Street,' I said, compensating for my apprehension with a welcoming tone, hanging my coat on its hook.

'That's right.'

'How did you get in?' I asked.

'Your niece opened the door. She went to bed a little while ago.'

When we shook hands, he gripped mine hard, as though to prove his greater strength. His fingers were heavily callused. I'd have guessed he was twenty, but the sureness of his stance made me believe he might be a good deal older.

'Thank you for coming,' I told him.

Grylek's jaw throbbed and he took a greedy puff of his cigarette, then stubbed it out in the clay ashtray that Adam had made for me and that I kept on the tea table next to my armchair. He took his time, as though considering what he needed to tell me.

More and more I divided the Jews of Warsaw into two categories – those who'd outlast the Nazis and those who'd join Adam. In my mind, Grylek elbowed and shoved his way right to the front of the first group.

'Were you able to put together a list of border crossings for me?' I asked.

'Yes, but before I give it to you, I have to explain how it works.' He looked at me as though I'd made trouble for him before. 'You'll have to be patient, because there are some things you need to know before I can give you what you want.'

'What things?'

He took off his coat, folded it neatly and placed it on the chair. His shoulders were broad and powerful, as though he'd been a boxer before our exile, and he seemed a man who enjoyed making others wait. He opened and closed his right fist as though testing his own capacities. *He wants to let me know he's capable of violence*, I thought.

'You're not to mention my name to anyone,' he began, his tone of warning obvious. 'And you are not to tell anyone in the Jewish Council about me. Or let on to anyone, in any way, that I was here. I can't take chances. And if you ever mention who gave you the list that I'm going to give you, I'll come back for you. Are we clear?'

'But surely the Jewish leadership all know about what you do,' I replied.

'Maybe yes, maybe no. For the time being, they leave me alone. But if they hear too much about my activities, especially from a man like you, they'll make my life hell.'

'Like me how?'

'Spare me the false modesty,' he replied, annoyance coarsening his voice. 'You used to be important and you know it. So are we clear or not?'

'I'd never inform on you,' I told him, offended.

'Maybe not on purpose, but Marcel, the young smuggler you met . . . he told me you'd mentioned me by name. You can't do that. So, do I have your word?' He looked at me coldly. I had the feeling he demanded absolute loyalty from those around him.

'I promise I'll never use your name,' I told him.

'Good. Now,' he said in a softer tone, 'if you'll forgive me some advice, don't use *anyone*'s real name or address. You'll end up in the barbed wire yourself if you do.'

'But why?'

'Haven't you noticed all the big *machers* at the Café Hirschfeld?' he said, switching to Yiddish. 'They're becoming King Midases on our imprisonment. And when their gold is threatened . . .' He drew a finger across his throat.

He spoke Yiddish to convince me I could trust him despite his hostility, but such a ploy only irritated me. 'Still,' I told him, 'I have to find out what happened to Adam.'

'And I want you to!' he assured me. 'That's why I'm here, and why I wrote out my list. Where can we sit together?' he asked eagerly.

'At the kitchen table,' I replied, gesturing for him to follow me.

'Sorry for speaking to you harshly,' he said, and when I turned to him, he smiled generously; his fever of anxiety had broken. 'It's like this, Dr Cohen,' he said as he sat down. 'I'm not naive. Things will go wrong for me sooner or later, but I want to put off that day as long as I can. You see what I'm saying?'

'Absolutely,' I replied. Sitting opposite him, I felt as if I was his opponent in a game that only he knew how to play.

'Your friend Abram made a mistake giving you my real name. Stupid risk. I've already had a long talk with him.'

'Abram was upset. I'd just told him about my nephew.'

'Upset?' Grylek raised his eyebrows questioningly and added, 'Wouldn't you say all of us are upset? Look, Dr Cohen,' he said in a more friendly tone, 'let me explain how it is. Everyone in my world uses false names. So if you need to refer to me, call me Rabe – an anagram for Baer.' He lifted out a square of paper from his shirt pocket and started to unfold it, then stopped. 'You know, if you're serious about investigating your grandnephew's murder, you should adopt an anagram too. I thought about it on the way over here. Try Honec – I once met a Czech novelist with that surname.'

'I'll consider it,' I replied – at the time, simply to please him.

Grylek unfolded his paper and handed it to me. I put on my reading glasses because his letters were tiny and irregular. As I scanned the seven addresses of border crossings he'd jotted down, and the names of their guards, he took out a tin of German cigarettes – Muratti Ariston – and offered me one, which I accepted.

'Smuggled?' I asked.

'You got it!' he replied, grinning proudly. He lit my cigarette with a theatrical flare to his hand movements, then set the flame to his own and drew in deeply. I had the feeling he'd had dreams of being a Hollywood star when he was younger – and even today enjoyed a dramatic role.

'Did you learn who asked my nephew to smuggle out an ermine jacket?' I asked.

'No luck, though I asked around.'

In my nightmares, Heniek, I have seen Rabe as two men, one of them with a murderous glint in his eyes, speaking Polish, the other a ghetto Puck on the lookout for mischief, and who talks to me in a lilting, happy-go-lucky Yiddish. Still, I'm grateful to him; he made me understand the stakes we were playing for were high.

'About the list – the names are all anagrams,' he explained. 'I've altered the street numbers as well.'

'But I'll never find the crossings this way!' I moaned, holding my head in my hands.

'You will!' he replied cheerfully, like a magician happy to teach a protégé one of his tricks, 'because I'm going to explain how it works.' He opened his right hand to show me numbers written in pairs on his palm. The first coupling was 7-2. 'When you see seven in an address, change it to two in your head. You got it?'

'I think so.'

'And once you know the code, you'll know all the ghetto's secrets,' he joked.

'I wish,' I replied.

'Just memorize the pairs now, and the street names, too. You'll be able to rearrange them into their real names if you just sit down with a pen and paper for a few minutes. I guarantee it.'

'I'm not so sure. I've never done anything like this before.'

'Look, I'm in no rush. When you tell me you've got everything safely in your head, I'll wash my hand.'

Committing his list to memory proved more difficult than I'd have imagined; I kept thinking of what delight Adam would have taken in this cloak and dagger work. Only after I'd finished – and as Grylek was scrubbing his palm at the sink – did I realize the obvious: my nephew had entered this underworld long before me.

CHAPTER 8

I do not dream that I am aware of, and I don't believe I even sleep, though I wish I could; there are times when I am so weary of mind and body that I could cry for not being able to disappear into nothingness. Worst of all, blackness never welcomes me when I close my eyes. Instead, sepia afterglows float and jiggle across my vision – of Heniek's face, his furniture, and all I have seen during the day. It is as if the barrier between outside and inside has faded.

Sometimes I think I may be dispersing slowly into everything I see and hear. I will end as nothing and everything – as the wind, the sound of a dog barking, the concerned gaze of the only man in Warsaw who can see me . . .

Though perhaps that's just my hope. Who wouldn't want a way of leaving the one life we have on earth without disappearing entirely?

Still, there may be benefits to my new nature; now that I am what I am, maybe the past can be bent around to meet the present . . . As dawn rose this morning, I pictured Adam and myself as childhood friends, flying our kites together in Saski Square, and the deeper I moved into the embrace of all that might have been, the stronger my certainty that it was, in fact, a memory.

Heniek insists on taking down my every word since he says that scribes are not editors, though he promises to add some annotations where necessary and to let me make as many cuts and modifications as I want when I'm finished.

'I'd like a happy ending, even if there really isn't one,' I've told him.

'We'll see,' he says, which means, naturally enough, that he doesn't think it's a good idea. Maybe he suspects I have an important favour to ask him when we're done and is trying to keep his options open. An intuitive man, our Heniek – perhaps even a minor prophet. After all, if he can see and hear me . . .

By now – judging from his questions – I suspect that his real reason for being so meticulous is that he's convinced a life-altering, kabbalistic moral to my story is going to burst out of one of my recollections, like a jack-in-the-box manufactured in Gerona or Jerusalem, and he doesn't want to miss that heart-stopping moment. Isn't that true, Heniek? (He's shaking his head, but I can tell from the twist in his lips that he's lying.)

In times past, I'd have said his neurosis takes the form of hallucinations meant to diminish his sense of powerlessness, but I no longer make such judgements.

I dictate and Heniek writes. It's our private cabaret act.

Our growing closeness makes me miss Izzy. More and more, I feel as if we were two halves of something that has no name. Will I ever see him again? And could it be that I've returned to tell not just my story, but his as well?

Heniek undoubtedly has his own ideas about why I've returned, but he doesn't share them with me. 'Secrets are my private blessing,' he told me just this morning.

As you can see, my host is also something of a poet, and before he retires to bed he sometimes reads me one of his recent verses. The soft, hushed sound of his voice is like wind over stone, which is just as it should be for poems written in a thousand-year-old city that is dying.

Yesterday, at the end of my first day back in Warsaw, after telling Heniek about Adam's death, I found it difficult to go on speaking.

Craving the reassurance of human warmth, I reached out to take his hand. It was my first attempt to make physical contact with him, because I'd been worried that my touch might prove dangerous to the living.

To my disappointment, my fingertips did not meet his flesh but instead eased an inch or so into him. To me, this overlapping of our borders felt pleasant – as if I was immersing my fingers in warm water – but not to Heniek. With a shriek, he drew back from me, nearly tumbling off his chair.

He told me the pain was excruciating, as though his skin were being peeled away.

After I apologized, I was silent for a long time, wondering if even talking to him could prove dangerous – if I might be turning him away from a better and safer path.

'Please, tell me what you're thinking, Erik,' he requested, and his tone was so gentle and respectful that I did.

With a smile of solidarity, that generous man then assured me that there was nothing he wanted more than to help me tell my story.

'I feel sometimes I was born for this,' he confessed. 'After all, why have visions of the dead, if you cannot be of any assistance to them?'

CHAPTER 9

The evening after my nephew's death, I apologized to Stefa for allowing Adam to leave the apartment. She received my words with her head down, unable to look at me. Unsure of what next to say, I started to tell her about having spoken to his friends.

'Stay away from me!' she hollered as if I were a criminal bent on corrupting her. 'And for the love of God, don't tell me anything about Wolfi and the others!'

Climbing into her bed, she hugged Adam's sketchbook to her chest and closed her eyes.

'Forgive me for being so inept, Stefa,' I told her, and I sat down next to her. At length, she took my hand and gave it a squeeze. I said nothing more, but the silence was filled with all my unspoken regrets.

After tucking Stefa in to sleep, I changed Gloria's water, then covered her cage and turned off the light. The darkness seemed my true home now. I sat by my niece, my hand on her shoulder so that even inside her dreams she would know I was beside her. I thought of her father and mother, who had adored her, and then my parents, and slowly, one by one, the room became peopled with everyone I'd ever loved. Adam brought my wife Hannah to me as though leading her towards a bed of wild flowers, and she was laughing at his merry insistence. Hannah had died just after Adam's birth, but in my dream the boy was about five years old. He climbed up on to my lap when I summoned him forward. My tears of gratitude dripped on to his hair.

'How's Gloria?' he asked me.

'Not so good,' I replied, and then I awoke and Adam's death seemed to fill my mouth with blood.

In the bathroom, I splashed cold water on my face. Removing the towel that Stefa had draped over the mirror, I stared at the skeleton-sockets I had for eyes, and at my cumbersome, blue-veined hands. Who was this useless man? How had I fallen so far?

I knew that an emptiness with exactly Adam's size and shape was awaiting me in my bed, so I fetched a woollen blanket and made a nest for myself in Stefa's armchair.

At dawn, I set out for the addresses I'd memorized. I showed my nephew's photograph to seven guards and a dozen smugglers, but no one recognized him.

At the funeral that morning, dread paralysed me, pounding so loudly in my ears that I barely heard the rabbi's condolences. The ground was stone-frozen, too hellishly hard to make a ditch, though two gravediggers had used their picks to chip away an inch down as a symbolic gesture. Seventeen homemade coffins made of bare planks of wood – the smallest being Adam's – were stacked around our quiet group, waiting for the spring thaw to be lowered into the earth. In the back of a horse-drawn wagon were six bodies wrapped in rough cloth; their families couldn't afford coffins.

Ewa, Rowy, Ziv and several other friends stayed close to Stefa during the ceremony. She had the frantic eyes of a lost child, but I didn't go to her.

Withholding oneself as a way of feeling the pain even deeper.

When Stefa finally looked at me, I saw that she wanted to keep some distance between us as well. Perhaps she was thinking – like me – that it would be impossible to ever forgive me for failing to protect Adam.

Stefa insisted on standing between the pale winter sun and the gravesite. I didn't understand why until I noticed how her shadow stretched into the soil that would receive Adam this spring. Maybe she imagined that her dark embrace would accompany him into his resting place.

A belief in magic can offer solace, even if we know it is a lie.

I am with you – that's what she was telling her son in the language of shadows.

At a discreet distance behind Stefa and her closest friends stood a middle-aged woman in a brown headscarf, with a searching, fox-like face. She carried a book, which I found curious. When she noticed my gaze, she turned away quickly.

Adam's friend Sarah shuffled up to me leading her parents. A merciless wind from Russia was buffeting our little group, and the girl's hair was swirling in her eyes. I put down the bag I'd brought with me and lifted her up. As I smoothed her hair back, she let her head fall against my chest, then shivered. I kissed her once and thanked her for coming, then handed her back to her father.

Feivel's mother soon came to me and told me – ashamed – that her son didn't understand that Adam was dead. 'He refused to come to the funeral. God forgive me, I couldn't even get him dressed.'

I kissed her cheek. 'He's better off at home.'

She handed me a sketch that her son had done of Adam and Gloria a few weeks earlier. Drawn with scratches of wild colour, the budgie was riding on my nephew's head. She was nearly as big as Adam.

Feivel understood my nephew better than I did, I thought bitterly.

Wolfi and his father then joined us, and the boy was crying silently. When I embraced him, his emotions loosened my own and I had to let him go. Izzy had guarded my back ever since our schoolyard snowball fights, and he hooked arms with me and took Feivel's drawing. Turning me round, he had me face away from the grave, which must have seemed scandalous to some, but for me it was a godsend.

Distance was my raft that day.

Izzy whispered prayers to himself in Hebrew, and after a time I hung on to the sound of his voice. Still, I was angry with him, because he'd seen my pain and helped me, and I didn't want to share my despair or diminish it.

A psychiatrist who can't cope, and who knows it. I'd fallen off a cliff, and the cliff was everything that Adam and I would never now do together.

After the rabbi delivered his sermon, two Pinkiert's men carried Adam's coffin to where gravediggers had fought hard to chip down into the soil. When my turn came to shovel earth atop the casket, I took my nephew's Indian headdress out of the bag I'd brought with me. On seeing it, I moaned; I'd forgotten about the feather I'd knocked off.

I held it up to Izzy. 'I should have fixed it. I wanted to put it on his casket.'

He kissed my cheek. 'Go ahead, Erik. What's perfect has no place in the ghetto.'

At the funeral of a child, the ground opens underneath you, and you tumble down, and you put up no resistance as the darkness throws its welcoming arms around you, because you cannot imagine sending a young boy or girl alone and naked into the underworld. If you have someone to live for – another son or daughter, a wife or husband – maybe you climb back out of the grave. Or maybe not. After all, people give up all the time.

I used to say they were irresponsible, but I'd been an arrogant fool.

I climbed out of Adam's grave. Stefa didn't. In a way, our destinies were as simple as that.

If they don't see that I'm under the ground with my son when they look in my eyes, then what's the use of telling them? I imagined Stefa was thinking that over the rest of the afternoon, and over the next days as well, because she refused to talk about her son ever again. That afternoon, around 1 p.m., her fever reached 39.2, and I discovered flecks of blood on her pillowcase. I'd sent everyone home by then and was sitting at the foot of her bed.

'I'll be right back,' I told her, getting to my feet.

'Where are you going?' she asked worriedly.

'To get a doctor. This has gone on long enough.'

A mother and her teenaged daughter were seated behind a pushcart outside our apartment, selling pickled cucumbers and carrots. The girl wore a Basque beret and a man's coat, which made me understand we were raising a generation of Jewish children living under the weight of their dead parents. I offered her three złoty to carry a note to Mikael Tengmann. Jumping up, she slipped out of her coat, kissed her mother's cheek and ran off.

The girl knocked on my door a half-hour later, sweat beaded on her forehead, her beret in her hands. 'Dr Tengmann says he'll be here at six sharp,' she told me.

I gave her a one-złoty tip. Thanking me, she took a pale blue calling card from her pocket and handed it to me. Her name – Bina Minchenberg – was scripted in elegant calligraphy imitating the lion's-paw shapes of Hebrew letters.

'Who's the artist?' I asked.

'I'm afraid it's me,' she replied, making an embarrassed face.

'You've got talent.'

'I'm also a very good cook,' she told me, 'and if you'll pay me to prepare a meal for you on occasion, I'll clean your apartment for no extra charge.'

'How old are you?' I asked.

'Fourteen.'

Her big brown eyes were full of hope, but she quickly realized I was going to turn her down and reached for my hand. 'Dr Cohen, I know what men need – even good men like you.' She pressed my palm to her breast and, when I tried to jerk it away, gripped it with both hands. 'I'll do whatever you want. And I won't tell anyone. I swear!'

'Oh, God,' I groaned, and my shuddering made her finally release me.

'Our savings have run out, Dr Cohen,' Bina told me, tears caught in her lashes.

I wanted to shake some sense into her, or simply walk away, but what right had I to judge her? 'Listen closely, Bina,' I told her. 'You're a brave girl. And you should do whatever you need to do to stay alive. But I'm not who I was. I don't know if I can—'

'All I'm asking is a chance!' she interrupted desperately.

'Very well, I'll send for you whenever I need a message delivered or a meal cooked.'

I thought I was lying, but how could I be sure any more of my own intentions? Or the consequences of even my most seemingly harmless actions?

We stared at each other for a long time, and because of what I now knew was possible between us, our solidarity terrified me. I don't know what she saw, but I saw a girl crawling through the trenches of a long slow war, and whom I was powerless to protect – and whom I resented because of that.

I handed her ten złoty, which made her rise up on her toes and give me a popping kiss on the cheek – transformed into a young girl again.

'Now go,' I told her. 'Your mother must be worried.'

As soon as Bina left, I headed to the bakery in our courtyard. Coming in from the arctic chill, the heat seemed tropical, and the workers were in their bare feet and shirtsleeves, with paper bags on their heads. Ewa wasn't there – she was at home with her daughter – so Ziv agreed to look after Stefa.

In the hour I had before Mikael Tengmann's arrival, I intended to search for more border crossings, but when I reached the sidewalk I heard my name called from behind me. Turning, I saw the fox-faced woman I'd spotted at the funeral, still carrying her book. Her ears and nose were red.

'Dr Cohen, excuse me for interrupting, but I need to speak with you,' she said.

Looking at her closely, I realized I'd seen her prior to the funeral, but I couldn't remember where. 'Why didn't you knock on our door?' I asked.

'I didn't want to impinge on your grief.'

'You must be frozen. Let's go upstairs.'

'No, your niece may react badly to what I have to say. Where else can we talk?'

'The Café Levone. We'll get you something warm to drink.'

As we started off, she said, 'I felt I had to be at the funeral. I'm sorry if I seemed out of place. I didn't know your grandnephew.'

'There's no need to apologize,' I replied.

She looked at me gratefully. 'My name is Dorota Levine.'

When I asked what she was reading, she turned the cover of Stefan Zweig's *Marie Antoinette* to face me. 'I take a book with me whenever I know I'm going to wait.'

It was then that I recalled that she'd come to the Yiddish Library a few weeks earlier and asked me to help her find books on butterflies for her son.

'I think we met briefly a couple of weeks ago,' I told her. 'At the library where I work.'

She smiled. 'You were very kind to help me.'

She grew silent then, and she rubbed her hand over her lips as if to keep from making further revelations. My curiosity about her made me fail to spot a puddle in time and I stepped through its ice sheet into the mud below. Sopping, cursing under my breath, I trudged on. Once seated inside the café, I kicked off my shoes, which were as ugly as two dead bats. My toes had been stained brown by my wet socks and my nails were yellowing daggers. A waiter fetched me a towel and then produced a dry pair of socks, insisting I take them, which was so unexpected that I was struck dumb.

The café smelled of cheap beer and cigar smoke. While we waited for our coffee, Dorota told me her cousin Ruti was married to the son of a university acquaintance of mine. The young man's name was Manfred Tuwim, and although he was stuck in Munich, far away from lonely Ruti . . . Dorota launched into one of those wordy explanations that Jews cobble together to prove that they're all part of the same club, linked through enough upstanding friends and relatives – and maybe even a rabbi or two – to fill up a bar mitzvah reception at the Berlin Sports Palace. My father had called this tiresome tradition *Jewish knitting*.

I cut her off. 'Why did you want to talk with me?' I asked.

She took a black-and-white photograph from the pages of *Marie Antoinette*. 'Because of my daughter, Anna,' she replied, handing it to me.

A slender girl stood by a fruit tree turned by springtime into a cloud of white blossoms. She wore a pleated skirt – dowdy and old-fashioned – and a dark, high-collared blouse that looked as if it reeked of mothballs. Their antiquity seemed to embarrass Anna, and she'd pulled her long tresses around to her front and was holding on to them for dear life. It was a pose that troubled me; children who cling to themselves generally have no one they can trust.

Putting on my reading glasses, I spotted fierce resentment in Anna's eyes, and saw, too, that she was leaning towards the right edge of the picture, anxious to flee. But the photographer's finger had clicked the shutter too quickly, sending her image into the future – and here to me. Beside the girl was a figure that had been cut away except for the small hand that held hers. I guessed that the missing person had been her brother, and that he had been the anchor keeping Anna from dashing away.

'That was a year ago,' Dorota told me. 'My husband took the picture in Bednarski Park – in Kraków. We were visiting my in-laws.'

I've learned from my patients to pay close attention to the first offering they give you. Keeping the photograph with her was clearly Dorota's way of proving to me that she'd never leave home without a reminder of her daughter – and that she was devoted to the girl. Yet why had she chosen such an unflattering shot?

'Anna didn't like being photographed,' I observed.

'No, she hated it – at least when my husband took the pictures.'

Dorota seemed keen to convince me that mistrust characterized the relationship between Anna and her father. 'Her clothes were an older sister's?' I asked.

'No, but the blouse had been mine.'

'Who was with her – holding her hand?'

'Her brother, Daniel. He was seven then.'

Our coffee had just arrived, and I was eager for the clarity of thought it would give me, but it was as bitter as acorns. Dorota was gazing away from me, and fidgeting with her collar. She seemed a woman who knew she was passing through life largely unseen. Under normal circumstances I'd have said she was leading a smaller life than was necessary, but inside our enclave, being overlooked could prove an advantage.

'Does Anna get along well with Daniel?' I asked, catching the waiter's eye and motioning for him to return.

'They used to fight like devils when they were little,' Dorota told me, 'but they'd become friendlier of late.' She gazed down, as though she'd already said too much.

Her retreat into silence – and use of *they'd* instead of *they've* – made me wonder if one or both of her children had died, though with any luck they'd merely been smuggled to Christian friends outside the ghetto.

The waiter came to me, and I asked for a shot of schnapps. As he left, a pigeon flew in the door. Landing on an empty table, he began pecking at crumbs.

I faced Dorota again. 'So your son is a fan of butterflies,' I told her, testing whether she'd use the present tense when discussing him.

'Yes, he thinks they're the most wondrous creatures in the world,' she replied, beaming as if I'd made her day.

So it was her daughter who resided inside the past. I handed her back the photograph. 'What's happened to Anna?' I asked.

Dorota looked around the café to confirm that no one was eavesdropping, then shifted her chair towards mine. 'She's dead,' she confided. 'The Nazis murdered her. She was tossed into barbed wire. Just like your nephew.'

Stunned, I raised my hand over my eyes as though to protect myself. 'I'm very sorry to hear that,' I told her. 'When did this happen?'

'A little over three weeks ago.'

'And you came to the funeral because you think there's a connection between Adam and her – from the way they were found.'

'Not just that. When she was brought to me, her right hand was missing.'

CHAPTER 10

'How did you find out that Adam had been disfigured?' I asked Dorota.

She took a quick sip of her coffee. 'I've a cousin in the Jewish police who saw your nephew after what the Nazis did to him.'

'So your cousin already knew about Anna.'

'Yes, I'd told him, but he warned me not to discuss her with anyone. A man from the Jewish Council also made it clear that I was not to tell anyone about how Anna died. I almost didn't come to talk with you.'

'Was it Benjamin Schrei who spoke to you?' I asked.

'Yes, do you know him?'

'Unfortunately,' I replied, furious; Schrei had known that Adam's death had not been an isolated killing and had lied to me. How many more children's bodies had been defiled? I gulped down the last of my coffee, savouring the burn of the schnapps I'd poured in. While I filled the bowl of my pipe, considering how best to confront Schrei, Dorota gave me a hard look.

'I'm listening,' I told her.

Leaning over the table, she circled her arms together, as though around a stash of secrets she'd accumulated since her daughter's death. 'Anna didn't return home on the afternoon of the twenty-fourth of January,' she began. 'It was a Friday, and she was supposed to help me prepare our Sabbath dinner. She was found by the Jewish police the next morning.'

'Excuse me for asking this, but was your daughter naked when she was found?'

'Yes.'

'And was there anything special about her hand that was taken?'

She looked at me as if I was insane. 'It was a girl's hand,' she told me resentfully. 'I'd say that was special, wouldn't you?'

I lit my pipe, eager for the comfort of an old vice. 'Were there any wounds on her body?' I asked from inside the swirl of smoke around me.

'None.'

'Was anything in her mouth?'

'I don't understand,' she replied.

'I found a piece of string in Adam's mouth. I think the murderer put it there.'

'I'm afraid I didn't look. But why in God's name would the murderer put string in the mouth of the children he kills?'

'I don't know.'

It occurred to me then that Adam might have been returning to the ghetto with valuable goods. Wanting to know whether robbery could have been a motive for Anna's murder – and the theft of her hand – I asked, 'Did your daughter wear a ring – maybe one she'd worn since she was tiny and could no longer remove from her finger?'

'No. She had a pretty garnet ring, but she stopped wearing it in the ghetto because she'd lost so much weight that it would slide right off her finger.'

'How about a bracelet?'

Dorota shook her head. 'She only ever wore pearl earrings. They were a gift from me – pink pearls dangling from a silver chain. But she didn't have them on when she was found. They must have been stolen from her. Though they weren't worth very much – I mean, if you're thinking that a thief may have killed her. The only thing that anyone might have found valuable was her hand itself.'

'What do you mean?'

She leaned towards me, her head low to the table, and whispered conspiratorially, 'The killer may be using parts of our children's bodies to make something inhuman.'

'What are you talking about?'

'A *golem*,' she mouthed, her eyes fearful, as if saying the word aloud might summon one from its hiding place.

'But why?'

'To protect us!' she declared.

I felt cornered by Dorota's beliefs. 'My God, woman, your daughter has been murdered! And a real person killed her. Don't you want to find out who it was?'

'All right, Dr Cohen,' she replied with controlled anger, 'maybe you don't believe that making such a creature is possible, but what if there's a lunatic out there who *thinks* he can?'

She showed me a challenging look, and I had to admit that madness might explain what had been done to Adam. Except that there was a problem with her argument. 'If a Jew killed my nephew,' I told her, 'then how could he have tossed the boy's body into the barbed wire from the *Christian side* of the border?'

She tapped her chest. 'I only know what I sense in here. And I know that there's more to these murders than we think.'

Eager to steer our conversation towards rational ground, I returned to the details of Anna's disappearance. 'Do you know if your daughter had snuck out of the ghetto before being murdered?' I asked.

Dorota leaned back in her chair. 'Yes, I'm fairly certain she went to see her boyfriend.'

'He doesn't live inside?'

'No, he's a Pole.' Sneering, she added, 'An Aryan.'

If Anna hadn't fallen in love with the wrong young man and refused to give him up, she'd still be alive. Although Dorota never spoke those words over the next half-hour, her resentment turned nearly all she said to accusations against her daughter. As we talked, it seemed to me that she would polish her grudge for years.

'And what makes you feel certain she went to see her boyfriend?' I asked.

Breathing deeply, as if she were entering dangerous territory, Dorota replied, 'Let me explain about my daughter.' She took off her headscarf and held it in her lap. 'Anna turned fifteen in June, and at her birthday party I looked at her and I realized my little girl was gone. But make no mistake, over the next few weeks, she proved she was still just a wilful child. *Belligerent and selfish* – that's how my husband always described her.' Dorota patted her thinning hair, as though putting her thoughts into place. 'And he was right – though you must think I'm heartless for saying so.'

'Not at all,' I told her, beginning to suspect her husband of ruining his daughter's life. 'Children can be difficult in desperate situations. They need our reassurance.'

'People who only met her once or twice – they didn't understand what she was like,' Dorota continued in a frustrated voice. 'Life was never easy with her – never! I can assure you of that. No punishment could make her do what she didn't want to. And she *believed* she was in love with a Polish boy. She couldn't live without him.' Dorota shook her head, clearly regarding her daughter's affection as absurd.

'What was his name?' I asked.

'Paweł Sawicki. Dr Cohen, how could my husband and I approve? The daughter of a Jewish tailor and the son of a Polish judge? I saw heartbreak ahead. Was I wrong?'

'I no longer know how to answer that,' I told her, holding back my criticism; by now, I realized that Dorota had chosen a photograph that would give me an idea of how difficult her daughter could be – and possibly, too, to help convince me that the measures she and her husband had taken to break the girl's will were necessary.

'When you told Anna you disapproved of Paweł, what did she say?' I asked.

'She shouted that I was a mean-spirited witch.' In a resentful voice, she added, 'My daughter used to call me Fraulein Rottenmeier.'

'Who?'

'The hideous housekeeper from *Heidi*. That was Anna's favourite book.' Dorota sighed. 'If only . . . if only I could talk to her just once more – make her understand.' The impossibility of that made Dorota gaze inside herself. 'Anyway, she refused to give up Paweł, so we quarrelled, and when my husband joined in . . .' She shook her head at the troubling memory. 'He threatened to use his belt on her. Which was when Anna promised she'd never see her boyfriend again. And maybe that really was her intention. I can't say. But if it was, then she changed her mind because she started leading a double life.'

'In what way?' I asked, concluding that if Anna had given in without a longer quarrel then it was probably because she'd felt the stiff leather sting of her father's belt before.

'You know the sort of thing girls do,' Dorota replied. 'She'd tell me she was going roller-skating with a girlfriend, then meet Paweł at a cinema. After we moved to the ghetto, I searched her dresser and found photographs of the two of them at a picnic in Saski Gardens.' She produced another picture from the pages of *Marie Antoinette* and slid it across the table to me as though pushing an evil talisman out of her life.

Anna was laughing freely in the photograph. Paweł was embracing her from behind, though only his hands were visible – his face and arms had been cut away. Given how Anna and Adam had been disfigured, it seemed dangerous for Dorota to have cut away pieces of the young man's image.

My uneasiness on holding the photograph seemed a bad sign for my own mental state; it was as if the ghetto were compelling me to believe in the power of amulets and spells, like Dorota and so many others.

'Did Paweł's parents approve of Anna?' I asked.

'My daughter told me they adored her, but I checked on the family and learned that the judge had become a vicious anti-Semite since the Nazi occupation.'

I asked if I could keep the photograph while I hunted for Anna and Adam's killer, and Dorota agreed. She went on to tell me that Paweł and his family lived at 24 Wilcza Street. 'He promised to visit Anna in the ghetto. At least, that's what she told me. He never came or even called that I know of. Then Anna announced that she wouldn't eat again until she saw him – announced it like a decree! That's why she lost so much weight and couldn't wear her ring. My husband started forcing her to eat supper, but after bed she'd sneak off to the bathroom and make herself sick. It took me two weeks to realize that's what she was doing. By then, she was a living skeleton. Dr Cohen,' Dorota said, opening her hands as if to make an appeal to reason, 'her wilfulness was killing our family.' She hunched forward, circling those secrets of hers again, though this time I sensed it was to hold something back. 'This will sound strange, but I felt I was living in a house that was falling to pieces. Every shadow was menacing. And Anna's appearance – it scared me. Once, I stood her in front of the mirror in my bedroom and showed her how gaunt she was, but she insisted she was disgustingly fat. Can you believe it? Of course, she blamed my husband and me for everything – for insisting she eat, for keeping her apart from Paweł. She put us through hell.'

'Did she ever succeed in speaking with him?'

'Not that I know of. When I called Paweł's mother, she told me she'd sent the boy to a boarding school. I told Anna, but she screamed at me that I was lying. She wrote letters to him. I allowed that in exchange for her agreeing to eat again. But she never received any replies – at least, not that I know of.'

I went on to question Dorota about her daughter's schooling and friends, hoping to chance upon a connection to Adam, and for once, Jewish knitting proved helpful; she soon told me that Anna had been very close to her maternal grandfather, whose name was Noel Anbaum.

'The musician – he's your father?' I questioned.

'Yes, do you know him?'

'I saw him perform when I was much younger. Dorota, Anna wasn't in a chorus, by any chance?'

'No.'

'How about your son?'

'No, why?'

'Adam was, and I saw your father at the concert.'

When I asked Dorota for her father's address, she looked at her watch and replied, 'If you hurry, you'll be able to catch him playing outside the Nowy Azazel Theatre.'

CHAPTER 11

The fingers of Noel Anbaum's black leather gloves had been cut away and his crocheted blue muffler had a corner that was unravelling in a *payot* curl, but he still cut a slim, dashing figure – a grey-templed, Roman-nosed Casanova – in his wine-red zoot suit and black gaucho hat. Standing on Nowolipie Street in front of the Nowy Azazel, his right foot up on a fraying green and gold brocade chair that looked as if it had been nicked from a local bordello, he was playing an undulating blues song on his accordion, bellowing the roller-coaster chord changes in and out with his left hand, the wizened fingers of his right coaxing a sensual vibrato out of the chipped and yellowing keyboard. He doubled the melody in his gritty voice, braving an English that was twisted into absurd shapes by Yiddish vowels. One line he must have improvised stuck in my head because he sang it with the provocative bravado of a gunslinger: *If I cabaret on Saturday and curse Herr Hitler all day Sunday, ain't nobody's business if I do* . . .

On the high notes, Noel's voice sounded like sandpaper being scratched, and its raspy imperfection made me fear he'd teeter off the melody, but he never did. His singing was a kind of high-wire act, which was probably why so many złoty had been tossed into the slate-grey velvet of his accordion case; after all, if his performance were effortless, would it be worth paying for? He himself kept his eyes closed, swaying luxuriously, as though his music were a slow tide carrying him deep into himself.

I threaded through the crowd towards a clearing that had formed around a bearded beggar sitting on the sidewalk about ten paces to Noel's left. The ribs of the bare-chested man jutted out dangerously, like a galley with its construction exposed, and his caved-in belly was criss-crossed by bloody scabies tracks. The stench of his having soiled himself made me cup my hands over my mouth and nose.

After Noel had finished his song and bowed to his audience, I went to him. 'My name is Erik Cohen. My wife and I used to see you play at the Esplanade. You were amazing.'

'That was during a previous lifetime,' he replied, laughing merrily. 'As you can see, I'm paying for my past sins in this one.'

'No, you're still wonderful!' I told him.

Smiling gratefully, he shook my hand. His trembled badly. Laying his hat on the seat of his chair, he picked up a Żywiec beer bottle from the ground. As he took a sip, he spotted me eyeing his shaking hand. 'Damn thing has a life of its own these days,' he told me. 'Except when it gets near a keyboard.'

'I need to talk with you.'

He cupped his hand behind his ear with sweet-natured eagerness and leaned so far towards me that he started to fall over and I had to prop him up. He was a bit drunk.

'Let's go somewhere warm,' I proposed.

'No, if I get comfortable now, I won't want to come back out. Let's stay here.'

'Listen, Noel, your daughter Dorota came to see me. She told me about Anna.'

His expression darkened.

'You see why I'd prefer to be alone with you,' I said.

'I'm sorry, but talking about Anna does me no good,' he replied.

After he showed me the smile of a man excusing a frailty, he put down his beer, lifted his accordion and started to play, but I grabbed his wrist.

'Why do you want to torture me?' he asked glumly, looking at me with so solemn a wish to be understood that I felt ashamed.

'Please, Noel,' I pleaded, 'my grandnephew, Adam, he was also murdered – just like Anna. All I need is for you to tell me why you attended a choral concert at the end of January. Twelve children sang Bach. Adam was one of them. It was—'

'I remember the concert,' he interrupted. 'I was there because of Rowy Klaus – the conductor. He studied piano and music theory with me when he was a boy.'

'So Rowy invited you?'

'Yes, we've stayed in touch all these years.'

'Thank you, Noel. I'm grateful.'

As I started away, he called my name and said in a resonant voice, '"May the angel who redeems me from all evil bless the children."'

After I'd nodded my agreement, his eyes fluttered closed and he entered the tide of another song. Its melody rose ghost-like out of my childhood, and though I was unable to identify it at the time, I later recalled that it was Schubert's setting of Psalm 92, which reads, 'My eyes have seen the defeat of my adversaries; my ears have heard the rout of my wicked foes.'

A marketplace had formed behind Noel, taking advantage of his popularity, and I zigzagged around shoppers until I was brought to a halt by a group of *ghetto mushrooms*: shoeshine boys sitting on wooden stools, their soot-smudged faces hidden in shadow by the peaks of their woollen caps, their hands stained black. One waif had a shaved head and a crone's joyless face. Cuttings of an old rug were tied around his feet. He looked at me with dull, lifeless eyes.

I ought to have led him off to buy boots or simply smiled at him, but I didn't – a measure of how far I'd let exile draw me away from myself.

Passing a small pyramid of cauliflowers in a pushcart, I realized they'd make a tasty supper. My heart soared to have happened upon one good and generous thing.

The seller was a miniature sphinx, of a kind common in Warsaw:

though barely five feet tall, and surely in her sixties, she had the coarse, big-boned hands of a locksmith. 'Two,' I told her, showing her the smile I'd withheld from the shoeshine boy, but she chose a pair from near the bottom of her pile that were covered with a nicotine-yellow ooze. She held them out to me, asking for four złoty each, as if they were the models of perfection she kept on top.

Frowning, I waved them away. I knew I ought to have simply eased my ten-złoty note and my disappointment back in my pocket and headed off, but I wanted to give her a chance to reconsider – a chance for grace. Though maybe I really just wanted to start a quarrel. 'Eight złoty for those *meiskeits*?' I questioned.

'That's the price.'

'Do you think I'm an idiot?'

'What do you mean?' she replied, outraged by my implication, raising a cauliflower triumphantly in each gnarled hand.

Taking a giant step towards her, I thrust up my thumb and index finger. 'How many fingers do you see?' I demanded.

She leered at me, sensing a deception. 'Two,' she replied hesitantly.

'So you're not blind, after all – which means you chose the worst ones on purpose! Tell me, what's it feel like to try to cheat a hungry man?'

Even as I spoke, I was aware that I sounded like a Dostoevsky drunk, but I couldn't stop myself.

'You old fool, get the hell out of here before I call my husband! He'll punch your face in!'

Her contempt backed me into a tight corner, and – stupidly – I chose the easiest way out. 'Impossible!' I scoffed at her. 'Whores don't have husbands!'

Her cheeks turned red and she leaned her head back, henlike. When she spat at my feet, I charged her, eager to get my hands around her throat and squeeze, but just as I grabbed the collar of her coat I flew forward on to my knees, crying out from the pain.

As I came to myself, I found I was lying on my side, my hands up by my face – a protective position I must have learned as a kid. The burly young man who'd knocked me over was cursing me in Yiddish. Was he her son? I never found out.

'*Ver di kapore!*' I snarled at him. That had been my mother's way of saying *drop dead!* I hadn't used it in half a century.

My attacker continued cursing me, but now in Polish, as if one language wasn't enough to express all his disdain. I stood up with difficulty and limped away, holding my wrist, which was very tender. Just past Pawiak Prison I stopped at a produce shop and purchased potato skins for soup and three wormy cabbages. I had a good cry in a bombed-out, ground-floor flat, sitting on the rim of the soil-filled bathtub that some clever soul must have been planning to use for planting vegetables in the spring.

Self-hatred stalked me home, though it comforted me to find Ewa and Helena watching over my niece, who was sleeping with her arm over her eyes. Helena looked at my torn trousers and dashed to me as I stood in the doorway, needing reassurance. I lifted her up and pressed my lips to her ear, her favourite spot for kisses.

'What happened to you?' she asked.

'I tripped on a cauliflower,' I replied, forcing a smile.

After I put the girl down, Ewa asked her to watch over Stefa, then led me into my room as though on a mission, easing the bedroom door closed behind her.

'I don't want Helena to hear our conversation,' she whispered.

'Very well,' I agreed. I tossed my bag of potato skins and my cabbages on the bed.

'Listen,' she said, brushing a tense hand back through her hair, 'my father says that Stefa has typhus. And she's had it a while – maybe too long.'

Ewa continued speaking, but frantic wings of panic were beating at my ears, blocking out her voice. 'Give me a moment,' I told her.

She helped me out of my coat and opened my collar. I sat down on the mattress.

'Over the next few weeks, Stefa will need nursing,' she told me. 'I can take over in the evenings, but you may have to quit the Lending Library. Her clothes were infested with lice, of course. To be safe, I had her sheets taken away to be washed. And Papa will have your apartment sprayed with carbolic acid later today. By all accounts, you should be under an order of quarantine, but he managed to avoid that. Listen, Erik, you may be infested, too.'

Her efficiency disoriented me. Ewa – with her small, determined eyes – now seemed one of those timid and reticent women who turn into Joan of Arc when their loved ones are threatened. A useful person in a war.

'Are there medications that will help?' I asked.

'Some ghetto physicians say that a Swiss serum has produced good improvements in patients, but it costs a thousand złoty a vial.'

'My God! Can your father get me some?'

'Yes, though I don't know how long it will take him.'

'I'll go and see him. I'll sell Hannah's engagement ring to raise the money.'

'No, please, don't do that!' she said sharply. Then, sensing she'd only heightened my sense of guilt, she added, 'I only meant there must be something else you can sell.'

'Not if I need to raise a thousand złoty in a hurry.'

Sitting on the floor in front of the clothes chest I'd shared with Adam, I opened the bottom drawer, clawed my way past his tangle of underwear and socks, and unhooked the ring from its hiding place. Holding it in my hand made me feel faint. My mouth was as dry as dust.

I held up the ring for Ewa to see. 'It's a two-carat diamond with a gold band.'

I got to my knees but was too dizzy to go any further. Ewa

helped me up and fetched me a glass of water. After a long drink, I sat down on my bed again.

'I'd appreciate it if you would sell it for me,' I told her.

'Me? My God, Erik, I don't know anything about selling jewellery.'

'Neither do I, but you're a pretty young woman, so you'll get a better price. You can say it's yours – for sympathy.'

When I held it out to her, she moved her hands behind her back. 'No, don't make me,' she pleaded. 'I'll get nervous and ruin things. Please, Erik . . .'

Tears appeared in her eyes and her shoulders hunched; she had transformed back into her usual self, so I didn't insist.

When I asked if she knew where Rowy Klaus might be, Ewa glanced at her watch and told me he was giving a piano lesson on Sienna Street, which was in the Little Ghetto, a relatively well-off section of our territory that was separated from the bigger – and poorer – section by Chłodna Street. In fact, Sienna Street was the most elegant address in the ghetto.

I left right away; I needed to question him about Anna and could elicit his advice on selling my ring at the same time. On the way, I got myself deloused at the disinfection bathhouse at 109 Leszno Street.

What unlikely marvels I saw in the shop windows that afternoon while waiting for Rowy! – six big fresh trout lying in a tub of ice; a burlap bag brimming with coffee beans from Ethiopia; and a bottle of Sandeman port from 1922. In the window of M. Rackemann & Sons, Tobacconists was a Star of David made out of twenty-four mustard-coloured packets of Gauloises cigarettes. The design had the unexpected, peculiar beauty of a Dadaist collage.

A blonde young prostitute with caved-in cheeks and frantic eyes soon caught my attention. She stood outside the Rosenberg Soup Kitchen, rubbing her spidery hands together, gazing around nervously, as though waiting for an unreliable friend. Had she been an art student? She dressed like the subject of an Otto Dix painting, with red stockings on her stick-figure legs and a lumpy, fox-headed stole slung around her neck.

When she asked me if I was looking for some affection, I thanked her for her interest but told her she'd have better luck with a younger man.

By the time Rowy emerged, the sun was going down. He was dressed in grey except for a crimson woollen scarf, which coiled around his neck and ribboned behind him in the wind like a banner proclaiming his youth. His walk was eager and untroubled – as though he were bouncing along on daydreams. I hailed him with a wave.

His face brightened on seeing me, which pleased me.

'Greetings, Erik!' he said as he approached.

'I like your scarf,' I told him, and we shook hands.

'Ewa – she knitted it for me,' he replied.

From the way he smiled, I could see he was deeply in love – and that his new way of walking was meant to let the world know. Maybe this was his first great passion.

'I just found out that you studied with Noel Anbaum,' I told him.

'Man, that was years ago!' he replied in jaunty German, adding in Yiddish, 'I hope you didn't come all the way across town just to confirm that.'

'No. What I really need to know is if you knew his grand-daughter Anna.'

'Sure did. She auditioned for the chorus. Noel set it up for her. Why?'

'She's dead – murdered just like Adam. And her hand was cut off.'

Rowy gasped, then swept his gaze across the rooftops behind me. He was likely trying to get a glimpse of his future, because he told me in a solemn voice, 'Makes you wonder if any of us will get out of here alive.'

'You'll make it. You're near the top of my list.'

He fiddled with the splint on his finger. 'You could be wrong.'

I grabbed his arm. 'Don't predict your own death – I won't allow it!' The clenched force behind my words made him draw back. I let him go. 'Sorry, forgive me,' I said.

'There's no need to apologize,' he replied, and I saw in the depth of his dark eyes that he would have embraced me had we known each other better.

'I'm not quite myself of late,' I told him.

'How could you be? Erik, I . . .' He struggled to find the right words, then shrugged defeatedly. 'I've wanted a chance to talk to you, but you left the funeral so quickly, and . . .'

'Rowy, I can't talk to you about my nephew just now. It would end any chance I have of doing anything useful. Now listen, I don't remember Anna singing at the concert. Was she there?'

'No. She passed the solfeggio exam, but she never showed up for any rehearsals. A few days later, I went to her home, but her mother said she wasn't well and was asleep in bed.'

'So you never talked to her again?'

'No, I did.' Rowy put on his gloves. 'I went back again a few days later because she had a soprano voice worth training, and she'd have added some needed balance to the upper end of the chorus. This time I saw her, and I begged her to go for her check-up with Ewa's father, but I never heard anything more about her.'

'How did she seem to you?'

'Unhappy. And fragile. The poor girl was just skin and bone.'

'She didn't by chance mention Adam when you saw her?' I questioned.

'No. Did they know each other?'

'That's what I have to find out. Rowy, listen, I've got something else to ask you that requires a little privacy. Let's go inside.'

The young man hooked his arm in mine as we walked towards a nearby apartment house. I imagined he was close to his father. The psychiatrist in me would have bet he was the youngest child in his family.

Once we were hidden on the stairwell, I took out Hannah's ring. 'Know anything about selling jewellery?'

'Just that you'll get a better price outside the ghetto.' He took the ring and studied it, then handed it back. 'Inside, it's become a buyer's market. I sold Papa's flute the other day and got next to nothing.'

As I'd guessed, that left me only one choice, but it was too late in the day for an excursion to the Other Side; I'd go in the morning.

I passed Rackemann's Tobacconists after Rowy left for home, and the French cigarettes in the window gave me the idea that the owner might be able to help me with an important request – or know someone who could. A woman in her fifties, with short, hennaed hair and too much rouge on her puffy cheeks, sat crocheting behind the counter. 'Is Mr Rackemann in?' I asked.

She laid her crochet work in her lap. 'My husband passed away in '37.'

'Then you must have made the Gauloises star in the window.'

'Yes, that was me. How can I help you?'

'Maybe you can put your hands on something unusual for me,' I told her. 'Two things, as a matter of fact.'

I waited an hour for my first request to be fulfilled by Mrs Rackemann. She told me then that my second item would require a great deal more work and would cost me the astronomical sum of 1,300 złoty if I wanted it by the next morning, as I'd indicated. I agreed to that fee, and since I couldn't pay her the full sum right away, I gave her as a deposit all the cash I had on me – nearly 200 złoty – as well as my gold wedding band.

It was just after five in the afternoon – morbid darkness in the

Polish winter – by the time I made it to Mikael's flat, which doubled as his medical office. In the waiting room, the tiny, quick-moving nurse whom I'd met briefly when Adam came for his check-up sized me up from her desk in the corner, and her disapproving look told me I'd failed whatever test she'd conceived for me. She told me in a stern voice that Dr Tengmann was with a patient, but she poked her head into his consultation room to let him know I was here. Too jittery to sit, I stood by the window and watched a water-seller accosting passers-by on the street below. A wooden bar was stretched horizontally across his shoulders, with a tin pail hanging from each end. He wore galoshes wrapped in what looked like birch-tree bark.

We were back in the Middle Ages, and the Nazis had dragged us there – which meant that the question we now needed to ask was: how far back in time would be enough for them?

A young woman with a plaster cast on her wrist soon came in and whispered to the nurse, who instructed her to sit and wait on the green velveteen couch to the side of the window where I was standing.

'Excuse me, but would you like to sign my cast?' she asked me after a minute or two, smiling hopefully. She held it up to show me it was covered with signatures.

She wanted to be nice to an *alter kacker* with grey stubble on his chin and dead bats for shoes, so I did as she asked, except that I wrote the name *Erik Honec* in extravagant Gothic lettering – what I imagined a professional writer might do.

She told me her name was Naomi. 'Are you Czech?' she asked me.

'Originally, but I've lived in Warsaw for twenty years now.'

My lie was a key clicking open a lock – the rusted one imprisoning me in myself. I felt as if I'd escaped a trap whose existence I'd failed to notice until now.

Mikael Tengmann saw Naomi and two more patients before

coming out to see me. It was a few minutes before six. By then, the nurse – Anka – had warmed to me and made us a pot of tea. I was on my second cup and was sipping it – as I'd learned from a Russian friend in Vienna – through a sugar crystal I kept between my teeth. The crystal was a gift from Anka.

'Hello, Erik!' Mikael exclaimed, shaking my hand exuberantly. He wore a white medical coat but kept woollen slippers on his feet. 'Sorry to have made you wait.'

'That's all right,' I replied. I took out what was left of my crystal and sealed it in an old receipt I had in my pocket as though it were a precious gem, which made his eyes radiate sympathetic amusement.

'I expect you want to talk about Stefa,' he said.

'Yes. I'm very grateful you came to see her. I want to buy serum for her. How long will it take you to get some?'

'A day or two. I know a young smuggler who specializes in medications. I'll get him right on it. But, Erik . . .' Mikael grimaced. 'It's expensive – a thousand złoty.'

'I know – Ewa told me. I promise I'll have the money for you tomorrow – the day after, at the latest.'

He waved away my concern. 'I trust you. The important thing is for Stefa to get well.'

Turning to his nurse, who was writing in the office appointment book, he said, 'Anka, I'm sorry to have kept you so late today. You can get going whenever you want.'

'Yes, Doctor,' she replied, smiling warmly. 'Thank you.'

'Listen, Mikael,' I said, 'I also need to talk to you about a girl named Anna Levine. Rowy Klaus told me she might have come to see you.'

'Anna Levine? I can't recall her.'

I took out my photograph and handed it to him. Mikael put on his tortoiseshell glasses, and I noticed now they were on a chain made of linked paper clips.

'Classy chain,' I commented.

He laughed brightly. 'Helena made it for me.'

Jealousy surged inside me, but I hid it as best I could. He studied the photograph. 'I remember this girl,' he told me, 'but Anna wasn't the name she gave me.' He handed me back the picture. 'And she never mentioned any chorus.'

'That seems odd.'

'Erik, I think we'll be far more comfortable in my office,' he said, gesturing me towards the open door at the back.

I sensed he didn't want Anka to hear any more of our conversation.

Once we were in his office, he offered me the chair in front of his cluttered desk. 'Make yourself comfortable.'

Behind Mikael were his sensual photographs of the Alps, and I speculated now that they were to remind himself that a monumental natural world – far beyond the control of the Nazis – still existed. And was waiting for him.

Sitting down, I asked, 'So what name did the girl give you?'

'I don't think she even gave me a name,' he replied, taking off his medical coat and hanging it on a hook. 'Whatever the case, I didn't write it down.'

'Why not?'

'Because she asked me not to take any notes about our conversation.'

He took a cigar from the box on his desk and offered me one, but I was feeling too tired to make the effort. 'If I remember correctly,' he continued, 'she came here without an appointment.'

'So you'd never seen her before?'

'No.' Kicking off his slippers, he sat down and leaned back with a grateful sigh. 'How do you know her?' he asked.

I told him about my conversation with Dorota, focusing on Anna's relationship with Paweł Sawicki. Mikael lit his cigar, sucking in so hard that his cheeks hollowed. He looked like the eccentric doctor in a children's story – off-kilter and endearing. Or was he making a great effort to appear that way and was someone else entirely? I again felt as though I'd wandered on to the stage set of a play, and that everyone had his lines but me.

When I finished my account, Mikael said in a horrified voice, 'This place, this time we're living through, it defies description.' He stood up, went to the window and opened the pane, taking in a bottle of vodka that had been chilling on the outside ledge.

'May I pour you a drink?' he asked, carrying the bottle to his desk.

'No, thank you. If I had any vodka, I'd fall right to sleep.'

He laughed sweetly. 'Still, you should have a smidgen.' He held his thumb and index finger an inch apart to indicate how much – the gesture of a man used to coaxing children to take their medicine. 'It'll help you relax,' he added. 'And keep you warm.'

Why are you being so nice to me? I wanted to ask. It should have been obvious to me that everyone sensed that I was barely hanging on, but it wasn't.

'I'll have a drink in a little while,' I told him.

Sitting down again, he took an amethyst-coloured shot glass from the bottom drawer of his desk and poured himself a drink. After gulping it down, he licked his lips like a cat. Added to his kindness, the intimacy of that gesture – as if we'd been friends for ages – undid me. 'Please help me, Mikael,' I pleaded, and hearing my suffocating tone of voice made me want to run.

'Listen, Erik, I'll help you any way that I can, but I can't tell you why the girl in your photograph came to me – at least, not precisely. I promised her that what we discussed would be kept secret, which is why I didn't keep a file on her. All I can really tell you is that she had a problem for which she needed a physician's help.'

'Did her mother know what was wrong with her?'

'I honestly don't know.'

'Was she very ill?'

'Erik,' he said gravely, pressing his palms together in a beseeching manner, 'don't make me lie to you.'

'She was very thin – her mother said she'd stopped eating. But maybe she couldn't eat because of dysentery. Was that it?'

'Erik, please stop!'

Despite Mikael's plea, speculations as to the source of Anna's troubles kept scattering through my head, though nearly all of them seemed ridiculously improbable. I even imagined that she was being slowly poisoned.

'Could she have gotten pregnant?' I finally asked. 'Was that why she was so desperate?'

'No,' he replied sourly.

He took a long puff on his cigar, then picked a shred of tobacco from his tongue. His gestures were quick and sure – the movements of a confident man who practised a valued profession, and whose grandchild was still alive.

I slapped his desk. 'Damn it! Someone must have known what was wrong with her! Please, Mikael, the Nazis cut off her hand!'

I knew I was making a scene, but I couldn't help myself. I wished I hadn't ever given him my real name; having a false identity would have enabled me to plead more desperately – or even threaten him.

Shaken, the physician put on his spectacles and refilled his glass slowly.

'Just tell me if she said anything about my nephew. I've a right to know that.'

He looked up, astonished. 'So they knew each other?' he asked.

'I can't be sure. Though there's one link between them – the chorus.'

'I see what you mean. But in that case, Rowy would be the person to talk to.'

A knock on the door interrupted us. It was Mikael's nurse. 'If there's nothing else, I'll be going, Dr Tengmann,' she said.

'Thank you, Anka. Goodnight.'

'Have a good evening, Dr Cohen,' she added.

'Thank you – and thanks for the tea,' I told her.

After the door was closed, I faced Mikael again. 'Rowy assured me that Anna never spoke of Adam to him. And my nephew never mentioned the girl to me.'

'So it seems we're at a dead end.'

He downed his second vodka, then pressed a troubled hand to his brow.

'Are you all right?' I asked.

'Just a momentary . . . what? I don't know how to describe it.' He lowered his hand. 'Despair comes to me when I least expect it. It's as if I'm in mourning.'

'For whom, if you don't mind my asking?'

'That's just it – I don't know.' He showed me a surprised look. 'It's like a new form of grief – for nothing and everything at the same time. I don't know any word for it.' He shook his head, displeased with himself. 'Though I have no right to talk of grief in front of you. I'm sorry.'

I saw I'd misjudged him; Adam was very much on his mind. 'Don't be sorry,' I told him. 'I'm grateful for your sensitivity to my feelings. And I realize you won't reveal any more about Anna than you've already told me, but do you know of anyone else who might be aware of what was wrong with her?'

'I'm afraid the girl hardly told me anything about her life. And now . . .' He took a second amethyst-coloured shot glass from his desk drawer and poured me a drink.

When I knocked back the vodka in one go, Mikael grinned in admiration.

'Better?' he asked.

'Few subjects could be less important than how I feel,' I replied, choosing honesty over politeness. 'But thank you just the same.'

Before leaving, Mikael handed me Adam's file. In his precise handwriting, in German, the physician had written: 'Excellent reflexes. Alert. No signs of any disease, but needs to put on weight!!!'

I'll never forget those three exclamation marks.

He had also written APPROVED FOR THE CHORUS in big letters.

I searched the page for a statistic I'd wanted to check and found it scribbled near the bottom. Adam had been four feet one and three-quarters of an inch in height at the end of November 1940, a quarter of an inch shorter than the measurement I'd recorded for him two weeks prior to that date.

In my mind, I saw myself tilting my pencil in a favourable direction; I hadn't realized I'd cheated.

'You can keep it if you want,' Mikael told me, and when I looked up to thank him, I discovered his eyes were moist. 'Adam was beautiful,' he told me.

I was back on the street when I heard my name called. Anka, Dr Tengmann's nurse, came hurrying towards me, her determined face wrapped tightly in a white headscarf.

'I could lose my job for this,' she told me in a rushed voice, 'but that girl, Anna, she never came to the office – at least not while I was here. And we kept no file on her. Ask yourself why!'

'But Mikael said that was because . . .'

Before I could say anything more, Anka turned and hurried away. She looked back at me once over her shoulder. I didn't see fear, as I'd expected. I saw anger.

CHAPTER 12

Before going home, I went to speak to Dorota. Clutching a floral shawl tightly over her shoulders, she tiptoed out into the hallway to speak to me. 'I'm sorry, but my husband won't let anyone come in,' she whispered.

I explained what I'd learned from Mikael.

Dorota shook her head sceptically. 'Anna refused to discuss her health with anyone. I can't believe she would have spoken to him or any other stranger.'

'So why would Mikael make up a visit from her?'

'I don't know.'

When I asked for a list of Anna's closest friends, along with their addresses, she slipped back inside to fulfil my request. A minute or so later, she slid an envelope under the door.

Dorota had written down two names in her precise script. Both lived across town in the Little Ghetto. I looked at my watch – ten minutes to seven. I'd have to return home to make supper. There wouldn't be enough time before curfew to question Anna's friends that evening.

On returning to Stefa's flat, I discovered that the ghetto health service had sprayed carbolic acid on everything except her bed, since she hadn't force enough in her coat-hanger arms to get up by herself and had adamantly refused assistance. I found her forehead burning. Her feet, however, were ice. As I covered them with an extra blanket, she said, 'No, don't, I have to wash Adam's white shirt in the tub. Help me stand up.'

'Why would you need to wash his shirt?' I asked.

'He's being photographed in the morning.'

'What are you talking about?'

From deep inside the delusion that had overwhelmed her, she replied, 'All the kids are being photographed for the start of school.'

Offering her the truth at that moment might threaten her fragile stability, so I told her that she was far too ill to do any washing, and that if I got Adam's white shirt wet now it wouldn't be dry by morning. 'But he has other nice shirts he can wear,' I added, trying to sound cheerful. 'I'll iron one after supper.' I intended to do just that if it would calm her.

'You're a bastard!' she snapped.

'Stefa, please don't say that. I'm doing my best.'

'But you're always criticizing me!'

Being thought of as an unfair uncle made me frantic, so I took the shirt she wanted out of the hamper in my room. When I brought it to her, she fought to sit up.

'For the love of God, stay put!' I ordered. 'I'll wash it right after supper.'

She began to cry in silence. Sitting down beside her, I told her I'd hang the wet shirt next to the heater in my room so it would be dry by morning. 'Don't worry – Adam will look like a prince for his photo.'

She gazed away. Her lips moved, and twice she mouthed her son's name. I imagined she was doing calculations about her own life and had discovered that nothing she could do in the future would ever even add up to zero.

'Stefa,' I began, but I couldn't finish my sentence; I couldn't think of how to phrase my wishes for us without seeming to betray the depth of our grief.

I sat alone at the kitchen table, feeling as though the walls of the room might collapse on me – and that it would be a fitting end.

Then I practised Erik Honec's signature until I settled on a highly ornamented script, with aristocratic flourishes on the E and the H.

The very movement of my hands gave me solace. It meant: *I still have options.*

At 7.30, Ewa arrived with Helena in order to check on Stefa before curfew. I had only just started on my cabbage and potato-skin soup, and all the people I needed to interview about Adam's death crowded in upon me as I stood over the stove. Helena stayed with me while Ewa talked to my niece. At the kitchen table, the little girl drew jagged pictures of needle-nosed aeroplanes flying over Warsaw. She told me they were Russian bombers. The city – a confusion of steeples and towers – was empty of people.

'But where is everyone?' I asked, fearing they'd been killed.

'On vacation,' she replied. 'It's summer.' She pointed to the big yellow sun at the top of her drawing.

I smiled at her, grateful for the warm days and nights in her imagination.

My niece must have told Ewa the nature of her quarrel with me; on hearing the taps in the bathroom running, Helena and I went in and discovered Ewa washing Adam's shirt in the bathtub. She hung it on a cord we strung across my room.

At just before eight, Ewa kissed me goodnight and led Helena to the door. I tried to give her money for a rickshaw – one of the bicycles mounted with a seat in front that had become common on our island by then – but she refused.

I propped Stefa up with pillows and spooned soup into her mouth, but she ate with inner-turned eyes and said nothing to me.

Then – God knows why – I sat at my desk and wrote a list of all the people I had known who were dead, starting with Adam and Hannah. I counted them when I was done: twenty-five. I spent another hour working on the list and came up with two more. But I still wasn't satisfied.

Only then did I remember that my mother became a frenzied list-maker after my younger brother was born. Papa and I would find her numbered inventories everywhere around the house. Years later, I asked her about it, and she told me it was the only way she could keep her head above the high water of having two children to raise.

On a whim, I inserted *Erik Honec* after my mother's name, and it was a relief to see my alter ego there; it meant I would escape the ghetto one way or another.

I settled into Stefa's armchair for the night. She stirred only once, some time after midnight, needing to pee, and her fever was down a little in the morning. She thanked me in a strong voice when I handed her a cup of hot tea sweetened with molasses and the sugar crystal I'd saved. I felt she'd returned home and kissed her cheek in welcome. After smearing rhubarb jam on her toast, I fed her pieces on the end of a fork. She joked about my aristocratic table manners, which seemed a very good sign, but while I was in the kitchen making myself some ersatz coffee, she called out, 'Is Adam's shirt dry yet?'

I went in to her. Maybe something in my expression reminded her of the truth; her eyes opened wide in horror and she brought her hands to her mouth.

'He's dead, isn't he?' she whispered timidly.

'Let's talk,' I said, rubbing her feet through the covers. 'You'll tell me whatever you want, and I'll make no judgements. I promise.'

I made that vow because I couldn't bear the thought of being remembered as an unfair uncle after I was gone.

'No,' she told me firmly. 'There's nothing to talk about.'

I stood up and retreated to the kitchen. There was a knock on the door while I was staring mindlessly into my coffee. I found Wolfi, Feivel and Sarah looking up at me from the landing. Their little faces were fearful; I suppose they thought that Adam's death might have turned me against them.

'Hello, Dr Cohen, we . . . we came to see Gloria,' Feivel told me hesitantly.

'She's not doing so good,' I replied. 'But you can come in and feed her if you like.'

While Feivel and Wolfi spilled seeds into her dish, Sarah carried the budgie's water cup back from the sink in both her hands, determined not to spill a drop. Her clenched determination gave me an idea.

'Maybe one of you could adopt Gloria,' I suggested. 'Adam would want that.'

Wolfi said, 'My dad hates pets. And he says birds shit all the time.'

Feivel gazed down, swirling his foot. Sarah bit her lip, looking as if she wanted to dash away.

'Forget what I said,' I told them. 'I was being thoughtless.'

'No, I'll take her!' Feivel announced, and he nodded hard when I looked at him, as if to convince us both.

As the two boys carried the cage downstairs, Sarah looked back at me for a moment, as though to fix me and the apartment in her memory, and I realized – with despair clutching at me – that I'd never see her or any of Adam's other friends ever again.

At 9.15, I left Stefa alone to visit Mrs Rackemann. She let me into her shop and locked the door with a firm twist of her hand.

The forger she'd hired – who went by the name of Otto – had typed me a document on Nazi stationery identifying Erik Honec as Sub-Director for the Warsaw District of the *Reichsministerium des Innern*, the Ministry of the Interior. I'd suggested the Reich Census Office, but Mrs Rackemann informed me that Otto had advised something more general, in case I ever embarked on another escapade demanding a slightly different government posting.

She grinned cagily on telling me that – she plainly adored trying to outwit the Nazis.

I tilted the stationery towards the light from her desk lamp. At the top of the sheet of off-white paper, the Nazi emblem – an eagle perched on a wreath centred by a swastika – looked sinisterly impressive. And the embossed stamp at the bottom seemed to be the real thing. As I ran my finger over its surface, Mrs Rackemann said, 'Otto's pretty damn good, isn't he?'

'A real pro,' I agreed.

'He produced papers for the Polish Interior Ministry for several years. He knows what he's doing – though he wished you'd supplied him with a photograph.'

'I might have lost my nerve if I'd gone home to get one. Besides, a Pole won't know what to expect, and I'm not planning on identifying myself to any German officials.'

After I promised her the rest of her payment the next day, Mrs Rackemann handed me a pen for the last detail. I signed my new name with the decisive flourishes I'd practised – a vow of revenge turned to ink.

Having had hundreds of Christian acquaintances before being forced into the ghetto, I'd decided that a change of appearance was in order before I ventured into the Other Side; after all, if someone recognized me and denounced me, I'd be executed on the spot. So before going home, I bought hair dye at a beauty parlour on Nalewki Street.

The homemade concoction turned into a frothy, milky-brown cream when I mixed it with water, and it tickled my scalp. I had my doubts about its effectiveness, but when I washed it off, my hair was black and shiny. The contrast with my ghostly skin and deep wrinkles made me look like an aged flamenco dancer clinging desperately to youth. My eyes seemed smaller, too, as if the *I* inside me were trapped in a deep cave.

Taking off my clothes and sitting close to my heater, I sponged off weeks of grime as best I could with our mushy ghetto soap. Then I shaved carefully, and dabbed my chin and cheeks with Stefa's rosewater perfume.

I dressed in my chestnut-brown woollen suit, which I hadn't worn since the day I'd moved into Stefa's apartment, but the heavy fabric sagged clownishly off my shrunken shoulders, so I put on a jumper underneath. I didn't wear my overcoat because it looked like a rag. Better to freeze than risk ruining my disguise.

As a last touch, I went to see Izzy to borrow his Borsalino. He'd recently moved his old army cot into his workshop because three newly arrived cousins of his were living in his apartment and he was feeling cornered.

On opening his door to me, he grimaced. '*Gottenyu*, Erik! What the hell happened to you?'

'I needed a new identity,' I explained, stepping inside.

'And it involves putting a dead crow on your head?'

'I'm a zookeeper in a Yiddish farce,' I quipped.

'They keep typecasting you!' he observed gleefully; even in grief – especially then – Izzy thrived on repartee.

'Tell me the truth – could I pass for the *me* I used to be?'

He sized me up, having to choose between humour and honesty. 'That depends on which *you* you intend to impersonate,' he replied. 'But why would you want to?'

'Never mind that. I'll need your Borsalino. Where is it?'

'So you're trying for the romantic lead, after all?' A lecherous spark went off in his eyes.

'Listen, if I don't come back, take any clothing of mine you want. And take my books.'

'If you're up to something dangerous, I want to know what it is.'

'It's a long story.'

'Tell me the condensed version or you can forget my help.'

After I told him about Anna, and showed him my Interior Ministry papers, he made clicking noises with his tongue – Izzy's code for a risky adventure – then slipped into the stationery warehouse behind his workshop to fetch his Borsalino. I needed to pee and went to the lavatory, which was a tin bucket hidden behind a folding screen. Hanging from the ceiling were paper arrows pointing towards Moscow, New York, Rio de Janeiro and the North Pole. A bigger one, facing southwest, read: *Boulogne-Billancourt: 1,300 kilometres*; Izzy's two adult sons – Ryszard and Karl – both worked as aircraft mechanics in that industrial suburb of Paris.

Back in his workroom, he handed me his hat. He already had his muffler on and was buttoning his coat.

'So, what's your problem, Dr Freud?' he asked when he was done, lifting those furry eyebrows of his; I must have been showing him a puzzled look.

'Nothing,' I replied; by then, I'd realized that having him join me was the real reason I'd come over.

'Watch this!' he said, and he pulled a white silk handkerchief from out of nowhere – a trick from his days of performing magic shows aboard the *Bourdonnais,* the French ocean liner on which he'd worked as a steward in his youth.

'What's that for?' I asked.

Folding it in a square, he put it in my breast pocket. 'Now you look a man not to be taken lightly!' he observed triumphantly.

'Or maybe just a well-dressed zookeeper,' I retorted.

Rabe hadn't yet arrived at 1 Leszno Street. We paid our ten złoty to a teenage guard wearing diving goggles; the cellar had recently become a rickshaw assembly plant and he doubled as a welder. About twenty men and boys – bare-chested and dripping with sweat – were hammering bicycle wheels, filing fenders, patching tyres . . . Izzy and I headed past them to the back, as we'd been instructed. The smell of burnt rubber and axel grease packed my nose. We climbed up a set of stairs to a scarred wooden door.

'Could it be this simple?' he asked.

I turned the brass handle and pushed open the door. We were in a dimly lit hallway. The guard we'd been told about had a grim moustache and dull eyes. He was eating an apple. Looking us up and down, he said in a gruff Polish, 'Take off your Jewish armbands.'

Once they were safely hidden in our pockets, he pointed to a rickety wooden staircase at the end of the hallway. 'One flight up,' he grumbled.

We came to a door giving out on a courtyard with a marble fountain at the centre: Pan balancing on one leg and playing his flute. Crossing over the flagstones, we entered the front hallway. Empty wooden crates were scattered around. We pushed through the front door into a sunlit street.

Izzy and I stopped right away, staring at the buildings around us like dazed insects after a thunderstorm.

The biggest difference was the smell, though I didn't realize that until we'd walked for twenty minutes and were standing under the spires of the Holy Cross Church. The pet-shop stink of the ghetto had disappeared.

We whispered our amazement in Polish; we dared not speak Yiddish outside our own territory.

Walking ahead, I tried to regain the confident gait of the Before Time – as I'd come to think of the time prior to the German occupation of Warsaw – but I kept lapsing into the hunched shuffle we'd all acquired. The ghetto paso doble, Izzy called it.

A dozen or so drunken German soldiers were singing disconnected harmonies on a melody I didn't recognize while wavering along the sidewalk in Zbawiciela Square. Hunching our shoulders, we made ourselves as compact as possible and rushed the other way around the traffic circle.

'We must look like two fucking matzo balls!' Izzy whispered to me.

In more favourable circumstances, I'd have burst out laughing.

Disappearing into the crowds on Marszałkowska Street made me shudder with relief. And good memories cheered me, too; Hannah and I used to come shopping here when we were courting – safe from our nosy parents and their gossip-greedy spies.

Feeling safe, I punched Izzy on the arm – hard enough to stun him but not to hurt.

'What's that for?' he asked, feigning anger.

'For trying to make me laugh in front of German soldiers.'

'So, what other choice do I have?' he asked, giving a Yiddish lilt to his question.

I turned in a circle to take in the dimensions of our temporary escape – and to gauge our vulnerability. No one was staring at us. A good sign.

'The thing that troubles me,' I told Izzy, 'is that I don't think anyone on this side of the border knows yet that Adam is dead. They probably don't want to know anything of what we're going through.'

Izzy spoke to me then about how my nephew's murder had damaged his faith, using his idiosyncratic clockmaker's metaphors – bent springs, wayward escape wheels . . . I listened closely to his stop-and-start confessions because I sensed he'd never reveal his heart to me like this inside the ghetto, and I was touched that he would risk talking to me of God, since I'd always been such an obstinate atheist. When he was done, I stared into the despair of his eyes, and it seemed that our friendship was the only way either of us would make it out of the frigid ocean we'd found ourselves in.

I whispered to him the one-line poem I'd been saving: 'Children are transformed into adults on passing through the threshold of Gehenna.'

'And what about adults themselves?' he asked.

'I'll have to think about that.'

As we walked on, I realized the time had arrived to broach a subject that had come close to drowning our friendship forty years earlier. 'Listen, Izzy, I'm sorry for disappointing you all those years ago. I was awful to you. Forgive me.'

He came to a halt, stunned.

'I should have apologized years ago,' I continued. 'I was a fool.'

It was good that we were speaking Polish; it was easier to venture out of my usual self in a language that wasn't the one I'd been living in of late.

He gazed down, unsure of how to reply. His jaw was throbbing. 'You didn't know what damage you could do. We were both too young to behave like men.'

For *men*, he risked using the word *mensch*, and its Yiddish nuances implied that we hadn't been ready to be good and generous with each other – let alone, with everyone else.

He and I stepped a little lighter across the rest of the journey that day, and I realized it no longer mattered that we'd never shared a bed; we were together now. Our renewed closeness was the one thing for which we owed the Nazis our thanks.

Soon, a troubling question came to me, however: might Adam's killer also have been freed from previous taboos by the German occupation?

Paweł's building was in the Stary Mokotów neighbourhood, an elegant section of the city guarded by broad, bare-limbed linden and birch trees. Two marble caryatids with smashed noses flanked the entryway. The tile floor – a checquerboard pattern – was sticky. The post box for 5B was labelled Sawicki.

'I really hope Paweł's mother will be as intimidated by Germans as most Poles,' I told Izzy.

He and I had reasoned that the boy's father would be at work.

'Growl at her every now and again – like you do at me,' he replied, grinning. He gave me a little shove towards the staircase – one soldier to another. '*Festina lente*' – hurry slowly – he added, shaking a teacherly finger; it was what our Latin professor, Dr Borkowski, used to tell us when the bell rang at the end of class.

Izzy waited downstairs. On the fifth-floor landing, I untied my scarf, took off my gloves and put on the Nazi armband that Mrs Rackemann had managed to secure for me. The swastika raised gooseflesh, but it also freed my imagination – the paradox of a good deception.

An attractive woman in a pink, floor-length nightgown – with silly carnation-like tufts of fur on her cuffs – answered my knocks. I'd have guessed she was forty, though her chestnut-brown hair was cut in a long fringe, which had the effect of making her look girlish. She had an intelligent face, but hard.

'Mrs Sawicki?' I asked, taking off Izzy's Borsalino.

'Yes.'

'My name is Honec. I'm sorry to bother you. I'm from the Reich Ministry of the Interior.'

I gave my voice the shading of an Austrian accent – I'd decided that, like me, Honec had lived in Vienna for a time.

We shook hands. Hers was cold but soft, and her long fingernails were painted cherry red; she plainly didn't need to do housework, even under German occupation.

'Is your husband in?' I asked.

'No, I'm sorry, he's at work, but perhaps I can help you. Is something wrong?'

'Nothing terribly important. It's just that we've lost track of a young woman – Jewish. I'm told that you might know her.'

'Unlikely – I don't socialize with Jews.'

'Very wise,' I observed. 'But I'd still like to speak with you a moment.'

'I'm not yet dressed, as you can see.'

'I have my orders,' I replied stiffly, 'and I wouldn't want you to have to come down to our office. It's way across town.'

'Do you have some identification?'

I took out Otto's handiwork and handed it to her. She scanned the text quickly – too quickly, as though trying to convince me she was absolutely fluent in German.

'All right, come in,' she said, handing me back my forgery but not bothering to hide her frown.

One test passed. I stepped inside. The floor was handsome, dark parquet, and the scent of fresh paint made my nose itch. I was evidently ready to embrace any clue, no matter how small; I pictured the blood from Anna's severed hand splattering against the walls, which had been given a concealing coat of whitewash.

Mrs Sawicki wore gold slippers tipped by tiny pom-poms of fur, exactly like the ones on her sleeves. It seemed so ludicrous a fashion that it could only work in the movies.

'Come this way,' she told me welcomingly.

Passing an antique wooden dresser and secretary, we reached a large sitting room in the centre of which lay a plush red rug the exact shade of Mrs Sawicki's fingernails. On opposite sides of the rug were a white leather sofa and three Art Nouveau armchairs whose backs were shaped like lyres and painted gold. The seats and legs were black.

I was dealing with a woman eager to go well with her furniture and decorations, but it was the space between and around things that put me on edge; having become used to our cramped clutter, this planet of comfort and wealth seemed menacing.

'Sit here, Mr Honec,' Mrs Sawicki told me, gesturing towards her sofa, which faced away from the windows. The buildings across the street crouched beneath the leaden sky, seeming to shrink away from winter. It was the tropics in here, however; the stove in the corner of the room – adorned with pink and white tiles in a geometric pattern – was radiating more heat than I'd felt in months. As I sat down, I thought bitterly of Stefa, one mile west and shivering under a mountain of blankets. Dislocation – heavy and hopeless – was the feeling that pulsed at the back of my head.

I was already hot, but I kept my suit coat on to appear more authoritative. I placed my hat beside me.

Mrs Sawicki sat opposite me in one of her small golden thrones.

It was obvious by now that she was royalty in her own imagination, and not at all intimidated by me.

'So, how is life at the Ministry of the Interior?' she asked, the amused twist to her lips telling me that she regarded my work as unimportant. Leaning forward, she took a cigarette from an ivory box on the glass table between us.

'With all the shipments of Jews coming in, we've been busy,' I replied, standing up and offering her a light. She brushed my hand as she took it – a studied gesture, and a cliché, but the twinge in my gut, like a bolt opening, meant she had achieved her effect. She funnelled the smoke towards the ceiling and crossed her slender legs.

I'd purchased a pack of Gauloises cigarettes to enhance my deception. Before sitting down, I stuck one in my mouth and lit it, then surveyed the room.

On the glass coffee table between us I discovered a stack of *Film Kurier* magazines. The cover on top showed Greta Garbo and Robert Taylor leaning towards a passionate kiss. I remembered how disgusted Dorota had been that Anna and Paweł had had secret trysts at the cinema.

'If you don't mind my saying so, you speak wonderful Polish for a German,' Mrs Sawicki told me.

'My family moved to Warsaw when I was thirteen,' I replied.

'How nice for you. Where did your family live?'

She was probably testing for the ghetto. 'Tamka Street,' I answered – it was where my uncle Franz had lived. 'So my father could walk to his classes. He was a professor at the university.'

'I see. Honec – that sounds Czech.'

'My father was from Prague and my mother from Vienna – which was where I was born.'

'An interesting upbringing, no doubt,' she observed generously, and yet she smoked with abrupt, irritated gestures.

Having repulsed her first attack, I grew bolder. By the entranceway to the bedrooms I'd spotted a Japanese watercolour of a yellow finch sitting on a tip of bamboo. Behind the exuberant little bird was a mist-covered mountain. I asked Mrs Sawicki if I could take a closer look.

'By all means,' she replied, energized by my interest.

As I stepped up to the watercolour, I brushed my hand against the wall, which proved to be completely dry – as it would be if Anna had been killed here on 24 January.

'It's by Sakai Hōitsu,' Mrs Sawicki told me. 'Japanese, late eighteenth century – Rinpa school.'

She was happy to show off her knowledge of Eastern art. I watched her smoke. She watched me watching. She adored the small spotlight I focused on her.

'The finch and the mountain seem to be made of the same substance,' I observed.

'And I believe that substance is called paint,' replied Mrs Sawicki, grinning.

A genuinely witty comment, and to please her I laughed.

All the artwork on her walls seemed to be from the Orient – and to be intended to tell guests that she was a cultured woman who had travelled far beyond the borders of Poland. So I ventured a guess: 'Was your father in the diplomatic corps?'

'I'm impressed, Mr Honec!' she replied, making a small, deferential bow. 'But it was Grandfather who was the ambassador in the family.' In perfect German – proving my earlier conclusion about her language skills to be wrong – she added, 'After finishing his career, he settled in Vienna. Whenever I visited him, he loved to take me out to dinner at the Imperial Hotel, on the Opera Ring. They had the best Sachertorte in all Austria – despite what the owners of the Sacher Hotel would like you to believe. Did you ever dine there, by any chance?'

Mrs Sawicki was trying to catch me out. Was I not acting my part cleverly enough?

'If you'll excuse a small correction,' I told her, emphasizing my Austrian accent, 'the Imperial is on the Kaerntner Ring. And I'm afraid it was beyond my father's means.'

'So it is, Mr Honec, so it is.' Her lips were pursed with amusement again; she was aware that I knew she'd been testing me. 'Now, if you'll excuse me,' she told me in Polish, 'I'll get dressed so we can talk properly.'

Mrs Sawicki still didn't seem to regard me as a worthy opponent. As though to prove her wrong, I stubbed out my cigarette as soon as she had swept out of the room and started searching her furniture for anything related to Anna or Adam. In the cabinet below the Victrola, classical symphonies predominated, but I found a record by Hanka Ordonówna with Paweł's signature on the centre label. Wouldn't he have taken a favourite recording with him to boarding school?

In the secretary in the foyer were envelopes printed with Mrs Sawicki's name in gold lettering, along with a dry inkwell and a puckered old apple that must have been hidden and forgotten, possibly by a younger sibling of Paweł's. On a sudden whim, I took three envelopes and stuffed them in my coat pocket. In the dresser were linens and a set of Jugendstil silverware in a wooden case. Easing it open, I lifted out six demitasse spoons. When I placed them beside the envelopes, the rest of my visit with Mrs. Sawicki was destined to beat with the damning evidence of thievery concealed in my pocket.

I'd needed to take something of value from her. I didn't know or care why. My belly was aching with hunger and anxiety, and that seemed far more important.

I sat back down when I heard Mrs Sawicki's footsteps approaching and lit another cigarette. She entered in a tightly fitted long blue dress. Her high heels were black and her lipstick blood red. Her eyes were thickly shaded with dark brown mascara, so that they looked bruised. She'd become the dramatic heroine of an Erich Maria Remarque novel.

Walking to the coffee table in front of me, she straightened the *Film Kurier* I'd noticed so that it was flush with the others and then sat opposite me again, joining her hands together in her lap as if afraid to be too expressive; perhaps my presence was worrisome, after all. Maybe her beloved Paweł had murdered Anna – or had been witness to a tragic accident – and she was worried I'd learn the truth and bring scandal on the family.

I took off my coat because I was sweating heavily. 'I'll get to the point,' I told my host. 'The missing girl's name is Anna Levine. I believe she might have come here. Her mother says that your son was her boyfriend.'

Mrs Sawicki forced a laugh. 'Paweł would never take a *Żydóweczka* as a girlfriend.' She pronounced *Jew-girl* as if spitting out dirt. I'd have liked to drag her back to the ghetto and leave her to fend for herself for a few weeks.

'Still,' I told her, 'I know she came here on the twenty-fourth of January.'

She pinched a piece of lint from the hem of her dress. 'That's impossible.'

'She'd needed to talk to Paweł,' I observed. 'She was ill, and she wanted his help.'

'I told you, my son didn't know any *Żydóweczka* named Anna.' Noticing the curl of ash at the tip of my cigarette, Mrs Sawicki moved the crystal ashtray closer to me.

'I'd prefer to keep our talk friendly,' I told her. 'Are you sure you never met Anna?'

'Absolutely.'

I tapped the ash on to the rug. She gave me a murderous look but didn't move. I had the feeling she could have held her hand over a candle flame to spite me.

'I have a reliable witness who told me Anna was here,' I challenged her; my anger was giving me a kind of reckless courage.

She stood up and walked to the window, her steps precise, barely

112

controlling her rage. When she turned, her eyes targeted me. 'Paweł and the girl went out a few times,' she told me, 'but as soon as I found out, I put a stop to it.'

'And Anna came here on the twenty-fourth of January.'

'How could I possibly remember the exact date? In any case, when she came to my door, I told her that Paweł was at boarding school, but the silly girl didn't believe me. She insisted on coming in – she even had the nerve to search his room without my permission.' Mrs Sawicki grimaced. 'She stank up the apartment – for a week it smelled like a stables in here.'

Because we have no hot water, and we have run out of proper soap, I wanted to shout at her. Instead, I said, 'Jews are filth.'

'No, Mr Honec, if they were just filth,' she replied in a lecturing voice, 'they wouldn't represent such a danger to us. I'm afraid they're much more than that.'

'Then how would you describe them?' I asked.

'As a subversive story that has finally come to an end.'

Her words rattled me, and I nodded my agreement to cover my unease. 'If only you're right,' I told her. 'Now, do you know where Anna went after she left here?'

'Back to her stables,' she replied, grinning as if she'd made another witticism.

'Did she say if she was going to meet a friend?' I asked.

'She told me nothing. She was only here a minute – less than that . . .'

'Did you see anything special on her hands – a ring or a bracelet?'

'Not that I recall.'

'Think back, if you can.'

'What are you implying?' she bristled. 'You can't possibly think she was wearing anything my son had given her! Mr Honec, this was just a minor fling for Paweł. It meant nothing.'

I stood up and handed her my photograph of Adam. 'Have you seen this boy?'

She shook her head.

'His name was Adam. Did Anna mention a boy with that name, by any chance?'

'No.'

'Did she give you anything? A letter?'

Mrs Sawicki glared at me over her nose as if I was trying her patience. I took a last puff on my cigarette and crushed it out on the windowsill. Tears welled in her eyes.

'If you're holding something back from me,' I threatened, 'then your husband will lose his job.'

'Mr Honec, it's clear to me that you don't understand the Poles. We're a proud people who have been oppressed for centuries, and we don't like being given orders by foreigners.' She was sitting up straight – she regarded herself as heroic and was posing for later recall.

'Who's giving orders?' I asked in an amused voice. 'I'm just asking questions.'

'Questions can be orders under certain circumstances.'

'You're a clever lady, Mrs Sawicki.'

'You better believe it!' she exclaimed, as if she were giving me a warning.

'But I don't need to be clever,' I told her. 'Because I make up the rules as I go.' I knocked my dead cigarette on to the parquet with the back of my hand.

The tendons on her neck stood out threateningly. 'You are, I suppose, aware you have no manners?' she demanded in an aristocratic voice.

'I'm only rude when my patience is being tested,' I retorted.

'The Jewish slut gave me a photograph for my son,' she admitted. 'She'd written something on the back, but I burned it.'

'What did she write?'

'I don't read Paweł's correspondence!' she snarled.

It was my turn to laugh.

'I don't appreciate being ridiculed by old Austrians!'

'Then who do you enjoy being ridiculed by?' I asked with a provocative smile.

'Who or what I enjoy is not your concern.'

'That's true – nothing about you concerns me,' I shot back with deadly contempt, 'except what you know of Anna Levine.'

'I didn't read what she wrote!' she shouted.

'Mrs Sawicki,' I said more gently, 'if we banter back and forth, we'll just keep offending each other. Just tell me what Anna wrote to Paweł.'

She straightened the shoulders of her dress, considering her options. At length, she said, 'She wrote that she couldn't understand why he hadn't called. She had important news for him. She begged him to call her or at least send her his new address.'

'Which he never did, because you never told your son that Anna had come here.'

'Of course, not. Why would I help her trap my son?'

'So you were worried he really was in love with her,' I observed.

She rolled her eyes. 'Do you really think a fifteen-year-old knows what love is?'

'Do you?' I asked pointedly.

'Mr Honec, you can be very annoying.'

'In any case, it's curious that Anna disappeared just after visiting you,' I told her.

'I know nothing about what happened to her after she left here.'

'Write down Paweł's new address for me.'

She went to the secretary in the foyer, took out a sheet of paper and scribbled quickly. Paweł's boarding school had an address in Zurich. Folding the paper in four, I put it in my pocket, and on a hunch, I said, 'Did you think you'd fool me so easily?'

'What do you mean?'

'Paweł is still here in Warsaw, isn't he?'

'Wait here.' She disappeared through the door at the side of the sitting room and returned with an envelope bearing a Zurich postmark. Taking out the letter, which was written on thin blue paper, she handed it to me. 'If you look at the date and signature, you'll see Paweł wrote it two months ago.'

She lit another cigarette as I confirmed what she said. Her contemptuous stare gave me an exaggerated sense of being nowhere close to where I wanted to be. I had the feeling the world was speaking to me, but at a pitch so high that I couldn't hear the message. I handed her back her son's letter, though, like Anna, I wasn't convinced that everything was as it seemed.

'Now get out of my apartment,' she ordered harshly, 'or I'll call my husband and have you arrested. He's an important judge, and Governor Frank is a family friend. So if you think you will ever do anything to hurt my Paweł, then you are . . .'

'If Governor Frank were such a friend,' I cut in, 'then why did you tell me the truth about Anna? You have to know that I suspect that you might be behind her disappearance. Or is it your son who's responsible?'

Mrs Sawicki shot me a hateful look. 'I only told you about the girl because she means nothing to me or my son – dead or alive.'

'I never said she was dead!' I declared.

'Hah!' she sneered. 'If you think you've caught me out, then you're a fool, Mr Honec. You must suspect she's dead or you wouldn't be here. In any case, I can't imagine why she means anything to the Reich Ministry of the Interior.'

'That, Mrs Sawicki, is no concern of yours,' I told her with poisonous calm, and before she could come up with a reply, I went to retrieve my coat and hat from the sofa.

When I returned to the foyer, it was clear from her contemptuous face that we had nothing more to say to each other. I nodded by way of goodbye and reached for the door handle, turning away from her. A mistake. I felt a burn near my elbow. She'd pressed something through my sweater into my skin. Stinging with pain, I swung out my arm and caught her on the mouth with the back of my hand, knocking her into the wall. Righting herself, she dropped her cigarette to the floor and crushed it out with the toe of her shoe. Reaching up to her lip, which was cut, she took some blood on to her fingertip and licked it.

Tears of shock and pain had welled in my eyes. I wiped them away roughly.

'Now you'll never go anywhere again without a scar from me!' she told me, and she laughed in a triumphant burst.

Mrs Sawicki was treacherous enough to have murdered Anna, and she was obviously given to violent outbursts, but why would she have taken the girl's hand?

Might Paweł have been so passionately in love with Anna that he gave her a precious family heirloom – a bracelet – without thinking of how angrily his mother would react? After all, Mrs Sawicki *had* become particularly defensive when I'd mentioned Anna's jewellery. Maybe Anna had kept the gift concealed from her mother and friends. On the day she ventured out of the ghetto, she somehow sealed the clasp so that it couldn't be taken from her without also taking her hand.

And yet with a judge for a husband, Mrs Sawicki would have found a legal way to recover any keepsake that Paweł had given Anna. She would have claimed, in fact, that the girl had stolen it. No government official would have believed Anna's word against hers.

Furthermore, it seemed impossible that Mrs Sawicki could have had anything to do with Adam's murder. How would she even have known of his existence?

In the lobby, I took Izzy's arm and rushed him away, sure that we'd be in danger as long as we remained nearby. Despite myself, I'd begun to fear that Mrs Sawicki could stop my heart with a single, well-directed thought.

117

She was gazing down at us from her balcony as we crossed the street. And all that day she would wheel above my thoughts like a bird of prey.

We made it to Jawicki Jewellers on Spacerowa Street at just past one in the afternoon. I recognized the balding shop manager who'd sold me a floral pin for Liesel two years before, but he didn't know me, which was a relief. Still, Mrs Sawicki had unnerved me and I fumbled Hannah's ring when I took it out of my pocket. It crashed on to his wooden desk.

He snatched it up with an agile hand. 'Got ya!' he exclaimed.

'Thanks,' I told him.

'You needn't have worried,' he observed. 'Diamonds are a lot harder than people.'

A surprising comment. Izzy looked at me sideways, which meant *don't let him trick you into saying anything about yourself.*

The jeweller put a loop in his eye and turned the ring to catch the diffuse winter light from his window. At length, he said, 'I'll give you two thousand seven hundred for it.' His toothy smile meant that he was giving me a great deal.

'It's worth three times that,' I stated for the record.

'Not to someone in your position,' he retorted.

The moist chill at the back of my neck was my fear that he *did* remember me – and knew I was a Jew. 'What the hell is that supposed to mean?' I demanded, figuring I might try to intimidate him.

'You badly need cash or you wouldn't be here.'

'Three thousand five hundred,' Izzy said, 'or we go elsewhere and you lose big.' He spoke with a Jimmy Cagney snarl to his words.

'Your bodyguard?' the jeweller asked me, smirking. His comment was meant to put Izzy in his place, since he wasn't quite five foot four even on his best day.

'As a matter of fact, I've been his bodyguard for sixty years,' my old friend replied.

And then he took a gun out of his coat pocket.

'Shit!' the jeweller exclaimed, jumping up from his stool.

'What in God's name are you doing?' I whisper-screamed at Izzy.

'Protecting us,' he replied calmly.

'Don't shoot me!' the man pleaded. Taking a step back, he held up both his hands as if to stop an onrushing carriage.

The pistol was bulky and black – and stunningly dangerous. 'Does it work?' I asked.

'You bet,' Izzy told me happily. 'It's German, and I just cleaned it the other day.' He jiggled it: 'Very sensitive – might even go off accidentally . . .' Here, he targeted his vengeful eyes on the jeweller – 'and kill the rudest person in the room. Now who do you think that might be?'

'There's . . . there's no need for violence,' the man assured him in a trembling voice.

'Glad we agree,' Izzy replied. He kissed the barrel of the gun, then held the tip to his ear, pretending to listen closely. 'Right, you got it, baby,' he said, as if he were a hitman speaking to his girlfriend. He slipped the pistol into his coat pocket. 'Marlene wants to know if we get our three thousand?' he asked. 'She's concerned. And when she's concerned, it's best to pay attention. You got that?'

'I understand. I'll give you . . . two thousand nine hundred.'

The jeweller still wanted to bargain? This was craziness! Izzy caught my glance and raised his shoulders to prompt my reply. I could see he was looking forward to bragging about his performance.

'It's a deal,' I said.

'It'll take me at least an hour to get the money,' the jeweller told us. 'Come back at two-thirty.'

'Why in God's name did you bring a gun?' I asked Izzy as we

hurried away. I was stomping over the cobbles, worried that someone had seen his weapon through the shop window.

'You should be thanking me,' he remarked contentedly. 'I've
cured your paso doble!'

I scowled at him, which made him flap his hand at me as if I was
being a pest. 'Look, Erik, 'Did you really think I was going to
venture into a city run by anti-Semitic cavemen with just Yiddish
curses to defend us? Sorry, but I ain't that *meshugene*.'

'Where'd you get it anyway?' I asked, conceding his point.

'It was Papa's. It's an 1896 Model 2 Bergman – five millimetre.'
Whispering, he said, 'Feels damn good in my hand. Maybe I was
born to be a gunslinger!'

'Do you really know how to use it?'

'Erik, it doesn't require a doctorate from the Sorbonne,' he
replied, snorting. 'It takes a five-round clip – couldn't be easier.
Besides, you learn a lot about a pistol when you take it apart and
give it a cleaning. It's a lot simpler to put back together than a Swiss
cuckoo clock, I can tell you that!' He took my arm. 'I thought it
was a good touch my kissing the pistol – and calling it Marlene.
Nobody would think a Jew would do that.'

As we walked down Spacerowa Street, Izzy and I debated whether
the jeweller would keep up his end of our bargain. We could easily
believe that his greed would win out over his anger – and whatever
suspicions he had about us – but we also knew he might simply
pick up the phone and call the police. So we decided to keep watch
on his shop from a fabric store down the street. We chose that
particular locale because Izzy was eager to buy a few yards of tweed
for a warm pair of winter trousers.

If no police showed up, we'd go back to get our money at
2.30.

I wanted to wash the burn on my arm with cold water, and the
shop owner was kind enough to let me use the sink in his loo,

where I inspected the damage. Mrs Sawicki was right – there'd be a scar. My skin was throbbing. Splashing water on it did little good.

Back at my post by the front door, I discovered that the coast was still clear. As the minutes clicked past, I began to believe that I'd been needlessly apprehensive. Hope that one has chanced upon the road back to the way things used to be is apparently a strong desire in those who've been locked outside their previous lives.

Izzy was looking at different herringbone patterns on the counter, delighted with his range of options. The mystery of Anna's connection to Adam was still nagging at me, and after a couple of minutes I went to him.

'Imagine you're fourteen years old,' I whispered. 'You're in trouble, and you need your boyfriend's help, but he's in Switzerland and his mother has just treated you like an insect. You can't talk to your parents, because you're a prisoner in their home. So where do you go?'

He closed his eyes to consider my question. 'I'm not sure, let me think about it,' he finally replied. A couple of minutes later, after he'd picked out the fabric he wanted, he called me over and said, 'Erik, Anna would have gone back to the one person who'd treated her well – Mikael Tengmann.'

'That's what I figured,' I replied, 'except that Mikael's nurse told me she was never at his office. But let's assume he did see her, and that she wanted to talk to him again, where would she have gone to see him?'

'At his home.'

'No, I don't think so – his office is in his home.'

A half a minute or so later, when I peeked out the door, a Gestapo officer was standing outside Jawicki's, about fifty paces away. He was putting on black leather gloves. Parked next to him was a black Mercedes.

I realized we'd been fools not to simply leave this part of town

121

and offer Hannah's ring to another jeweller. We were colossal amateurs at this life of subterfuge.

'Is there a back door that leads to some other street?' I asked the owner, who was ringing up Izzy's purchase.

He frowned at me, and I could see he thought that we were up to no good.

Grinning in what I hoped was a charming way, I told him I'd spotted someone I owed money to walking down the street; a stupid lie, but what could I say?

He told me there was only the front door, so I made Izzy pay quickly and then steered him there. 'The Gestapo are on to us,' I whispered. 'When we get outside, don't look towards Jawicki's. Just walk slowly to the right.'

Stepping on to the sidewalk, we heard no screams or whistles, but after twenty or so paces, when I looked back to see what was happening, the Gestapo officer had his gun drawn and was staring at me; the jeweller must have told him what we looked like. My turning round had only confirmed that we were the suspects he was after.

I must have groaned or given away my panic in some other way; Izzy looked back.

'We're fucked!' he whispered.

'We've got to run!' I told him.

We took off west on Szucha Street and made it to Rakowiecka before Izzy's arthritis made him double over. Panting, he pushed me off. 'Get going!' he ordered. 'I'll shoot the Nazi when he gets close.'

I felt as if everything I'd ever lived for were turning slowly around this one moment, but I wasn't about to let Izzy sacrifice himself for me.

'I'm too tired to run,' I replied. 'You're stuck with me.'

By now, the Gestapo officer had turned the corner – no more than sixty yards from us. He was in good shape, and young. A sense of doom pounded in my chest.

'Erik!'

Izzy had stumbled forward into the doorway of an apartment house and was waving me towards him.

I joined him in the dark hallway. My throat felt as if it had been scraped with a rasp. The burn on my arm was aching.

'You think he saw us come in here?' Izzy asked in a whisper.

'Probably. And anyway, people on the street noticed and will denounce us. Come on,' I said, grabbing his arm, 'let's get out of here!'

We pushed through the rear door into the courtyard, which had been dug up to make a garden, though winter had starved it to a barren tangle of skeletal vines and brambles. A strongly built, middle-aged woman in a dark headscarf, plaid overcoat and frumpy woollen slippers was bent over in the far corner, pulling out metal stakes around which clung the withered tendrils of dead sweet peas. Behind her, the remains of tomato plants tortured by the wind and cold crumpled against a rusted trellis. The woman's torn gloves dangled from the rim of her lopsided wooden barrow, which looked like a relic from the Iron Age.

Today, in my mind, I see her as though she were symbolic of all the women who bear misery with lips sealed to silence.

She looked up at Izzy and me, staring at my armband.

'We mean no harm,' I assured her in Polish.

She picked up her spade, but not in a threatening way. She stood with it, her posture rigid, as though she were posing for a portrait. I threw down my armband. 'We're not Nazis,' I told her, opening my hands. 'We're in the Resistance and we're in trouble.'

The woman's face showed the indifference of stone. After leaning her spade against her barrow, she bent over, pulled out another stake and tossed it with a harsh clang into the pile she'd made.

Izzy and I were still gasping for breath. To be sixty-seven years old in the Polish winter is to know the limits of the body.

Richard Zimler

'Thank God we didn't go far away from Jawicki's,' Izzy told me.

'What do you mean?' I asked.

'If we'd come back only when we were supposed to, the Mercedes would have been hidden around the corner. We'd have never known that that son-of-a-bitch called the Gestapo until it was too late.'

A brick wall, five feet high, separated us from a second apartment house at the back. A cane-work chair had been put there – for kids to hoist themselves over the wall and take a winter shortcut to the next street, most likely.

'Come on!' I told Izzy, pointing to the chair. 'Let's try our luck.'

We'd just started forward when the door behind us opened. Out stepped the Gestapo officer who'd been chasing us. He was holding a pistol.

124

CHAPTER 13

'Don't move!' our assailant ordered in German.

He was no more than twenty years old, with copper-coloured hair shining under his cap and long blond eyelashes. He's *just a rabbit of a boy, and if I don't lose my nerve* . . .

'I'm from the Reich Census Bureau,' I told him, 'and this man is helping me.'

He looked at my swastika armband on the ground and frowned. 'I know who you are, so shut up and put up your hands!'

We did as he said, but Izzy gave me a sideways look, as if he was about to pull the cord of some mad plan.

'Not yet!' I whispered to him in Polish; I thought I could still talk my way out of this.

'Shut your snout!' the German yelled.

Below my frantic heartbeat, I heard the metallic scratch of another stake landing in the woman's pile. She was still gardening – it might have been comic under other circumstances.

'Stay still!' the Nazi ordered Izzy. 'And you, get on your knees!' he told me.

'If you let us get on our way,' I told him, 'I'll give you five hundred złoty.'

'If you want a bullet in your head, keep talking!' he growled.

I thought he was going to search me for the pistol that the jeweller must have warned him about, but when I was kneeling he jabbed the muzzle of his gun into my ear. Panic surged through me from my legs up to the top of my head. My bladder opened, and in a trembling voice, I said, 'You're too young to want my death on your conscience.'

'I told you to shut up!' he shouted. 'And don't move!'

'You!' he snarled, turning to Izzy, 'throw down your gun! And do it slowly.'

Out of the corner of my eye I could see Izzy lifting it out.

'That's it . . . Toss it near my feet.'

The pistol landed by the German and made a little hop. *It's over for us now*, I thought.

Behind us, a window squealed open. I closed my eyes, and a deep silence opened around me. I imagined I was falling into it, and I wanted to keep falling – for each second to stretch towards the infinite. Who wouldn't want more time?

'You!' the Gestapo man called to the woman behind us. 'Get over here!'

I opened my eyes to find the Nazi sneering at her. 'Who gave you permission to dig up this courtyard?' he demanded.

I realized that boys holding guns were brutalizing women all over Europe.

She made no reply. She clutched her thoughts deep inside her – as though they were children she'd never give up to an enemy.

'Do you speak a little German?' the young man demanded of her.

'*Ja*,' she replied indifferently, wiping her runny nose.

He licked his lips. 'Go to Jawicki Jewellers on Spacerowa Street. You understand?' When she nodded, he added, 'Tell the Gestapo officer there to come right here. And don't dawdle. If he's not here in two minutes, I'll put a bullet in your friend's head!'

She took two steps, then swivelled around with quiet grace. Standing at the centre of a world over which no man had any power, she opened her eyes wide enough to hold all her fury and raised her spade.

The German was staring down at me. He'd already forgotten about her.

In the second before she swung, she drew her lips back over her chipped brown teeth. I'll never forget her look of spiteful hate; the transformation seemed worthy of a devil in a painting by Bruegel. Then I heard her sharp intake of breath. So did the Gestapo officer. Turning, he caught the blow on the side of his face. With a guttural scream, he fell to one knee. His cap landed several feet away, on a patch of muddy ice. Clamping his hand over his battered and bloody ear, he pointed his gun at her, but before he could pull the trigger, she clouted him again, grunting. It seemed an act of vengeance against years of mistreatment. His nose and cheekbone shattered. I'd never heard bone breaking before, but the crack was unmistakable. An explosion of blood splattered over my face and on to my coat. I wiped the spray off my cheeks as the German fell forward on to his belly, his hands splayed out, his fingers arched like a crab's legs. His breaths came in desperate gulps. While trying to raise himself, he groaned. He spoke in a low grumble, as well. I made out the word *unrecht* – wrong.

Did it seem wrong to him that an illiterate Polish woman hadn't followed his orders?

I stood up. The German's right hand had curled around his gun. I stepped down hard on it, and the crunch of his fingers was the sound of the new identity I was making for myself. Shrieking, he collapsed forward. 'God, no!' he shouted.

Bending down, I took the pistol. I pointed it at his head. I expected him to look at me, but he pressed himself down into the ground. His lips moved. Maybe he was praying to the earth – or to whatever god he hoped was watching.

We'll never know if I'd have fired; carefully, patiently, as though all of nature were on her side and nothing could go wrong, the woman put one foot on each side of the Nazi's legs. I knew what she was about to do, but I didn't stop her. Instead, I took a step back to give her room.

Regret for that comes to me only infrequently, and only when I think of his parents.

It isn't that hard to murder a man. A silently enraged Polish woman taught me that.

And yet it must have seemed impossible to the German. How could he meet death in a rusted curve of Slavic iron, five hundred miles from home?

The brutality of her strike made Izzy gasp, then reach for me.

She opened a gash so deep in the Nazi's forehead that I saw a white flash of bone before blood flooded the wound. His life sluiced down his cheek and spilled on to the earth. With a gurgling sound, he tilted to his side and his jaw fell open.

Heniek, what do you suppose young men think of when they know that they will never again see their home, and the fifty years of future they'd counted on is gone?

What could I have done differently . . . ?

Ask my parents to forgive me for dying young . . .

No, I don't know either. I went to my death already an old man. The expectations are different.

The youth's head sagged. His eyes were open but saw nothing.

The woman was alone in the world with Izzy and me. We three shared the fractured skull of a young man whose name we would never learn. With our eyes, we passed the finality of his death between ourselves like a crust of hard bread.

Izzy picked up his gun.

It was the puddle of blood spreading beneath the young German's head that made me want to run. I imagined the brown icicles that would hang from his chin that evening. I reached into my coat pocket and handed the woman the demitasse spoons I'd stolen from Mrs Sawicki. She took them in her dirt-encrusted hand and nodded her thanks.

'*Był cięnżki, potrzebuję taczkę,*' she grumbled – 'He looks heavy – I'll need the wheelbarrow.' Those were the only words she ever spoke to Izzy and me – the woman who saved our lives.

CHAPTER 14

Izzy had done business for years with Wysocki Jewellers on Elektoralna Street. Though just a small neighbourhood shop, it had the advantage of being on our way home.

To avoid being spotted, we walked a mile east to the banks of the Vistula and made our way north along a tangled path towards the medieval-looking towers of the Poniatowski Bridge. From there, we headed west into the city centre. We went slowly, stopping often, too exhausted and troubled to exchange more than a few words.

It was nearly two hours later when we finally made it to the jewellery shop. Only then did I notice that Izzy no longer had his tweed fabric.

'I tossed the bag away while we were running,' he told me, shrugging off his irritation.

Inside the shop was a wiry young man sitting behind a bulky, old-fashioned desk, hunched over a book, lost to the world. Despite the cold, Izzy and I were sweating heavily, and his arthritis had him close to tears.

'That's Andrzej,' he told me, 'the eldest, and a good boy, but' – here, Izzy tapped his temple and added, 'not much up here – *der shoyte ben pikholtz.*'

Andrzej looked up on hearing the bells on the door tinkle. 'Mr Nowak, what a surprise!' he exclaimed gleefully, coming around the counter with his arms open.

After hugging Izzy, the young man remembered that nosy

neighbours might be watching. Locking the door with a decisive click, he invited us into his storeroom. Once we were safely out of view, I introduced myself and shook his hand.

Andrzej's hair was a brown skullcap, but he'd left a four-inch whip in front that dangled between his eyes. In his thick, black-rimmed spectacles, he looked like a cross between a Talmud student and a jazz musician.

'So, tell me about the ghetto,' he said to us in a fearful tone. 'Is it bad?'

I deferred to Izzy. He was already seated in the armchair in the corner and was pressing at the shooting pains in his right hip. 'Don't ask,' he replied wearily. 'Listen, Andrzej, we're in a hurry. We need to sell a wedding ring. Show him, Erik.'

While the young jeweller examined the diamond, I dropped down on the bench along the wall. After a minute or so, he lowered his ivory-handled magnifying glass. 'Times are hard, Dr Cohen, so if you'd be willing to accept two thousand, then . . .'

'Where's your father?' Izzy cut in.

'Papa's got a cold. So I'm not sure I can . . .'

'Get him on the phone.'

'The phones are down. I think that . . .'

'It's worth eight thousand and we won't take less than four!' Izzy announced, using a jabbing finger to intimidate Andrzej.

'Papa has set a two-thousand-złoty limit for me,' Andrzej replied sadly.

They began to haggle, and their words became needles poking into my fragile composure. When Izzy began to plead, I told them I'd wait in the shop. Seated at the desk, with the door to the store-room closed behind me, I eased open the top drawer and found a handsome silver letter opener on top of a ledger book. I slipped it in my pocket. I lit a cigarette, then leaned down to undo the laces on my shoes. The smoke made my eyes tear, which gave me an excuse to shut them. To never open them again seemed my best option.

Izzy was sputtering curses in Yiddish and French when he hobbled out. Andrzej trailed behind him like a punished puppy. He came to me and apologized for not being able to offer a fair price, desperate for forgiveness, and I gave it to him, but I curled my fingers around the letter opener in my coat pocket as though its theft were my real reply.

After I'd done up my laces, Izzy handed me a stack of notes – two thousand four hundred złoty. 'Let's go,' he told me, and after twisting the deadbolt, he pulled open the door as if he was ready to clobber the first person we met on the street. I faced Andrzej and asked if he knew of a nearby crossing point back to the ghetto. He said no, but Izzy didn't believe him. To shame the young man, he tried to stuff a ten-złoty note into his coat pocket, saying, 'Here's what you Christians need to make you charitable!'

Andrzej pushed the money away. 'For the love of God, Mr Nowak, stop!'

Outside, shivering, the young man pointed towards a bakery down the block. 'I've seen delivery men loading sacks of flour on to wagons. I'm not sure, but try there.'

Izzy marched off without shaking Andrzej's hand. When I caught up, he snarled, 'I know I behaved badly, but don't you dare start with me!'

At the bakery, the owner's wife advised us to go to a garage on Freta Street. 'Ask for Maciej.'

Maciej came to the door reeking of gasoline, his face streaked black with grease. 'No, no, no,' he told us when we asked after a crossing point, shooing us away like mosquitoes, but Izzy held up two ten-złoty notes and said, 'Abracadabra!'

Maciej and another mechanic pushed a black Ford into the corner of the garage, revealing a two-metre square of corrugated iron on the cement floor. Sliding it to the side gave us access to a hole the size of a wagon wheel.

'What's down there?' I asked, peering in and seeing only sandy earth at the bottom.

'A tunnel. And despite the rumours, I haven't spotted a single albino crocodile inside – though I can't guarantee you won't find frogs.'

'Frogs?' Izzy asked.

'A smuggler came back with a handful the other day. They must breed somewhere down there in the dark. Our theory is that they're a bit shy when it comes to fucking.' Grinning, he added, 'Like Jewish girls.'

I expect he thought that was witty. Izzy and I failed to laugh, so he apologized. He seemed a good man, but I didn't trust him; he was a Christian, after all – with a wholly different destiny from ours, whether he wanted it or not.

'How far do we have to go to reach the ghetto?' I asked him.

'After twenty-five metres you'll reach another hole leading up. Just call out – the women will open the trap door.'

'Women?'

'They sew children's clothing for the Germans.'

A candle cost us fifty groszy; use of a ladder was free. Izzy climbed down while I showed Maciej my photos of Adam and Anna, but he didn't recognize either of them.

The tunnel's entrance was only a few inches wider than our shoulders. The candle succeeded in pushing the darkness back just four or five metres. Wooden beams held up the ceiling; it looked like a tiny mineshaft. And it didn't look like it had been built to last very long.

'We're going to have to crawl,' Izzy told me morosely.

'Listen,' I replied in an urgent whisper, 'we have no proof this even leads to the ghetto. We could be buried alive.'

'Why the hell would Maciej want to trap us?' he asked.

'Why wouldn't he? There are rewards for catching Jews.'

Izzy scoffed, but then climbed back up and talked to Maciej. I stood on the second rung of the ladder and watched, but they kept their voices down, so I couldn't make out what they said. At one point, Izzy took out Marlene. The burly mechanic patted his shoulder and smiled, as though they were old army comrades.

'What did you tell him?' I asked Izzy after he'd climbed back down.

'That if we had any trouble I'd come back and blow his brains out.'

'And what did he say?'

'That I was sure as hell one angry Jew, but that he didn't mind, because it was about time the Jews got fed up.' He grinned boyishly. 'He also said that my Jimmy Cagney imitation was excellent.'

'Did he really say that?'

'No, but I could see he wanted to!'

I laughed – and for a few moments all that mattered was Izzy's unstoppable sense of humour. Then his face grew grave. 'I'm going to tell you a secret, Erik,' he told me.

'What?'

'When you laugh, your eyes twinkle and you look like you did when we were seven years old and planning adventures in our neighbourhood. It's the best thing about you, your laughter, and the thing I've always loved, and that Hannah most loved, and though you probably think other things about you are much more important and profound, they aren't. Because the way you can switch from grief or dread to absolute joy in an instant . . . like there's a spring always ready to push you towards what's best . . . It says something significant about the way you are – and it makes people side with you. And one other thing,' he added, taking my arm, 'it's what Adam adored about you more than anything else.'

I wanted to say something equal to my feelings, but the words wouldn't come.

Izzy came to my rescue, as always. 'I'll go first, Dr Freud,' he said cheerfully.

'Why you?'

'Because I want to play the lead for a change! Besides, I've got the candle. You take Marlene.' He handed me the pistol. 'If you see anything furry that resembles Mickey or Minnie, pow – right between the eyes!'

Izzy started ahead. I followed close behind. The tunnel was filthy with scum, and the rotting-wood stink was nauseating. The scabs on my knees opened. The air became stale and the heat grew stifling. Hearing a metallic clang behind us, I looked over my shoulder. Blackness pressed against my eyes like a blindfold. We were sealed in.

With my pulse racing, I tried to slip out of my suit coat, but there wasn't enough room. Panic covered me like netting. I pushed out on the wooden planks of the tunnel. 'I can't go on!' I announced.

'Erik, if we aren't there in two minutes, we'll turn back.'

Water dripping from the ceiling stepped its fingertips across my neck as I edged forward. My ears seemed stuffed, and I felt dizzy. The air became too thin to fill my lungs. Izzy's candle grew dim and sputtered out. By my count, we had crawled thirty metres.

Purple and red shapes floated around me. My thoughts were arrows flying out in wild directions. 'Maciej tricked us!' I said, sucking in air, then sucking again, because my lungs weren't filling.

'Give me your lighter!' Izzy ordered.

'No, I'm going back,' I answered between gulps of air. I must have looked like a fish tossed on land. I tried to turn around, but it was too tight.

'Erik, hand me your goddamned lighter!' he repeated.

I found only the letter opener in my coat pocket. 'It's gone,' I said, panting. *Get out of here now!* was what the booming against my ribs meant.

'You've still got it – try in your other pockets!' he told me.

I found it and held it out. 'Take it!'

His fingers groped along my arm and snatched it, but he couldn't raise a flame. Fighting for breath, he whispered, 'It doesn't matter. I saw the exit just ahead.'

I could tell he was lying, but before I could say so, my hands gave way and I slipped on to my belly. I was too weak to move and I was falling into darkness.

I awoke pierced by light. Izzy was staring down at me, and his face seemed too big. A young woman with pretty brown eyes was also gazing down at me. Her eyelashes were long and delicate – like fern tendrils.

'Yes, you're alive,' Izzy assured me. 'We pulled you out with a rope.'

'Out of where?' I asked; my memory of the last hour was gone.

'The tunnel.'

'And where are we?'

'Where would you like to be?'

'London – the British Museum.'

'Good choice! Anything I can get you?' he questioned.

'Some tea. And a scone. And maybe a thunderstorm.' Strange things to ask for, but I was thinking that there was a lot to be said for English clichés when one has been crushed by German ones.

'Sorry, we took a wrong turn somewhere near Brussels,' Izzy replied. 'We're back home. How about a week-old *sheygets* and some ghetto water?'

He sat down beside me and lifted a cup of water to my lips. I drank gratefully. My head was pounding.

'So, how are you feeling?' he asked.

'That I wish I'd gone first. *I* wouldn't have made a wrong turn near Brussels.'

Smiling with relief, he helped me sit up. The woman beside him took his cup and held it to my lips again. I felt bruised and tender, as if I'd been stepped on. I looked around the room. Five women sat at sewing tables, pedalling like demons. I held up my hand and waved. Two of them noticed and smiled. They had sympathetic eyes and the same gaunt features we all had – starvation would make us all cousins before the Germans were through with us. Still, the whirring sound of the sewing machines was reassuring – a noble percussion that meant: *we Jews are fighting on.*

I was lying on a lumpy couch, covered by a woollen blanket. I lifted it up. I was in my underwear. My knees were crusted with blood. And my arm was throbbing – I looked again at the angry burn Mrs Sawicki had given me.

'Checking on your *petzl*?' Izzy asked, raising his eyebrows.

'I thought it might be prudent to make sure it's still there,' I told him.

The women laughed.

The air had become warm and full. My trousers were folded neatly on the seat of a chair by my head. My coat and shirt were hanging over its back. When I reached for my pants, an old season ticket for the omnibus fell out of my pocket. And just like that, I seemed to have entered one of Papa's jokes: a skeleton crawls out of his grave five years after burial and finds a receipt in his coat pocket for the trousers that he'd been having altered when he died, so he goes to his tailor, presents the receipt to him and says, 'So, Pinkus, are my pants ready?'

For the life of me, I couldn't remember the punchline of the joke, but I giggled anyway. Izzy looked at me inquisitively.

'Too little oxygen,' I told him, which must have been partially true, but I was mostly giddy at finding myself still alive.

At home, Izzy and I found that Stefa was still unable to leave her bed. After I slipped into fresh clothes, I emptied her chamber pot, and she asked me what had happened to my hair. I reached up to check it was still there. Then I remembered. 'I needed a disguise,' I told her.

She sighed as if I required great patience. 'I'm sore all over,' she moaned. 'And my feet are still frozen. Could you make me some hot tea with lemon?'

We had no lemons, so I trudged over to the Tarnowskis' while Izzy massaged Stefa's shoulders. As I stood in the doorway, Ida Tarnowski asked about my hair as well. 'I'm up for a part in a Yiddish production of *Don Juan in Hell*,' I told her, which I thought was witty, but she asked me when I'd know if I'd passed the audition.

'Sorry, I was just kidding,' I replied, and I asked her for a lemon, but she told me she couldn't even remember what one looked like.

I tried several other neighbours without luck. When I returned home, Stefa was snoring and Izzy was flat on his back in my bed, in all his clothes, his mouth open – an ancient cave with hidden gold. I chopped off most of my hair at the bathroom sink and ended up looking like a prisoner of war, which seemed right. Then I left a cup of hot water on my niece's night table – sweetened with molasses – and climbed under the covers. The sheets were Siberian ice, but I was too exhausted to care.

I woke up when I heard Izzy clomping around the room. He was munching on a piece of matzo. He sat down at the foot of my bed. 'Your raven has flown away,' he noted.

'Gloria told him that Poland was no place for a bird.'

We talked about our next moves. I needed to make some food for Stefa, so he agreed to go to Mikael Tengmann's office and hand him the thousand złoty, then head to Mrs Rackemann's shop, pay her what I still owed her and pick up my wedding band. I put Mikael's money in one of Mrs Sawicki's envelopes and asked him to note if the physician showed any unease or surprise on seeing her name; it occurred to me now that the killer – who must have lived outside the ghetto – might have had an accomplice inside. And Mikael was one of only two people I knew of who had known both Adam and Anna, the other being Rowy. Maybe one of them was conspiring with Mrs Sawicki.

An hour and a half later Izzy was back. I was frying up some wild onion to add to the borscht I'd made out of two withered old beets.

'Mikael is getting the anti-typhus serum tomorrow,' he told me. He stuffed the money in my coat pocket, since my hands were busy, and he put my wedding band down on the counter.

'You could have paid Mikael already,' I observed.

He took a long sip of ersatz coffee out of my cup, then said, 'He told me not to – not until he had the serum. So he hasn't seen the envelope yet.'

'What are you two talking about?' my niece called out from her room.

When I explained to her that we'd soon have the serum, she announced, 'No one is injecting me with anything!' Her voice was strong, but she gave herself a coughing fit and got bloody phlegm on her sheets.

'I didn't risk my life so you could put up a fuss,' Izzy told her as I fetched a hand-towel from her wardrobe.

'How did you risk your life?' she asked, squinting suspiciously.

I glared at Izzy to keep the truth hidden, but he'd already figured that out. 'Every outing with your uncle puts me in danger of a fatal moral decline,' he said dryly.

'Go away!' she told him nastily. 'And you, too!' she added, turning to me.

The next morning, I awoke just after dawn, eager to speak to Anna's friends before heading to Mikael's office. Stefa looked fast asleep when I tiptoed into her room, so I turned round, which was when she spoke, making me jump.

'I'm up,' she said in a drowsy voice.

She dared open her eyes only a sliver; the light streaming through the window made her head throb. She instructed me to look for a small book with a leather cover in the top drawer of her dresser.

Once I'd found it, she had me open it to the first page. Written in her neat square handwriting – in Polish – was the following:

> *Adam Liski*
> *Birth: 4 August 1932.*
> *Weight: Seven pounds four ounces.*
> *Length: Nineteen inches.*

Glued near the bottom of the page was a sprig of her son's downy blond hair. On subsequent pages, I discovered records of his childhood diseases and medical treatments, as well as drawings of his hands and feet, and a portrait of him that she'd done when he was five. She had artistic talent – who would have guessed? Among a series of old sketches of her husband Krzysztof, I also discovered – to my surprise and delight – that she'd drawn me huddled over a book. I was smoking the meerschaum pipe I'd inherited from my father. She must have done it about ten years before. Had I really ever looked that strong and young?

'Uncle Erik,' she pleaded, 'you have to hold on to Adam's record book for me.'

'Me? Why?'

'Just do what I say for once!'

'All right, I'll keep it safe. But you're going to be fine. You just need to stay warm.'

'Hide it!' she said in a hushed whisper, as if the Germans would need to know Adam's height to win the war.

'I'll put it under the mattress in my room,' I told her, but once I was out of sight I slipped it into my coat pocket instead.

I sat with Stefa for a time, smearing *schmaltz* on her chapped lips and combing the tangles out of her hair. She declined my offer of borscht.

'Listen, Ewa has been helping me write cards to our friends outside the ghetto,' she told me. 'We're going to have a courier post them on the Other Side.'

'Why are you sending notes?'

'Our friends need to know about . . . about things with us,' she replied, unwilling to speak Adam's name. 'Is there anyone you want me to write to?'

I thought about that. 'No, thanks. I wouldn't know what to say.'

I told my niece I had to go out for a while but would ask Ewa to check on her from time to time. Down in the bakery, the young woman promised me she'd do just that.

I was too exhausted to walk anywhere, so I splurged on a rickshaw. My driver was a former chemical engineer named Józef. He wore a red velvet vest under a high-collared russet coat. 'My daughter made them for my birthday,' he told me.

When I replied that she was a genius with a needle and thread, he turned away from me as if I'd offended him, but I didn't ask why; everyone in the ghetto kept a misery on his shoulder that could easily justify odd behaviour.

Though Józef pedalled hard, the younger competition passed us. I spent the journey across town looking through Adam's record book. Near the end, I discovered lists that Stefa had made of the advantages and disadvantages in the personalities of her friends. I'd never known that she'd been a list-maker, but it didn't surprise me.

I remember Izzy's inventory better than all the others because it showed off my niece's wit.

Advantages: Perfectly manicured hands, delights in his own humour, can fix anything, speaks French, walks as slowly as I do, eyebrows like furry caterpillars, has not an evil bone in his body, hardly ever raises his voice, is easily overcome by my anger, keeps Adam entertained and Uncle Erik out of my hair, has sad eyes (like the surface of a warm lake!), makes me feel motherly when he is down, and is loyal, loyal, loyal.

Disadvantages: Delights in his own humour, is unable to tell when I don't want to be teased, sulks when he's yelled at, can hold grudges (despite his denials), walks as slowly as I do, has the table manners of a

beagle, will never understand evil people (he excuses my sniping as harmless eccentricity, poor man!), makes me feel motherly when he is down, is too loyal, and encourages Adam to leave his shoelaces untied, lick his plate, play with stray dogs, etc.
Unspoken motto: Once you're on board, you're along for the whole ride.
Food would most like to have in the ghetto: lox.
Favourite movie star: Jimmy Cagney (his imitation isn't all that bad, but Cagney in Yiddish sounds a bit meshugene).
Mystery: Was Róża pregnant when he married her?
Wish for him: May he find a man who appreciates his goodness.
Immediate prospects: Loneliness (given Róża's health and the state of the world with regard to his sexual proclivities).

I looked for the list of my own pros and cons, but several pages had been torn out and she must have destroyed it. Most of all, I wanted to know what her wish for me had been.

It didn't occur to me till much later that Stefa left Izzy's page for me to see for a reason: so that I wouldn't take him for granted, which was always what she'd accused me of – and rightly, at times.

She hadn't destroyed her lists for Ewa, Helena, Ziv and Adam. I read all of them but my nephew's. I had to close it as soon as I read his first advantage: *loves everyone around him, even me.*

Józef dropped me near the Chłodna Street crossing to the Little Ghetto; I'd walk from there. As I got out of the rickshaw, he wiped his brow and apologized for being passed by other drivers.

'We got here in one piece,' I told him, handing him his payment, 'which is all that counts at the moment. Besides, my nephew always complained that I moved as slow as a . . .'

I was about to say *tortoise*, but Adam – the misery always sitting on *my* shoulder – held his hand up for me to say no more about our life together. Józef showed me a puzzled look. 'Some things are best left unspoken,' I said. I shook his hand and walked off.

141

Two body collectors cut in front of me almost immediately. They were hauling a dead man wearing only a tattered undershirt. His hair was thick and black, but he had the sunken eyes and caved-in chest of a battered grandfather. His arms were bamboo reeds ending in dirty claws.

Whiskers dusted his chin but his cheeks were hairless – could starvation take away a man's beard?

The ghetto funeral stretchers were slatted ladders with wheels on one end, but this one also had knotted white tassels – *tzitzit* – at its corners. That made me curious, and I eavesdropped on the collectors' conversation. They were talking about a reading a fortune-teller had given one of them.

'She told me I was going to take a long trip soon,' the shorter of the two said.

'Somewhere warm?' his partner asked hopefully. He wore black spectacles held together by tape; they kept slipping to the end of his nose.

Leaving their cart on the sidewalk, they gazed around, exchanged a few words I didn't catch, then shuffled over to a wooden stall set up in front of a clothing shop. Inside was a walnut-faced iron-monger sitting on a three-legged stool, surrounded by piles of door handles, keys and rusted junk. On the walls he'd hung hand-sized wire animals – dogs, cats and swans. A naked woman was slumped at his feet, her face angled down and chin pressed against her chest, but he didn't seem to see her; he concentrated on the wire he was twisting into the shape of a poodle standing on its hind legs.

The woman's hands – with red, swollen knuckles – were joined together as if she were still holding a beggar's cup. The spectacled collector spoke to the ironmonger in a whisper. Then, leaning down, he shook the woman, and her head – gaunt and waxy – flopped to the side. He grabbed her ankles. His partner took her arms.

'*Eins, zwei, drei,*' they said in unison.

142

They lifted her up. Her hips jutted out from around her sunken triangle of sex like shovels.

The ironmonger never looked up to watch her go, but his hands stopped twisting his wire for a few seconds and he closed his eyes.

People go on with their lives the only way they know how. Hannah once told me that and I thought she was being glib, but living in the ghetto convinced me she was right.

As they carried the woman to their cart, the body collectors folded her together, then pulled her apart. Carelessness or a morbid comedy routine?

When they passed, her grey eyes stared at me. I imagined that she wanted to tell me about her life.

If you could say only one thing to me what would it be? I asked her in my mind.

'*I died of thirst for so many things,*' came her reply. Her voice was shadowed by bitterness and regret.

The dead want us to know what killed them, I reasoned – though maybe I only came to that conclusion because it meant that Adam would want me to learn the identity of his murderer.

'No, she said it would be cold where I was going,' the short collector told his partner, resuming their previous conversation.

'She must have meant you'd be heading off to Mogiła Street!' his partner replied with a quick laugh, since *Mogiła* meant tomb in Polish.

They dumped the woman atop the dead man they'd previously collected. The bones of her back – jutting fins – crushed his face, and her head dangled back and to the side, threatening to fall off her spindly neck. Her breasts, shrunken, sucked dry by hunger, were wrinkled pancakes pressed against her ribcage.

No one rushed to cover her. Or to claim her.

CHAPTER 15

Janek's mother invited me in when I explained my visit. She said I looked faint and brought me a glass of water right away.

The studious-looking, wiry-haired young man was uncomfortable discussing Anna with me, but after I told him I suspected that she had been gravely ill, he confessed he'd had a quarrel with her over twenty złoty she'd borrowed from him and couldn't pay back. They hadn't spoken since early January.

'Listen, son, why did Anna need the money?' I asked.

'She wouldn't tell me,' he replied, which made his mother smack the back of his head. 'I swear, Mama!' pleaded the boy, ducking away from her. 'You know how secretive Anna could be. All she told me was that she was in bad trouble.'

Anna's other close friend, Henia, lived on Pańska Street, near the Nożyków Synagogue, where my mother and I had attended services on high holy days. She answered my knocks dressed for school, in a pretty burgundy jumper and dark woollen trousers. Her cheerful face was framed by blonde braids, which made her look as though she'd stepped out of a Bavarian children's story. In her hand was a half-eaten hard-boiled egg.

Her mother called out to ask who was at the door.

'A friend!' the girl shouted back. To me she mouthed, 'Wait downstairs.'

She came rushing into the hallway a few minutes later. 'I'm late,' she said. 'Let's talk as we walk.' She buttoned her coat and put on a black leather aviator's hat with sheepskin earflaps, tucking her braids underneath. She looked like a teenage boy.

'I have to cross over to the Big Ghetto to get to school,' she explained, 'and the German guards used to grope themselves when I passed the gate. A big ugly one even tried to kiss me once. Now, they leave me alone.'

She burst out through the door as if to take on the Nazis and the rest of the world, holding her book bag tightly against her chest – undoubtedly to hide the sleek rise of her breasts.

I liked Henia immediately. And do you know why, Heniek? Because survival was shining in her light brown eyes. I blessed her for that.

'Do you know what was wrong with Anna?' I asked her.

'Wrong?'

'I have reason to believe she was ill.'

'She wasn't ill – the idiot got herself pregnant.'

'That's impossible. A doctor who examined her told me she wasn't.'

'Then he lied to you.'

'Why would he do that?' I demanded.

'Why wouldn't he?' she said, irritated. 'What right do you have to know intimate details about Anna's life?'

I remembered Mikael begging me not to force him to lie. 'But her mother said she had gotten dangerously thin,' I told Henia.

'Yeah,' the girl replied, 'that was quite a feat, wasn't it? She had everybody fooled.'

I stopped. Henia didn't. 'So you're certain she was pregnant?' I called after her.

She turned round. 'Yup,' she replied casually, walking backwards. 'Three months along. If you looked really closely, you could kind of tell in the curve right here, even though she wasn't much more than a skeleton.' She designed a contour in front of her belly with her hand.

I caught up, then grabbed the strap of her book bag to keep her from rushing ahead. 'Did her parents know?'

'No. Anna didn't trust them. She wanted an abortion. But we didn't know where to go. We were afraid that if we asked her doctor or any other adult, it would get back to her parents. So she just stopped eating.'

'But sooner or later, her condition would have become obvious.'

'I'm sorry, Mr Honec, but we have to keep walking – if I'm late for school, the director won't let me in.'

I let go of her strap. Henia shifted her book bag to her other shoulder and we started off again. 'Anna read somewhere that starvation can cause a miscarriage,' she told me. 'So she could hide her pregnancy *and* get rid of it at the same time. It was a neat trick – if you don't mind starving to death, that is.'

'So did she lose the baby?'

'No. Though we didn't talk for a couple of days before she was killed, so I suppose she might have lost it then – or even found someone to give her an abortion.'

'Do you know if she intended to tell Paweł's mother?'

'I've no idea.'

'And did Paweł ever give her a ring or a bracelet – something valuable?'

Henia shrugged. 'If he did, she never showed it to me.'

'Is it possible that Anna got his name tattooed on her hand? Or maybe his initials?'

Henia burst out laughing. 'Do you think she wanted to look like a sailor, Mr Honec?'

We were crossing the scruffy park in Grzybowski Square, steering around the low-hanging branches of a hazel tree stripped naked by winter. Henia's expression turned troubled. 'There's something that's been bothering me,' she said hesitantly. 'But I don't know if I should tell you. Anna wouldn't like it.'

'She's been murdered. What else could go wrong?'

'Plenty! So why don't you tell me what you want to know about her and I'll see how much I want to say.'

I spoke of my nephew's death until she gripped my arm. 'I'm sorry,' she interrupted, 'but please don't tell me any more about Adam. Since Anna's murder . . . Look, what's been bothering me is that she refused to tell me who the father was, and that started me thinking. I thought it was probably Pawel, but she wouldn't confirm that – or deny it.'

'Who else could it have been?'

'Your guess is as good as mine. But listen, whatever you do,' she said, grimacing, 'you can't tell Anna's parents about any of this.'

'Why not?'

'Mrs Levine has a temper. She drinks. And she used to beat Anna with a wet towel.'

'Why a wet towel?'

'It hurts like hell but doesn't leave marks.' Henia sneered. 'Anna always said her mother was clever – *ugly but clever*. She used to call her Fraulein Rottenmeier – from *Heidi*.'

'Yes, I know,' I replied bitterly; Dorota had fooled me; she'd been protecting herself, not her husband. The unflattering photograph of her daughter had been meant to show me that Anna deserved the abusive treatment her mother meted out.

'No one knows what I'm telling you,' Henia continued. 'I'm not even sure Anna's father knows how bad things were, though she was furious at him for never protecting her. I don't know how Fräulein Rottenmeier will react if you let on that you know what she was up to. And if you tell her Anna was pregnant . . .' Henia groaned to indicate the disaster that would engender.

I stopped to consider whether Anna's own mother might have been involved in her murder. It seemed impossible, yet so did Adam's death.

'No more questions?' Henia asked.

'I don't think so.'

'Bye, Mr Honec,' she said cheerfully, and then she strode away.

After a few seconds, I called out to her. 'Henia, did you lend Anna money?'

She hesitated, then rushed on.

'You have to tell me!' I shouted.

She stopped, unsure what to do. Trudging back to me, as though punished, she took off her aviator's hat. Her face was solemn. 'How did you know?' she asked.

'I'm beginning to understand more about what you children are going through.'

She bit her lip. 'I gave her twenty złoty. But you can't tell anyone!'

'I understand. An abortion is . . .'

'No, you *don't* understand, Mr Honec! I didn't care whether she had an abortion or not. I did something unforgivable, something that . . .'

'You stole money from your parents,' I cut in – to relieve her of the need to speak her crime aloud.

'No, from my younger brother,' she whispered, and her eyes moistened. She rubbed the tears away roughly, as if she didn't deserve them. 'God forgive me, I took two ten-złoty notes out of his wallet. He'd been saving them for months. Mr Honec, he'd even ironed them to make them perfect. He cried for days when they went missing. And my parents were furious with him.' Henia shook her head at her own treachery.

'Anna was desperate,' I told her. 'You helped her. You were a good friend.'

'But I betrayed my brother – badly.'

I gazed into the distance, at the brick wall blocking off Próżna Street, trying to read what to say to Henia in our landscape of confinement. 'On this island, even a *mitzvah* can cause harm,' I told her. 'Though I wish none of us had to learn that.'

'Making my brother feel hopeless wasn't a *mitzvah*!' she declared, unwilling to be prised free of the moral trap she'd stumbled into.

'And I couldn't ever face my parents or brother again if they found out what I've done. Never! So you can't say anything!'

'I won't say a word. I promise.'

Henia put her hat back on. 'Mr Honec, do you . . . do you have any idea why the Nazis killed Anna?' At that moment, she seemed a small girl imprisoned high up in the tower of her best friend's death.

'No, not yet,' I replied.

'Then I want you to do me a favour. If you find out, don't tell me – at least, not until we get out of here.'

'But why?'

'Because I'd kill myself if I was in any way responsible.'

'Don't say that!' I pleaded.

'But it's true.' She fixed me with a hard look. 'And my death would only make things harder for my parents and my brother.'

Anna had needed to talk to Paweł because she was pregnant – and possibly for him to contribute to the cost of her abortion. Had Mrs Sawicki found out about the girl's condition? Maybe Anna had demanded that Paweł marry her, and his mother had murdered her to safeguard his independence.

Or maybe Mikael had performed an abortion on her – one that ended tragically. Terrified of being held responsible, he'd discarded her in the barbed wire, so that we'd assume the Nazis were responsible. But to do so, he'd have had to obtain permission from the Germans to cross over to the Christian side, and they would have surely discovered he had a girl's body with him. It seemed highly unlikely. And in any case, neither of these scenarios could explain why Mikael, Mrs Sawicki or anyone else would want Anna's hand.

I headed off to Mikael's office to speak again to Anka, his nurse, and to see if he'd already secured Stefa's anti-typhus serum.

At first, Anka spoke to me brusquely, insisting she had nothing more to say to me, but by telling her about Adam and his connection to Anna, I managed to draw her out to the stairwell, where we could talk alone.

'You don't approve of abortions,' I whispered to her as soon as we were hidden.

'So you found out.'

'As you wanted me to.'

She crossed her arms as though to defend herself and said, 'Let's get one thing straight – I *do* approve of abortions. These starving girls can't bring a baby into this goddamned mess! But one girl died after her operation.'

'And you were there when that happened?'

'No, Dr Tengmann performs the procedures in the evening. But this girl, Esther . . . After going home, she went to bed, saying she was feeling a cold coming on, but in the morning her parents found her soaked in her own blood, unconscious. It was too late to save her. Maybe we'd never have found out, but her father came here asking questions. He'd known his daughter was pregnant, though he wasn't sure she'd come here. He caught us off guard. Dr Tengmann admitted that he'd seen her, but he denied having given her an abortion. That was very wrong!' At the thud of a door closing somewhere in the building, Anka flinched. When she spoke again, it was in a whisper. 'I can't forgive him for lying. And I can't trust him any more. I've tried, but I can't.'

'If you didn't help with the operation, how can you be so sure of all this?' I asked.

'I know a nurse who assists Dr Tengmann at night.'

'Then she can tell me if Anna also got an abortion!'

'I've already asked her. She never met any girl with that name.'

'Anka, I'd like to talk to her myself. Can you give me her name and address?'

'No, I'm sorry – she wants to keep her identity a secret.'

'Then would you be willing to show her my photograph of Anna?'

'Of course.'

I handed her the picture.

'I'll send you a message with what I find out,' she assured me.

'Listen, was anything . . . a hand, a leg . . . taken from Esther?'

'Her father didn't mention anything like that. God, I hope not!'

'Can you give me his name and address?'

'If you want. But I need my job here – you'll have to be discreet.'

'You have my word. Do you know if Dr Tengmann keeps records of his abortions?'

'If he does, I don't know about them – or where they'd be.'

Back in the sitting room, Anka wrote me out the name of the dead girl's father – Hajman Szwebel – and his address. He lived on Solna Street, just two blocks from where Adam and Anna had been tossed in the barbed wire.

I waited a half-hour before I could get in to see Mikael in his office. After shaking my hand warmly, he held the serum up to the light. 'Here it is!' he enthused.

Our hopes resided in an amber vial.

'I'll go with you now to administer it,' he told me.

'But what about your other patients?'

'They'll have to wait – typhus is serious business.'

'Look, Mikael, I'll never be able to repay you,' I replied, 'but at least I can give you this . . .' I handed him my envelope of money, making sure that Mrs Sawicki's printed name was facing him.

Spotting the embossed lettering, he grinned. 'I see you're still playing at detective.'

'I'm not *playing* at anything!' I replied gruffly, more aggressively than I'd intended, probably because I'd been secretly hoping that the name Sawicki – and the implication that I'd spoken to her – would disquiet him.

'I'm sorry – that came out wrong,' he told me. 'Forgive me, Erik. It was a stupid thing to say. It's just that I'm worried about you.'

'I'll be fine. The worst has already happened. But listen, you might want to count the money.'

'There's no need – I trust you.' He took his coat down from its hook by the door, tucking the envelope and serum away in an inside pocket. 'So were you able to speak to Paweł?' he asked.

'No. Mrs Sawicki told me he was in Switzerland – at boarding school.'

'I see.' Putting his coat down on his desk, he tucked his glasses into their case and rubbed his eyes. 'Do you understand now why I couldn't answer all your questions? And why I lied about what was wrong with Anna? You gave me no choice.'

'Yes, I can see that now. But you no longer have any reason to hide the truth. So I need to know if Anna was certain Paweł was the father.'

He started. 'Do you have reason to believe he wasn't?'

'One of Anna's friends told me she had her doubts.'

'All she told me was she was in love with Paweł and that her parents didn't approve of their relationship. That's all I know. I help the girls the only way I can. To tell you the truth, I don't want to know more about their lives. I just can't take it.'

We took a rickshaw to Stefa's flat. Mikael gazed away, troubled. Guessing what was on his mind, aware now of how fate had trapped him, I patted his leg and said, 'Given our circumstances, what you do is a good thing.'

'You think so? I'll be honest, Erik. I have my doubts at times, but when the girls plead with me, how can I refuse? And you know what they fear most? That their baby will die of starvation inside their womb. How's that for something to keep you awake at nights?' He surveyed the massive, swirling crowds on both sides of the street as if looking for strength. 'I just want Ewa and Helena to be able to get out of this place alive,' he added. 'That's the only reason I keep going.'

Kids in little more than rags began running after us, shouting for money. Mikael tossed coins to the pavement. The boys and girls, hollering, swarmed upon them.

For the first time, I saw how the youngest among us would lead us into the grave. That was now the meaning of Adam and Anna's death.

Mikael and I sat in glum silence. The low-lying winter sun was blocked by the tenement roofs, leaving the streets in deep, penetrating shadow. I couldn't stop shivering.

Finally, I asked, 'So Anna never confirmed to you that Paweł was the father?'

'No, I assumed it.'

'Did she come right out and ask you for an abortion?'

'Yes. And I agreed to help her, but on the evening of her procedure, she didn't show up.' I started to ask a question, but he raised his hand. 'I have no idea why not. I never heard from her again.' He shrugged. 'And then you appeared, telling me she was dead. That's all I know.'

'Was her abortion scheduled for the twenty-fourth of January?'

'It's hard to recall, though that sounds about right. But how did you know?'

'That's the day she went missing.'

The icy wind pushed against our faces. I lifted my muffler over my mouth, so the rest of our brief conversation seems to me now to be textured by thick, dark wool.

'Have all the girls recovered well from their procedures?' I questioned, wanting to test Mikael's honesty.

'What do you mean?'

'No complications, infections . . . ?'

He glared at me. 'All the girls have left my office healthy – tired and upset, but healthy. What happens to them after that, I can't control. Or do you think I can?'

*

Ewa was waiting for Mikael and me in Stefa's apartment, sitting on my bed, her arm over Helena's shoulder, her eyes red and puffy.

'What's happened?' I asked, rushing to her.

'It's Stefa,' Ewa moaned, and she pointed to the window. 'She's in the courtyard, but . . .'

Looking down, I saw a woman's body covered from the waist up by a newspaper and two men standing nearby – our building supervisor, Professor Engal, and a Jewish policeman. The policeman held Stefa's Moroccan slippers, one in each hand.

I clambered down the stairs. Two bricks had been placed atop the newspaper to keep it from blowing away. Kneeling, I tossed them aside.

Ewa told me later that on seeing Stefa's face I immediately let out a cry for Ernst – my younger brother and her father. I have only the most vague recollection of that.

Silver coins covered her eyes. That's what I remember clearly.

I began shaking. The Jewish policeman helped me to my feet and told me my niece had jumped.

'No, no, no – she was too weak to do that,' I insisted.

He pointed to the window of my bedroom. 'She sat on the ledge and pushed off.'

Turning round, I noticed Ziv sitting in the corner of the courtyard, rocking back and forth like a lost child. I called to him, but he didn't answer.

I sat with Stefa for a time, holding her hand, whispering to her about when I'd first seen her as a baby. While clinging to the soft, searching sound of my voice, I realized why she had me keep Adam's medical history and the portraits she'd drawn of him.

I took the złoty coins off her eyes; I didn't believe in ghostly ferryboats across mythological rivers. Professor Engal told me they were Ziv's, so I tossed the money by his feet, hoping to get his attention, but he didn't stir.

While caressing Stefa's hair, I apologized to her again for not protecting Adam, speaking to her in Yiddish and Polish, because each language had its own nuances of guilt and remorse, and ways of asking for what could never now be given to me, and I wanted her to hear them all. When I trudged back upstairs to try to figure out how she'd managed to end her own life, I found Mikael seated on my bed. He stood up to embrace me, telling me how sorry he was. He said that Ewa had taken Helena home.

On handing me back my thousand złoty, he said, 'Stefa had to do it now – she didn't want to waste the serum. I've seen that sort of sacrifice before. I should have warned you. I apologize for being thoughtless.'

I understood then why my niece had been so angry with Izzy and me for finding anti-typhus serum. Maybe she hadn't been ready to meet Death in a Warsaw courtyard, but she knew she couldn't wait.

CHAPTER 16

Stefa must have crawled out of bed and used all that was left of her strength to drag our armchair to the window. I know that because two parallel scratches from the chair legs marked the wooden floor. The window had been shut tight to keep out the frigid wind. My niece had been unable to lift a spoon to feed herself, but she must have somehow managed to throw it wide open.

Later, when I questioned Ewa, she swore to me that the door was locked the last time she came to check on Stefa. As always, she'd let herself in with her spare key. There was no sign of anyone having been there to help her commit suicide. Stefa had been asleep in bed.

'Or she looked asleep,' I noted.

'Or that,' Ewa agreed.

Why did my niece put on her slippers before jumping? True, her feet were always cold of late, but she must have known she'd feel no discomfort soon enough. Maybe she didn't want the person who found her to see the open sores between her toes. I'd known nothing about that small corner of her misery. She'd hidden quite a lot, as it turns out.

In any case, she put on her red and gold Moroccan slippers, climbed up on the chair and eased herself down on the window ledge. Her brittle arms must have been trembling under the strain. One after the other, she swung her legs over the rim until she was sitting on it and facing out – a complex manoeuvre. I know that because I tried it myself, and I'd swear in any court that it required a dexterity and strength that were beyond her.

Ziv was on break and sitting outside the bakery, reading a chess newsletter that had been printed in the ghetto; it had an article on Szmul Rzeszewski, one of his heroes.

Did Stefa hear him call out to her not to move, that she was in danger of falling?

'I'll be right up!' he shouted. 'Wait for me!'

What did she think as she pushed and swivelled herself closer to the edge? Perhaps that gravity was a blessing.

I hope she imagined she was about to see Adam again, but maybe it would have been best if she was thinking nothing at all.

Ziv told me later that she didn't seem to hear him or even notice he was there.

'As soon as she hit the ground, she was dead.' That's what Professor Engal told me when I returned to the courtyard, which was what he had heard from Ziv. Maybe they wanted to spare me more anguish. Still, thirty feet is a long way for someone to fall, and maybe he was right.

Ziv rushed to her but couldn't find a pulse. He dashed into the bakery for help. Ewa and several others tried to revive my niece, but it was too late.

Stefa's slippers had fallen off. Ziv retrieved them while waiting for the Jewish police to come, then sat down in the corner of the courtyard, his head in his hands. He didn't move from there all afternoon and slept there that night. I brought him a blanket, and he let me cover him with it, but he refused to speak to me or come inside.

I'd learned by then that going on strike against the world's injustice was a common ghetto strategy. Not that it ever changed anything.

I'd never previously considered that he'd been in love with Stefa. After all, she was seventeen years his senior. Still, if I'd have been paying attention, I'd have understood that the rose blossom and fresh eggs he gave her on the evening of our first Sabbath banquet represented his opening gambit in what was probably a ten-move strategy. And maybe age differences are unimportant to those who live with queens and rooks dancing through their dreams.

My niece's corpse waited all night for the body collectors. They only came at ten the next morning, explaining that disease and starvation were taking a hundred residents a day and they couldn't cope. By then, I'd dragged her into the hallway of our building; it had started drizzling. I'd wanted to hire some boys from the street to carry Stefa up to her apartment, but Professor Engal told me that the collectors would resent having to walk up the stairs – and might even refuse.

Stefa's miracle . . .

At 3 a.m. on the morning after her death, standing at the window in my room, I looked down at her in the courtyard, and I noticed Ziv jump up and chase after a vague, darting shape. Fearing it was a feral cat or worse, I threw on my coat, hurried downstairs and sat with my niece. Ziv was back tucked into his corner by then, but now he was whimpering to himself. A little later, I looked up to the window of my bedroom, and in the hazy moonlight it seemed the entranceway to a fairytale world, out of which magic had spilled into this place only a little while before. My wonder at how Stefa had found the strength to open her window, climb out on to the sill and jump now seemed to contain everything I'd ever failed to grasp throughout my life – even how men and women could believe in God. And that's when I realized that miracles do indeed occur, though – unfortunately – they aren't always the glorious affirmations of transcendence that we have all been led to believe.

PART II

CHAPTER 17

I'll have to be more wary on my excursions. Early this afternoon, Heniek, while you were working at your factory, I crossed the bridge to the Praga district to make sure my old friend Jaśmin was still alive. Unfortunately, the entrance to her apartment house was locked. I waited outside, watching the passers-by, until, finally, after a couple of hours, she appeared at her window, gazing at the powdering of snow that had begun to fall. I stayed there a long time after she went back to whatever she was doing, grateful that Izzy and I hadn't caused her death. But on the way home, feeling my strength renewed and wanting a small adventure, I decided to go to the Little Ghetto to see what wonders were gracing the shop windows of Sienna Street. A mistake.

I never made it there; I found a crowd swarming out in front of All Saints Church, and at its centre was a burly butcher hacking away at the emaciated, mud-brown carcass of an old mare. Hot blood kept spurting on to his grimacing face. I could tell from the way the poor beast's ribcage stood out that she'd been an underfed, work-damned tram horse. A poisonous-looking steam was rising from the wormy ravine of her open belly.

The ghetto devours itself and will never die, I thought.

I'd never seen a horse without a head and backed away slowly.

'You've grown silent again,' Heniek tells me.

'I thought I was telling you about a dead horse,' I reply.

'No, you haven't said a word in twenty minutes.'

Heniek says I can go an hour or more without speaking, even though I can hear my voice clearly and am sure I'm talking to him. He says my silence scares him, because my edges begin to darken, as though I'm being engulfed by a greedy shadow.

Though he tries to wake me from my trances by calling my name, I show no sign of hearing him.

It is our fourth day together by my count. My seventh, according to him. I do not know how so many days disappear.

After Stefa's husband Krzysztof died of tuberculosis in 1936, my niece would shut herself inside her bedroom and sob. Adam was five then. The little boy once told me that the scrape and click of her turning her key in the lock made him feel like crying out for help, but whose name would he have called? Hearing his mother's weeping, he'd plead with her to let him in while squatting on his heels by her door. He'd scratch like a cat and jiggle the door handle but nothing could convince her to open up.

After confessing these details, he added, 'But it's not so bad. I don't even cry any more. Though I keep scratching. Or else Mama might forget I'm there.'

Amazingly, he didn't show any resentment; he was proud of his ability to cope on his own.

Had Stefa been a good mother? Is anyone *always* a positive influence? All I know is that Adam adored her.

When she finally let her son into her room, she'd pretend nothing had happened. They would sit cross-legged on her bed and nibble bread and cheese, and play cards. My goodness, how the two of them could live on cheese. They were like giant mice!

After the boy had won all his mother's coins, she would open a novel and read aloud to him. Or they'd nap together; her fits of sobbing always exhausted them both.

Ever since she was a teenager, Stefa had devoured detective novels – books by Zangwill, Gaboriau, Groller . . . 'It's like this,

Uncle Erik,' she explained to me once, just after her Krzysztof's death, 'mysteries have solid endings. When you finish the last page, a door locks behind you. So people like you and me and Adam, we can't ever get stuck inside.'

Jumping to the courtyard must have meant that not enough doors had closed behind her over the course of her life; she'd become a prisoner in a story she could no longer go on reading.

Two Pinkiert's men came for her in the morning. It was drizzling. As they picked her up, the world receded. I was encased in thick glass.

Outside, as their cart trundled away over the cobbles, the tense, grinding sound of the wheels gave me the impression we were fighting a losing battle. Upstairs, I got out my list of the dead and chanted the names of everyone I'd ever loved.

I drank vodka and chanted until my voice was gone.

I wanted my parents to come for me. And I wanted out. So I closed the curtains and crawled into the frozen arms of my blankets. I'd promised to go to Pinkiert's headquarters to schedule and pay for the funeral, but it was my turn to go on strike.

Turning on my side, I stared at the window through which Stefa had left our world. To die seeing the sky – even if it was heavy with coming rain – would be comforting. Would it be too much to hope for that my niece had looked up instead of down as she fell?

I slept a drugged sleep and awoke unsure of where I was. Sitting over the side of the bed, I let my pee slide down my legs on to the floor. I suppose I needed to feel I still had a working body.

Maybe that's why the inmates of sanatoriums sometimes soil themselves – to remind themselves they are alive. Pee and shit as the only mirror they have left.

I exist.

While gazing at myself in the real mirror in the bathroom, I repeated that small incitement to life over and over, but in truth I seemed to be just a vessel for one more breath and then another, an instant in time receding towards a quiet so deep it would never end.

Our thoughts don't make us alive. Something else does. But what?

The ghetto taught me to ask that question but never gave me the answer.

If you want certainties then I'm afraid you'll have to read about a different time and place. And different men and women. In Warsaw in 1941, we had none to give you.

A knock at the door woke me to myself. I found Izzy standing on the landing.

'I just heard about Stefa,' he told me.

He embraced me so hard he nearly knocked me over. Afterwards, we sat together on my bed. I couldn't speak. But there was nothing to say.

We were old men exiled from the lives we'd expected to have.

When I could talk, I told him where to find money for Stefa's funeral. He promised he'd organize the ceremony. He put me back to bed.

I awoke on and off all day. He was there watching over me the whole time. Then night fell. I awoke once just after midnight. Fearful, I shouted for Izzy, but he'd gone home. I went to the window. Standing in the darkness, I imagined that if I offered up my life to God, he might spare someone who wanted to live – a child with decades of life left in him. But even if I could convince the Lord to make that bargain with me, how could I decide who was most worthy?

I awoke the next morning to a young woman in bare feet bringing me breakfast in bed. A fried egg looked up at me sceptically from the centre of one of Hannah's Chinese dessert plates.

'Time to eat!' the girl said cheerfully, throwing open the curtains. The light caught the floor and travelled up the blankets to my eyes, making them tear.

The girl had dark hair cut in a pageboy, and an olive skin tone. She wore a man's coat that fell to her knees. She walked with an upright posture, and gracefully, like a ballerina.

'Bina – is that you?' I questioned.

'That's right,' she replied, beaming at me as though I were her prize patient.

'You can't be here,' I told her in a tone of warning.

'Why not?' she asked, her eyebrows knitting together theatrically.

'For one thing, you've let in too much light,' I said, shading my eyes.

She tugged the curtains together but left them open a crack. 'A little light will make you feel better,' she suggested.

'You can't really think the sun can bring back the dead.'

'No,' she agreed, gazing down, adding timidly, 'not even our prayers can do that.'

'Just leave,' I pleaded, but she stood her ground.

'Will you at least drink some tea?' she asked in a small voice.

I changed tactics. 'How on earth did you get in here?'

'Izzy gave me the key.'

'You know Izzy?'

After stooping to pick up one of my socks, she replied, 'I met him yesterday evening when he left your building. And this morning, when he came back, I asked him what was the matter with you. We talked. He's a nice man. He bought some gherkins from me and my mother.'

She picked up another sock and an undershirt. Without looking at me, she said, 'I wanted to tell you I'm very sorry about your niece.'

'Did Izzy come by this morning?' I asked, passing over her sympathy, since the last thing I wanted was to discuss what had happened.

'Yes, he brought coal for you. When he came out to the street, he told my mother and me that you slept through his visit.'

It was only then that I noticed that the room was warm for the first time in months.

'Where the hell did he get coal?' I questioned.

'He didn't tell me.' She folded my trousers neatly and draped them over the back of the armchair. 'You need nourishment,' she observed.

'My God, girl!' I snapped. 'How could you think hunger is my problem?'

She ran into the kitchen. I was sure I'd achieved my goal of making her burst into tears, but I didn't hear any sobs. When she returned, she sat down in the armchair, on the front edge of the cushion, and looked at me as if ready to wait for me to tell her what to do. Her eyes were so needful that I turned away. After a while, I noticed her staring at my breakfast plate. I didn't want to be kind to a girl who didn't have the courage to ask for food when she was famished, so I said nothing.

'Do you mind if I eat your egg?' she finally asked in a fearful voice.

'Be my guest.'

After she'd gobbled it down, she licked the plate. Then she realized how she must have looked and blushed.

Imagine living like an insect for the last six months and worrying about etiquette. Only Jews could raise such absurd children.

I threw off my blanket and kicked my legs over the side of the bed. My feet found the puddle of urine I'd made. Good for me.

I asked her to turn away from me while I dressed. While I was buckling my belt, I said, 'Bina, for the love of God, find someone else.'

'What do you mean?' she asked, looking at me with a puzzled face.

'Go earn some points with God where you're wanted!' I told her.

But even my bullying didn't make her cry. Tightening her lips, she did her ballerina walk to the front door and left. She never looked back, thank God.

Leaning back against the wall for support, I told myself I had saved her from wasting her time on me, but in truth I'd wanted to slice one more wound into the only enemy I could reach.

Izzy came over again late that afternoon. I was sitting in bed with my dream diary, scribbling a list of all the cities I would have wanted to visit if I weren't where I was.

'You're up!' he exclaimed, astonished. 'What are you writing?'

'I'm deciding where I'll go when I get out of here.'

Only after that reply popped out of my mouth did I realize it was true. I went over what I'd written. Genoa seemed my best option – a former colleague of mine from Vienna was living there, and I could probably catch a steamer to Izmir. Or England. Hannah and I had spent our honeymoon in London – and two other vacations there – and we'd always loved it.

'A man from the Jewish Council came over last night,' Izzy told me, sitting down at the foot of my bed. 'He said his name was Benjamin Schrei.'

The mattress sagged towards Izzy. I felt I was made of broken and rusted metal, and all those useless pieces inside me were sliding in his direction.

'I told him you were sleeping, but he wants to talk to you,' Izzy continued, and then he poked around his mouth with his tongue and spat something into his hand.

'What's that?' I asked.

'A tooth,' he replied. 'They've been falling out.'

167

'Open your mouth,' I told him.

I looked in. His gums were bleeding and his breath was putrid, like mouldy bread.

'What the hell is happening in there?' I asked.

'Scurvy,' he replied. 'I managed to buy some oranges, but they haven't helped yet.'

'Lemons would be better,' I observed.

'So find me a lemon.'

'Does it hurt?'

'Only when I eat or talk,' he replied dryly. 'So what do you think Schrei wants?'

'Who gives a damn!' I replied, and I realized that that was what Stefa would have said. Was that how I would go on – by imitating the sound of her voice in my head? After I'd drawn one tight circle around Genoa, and another around London, I added gruffly, 'You shouldn't have told Bina she could help me.'

'Why not?'

'Because she can't!' I declared.

'You know, a little solidarity right now might help,' he advised me, examining his tooth keenly, as if it were a precious artefact from the Dead Sea.

'But what could Bina possibly do for me? I don't want anything to eat, and she doesn't know who murdered Adam or Anna, and . . .'

He threw the tooth and hit me on the side of my head. 'I meant *you* could show a little solidarity towards *her,* you nincompoop! The girl is starving to death under that big coat of hers.'

Izzy made turnip soup while I worked on my list of escape routes. A half-hour later, while we were slurping away, I jotted down the names of the places I'd go if I could live out my fantasies of reaching a tropical paradise – Bangkok, Rangoon, Mandalay . . .

I wanted to wake up to warmth every day, and green, luxuriant life creeping through every crack in the sidewalk, overgrowing rooftops, walls and barricades. I wanted to eat red and yellow handfuls of tropical fruit for breakfast and spit the seeds into the moist soil of my garden, and watch them sprout, and go swimming in an ocean where fern-tailed seahorses and puckered moonfish peeked out at me from their hiding places in coral thickets. I wanted to wake up to the finch-like cries of boys and girls playing naked on the beach. I wanted to be where no one had ever heard German.

CHAPTER 18

I couldn't know when I was fifteen or even fifty what would break my heart, could I? I ask that because it often now seems as if I'd always known that Hannah, Adam and Stefa would die before me.

Imagine black dye running off into every memory. Nothing survives that isn't grey.

CHAPTER 19

Rowy, Mikael, Ziv, the Tarnowskis and other friends came by to check on me over those first days following Stefa's death, but I remember very little of what they said. The only conversation I remember clearly was Rowy telling me he'd obtained funding to buy new musical scores, as well as cheap fiddles, recorders and other instruments; he'd decided to organize a youth orchestra.

The Adam who resided inside me now made me listen to his plans clearly.

With his eyes focused on a brighter future, Rowy also told me that Ziv had generously volunteered to help him search for talented street performers throughout the ghetto on his day off.

Curiously, Ewa and Helena never visited me.

I tossed words back and forth with all my guests, but most of the time I was thinking of how I'd have preferred to be alone. And how I wished I'd taken Stefa and Adam to be photographed. So many lost opportunities rattled in my head after my niece's miracle, but I didn't want to ever free myself from them.

Do I need to tell you why, Heniek? Maybe it's not a bad thing to risk being too clear on occasion: they were proof of all my niece had meant to me.

Sunday was the funeral. I refused to go. I smoked my pipe and watched the rain pelting my window.

Izzy came over afterwards. He collapsed on my bed, face down, the crook of his arm over his eyes. He was sopping wet. He smelled like mud.

I dropped down next to him and held his shoulder. 'I've decided to help Bina,' I told him; I wanted to please him.

But he wouldn't look at me.

I took off his shoes and socks, dried his face and arms, and got him under the covers.

While he slept, I retrieved my dream diary, turned to my list of the dead and added Stefa's name, shivering with relief. I'd almost forgotten to do that. It scared me how we could forget our most important duties.

That night, I woke with a start and lit my carbide lamp, unsure now whether I'd really added her name. Staring at *Stefa Liska*, I wondered about the power of our names to alter our destiny, until the letters lifted off the paper. Soon, all the names of the dead – *my* dead – were floating in the pearly blue light, like butterflies kept aloft by a wind made of my own thoughts. The effect was pretty, but I knew it was only an optical trick; and yet the longer I kept my eyes on them, the more Stefa's and Adam's names seemed wrong – misspelled or mistakenly given to them. So I started rearranging their sequence of letters, which was when it occurred to me that this must have been why I'd made the list in the first place: to find the new names we ought to have given ourselves to protect us from the Germans and all the evils they'd brought with them.

I spent most of the next five days in bed. I slept in and out of twisted half-dreams, and their incompleteness gave me the troubling impression that Adam had wanted to tell me more about his thoughts and feelings – things only I would have understood.

I told all my visitors I felt abandoned and fragile, which had the advantage of being both true and what they wanted to hear, since it gave them the chance to offer me sympathetic looks and words of comfort. They also wanted to be reassured that I'd never give up so that they could believe in the quiet heroism of men and women – and more particularly, of the Jews.

I don't mean to sound cynical about my friends; they were caring people, and they were under no obligation to give up their hopes for a happy ending.

To myself, however, I made the promise that I'd take Stefa's way out after finding Adam's killer.

That week, couriers delivered three letters smuggled in from the Other Side – from Christian friends to whom Stefa had written about Adam's murder. Among them was one from Jaśmin, my former patient. At the end of her long and moving letter, she told me she was talking about the wretchedness of the ghetto to whoever would listen – even foreign journalists – and that I mustn't give up hope of getting out.

She worked only a few blocks away but it was clear by now that we inhabited two separate countries, and that mine would one day disappear from the face of the earth, leaving nothing but a crater of memories for those few who managed to survive.

Sunrise would wake me every morning as if I'd been thrust from a moving train. Sitting up, watching the roaches making zigzag journeys across the cracks in the walls, I'd put myself in the killer's place. He'd obviously wanted a piece of the lives he'd destroyed – as trophies, perhaps. But why a hand and a leg?

And the string – had Adam put it in his mouth or had the killer?

Izzy brought me bread every morning before work, and made me breakfast. Once, standing by the window, he spoke in a hesitant voice of how desperate he was for a chance to apologize to his wife for creating problems in their marriage. Rising to the challenge of his honesty, I confessed all I'd done wrong as a father – a last chance to make amends, I suppose. And a last chance for both of us to reveal secrets we'd kept deep down in our pockets for decades.

Izzy was convinced that he'd made a wrong turn early in his life, when he came back to Warsaw from France. 'I never found my way back to myself after that,' he told me.

Opening an envelope he'd brought with him, he took out four sepia-toned photographs of young men posing in front of a ship's railing. 'My lovers during the six years I worked on the *Bourdonnais*,' he explained, handing them to me.

As I looked at each of his old friends, Izzy's eyes grew worried. I realized he needed to show me all he was, and for me to give him my blessing; there was no time left for waiting.

'You travelled far,' I told him. 'That was a very good thing.'

But his error-of-a-lifetime would give him no peace. Through a surge of tears, he whispered, 'I married Róża to prove to myself I could be the man everyone wanted me to be. I could have had another life – a truer life. Róża, too.'

'One thing I learned from my patients,' I told him, 'is that we *all* spend our lives living beside the people we could have been.'

'Not like me, Erik. I hurt the people I cared for most.'

'Do you still hear from any of your old lovers?' I asked, a plan forming underneath my words.

'One – Louis. Another steward. We write to each other for New Year's.'

'Did you love him?' I asked.

'Very much.'

'Where is he now?'

'He's in Boulogne-Billancourt. That's why I sent the boys there. He found them jobs. He used to work as an airline mechanic. The boys even stayed with him for a while, though they aren't aware of what he and I once meant to each other.'

'When the ark comes for us, you'll go to him,' I told him as if it were an order.

'Erik, I'm too old,' he replied. 'And all of me is unravelling. Besides, there's Róża. I can't leave her.'

'Izzy, she's had a major stroke. She's not going to get any better, and she doesn't know who you are. Let her stay with her sister. Or if you have to, take her with you and let her move in with the boys. You've punished yourself long enough, don't you think?'

One evening, Rowy finally told me why Ewa hadn't visited me; Stefa's suicide had shaken both her and Helena badly, and the little girl had suffered a diabetic shock. She'd nearly died. The young man added that he and Mikael had kept the bad news from me during the worst of my grief so as not to make me feel any worse. Helena was better now, but still weak.

On the afternoon of Friday, 28 February, eight days after Stefa's death, a ghetto courier brought me a note from Gizela, the young woman who was looking after my home. She informed me that a lieutenant in the SS had requisitioned my flat a few days earlier. Gizela and her husband were back living with her in-laws. She asked me not to write to her, since she was convinced that all her mail was being read.

Thinking of a Nazi in my bed made me storm out of the apartment, shaking with rage. I ended up only a block from Weisman's dance school, which started me thinking . . . Checking my watch, I realized I could make Rowy's afternoon chorus rehearsal.

The young musician made a fuss over me as soon as I arrived, introducing me to all of his little singers as a great friend of the chorus. I was impressed with his ease with them and how they tugged at his shirtsleeves for his attention.

When I explained my purpose, he asked, 'Are you sure you're up to it?'

'Yes, it won't take long. But I'll need to see each kid separately – and alone. I don't want them influencing one another.'

That was a lie: in truth, I was afraid that if any of the children had anything unusual to say about Rowy, his presence would intimidate them.

I talked to the eleven youngsters one at a time, behind the closed door of a dressing room. Unfortunately, none of them knew anything about Adam's smuggling activities, and the most damning secret they could tell me about Rowy was that he ate half a chocolate bar after each of their performances.

The next day, Saturday, Anka came to my door early in the morning. She refused my invitation for ersatz coffee. 'I'm in a rush – I make house calls on Saturdays,' she told me, standing in the doorway. 'Listen, I'm sorry it's taken so long to get back to you. My nurse friend has been off with dysentery, but I went to see her yesterday and she told me that Anna never showed up for her procedure. She said that she doesn't know if Mikael keeps records of the abortions. She wasn't sure of the date Anna was scheduled for, but that the twenty-fourth of January sounded right.'

So Mikael had been telling the truth. Perhaps Anna had gone to see Mrs Sawicki hoping to get more money to pay for her abortion, and on the way home she'd been attacked – except that her mother said there'd been no signs of a struggle on her. Just like Adam. Which meant that the two children had either been caught completely by surprise or had known – and trusted – their killer.

Could Rowy or Mikael be working secretly for the Germans and have obtained authorization to cross the border on a regular basis? After all, if Anna or Adam had met one of them on the Other Side, they would have suspected nothing.

How important is personal geography to our destinies? I ask, Heniek, because the only reason I chose to follow Mikael first was that his apartment on Wałowa Street was closer to Stefa's.

I got to his front door just after nine, but I didn't go in. Instead,

I stood vigil down the block. An elderly man rented me a chair for one złoty an hour.

Mikael came out near noon, dressed smartly in a tweed overcoat and carrying a black leather case. He hailed a rickshaw right away. Rushing into the street, I was able to flag one down myself. I told my driver to follow at a safe distance behind his colleague.

A short time later, Mikael got out on Nowolipki Street and entered the door to a five-storey apartment house. I had my driver drop me fifty paces away and knocked at one of the ground-floor apartments. A boy of thirteen or so, wearing a knitted yarmulke, came to the door. At the back of the room, two old women in dark shawls and headscarfs were working over a stove. The place reeked of boiling cabbage.

'Are there any clinics in this apartment house?' I asked the young man; I was guessing that Mikael was carrying medical supplies in his case.

'What do you mean?' he asked.

'Why would a doctor come here?'

'How the hell should I know?' he replied, scowling as if I were a beggar.

I went back outside, stood on the sidewalk and looked up at the façade of the building. A hand-lettered sign in a second-floor window made immediate sense of Mikael's visit: *Jerusalem Photo Studio – Develop Your Own Pictures*.

I knew nothing about photography, but the case Mikael was carrying must have held his plates or film, or maybe even a camera. He'd probably spend a few hours there developing his negatives.

Realizing that it could take weeks to learn something damning about him or Rowy, I headed off through a fog of self-doubt.

On reaching home, the silence of Stefa's apartment pressed down so hard on me that I fled right away. I ended up at the Café Levone. A middle-aged woman with shoulder-length silver hair, intelligent eyes and silver lily-of-the-valley earrings approached me shortly after I was served my tea. 'Sorry to bother you,' she said with an apologetic smile.

She wore an old black jumper whose fraying sleeves she'd accordion-bunched at her elbow, which I found both comic and attractive.

'Why is this so difficult?' she asked, irritated with herself. Her sensitive green eyes drew my sympathy.

'Don't be embarrassed,' I told her, reaching into my pocket for a złoty.

She waved away the coin I held out. 'Oh dear, what a ridiculous sight I must be in these old clothes!' she said, shaking her head. 'I just thought you might like some real sugar.' She held out to me a handful of brown crystals. 'I find it's the only way to keep the ghetto tea from making my taste buds want to run and hide.'

Smiling appreciatively, I picked up a crystal and thanked her. Next to her slender pink hand, mine seemed ungainly and hairy, like an orangutan's, but that was all right with me because it was a reminder that I was a man and she was a woman. 'Please, sit,' I told her, since she, too, looked as if she could use some company.

Once seated, she dropped her crystals into a white linen handkerchief, folded each corner towards the centre, tied it together, and stowed her treasure in her leather bag. Her gestures were quick and practised, which charmed me. When she looked at me again, I put my crystal between my front teeth and took a sip of tea across its smooth surface. She watched me with a serious look, and neither of us turned away for far longer than would be considered appropriate for two Jewish dinosaurs.

Who can explain the ways of the body? My dormant, under-nourished *shmekele* began to grow. And my thoughts turned to hopes long extinguished.

What kind of man would long for sex after the death of the two people he most loved in the world?

The woman introduced herself as Melka Wilner. She told me

she knew who I was because her niece Zosia Kleiner was married to Dawid Kornberg, the son of a former neighbour of mine, who just happened to be in Amsterdam on business when we were ordered into the ghetto . . .

To play by the rules of Jewish knitting, I listened patiently before steering us towards more interesting topics. The rest of our conversation was filtered through the sensual feel of the sugar crystal melting between my teeth.

We ended up talking of travel. I spoke of my honeymoon in London and she told me she had lived in Palestine for five years, from April 1902 to December 1907. She'd married a judge named Timmermann on returning to Poland. 'He always knew right from wrong, which seemed a good thing until I realized *he* was always right and I was always wrong!' She laughed in a burst, and light radiated from her eyes.

I envied how she talked so easily of the events around which her life had turned.

The deed was done in her slender bed, behind a rose-patterned curtain strung from wall to wall; it separated her side of the room from her cousin Zosia's. Melka sensed my nervousness and took control. She was gentle with me, and her kisses were so passionate that she left me disoriented – as if outside my body. Our acrobatics themselves proved painful, limited by the demands of bodies that had been given bony angles by cramped hunger and age. Still, to our credit, we managed to make a pleasant mess on ourselves and the sheets.

God knows why she chose me.

I floundered like a wounded animal afterwards, in a dim grey twilight between waking and sleep. I was giving Adam a bath, and he was splashing. I knew it wasn't real, but I wanted to stay with him. I wanted to become sopping wet with the very sight of him.

'When was the last time you made love?' Melka asked me, tugging me fully awake.

She was sitting at the foot of the bed. Sensing my confusion, she caressed my leg and repeated her question.

I sat up, already so far from Adam that it petrified me. Trying to disguise my feelings, I replied, 'As best I can recall, Nero was emperor in Rome.'

She laughed, which made me feel a little better. 'And you?' I asked.

'Three or four days ago,' she replied. 'I've a . . . a friend.'

I examined my feelings and couldn't find bitterness or jealousy. What else had I a right to expect?

'I'm sorry, Erik,' she said, rubbing my foot.

'It's all right.'

I noticed now the smell of mildew in the room. It seemed to be coming from beneath the bed. I decided not to look.

'Tell me what you're thinking,' Melka requested, smiling encouragingly.

'Do you really want to know?' I asked in a tone of warning.

'Yes. At the very least, we can help each other by listening.'

As I explained about Adam and Stefa, and all the detective work I'd done that had led me to Rowy and Mikael, which now seemed like nowhere, Melka got up and went to the window, peeking through a crack in the curtains. I had the impression she was listening to her own inner voice rather than me, but I needed to confess myself to a person who hadn't known all the people I'd failed, so I kept on talking.

'What will you do now?' she asked after I'd finished.

'I don't know. I suppose after I find out who killed Adam, I'll go back to work at the Lending Library and wait for the Germans to shovel our skinny corpses into the river.'

Melka opened a chink in the curtains again. 'God, I hate the Polish winter,' she said, sighing despairingly.

'We'll hope for an early spring,' I replied, trying to sound encouraging.

'Maybe you need to let your niece and nephew go,' she said without turning round. 'You still have a chance to make a new life.'

'You can't be serious?' I replied.

'Sorry, what I said was thoughtless,' she told me, smiling sweetly. 'Forgive me.'

When she slipped on her pullover, I recognized my cue. After I was dressed, I pressed a slip of paper with my address into her hand, but her easy thank you and friendly peck on the cheek meant that we would never do this again.

My guilt that afternoon and evening was crushing. I drank vodka until I passed out.

Ewa finally came over the next day, Sunday, 2 March, while I was napping off my hangover.

'I want you to know I think of Stefa and Adam every day,' she told me, moving her worried gaze over the floor between us. 'They will be with me always.'

Ewa seemed to speak to me from out of a deep thicket inside herself. I didn't think it was fair that she should have to lug my dead behind her, and I wanted to tell her that, but her air of defeat angered me. *You have your health and your daughter, so you don't have the right to give up!* I wanted to shout.

She sensed my ambivalence towards her and started to cry. After handing me a note she'd meant to send me earlier, she rushed out the door.

The note read: *Everything has gone wrong. The happiness we once all had now seems so distant. It's as if we never had a chance. I'm sorry, sorry, sorry . . .*

Perhaps it was my irritation at seeing Ewa so withdrawn – and at my selfish reaction to her – that awakened me to all I still needed to do. After putting her note under Stefa's pillow, I brought back to my bed the books on child abuse by Ambroise Tardieu and Paul

181

Bernard that I owned; I was looking for what would motivate a killer to take a boy's leg and a girl's hand.

I read until nightfall about kids who'd been raped, beaten and starved – usually by their parents or other relatives – but I couldn't find any who'd been mutilated like Adam and Anna.

Of the unfortunate children I read about that day, I remember a French girl named Adelina Defert most of all. Her parents had locked her in a small wooden box from the age of eight to seventeen. They'd tied her down, whipped her and burned her with red-hot charcoals, and to torture her further her mother had washed her wounds with nitric acid. When Adelina was finally rescued, her straw mattress was teeming with insects, and the rags she used for blankets were soaked with pus.

Reading about Adelina gave me the idea that her parents would have adored running the ghettos across Poland. An insight? Maybe Adam's murderer wanted nothing but the pleasure of disfiguring what was beautiful.

Gratuitous cruelty . . . We have to admit it never goes out of style, and the Nazis had raised it to the level of a philosophy.

All temples are metaphors for the human body; and it was the body that gave birth to the notion of holiness. A professor of mine had told me that in Vienna, but I'd been too young to understand. Now, I realized he'd been right, and what that meant to me now was that the murderer wanted to sever all holiness from the world.

Ziv knocked at my door that evening. He'd come over a few times after Stefa's death but he always looked as if he was about to burst into tears and only stayed a couple of minutes. Since her suicide, he'd become as pale as ivory, and so gaunt that his pimply forehead jutted out over his eyes.

Under his arm he held his alabaster chessboard. 'How about a game before bed, Dr Cohen?' he asked, trying to sound cheerful.

'I don't think so. My mind . . . it's all over the place.'

He looked so forlorn that I invited him to talk with me in the kitchen. I offered him one of the potato pancakes that Ida Tarnowski had made for me, but he turned me down. Looking at his unhappy face, I said, 'All right, let's see if I can beat you this time.'

His reply was a glorious smile.

As we played, I pretended not to notice he was losing on purpose, but not even the village idiot in a Russian novel could make such numbskull moves.

To Ziv, losing on purpose must have meant that we could be generous to each other – why else make such a sacrifice? I guessed that not many people had ever treated him well. And that he'd been building up his courage to give me the gift of his loss since Stefa's death.

Early the next morning, I took a rickshaw to Ogrodowa Street to question the father of the girl who had died after her abortion; I had to make sure she hadn't been disfigured.

Mr Szwebel had oily black hair falling over his ears, wild green eyes and a scruffy beard. He wore long flannel pyjamas and a stained old prayer shawl over his shoulders – a Jewish Rasputin. I told him that Mikael Tengmann's nurse had given me his address, but that he must never tell that to anyone, and he agreed.

When we shook hands, I noticed his fingernails were long and filthy. I feared that his answers to my questions would become manic rants, but throughout our conversation he spoke to me in a quiet and well-considered voice. We sat at his kitchen table, and he poured mint tea for us into slender glasses.

'I've come about your daughter,' I said to him.

'I figured that's what it was.'

'I understand she had an operation.'

'Yes, but I'm afraid I don't know much about what took place,' he replied.

'But you know that Mikael Tengmann performed it?'

'That's what I've been told. He denied it.'

'You don't seem angry about that.'

'Anger is of no help where we live, Dr Cohen.'

'His nurse, Anka, said you knew your daughter Esther had been pregnant.'

'Yes.' He stood up and took a bowl of stewed prunes from the counter, then grabbed a tarnished spoon and handed it to me. 'Eat something,' he told me, putting the fruit in front of me. 'You're way too thin.'

'So are you,' I observed, smiling.

'That's because I don't want to leave the ghetto with anything weighing me down,' he replied. 'But it's different with you. Your time hasn't come yet.'

'How can you be so sure?'

'Let's just say that traumas can sometimes improve our vision.'

To please him, I spooned up one of his prunes, but its burst of sweetness only served to distress me; I didn't want to let myself believe that I could one day return to a life of small delights.

'Did Esther ever say if anyone had threatened her in any way?' I continued.

'No.'

'What did she tell you about Dr Tengmann?'

He took a thoughtful sip of his tea. 'We'd only heard of him – of the procedures he performed. We hadn't been to see him. In fact, we'd agreed that she would continue with the pregnancy – at least that's what I *thought* we'd agreed. Esther went to him without telling me.'

'And do you know who the father of her baby was?' I was testing for anyone who might have known Adam or Anna.

'Her fiancé, Felix Perlmutter.'

I didn't know him. I explained briefly about Anna and Adam. Mr Szwebel looked away, revealing emotion only in his frequent blinking. In answer to my subsequent question, he shook his head. 'No, nothing was cut from Esther,' he told me. 'At least nothing outside her body. She haemorrhaged badly on her inside.'

'Do you know if she could sing?' I asked.

'What?'

'Had Esther a good singing voice?' I clarified.

'I'm not sure. She wasn't a musical girl. But I don't understand what that has to do with anything.'

'I've a friend who started a chorus for boys and girls. I'm wondering if she ever met him. His name is Rowan Klaus.'

'No, she never spoke of him. Though I suppose it's possible she was keeping one more secret from me.'

CHAPTER 20

It started to snow as I made my way home, and the moonlit cascade of those cold blossoms endlessly falling on to me and the rooftops and streets, covering all the muck and disorder, was so wondrous and complete that for one moment everything in the world seemed to be united against a common enemy.

The flakes stuck to my gloves – crystalline and perfect – then melted for ever.

I was moved.

Except that when my feeling of transcendence vanished, I hated all the beauty around me as one can only hate what one has loved as a child.

I spotted Bina and her mother down the street, selling their pickled vegetables, but I didn't dare go to them.

Izzy was waiting for me in my apartment, seated on my bed. He'd taken down a figurative print by Kokoschka that Stefa had kept over her bed – a no-nonsense young woman with her hand on her hip, ready to vanquish any and all opponents. I'd bought it for her because the woman reminded me of her. He was polishing the glass.

'Was it very dusty?' I asked.

'Filthy!' He held up his rag to show me the yellow-brown grime he'd removed, then stood the print in his lap and sat up straight. 'I've just heard that the Jewish Council is assigning tenants to move into the apartments of people who've died – to cope with the thousands of new arrivals from Danzig and everywhere else. So before you have someone move in that you can't stand, I suggest you take in Bina and her mother.'

'Izzy, you're obsessed with that girl!'

'You'd prefer she starve to death under our very eyes?' he demanded.

'But she's like too soft a pillow. She irritates me.'

I made that silly criticism because I couldn't think of a real reason to dislike her.

He eyed me angrily. 'You're behaving miserably! We have to help.'

I sat down beside him and took off my shoes. 'Look,' I told him, 'how can anyone move in? All of Stefa and Adam's things are still here. And I won't pack them up. I couldn't bear to look at them.'

'I'll take care of that,' he said gently. 'We'll put them in my workshop. Nothing will be lost.'

'Very well. Make a copy of your key for Bina and tell her that she and her mother can move in as soon as they want.'

'There's a slight problem – I think she also has an uncle living with her,' he told me warily.

I gave a little laugh at the absurdity. 'Well, I guess one more passenger won't make much difference.'

He embraced me gratefully.

After Izzy left, I looked into Adam's chest of clothes, to feel my pain as deeply as I could before giving it up. Afterwards, while splashing water on my face, there was a knock on the door.

Benjamin Schrei stood on the landing. He wore a pinstriped grey suit, and shimmering on his lapel was a golden Star of David that meant: *I represent authority!*

I stank to high heaven, and I hadn't shaved since Stefa's death, but I was glad for it; I wouldn't have wanted to be anything but a rumpled, smelly eyesore.

'What the hell do you want?' I demanded, tossing my towel behind me on my bed.

'I was sorry to hear about your niece,' he told me, taking off his hat.

'Sure you were,' I replied with a sneer, more than anything else because his slicked-back hair was Hollywood-perfect. Imagine a man preparing for a grievance call as if he had a date with Carole Lombard!

'We need to talk,' he told me, which meant, *you need to listen!*

'No, *I* need to talk and you need to shut up!' I retorted, gratified by the snarl in my voice. 'You told me that Adam was the only child who'd been mutilated, but a girl named Anna had her hand cut off – and you knew it!'

'How did you find out?' he demanded.

'None of your business!' I snapped back.

'Everything that happens in the ghetto is my business.'

'*Oy gewalt*,' I replied, rolling my eyes. 'Did some Hollywood rabbi make you memorize that line for your bar mitzvah?'

'What makes you think that I was under an obligation to tell you about Anna?' Schrei retorted, seething. 'Because you were once an important man? You assimilated Jews make me sick!'

So, Schrei's playing Clark Gablewitz in the Yiddish gangster movie of his own making was all about turning the tables on the Jewish elite. Didn't he realize that his pinstriped suit – even if tailored by a Hasidic hunchback – implied assimilation? 'You don't need to remind me that I'm nothing in here,' I told him, 'or that the man I was outside the ghetto has vanished. I've no illusions – the Germans will grind up my bones and make glue out of me. But I'll tell you this, Schrei – before I'm sold for four pfennig a jar in Munich, I'm going to find out who murdered Adam! So why don't you just save us both some time and tell me if any other kid has been killed.'

I saw from his throbbing jaw that my brutal honesty had unnerved him. 'Look, I'll tell you what you want to know,' he said in a voice of restraint, 'but only if you tell me what you've found out about Adam and Anna.'

'Why should I bargain with you?'

'Because,' he observed, eager to prove we were playing on the same team, 'we both need to know who killed your nephew.'

'Why do you need to know?' I questioned.

'To keep order in the ghetto.'

'Is there an order in the ghetto?'

'There is, even if *you* can't see it!'

'So the God of Moses and Abraham isn't the only invisible being you believe in.'

'I'm afraid you've lost me.'

'Probably because I don't trust you.'

'The council doesn't pay me to be trusted.'

I laughed maliciously. 'There you go again with your bar-mitzvah lines. So you consider yourself a martyr to the Jewish cause? Do you often dream you're on Masada holding off the Romans, by any chance?'

'Has anyone ever told you you're too clever by half?' he asked.

'Just my wife. But I'm pretty sure I've gotten dumber since she died – especially over the last few months.'

'Look,' he said, sighing with exasperation, 'I know you don't like me, and I *know* I don't like you, but I've had a hell of a day and I need to get off my feet.'

'That's the first thing you've said that makes any sense,' I told him admiringly. I gestured for him to step inside. 'Take the armchair,' I told him.

He dropped down and undid his coat as if he might not move again for quite some time. I sat on my bed.

'Do you mind if I smoke?' he asked, taking out his cigarette tin.

'Not if you give me one.'

He lit mine – a gentleman even to his enemies, I had to give him that. I fetched us the clay ashtray Adam had made and plonked it down on the arm of his chair.

'Well?' he prompted.

'Well, what?' I replied.

'What have you found out about your grandnephew?'

'For one thing, he led a double life, as you suspected. Though I haven't found out yet where he used to cross to the Other Side. He left the ghetto on the day he was murdered to try to find coal. What else he was smuggling, I've no idea – probably cheese. He and his mother could live on cheese. We come from a long line of mice.'

'And Anna?' he asked, unamused.

'The way this works, Mr Schrei, is you ask a question, then I ask one. That can't be too hard for you to understand even if you're too pooped to punch me in the face.'

He grinned, since I'd read his thoughts accurately.

'Have any other kids been mutilated?' I asked.

'One, a boy – ten years old. Just three days ago.'

'What was missing – a hand or a leg?'

'It's my turn, Dr Cohen,' Schrei told me. 'What did you learn about Anna?'

'She had a boyfriend outside the ghetto – a Pole named Paweł Sawicki. By the way, when you found her body, were there any signs of her having put up a struggle?'

'No.'

'So maybe she knew whoever killed her. Or whoever betrayed her to a murderer living outside the ghetto. Maybe Adam did, too.'

'That seems possible,' he agreed.

'So what was missing from the murdered boy?' I asked.

'The skin over his right hip – it was sliced away.'

I cringed. 'How much skin?'

'A lot.' He held his hands half a foot apart. 'Tell me about Paweł.'

'A nice boy, by all accounts. Went to the cinema with Anna, took her on picnics. Only one problem: his mother is a Jew-hating witch who banished him to Switzerland to keep him away from Anna. So was there anything special about the skin that was taken from the boy?'

'We can't find anyone who knew him well enough to say. Was there anything special about Anna's hand?'

'Her mother didn't think so. What was the boy's name?'

'Georg.'

'And where was Georg found?'

'Chłodna Street – in the barbed wire, just like Adam.' Schrei smoked thoughtfully and disregarded my next question. 'So maybe Paweł's mother had Anna killed,' he conjectured in a slow, cautious voice. 'Anna knew her, so maybe she could have been lured somewhere to be murdered by her, or by someone helping her.'

'Maybe. I mean, that's what witches do – kill children. But I've no reason to believe that Anna ever met Adam, and in any case, it's nearly impossible for me to believe that Mrs Sawicki knew anything about him, so why would she have had him murdered?' I went to the window and gazed down into an image of Stefa lying under the *Berlin Morgenpost*. Schrei tossed me his next question, but I let it fall between us. 'You know what Mrs Sawicki told me?' I said to him. 'That our story is over – the Jews, I mean.'

'She may be right,' he replied glumly.

Schrei closed his eyes and angled his face up, as though trying in vain to recall the warmth of summer sunlight, and just like that we *were* on the same team – fighting to keep *The End* from being written into our four-thousand-year-old autobiography.

'You want something to drink?' I asked him in a conciliatory tone. 'I've still got a little schnapps left.'

'Any coffee?' he asked.

'Some chicory substitute that isn't too bad.'

On the way to the kitchen to boil water, I patted his shoulder. Surprised by my gesture of friendship, he stood up and accompanied me.

'Georg – did anyone see who left his body in the barbed wire?' I asked.

'No. Was Anna smuggling?' he shot back, leaning against the cabinets.

191

'I don't think so. She left the ghetto to see Paweł, but he was already in Switzerland.' To keep my word, I refrained from revealing she'd been pregnant. 'She never made it back inside,' I added. 'Not that she had much to return to.'

'Go on,' he said.

'There's a second witch in her story.'

'Who?'

'Her mother forbade her to date *Goyim*,' I replied, 'and she beat Anna when she refused to give up her Polish Prince Charming. Do you know if Georg had ever met Adam or Anna?'

'No, I've no idea,' Schrei replied.

'And you know where he lived?'

'He'd been in the Krochmalna Street orphanage, but he'd run away.'

'The orphanage run by Janusz Korczak?' I asked.

'That's right. Have you discovered anything that Adam and Anna had in common?'

'They had the ghetto in common,' I replied.

Thinking I was trying to be funny, he grinned – a tough guy's grudging smile – and took a quick, determined puff on his cigarette. He was starting to like me and getting his energy back.

'And what else?' he asked.

'Being half-starved . . . becoming adults before their time . . . wanting to get to a warmer climate.' I refrained from mentioning Mikael or Rowy just yet; I didn't entirely trust Schrei and couldn't risk him alerting my suspects that I'd be following them. 'How long a list do you want?' I asked him.

'I meant,' he said, sighing mightily, 'have you found anything *specific* they had in common?'

'Not yet,' I lied.

'Were Anna and Adam friends with any of the same kids?' Schrei asked.

'Not that I know of. Was there any string in Georg's mouth when you found him?'

'String?'

'Adam had a small piece of white string in his mouth. Did anyone look in Georg's?'

'No, but he might have been keeping a tiny square of gauze in his fist.'

'*Might have?* What's that mean?'

'We found a piece of gauze in his fist. But maybe it had been in the barbed wire and got stuck to him when he was tossed there. It had been raining – the gauze must have been wet and clingy.'

'What kind of gauze?'

'The kind used in wedding veils, that sort of thing.'

'Did you save it?' I asked.

'No.'

'Why the hell not?'

'It didn't seem important. Look, Dr Cohen, hundreds of Jewish kids die each month in the ghetto – should we save everything they've got in their hands?'

'Was the gauze bloody?'

'No, it was clean.'

'Which means it may have been put in his fist after he was murdered. Or he may even have snatched it up.'

'Why would he do that?' Schrei questioned.

'I don't know. What was Georg's surname?'

'If I tell you that, you have to promise not to go public with anything you find out.'

'Whatever you want,' I agreed. 'I'll even leave you my first editions of Freud in my will. You *can* read, can't you?'

'This is serious, Dr Cohen. You're already in trouble.'

'With whom? Besides God, I mean – for being an assimilated Jew.'

I thought that was witty, but he glared at me as if I'd gone too far. 'With . . . me,' he said slowly and darkly, and he took a long and greedy puff. He had fantastic lungs – I'd give him that.

'*Mazel tov!*' I told him sarcastically. 'God and Benny Schrei regard me as too clever by half. Do you and He perform together often?'

'This is useless,' he concluded, frowning. '*You're* useless. And I'm too sick of my life to go on hitting verbal ping-pong balls back and forth with a crusty old bugger like you.' He strode past me, chin high and elbows swinging, just like the cowboy hero in a Karl May Western.

'I'm sorry,' I told him, and when he faced me at the kitchen door, I said, 'I really am, but what can I do?'

I saw in the willingness of his eyes that he'd wanted someone to apologize for a long time – for what, I didn't know, but every Jew in Poland woke up with an urgent need for someone, even a stranger, to tell him he was sorry.

'You want me to follow your orders,' I went on, 'but I'm exhausted, and underneath my exhaustion is an anger so deep it's probably bottomless. And besides, I've always been bad at doing what other people want.'

The water was boiling by now, but I'd used up all my strength bantering with him. I sat at the table and propped up my head with my hands.

'When was the last time you had a good meal?' he asked me.

'Define good.'

'I'll make the chicory,' he told me.

'It's in there,' I said, pointing to one of the cabinets.

'So what are you going to do when you find out who killed Adam?' he asked me, taking out the tin. He also found a wedge of cheese that Stefa must have hidden for an emergency.

'Have you ever been to London?' I asked.

'No,' he replied.

'How about Paris?'

'Once, why?'

He took a paring knife from the towel on which I'd let the

washed silverware dry and started scraping the outside of the cheese.

'Was Paris exactly as you thought it would be?' I questioned. 'I mean, when you were walking along the Seine did you feel just as you thought you'd feel?'

'No, of course not.'

'So how can I know what I'll do when I reach the final page of this mystery?'

He scowled as if my comparison was silly. 'Do you have any bread?' he asked.

I pointed to my stash of matzo on Stefa's spice shelf. He took a rectangle and cut two reasonably mould-free slivers of cheese on top. 'Eat this,' he said, putting it in front of me.

It was comforting to be given an order. While he made our ersatz coffee, I nibbled away – the third mouse in my family, and the only one who hadn't yet had his neck snapped in two.

We let silence settle the quarrel between us. I was grateful for that.

'I want you to come to me when you find out who murdered Adam,' he told me, putting a steaming cup of chicory in front of me. 'Before you do anything stupid, I mean.'

'All right, but I'm prone to doing stupid things. It's a personality flaw.'

Sniffing, he said, 'No offence intended, Dr Cohen, but are you aware you smell like a dog's behind?'

His *no offence intended* made me laugh. I liked him more and more.

To give ourselves a rest, we talked about the wretched weather for a time – a favoured subject in Warsaw for at least nine months every year. Then he asked about Stefa, and I told him how she'd given me back a belief in miracles. When I spoke of her Moroccan slippers falling off, and of the sores I discovered between her toes, he closed his eyes as if he might give up his Hollywood gangster persona and turn back into the softer man he undoubtedly was in the Before Time.

'Hey, give me some more cheese,' I asked, to move us beyond our impasse.

He cut me a big slice, pulling the knife towards his thumb like a peasant, which made me realize how far he'd come.

'Got a pen and paper?' he asked while I was licking the crumbs from my palm.

'What for?'

'I'm going to write down what I know about Georg.'

I told him to fetch my dream diary from under my pillow and my inkstand from my desk. In the thirty seconds he was gone, I realized the obvious: he was too overworked to solve the murders of Adam, Anna and Georg; he wanted me to do that for him. And I also realized that he must be sure a Jewish accomplice inside the ghetto was at least partly responsible for Adam's death or he wouldn't be worried about what I'd do.

'Who are the letters under your pillow from?' he asked when he returned.

'My daughter. She lives in Izmir. She's an archaeologist. She likes old things.' *Except for her father*, I almost added, but I hoped that was no longer true.

'Thank God she's safe,' he told me.

'Yes, that's a very good thing. Listen, Schrei, after I find out who killed Adam, Anna and Georg, what'll you do with me?'

'Do with you? I won't do anything with you.' He was offended by my implication.

'If the murderer turns out to be a wealthy smuggler who's collaborating with the Germans, you won't put a bullet in me?'

'Not if you keep his identity to yourself.'

'And if I don't?'

'Dr Cohen,' he replied wearily, 'if I were a betting man, I'd wager you'll never find out who the murderer is. But if you do, you can be sure I'll take care of him – even if he turns out to be Keranowicz.'

'Who?'

'Sorry – it's my anagram for Czerniakow.'

Adam Czerniakow was the head of the Jewish Council – and the most famous man in the ghetto.

'You too?' I exclaimed.

'Me too what?'

'Rearranging things to fit the new world we're living in.'

'What else can I do?' he replied, shrugging. 'Anyway, I'll take care of the murderer – *if* you find him. That's my job.'

He spoke so matter-of-factly that I believed him. He wrote a name in my dream diary – Georg Mueller – then the address he'd lived at before being orphaned: 24 Brzeska Street, which was in the Warsaw suburb of Praga.

He also wrote down his own address. When he handed me my diary, he said, 'Get in touch with me if you find out anything more – any time, day or night.'

'You're sure Georg's parents are dead?' I asked.

'That's what the boy told the people at the orphanage. And we managed to send someone to his home address, but none of his neighbours knew of any relatives in the area.'

'He must have someone – an aunt, an uncle . . .'

'He said he had cousins in Katowice.'

As I wrote that down, I asked, 'And how did his parents die?'

'The Nazis sent his father away on a labour gang and he never came home. Pneumonia killed his mother.'

'Do you have a photo of him?' I asked, and when Schrei shook his head, I added, 'How about an identity card?'

'Nothing. He was thrown naked into the barbed wire.'

'From the Christian side?'

'Yes.'

'You said he'd run away from the orphanage. So where was he living?'

'On the street. A nurse who worked at the orphanage said she used to see him juggling outside the Femina Theatre. But listen,

Mueller may not be his real name. That's the name he used, but he might have made it up. Apparently, he was that kind of kid.'

'What kind of kid is that?'

'The kind who lies to adults.'

'You don't get it, do you?' I told him. 'In here, all kids lie. That's one more way we can be sure we've been exiled to *Gehenna*.'

CHAPTER 21

A barber at a makeshift stall near the Femina Theatre confirmed to me that kids often performed there starting at noon and, sure enough, five boys and one girl, all in homemade black leotards, arrived only a few minutes after the hour. A crowd formed as they spread a worn red rug along the sidewalk.

They performed flips and handsprings to much delighted applause. Only one of the kids – a boy with a shaved head who was maybe ten or eleven years old – seemed to be a trained gymnast, however; he did a twisting handspring into a back flip that made everybody gasp. But he never smiled; he seemed to be embarrassed.

For a finale, the children formed a three-tiered pyramid. An imp with a shaved head stood at the top. He wore a gold papier-mâché crown and gripped a sceptre in his fist – a metal bar painted silver, with a blue light bulb fastened at the top. Surveying the onlookers, he held his head high, as if they were his subjects. He tried his best, but the whole amateurish spectacle only revealed to me how far we'd fallen.

As soon as the show was over, the capable gymnast walked through the crowd with a black derby, asking for donations. I dropped a złoty in and asked if he'd known a young street juggler named Georg. He told me that he hadn't, but the miniature king who'd reigned atop the pyramid overheard us and hollered, 'I knew him!'

'What's your name?' I asked.

'Zachariah Manberg,' he replied proudly.

'He's *Tsibele*!' the slightly older acrobat beside him shouted with malicious glee.

''Cause he smells like an rotten onion!' another shouted.

'We all smell like onions!' I challenged them.

'Not you, *Reb Yid*!' yelled the girl acrobat, hoping to win some coins in exchange for flattery.

'True,' I acknowledged. 'I have it on good authority that I smell like a dog's rear end.'

She was too shocked to laugh. And Zachariah was too curious of me.

'Come here,' I told him, motioning him over. He had merry green eyes – intelligent and wily – and I imagined from the serious way he stared at me that he was trying to assess whether I was a hundred, or maybe even a thousand, years old. I felt an immediate affection for him.

'My name is Erik Cohen and I'm sixty-seven,' I told him. 'How old are you?'

'Seven and a half,' he answered proudly, puffing up his chest like a rooster.

'Do you know if Georg was smuggling?' I asked.

He held out his palm, stuck the pink tip of his tongue between his lips and gave me a cheeky look. I reached into my pocket and took out a one-złoty coin, then gave it to him, which made his eyes pop. The four other boys and single girl in his troupe circled around us.

'I'm sure he was smuggling,' Zachariah told me.

I squatted to his level so he'd trust me, but my knees were so sore that it felt as though broken glass were sticking into them. I dropped down on to my bottom to relieve the pain. When I asked my little friend to sit with me, he dropped down and crossed his legs.

'Where's your coat?' I asked him.

'My sister is holding it.'

'Where is she?'

'She went for food.'

I took off my muffler and twirled it twice around his neck. 'There, that's better,' I told him. 'Now, what kind of goods did Georg smuggle?'

He held out his hand again. I gave him another złoty. He inserted both coins into his sock, then told me happily, 'I don't know.'

'I paid you so you could tell me you don't know?' I made an exaggerated, silent-movie frown. 'You're taking advantage of an *alter kacker*!'

He giggled and squirmed. The ghetto hadn't yet murdered his sense of humour, which was worth paying for. But more than that, I realized I'd found the child I wanted.

When I learn who killed Adam, take me, but let this boy survive, I whispered to God – or maybe to Satan. It didn't seem to matter which, as long as my wish was granted.

'Do you know which secret passage Georg used to get out of the ghetto?' I asked.

He held out his palm for more money. I snatched his hand. 'Listen, Zachariah, this goes beyond money – I need to know very badly.'

'Georg went right through the wall,' he answered. 'He and some other boys knocked out some bricks one night.'

'Where?'

'I don't know.'

'On Okopowa Street, near the cemetery,' an older boy with a scab on his chin told me. 'I was with him.'

I motioned him over and he squatted down beside me.

'Did he ever speak about meeting anyone dangerous or threatening?' I asked.

'No.'

Zachariah agreed with that. He rubbed his eye with his knuckle.

I noticed a louse crawling in his eyelashes. I took his shoulder. 'Don't move,' I told him.

I pulled out the wretched parasite between my thumb and forefinger, then crushed it with my nail.

'What was that?' he asked.

'Just a bug,' I replied, tossing it away. 'Listen, did Georg ever say why he didn't go back to the orphanage?'

'He hated being cooped up!' Zachariah exclaimed, as if that answer might win him a ticket to the cinema.

'And do you know where he was living?'

'On Nowolipie Street.'

'What number?'

Zachariah made a face and hunched up his shoulders to indicate he didn't know.

'Georg was kind of secretive,' the older boy said solemnly.

'What did he look like?'

'He had big ears – like an elephant,' Zachariah told me. He tugged on his earlobes.

'Did you ever see him naked?'

'Naked how?' he asked, puffing out his lips in puzzlement.

'I need to know if he had any identifying marks on his hip.'

As soon as I finished my question, a jolt of understanding made me gasp. I realized now what might have made Adam's leg special.

'No, I never saw his hip,' the older boy told me.

'Me neither!' Zachariah chimed in.

I got to my feet. The two boys did, as well. I continued my questioning, but I felt as if I'd crossed an invisible portal into a myth, in which the only way to identify brothers and sisters separated at birth was by a telltale sign on their skin. And Adam's telltale sign was on his ankle – his *right* ankle: a line of four birthmarks. But of what value could they have possibly been to anyone? And could something so small and insignificant really have summoned Death to my nephew?

'How about Georg's clothing – anything unusual?' I asked the acrobats.

'I know the answer to that one!' Zachariah exclaimed, his eyes brightening. 'He had newspapers stuffed into his shoes!'

'That's all?' I asked.

'And he wore a chain around his neck,' the older boy told me.

'What kind of chain?'

'With a little Virgin Mary at the end. He said his mother was Jewish, but that his father was Russian. His father had hung that necklace around his neck when he was just a baby. He never took it off.'

'And Georg juggled, right?'

Zachariah nodded.

'Did he do anything else to earn money?'

'No,' the little boy replied, but the older acrobat added, 'Georg sometimes sang while he juggled. Mostly Yiddish folk songs. He said it got him a bigger crowd.

'Was he any good?'

'Pretty good, but he wasn't the best juggler in the world. He could do only four pairs of socks. And sometimes one would fall.'

'Socks?'

'That's what he juggled – he rolled each pair into a tight ball.'

By now, I'd realized that Rowy or Ziv was sure to have noticed him sooner or later while looking for new singers. Was it possible that they were both involved in Adam's murder? Rowy was terrified of being conscripted again into a labour gang, and perhaps he had exchanged the lives of three Jewish children for a guarantee of safety. As for Ziv, what did I really know about him, other than that he was shy and awkward, and an exceptional chess player?

'Did Georg ever talk about singing in a chorus?' I asked Zachariah and his colleague.

'He said something like that once,' the older boy replied. 'He mentioned to me that a man told him he could sing at a concert he was going to organize.'

'Did Georg tell you the man's name or what he looked like?'

He shook his head. 'Sorry.'

I gave him a złoty with my thanks, and he ran off.

'Where's mine?' Zachariah whined.

'If I give you more money, I need you to do something for me,' I told him.

'What?'

'I want you to get disinfected at the Leszno Street bathhouse. You know where it is?'

'Of course.'

'Good.' I dropped two złoty – one after the other – into his excited hands. I wanted to tighten the scarf I'd given him around his neck – as an excuse for holding him once more – but he dashed off before I could, one hand securing his crown.

CHAPTER 22

Dorota refused to let me into her apartment once again. 'My husband isn't home,' she confessed, 'but if he ever learned that a man asking about Anna had been here . . .' She shook her head as if dealing with his temper was a constant burden.

'Just tell me about your daughter's hand,' I told her gruffly.

She drew back her head like a surprised hen. 'There's nothing to tell.'

'Did it have any birthmarks?'

'No.'

'Anything else that would make it identifiable to someone who'd never seen her before?'

'I don't know – just a small patch . . . a discoloration on the back,' she said doubtfully. 'But why are you—?'

'What did the patch look like?' I interrupted.

'It was tiny and red – like a stain. On the skin between her thumb and index finger. People were always trying to wipe it clean when she was little.'

'Why in God's name didn't you tell me that before?' I demanded angrily.

'It was so small. And it seemed so unimportant. Besides, Anna was ashamed of it.' She reached for my arm. 'The poor girl hated it!'

Outside Dorota's apartment house I took my first steps too quickly and slipped on the fresh snow. The trunk of a beech tree saved me from a bad tumble. Embracing it, standing apart from the people hurrying past, I saw that Adam and Anna had both been marked at birth. And if I was right, then Georg had been, too. Someone had wanted their skin blemishes and birthmarks. But why?

Everything pointed to their having been murdered outside the ghetto and then dumped in the barbed wire. And it seemed clear now that Georg was recruited by either Rowy or Ziv. One of them must have identified the children to the murderer – a German or possibly Pole – who had had the kids followed and snatched.

I was anxious to question both men, of course, but doing that would do little good, I reasoned; if one or both of them were guilty, they'd try to cast the blame on someone else – probably on Mikael, since there was no reason why they wouldn't be able to make the same deductions I had. Or would they simply tell me that they couldn't have known that Adam and Georg had any skin blemishes? After all, it was unlikely that they'd seen either boy naked or – during our frigid winter – in short pants. Only one person could have – Mikael.

Maybe Anna had threatened to denounce him for his abortions and he had asked whoever was working with him on the outside to kill her when she left the ghetto. In that case, the murderer had waited until she visited Mrs Sawicki, then lured her away.

I hailed a rickshaw, sure of only one thing: I'd resume following Mikael as my most likely suspect. But as soon as we set off for his office, a fact I'd overlooked made me call out to the driver that we needed to change our destination.

I discovered Stefa's apartment door open. A squat young Gestapo officer with his cap in his hands was gazing out the window. Another Nazi, older, his hair turned to silver by the light from my carbide lamp, was reading.

They've learned I was on the Other Side and did nothing to prevent the murder of a colleague of theirs, I reasoned.

Before I could slip away, the younger man turned to me with a surprised expression. Sensing a change in the room, the German at my desk also faced me. Putting down his book, he showed me a cat-like grin.

My legs tensed, and if I'd been younger, I'd have raced down the staircase. Instead, I slipped out of my coat and stepped inside. At times, the state of one's body can determine everything.

'Are you Dr Erik Cohen?' the German who'd been reading asked me. He put on his cap and stood up.

'Yes.'

'We need you to come with us.' His Prussian accent made me shrink back.

'Where?' I asked.

'Out of the ghetto. I'll explain in the car.'

I hung up my coat to give me time to take a couple of deep breaths. 'I've done nothing,' I told him.

He smiled, amused, revealing fine Aryan teeth – the teeth of a man who ate satisfying meals served by starving Jews.

'We're not going to kill you just yet – that would be too kind,' he told me.

Apparently, that was what passed for wit amongst the Nazis; the young German laughed in an appreciative burst.

'Why do you want me?' I asked.

'I'll explain on the way down the stairs.'

'Do I need to bring a change of clothing?' I was trying to learn if I'd be incarcerated.

'Do you *have* a change of clothing?' he replied sarcastically, looking me up and down as if I were a peasant, and the two men had another good laugh at my expense.

I waited for the Nazi comic to give me a real reply, but none came.

'I need to check one thing before we go,' I told him.

'We're already late.'

'I'll only need a minute.'

Frowning, he gave his permission with a patronizing twist of his hand.

I rushed to my desk and got out the medical folder on Adam that Mikael had given me. My heart was thumping, and I fumbled my reading glasses. Once I had them on, I discovered that at the bottom of the second examination sheet, Mikael had written in his neat script: 'Four birthmarks at the base of his right calf muscle, the largest 1.5 centimetres in diameter and hard-edged.' He'd also drawn them.

Birthmarks – *Geburtsmale* – was in German, but the rest was in Yiddish.

My intuition had been right; as chorus director, Rowy could have had access to this examination sheet, and it was just possible that he might have mentioned something to Ziv about the peculiarities on Adam's leg – in passing, thinking nothing of the consequences. Indeed, Stefa might also have made some innocent remark about them to either man. So neither of them would have had to see Adam naked to know he was marked for death.

The Gestapo comedian and I rode in the back of a Mercedes down Franciszkańska Street. He carried the book he'd been reading. It had been Adam's: a German edition of *The Lost World* by Sir Arthur Conan Doyle, that I had bought for him. He held the book with the title facing out, undoubtedly eager for me to protest in an outraged voice so that he could laugh in my face. But his thievery didn't concern me; by now, I believed that Rowy – maybe with Ziv's help – had betrayed Adam and Anna to a Nazi murderer; after all, if Mikael were guilty, he wouldn't have let me keep Adam's medical file, which was clear evidence that he had noticed the boy's birthmarks.

I'd have to follow the young conductor to try to learn whom he was working with on the outside.

We exited the Okopowa Street gate, with the Jewish cemetery on our right.

'They start with the eyes and lips – anything soft,' the Nazi beside me told me lazily, as if in passing.

He pointed to a group of crows huddled on the cemetery wall, probably waiting for mourners to leave a frozen burial site.

'They'll tear their beaks into anything, and they'll wait hours if need be,' he added. 'I've even seen them tug the lid off a casket. Admirably intelligent creatures.'

I said nothing; I'd learned in my work that there are people who are barren inside – who feel no solidarity for anyone. The amazing thing was that they looked just like the rest of us. And now they had the world's most powerful armaments and their very own empire.

'I suppose in the long run the mass graves are a blessing,' he observed, giving me a playful nudge. 'The grass will grow better with all that fertilizer. What do you think?'

'Me? I don't think anything,' I replied, refusing to look at him.

Outside my window, dismal apartment houses and grubby streets zoomed by. Both Germans tried to bait me several more times, but their comments soon decayed into centuries-old clichés. I played with the coins in my pocket to keep calm – an old strategy for dealing with Jew-hating colleagues in Vienna.

Still, maybe their antagonism had an effect on me; the bump and tumble of the car, the glide of winter landscape, the musty leather smell in the car – everything soon left me panicked that I'd be killed before taking vengeance. And the further we moved from the ghetto, the deeper my sense of vulnerability became.

As we pulled into the gravel driveway of a three-storey villa with Palladian windows, my travelling companion elbowed me. 'Get out,' he growled.

A handsome, middle-aged woman met us in the foyer, which was floored with black and white marble squares, as in a medieval Italian painting. She was tall and slender, with a man's closely cropped blonde hair. Her healthy face was red-cheeked, and her blue-blue eyes were the stuff of Aryan mythology. Scandinavian, I'd have bet. And eating three square meals a day, just like my German escorts.

I will always remember the first lingering look she gave me, her eyes moistening, as though she had been hoping to meet me for years, and the way, too, that she breathed in slowly, filling herself with this moment.

'Thank goodness you're here!' she exulted in French-accented German, and she reached out for my hand with both of hers. 'It's an honour to meet you, Dr Cohen. I've heard so much about you. My name is Sylvie Lanik.'

The Gestapo men stood stiffly by the door, which meant that my host was a powerful woman.

'*J'aimerais savoir pourquoi vous m'avez convoqué*,' I asked her.

I tried my rusty French because I preferred the Germans not to know that I was asking why I'd been summoned.

'It's Irene . . . it's my daughter,' Mrs Lanik answered, also in French, embarrassment reducing her voice to a whisper. 'She's not well. I'm hoping you can help her.'

'Send the Germans away,' I told her.

'Yes, whatever you want.' Mrs Lanik summoned her elderly housekeeper and asked her to give the men coffee and cake in the kitchen. The Gestapo comedian showed me a predatory smile as he strode off, no doubt envisaging the revenge he'd take. The only question was whether I'd survive.

'You must be important,' I remarked in German as soon as they'd left.

She flapped her hand. 'My husband is the important person around here.'

'Is he a Nazi?'

'Yes, though he and I both know that what Hitler says about Jews is all lies.'

Did she expect me to thank her for not hating me? I forced a laugh.

'Have I offended you, Dr Cohen?' she questioned fearfully.

I despised her for being a traitor to her own beliefs and refused to give her the satisfaction of an answer. 'Where's your husband?' I asked roughly.

'He left yesterday morning and will be gone until tomorrow.'

'Does he know I'm here?'

'I told him we were sending for someone who could help Irene.'

'But not a Jew.'

'No, that was my decision,' she said firmly.

'Mrs Lanik, I may have been reduced to nearly nothing, but that doesn't mean I don't have a life. I have to get back to the ghetto.'

'Dr Cohen, please just give my daughter a half-hour of your time. She needs help. I'll pay you whatever you want.'

I grinned maliciously. 'Why do you people always think you can buy a Jew with money?'

'You know that's not what I meant,' she replied angrily, but she added in a contrite voice, 'though I suppose I deserved that.'

'Look, why should I help you?'

'Given the unfairness of the world and all that's happened to your people, maybe you shouldn't,' she observed.

Her honesty impressed me. 'Very well, tell me what's wrong with your daughter,' I requested in a business-like tone.

'A few days ago, she tried to take her own life – with pills. She won't talk to me about what's bothering her. She'll only talk to you.'

'Me? How does she know about me?'

'Irene found out you were a well-known psychiatrist before you were . . .' She searched for the word; her German was excellent, but she was clearly under an enormous strain.

'*Emprisonné*,' I suggested.

'Yes, imprisoned,' she agreed.

I discovered that day that Mrs Lanik stepped cautiously through her thoughts, as though searching for hidden motives in herself and others. As a consequence, all her responses were delayed. It was unnerving. I began to believe she led an isolated life – and conversed with very few people.

'Where is your daughter?' I asked.

'She refuses to leave her room. I'm losing my mind.' She clutched at the collar of her blouse. 'If . . . if Irene should die . . .'

She loves her daughter as I loved Adam, I thought, and that changed the direction of all my subsequent actions.

'Mrs Lanik,' I said more gently, 'how did you find my address?'

'My husband is the chief physician for the German forces in Warsaw. It wasn't hard to locate you.'

'I don't have much time. Take me to her.'

On the way up the curving central staircase to the gallery, I told her, 'I'll want to bring some things back to the ghetto with me – food mostly.'

'What would you like?'

'Find me a dozen lemons – two dozen if you can. I'll also want cheese and meat, and good bread and coffee. And pipe tobacco – Achmed, if you can find it. And I'll take you up on your offer to pay me – two hundred złoty per session.'

'Of course, though it might be difficult to find so many lemons.'

'If you can't get them, I'll need oranges or fresh cabbage.'

Standing in front of her daughter's door, I faced Mrs Lanik again. To my surprise, I was embarrassed now about my shabby clothing and withered state – suddenly arm in arm with my desire to return to a normal life.

'I want you to order the Germans to take me home in silence,' I told her. 'I won't see your daughter unless they promise not to speak to me – or hurt me in any way.'

'Very well. I'll take care of it.'

'And tell them not to touch any of the food you give me. You're going to have to threaten them with reprisals.'

'Leave it to me,' she assured me. 'Can we go in now?'

When I gave my permission, she knocked. 'Irene . . . ?' she called softly, but there was no reply. 'Dr Cohen is here. We're coming in.'

She tried the door handle, but it was locked.

'Irene, this is Dr Cohen,' I began. 'I don't have much time. Let me in, please.'

The girl whispered through the door, 'Only you, Dr Cohen, not my mother.'

Mrs Lanik shook her head violently, as if her daughter was sentencing her for a crime she hadn't committed.

'Irene will be safe with me,' I told her. 'Sit in the foyer, and when I come out we'll talk about what I've learned. And bring me strong coffee, as well,' I added, since the efficient heating in the house was making me drowsy. 'When it's ready, have your servant knock on the door and leave it on the floor. I'll come out and get it.'

Mrs Lanik looked back as she crept down the stairs. She gripped the railing hard; I realized she was close to fainting.

I called to Irene through the door in German again, telling her that we were alone. After a few seconds, I heard the latch click. A blue eye peeked in the doorway.

CHAPTER 23

Irene was a willowy girl, and nearly six feet tall, though she had the hunched posture of someone who had been taunted for years about her height.

After opening the door, she marched to the back of the room, anxious to put some distance between us. She had her mother's short blonde hair and mesmerizing eyes. Her earrings were tiny silver bells.

She smiled at me fleetingly, standing between the head of her bed and a leather armchair positioned for a view out the window, then turned to the side abruptly, as though having just remembered to withhold her feelings. The oblique light from the afternoon sun made crescents of deep shadow under her eyes. The way she held her hands knitted tightly together seemed a bad sign.

She wore modest, impeccably pressed clothes – a silvery-green woollen skirt and an embroidered Ukrainian blouse. I had the sensation that they weren't what she liked – that she dressed this way to please someone else.

Her shelves were neatly packed with books and stuffed animals. A Picasso print of a sad-faced harlequin was framed behind her bed.

'Thank you for coming,' she told me in an unsure voice. She spoke in German.

'Thank you for letting me in,' I replied.

She grabbed one of the blue silk cushions from her bed, took off her furry slippers and sat down in the armchair, folding her bare feet girlishly underneath her bottom. Placing the cushion over her lap, she leaned towards the window and gazed at the lawn below as if concerned about what might be taking place down there in her absence. Whether on purpose or not, she gave me a good look at the bald spot at the crown of her head where she must have been pulling out her hair.

A patient's initial gestures often indicate how forthcoming they intend to be, and Irene had chosen to show me a symptom of her misery before even saying a word.

I sat down on her bed. Though the girl didn't speak or look at me, I was at ease; this silence between myself and a patient had been a kind of home to me for many years.

'Now, Irene, I'm just going to ask you some questions. Is that all right?'

'Yes, I suppose so.'

I didn't have much time, so I tried a shortcut that had worked for me in the past. 'If you could go anywhere in the world, where would it be?' I asked. I was hoping she'd accidentally reveal what was pursuing her by telling me her fantasy of escape.

'You mean, where in Warsaw?' she questioned.

She was afraid to dream too ambitiously, which likely meant she felt powerless to flee her predicament. 'No, anywhere,' I replied. 'London, Rome, Cairo . . .' Finding my professional voice again gave me confidence.

'I'd go to France,' she replied. 'To Nantes.'

I heard Swiss vowels in her reply, though she was speaking High German.

'Why Nantes?' I asked.

'Because my grandparents live there.'

'Would you feel safer with them?' I questioned.

Grimacing, she moved her cushion over her chest and clutched it tightly.

'Are you all right?' I asked.

Straining for breath, looking at me directly for the first time, she replied, 'There's a constriction in my chest that comes and goes. And when it's bad, it's like a big rough hand is pressing down on me. Sometimes I think I'm going to suffocate.' She fixed me with a desolate look. 'Dr Cohen, it's this house . . . it terrifies me.'

When tears came, she faced the window again, afraid to see my reaction.

'What about this house scares you?' I asked.

For a long time, she made no reply. I took out my pipe and examined the bowl to keep from looking at her and making her more uncomfortable.

'I often think someone is hiding underneath my bed at night,' she finally told me. 'Or in my wardrobe, or in the dining room – a person who wants to kill me. I check everywhere I can think of, but it's too big a house to be sure I haven't missed something – or that the killer isn't one step ahead of me.'

A knock on the door startled me. 'Your coffee, Dr Cohen,' a woman called out.

I asked Irene to excuse me a moment. Opening the door a crack, I saw an elderly maidservant walking away. On the floor was a wooden tray on which she'd placed an elegant porcelain coffee pot – white, with a black handle – and a matching cup. I carried the tray inside and put it on the girl's bed.

'Irene, this is a mansion, and it must have lots of hidden corners and passageways,' I told her as I poured a first cup. 'Our deepest fears tend to hide where we have trouble finding them. But I'm going to help you find them.'

She nodded her thanks, but guilt entered deeply into me; who could say if I'd ever come here again? I stole a look at my watch. It was 2.20. I wondered where Rowy and Ziv were at that moment. I decided to stay with Irene until three.

I took a first sip of coffee, but its dark flavour was so redolent of better times that I wasn't sure I ought to drink it.

'How long have you lived here?' I asked the girl.

'Four months.' She looked far into the distance out her window. 'Sometimes I imagine that the killer is outside the house and . . . and trying to get in any way he can,' she told me cautiously, and with the effort of recall, as though groping her way through memory. 'I start worrying that my parents might have left the front door open, which would allow him to get inside, so I check that it's locked before going to my room. And I end up coming downstairs several times in the night to make sure it's still locked.'

'Do you think your parents might leave the door open on purpose – or unlock it after you've locked it?'

Those were risky questions, since they touched on her relationship with her parents. Irene faced me and held my gaze, wanting to see the kind of man who would ask them – above all, whether I would give up on her if she spoke to me honestly and revealed something of which other people might disapprove. So I looked at her hard and long. It was an important moment – the hub around which our subsequent conversation would turn. She didn't flinch or even blink. I began to believe she was a courageous girl.

'Please tell me what you're thinking,' I prodded.

'I never before imagined that the door . . .' She raised a hand over her mouth, assaulted by fear. At length, she said, 'I love my parents. I want you to know that.'

And yet one or both of them is threatening to hurt you, I thought.

'I believe you,' I told her, 'but it's hard to trust even the people we love most when we find ourselves in a new environment. I learned that when I moved into the ghetto.'

She started; she hadn't expected me to talk about my own life. Drawing her knees into her chest and hugging them, she asked, 'Is it . . . is it very bad in there?'

'Yes, it's bad, but there's nothing any of us can do about it at the moment.'

'No, maybe there is,' she declared.

'What do you mean?'

'We can each play our part in preventing worse things from happening.'

I was impressed by her solidarity, but at the time she seemed hopelessly naive.

'Maybe so,' I told her. 'But we need to talk about you for the moment. Now, Irene, can you tell me what the murderer looks like in your imagination?'

'I'm not sure. I don't recognize him, if that's what you mean. But I sometimes see he has an awful face, and he looks at me in a dreadful way.'

A sense of déjà vu made me halt as I reached for my coffee cup. Where had I heard her last words?

'What makes his look so dreadful?' I asked.

'Something in his eyes – something dark and purposeful,' she replied, moaning, and she began twisting the hair on top of her head.

'And do you have any idea why he would want to kill you?'

'No, I don't know!' she replied in desperation. Taking a deep breath, she tugged out the tangle of hairs she'd twisted around her index finger.

I grimaced, but she said reassuringly, as if I were the one in pain, 'It's all right, Dr Cohen, it doesn't really hurt. And even if it does, it's a good kind of pain.'

'Why is it good?'

'I'm not sure. I only know it is.'

'Because you're the one causing it?' I asked, hoping I'd come near the truth; I needed to build up her confidence in me if I was going to help her.

She thought about my theory. 'Maybe you're right,' she told me, but she didn't sound convinced.

To my subsequent questions, Irene went on to tell me that the killer wasn't interested in robbing her. She pictured him stabbing her in the heart. She would bleed to death.

'When did you start believing your life was in danger?' I asked.

'Maybe a couple of weeks ago.'

'Did something unusual happen then?'

'What do you mean?'

'Did you get ill? Or did you have a quarrel with your mother or father? Maybe it was something that you—'

'My father is dead to me!' she interrupted roughly, probably hoping to shock me; perhaps my questions about the timing of her troubles were too threatening, and she wanted to push me away.

'Dead to you, how?'

'He's never wanted anything to do with me.'

'I don't understand. I thought you lived here with your—'

'Rolf Lanik is my stepfather,' she cut in. 'My father is a radiologist named Werner Koch. He lives in Switzerland, though he visited us here in Poland – once, two months ago.'

'How long has your mother been married to your stepfather?'

'Let's see, I was six, so that makes . . . eleven years. He's a good man. In fact, Rolf is the best thing that ever happened to me.'

She spoke as though I'd obliged her to defend his honour, which led me to believe he might have been her tormentor, though he might not have been aware of the damage he was doing.

'Why is he so good for you?' I asked.

'Because he gets us whatever we need. And I'm in an excellent school for foreigners. He's kind and generous, and he loves us – me and my mother.'

'And yet he's made you move to a house that you hate.'

'That's not his fault, Dr Cohen! Or do you think it is?' she snapped.

I was glad that she felt secure enough to reveal her anger. 'I'm not in a position to say,' I told her. 'But tell me, what does your mother think of your new surroundings?'

'Mama? She loves it here,' the girl replied resentfully. 'She certainly doesn't say otherwise.'

Irene seemed to have concluded that her mother valued their new house – and her husband – more than her daughter.

Sensing that her father's sudden appearance two months earlier might have touched off Irene's current problems, I returned to her mother's first marriage. The girl told me that it had ended in divorce after six years. She had been four when her parents separated. Her mother had lost everything, and had started a new life in Zurich, where they had relatives. She'd found work as a barmaid in a small hotel.

'Ah, so that explains your Swiss accent,' I observed.

Sticking out her tongue and groaning, Irene replied, 'So you noticed.'

'Yes, but you don't sound too pleased.'

'Should I be?'

'I don't know. All I can say is that, in my opinion, your accent is charming.'

She smiled, hesitantly at first, then broadly, and for the first time she looked relaxed. My compliment changed her; in a voice that raced ahead into her emotions, she went on to tell me that she and her mother had lived for two years in a one-room garret that was infested with bedbugs and had a leaky roof. 'Mama even lost her reputation,' she told me, outraged.

'What do you mean?' I asked.

She crossed her arms over her chest. 'Thanks to my dear father,' she said, sneering.

To my subsequent questions, Irene told me that he had spread malicious rumours about an affair that her mother had carried on with a Jewish surgeon, which, in their circle, had sentenced her to ridicule. She told me several stories of how her mother had been made to suffer – and how she'd fought back through guile. It was clear that Irene admired her mother and had formed a close identification with her.

The girl had only seen her father three times since the divorce, the last time in early January when he'd shown up one Friday evening at their home without warning.

220

'I have reason to believe,' she told me, using a wily tone that implied she'd done some eavesdropping, 'that he came here to get money out of my mother.'

Could he have been blackmailing Mrs Lanik with information about her previous life?

'Did your mother actually tell you that?'

'No, she refused to talk about him with me, but he was looking wasted – as if he was drinking again.'

'Did you have a chance to talk with him?' I asked.

'No, he said hello to me, then spoke to my mother for a few minutes, and then he staggered off.'

Irene's replies turned evasive when I asked about her feelings as a child with regard to her father. She clearly wasn't ready to revisit that part of her past, so I returned to her stepfather. She told me that Rolf Lanik had grown up in Zurich and moved to Hamburg after medical school. He'd fallen in love with her mother eleven years earlier, while vacationing with his parents. Irene had lived in Hamburg with her mother and him before moving to Warsaw. Now, he had an office in the centre of the city and only came home late at night. In a disappointed voice, she added, 'Once we moved here, he started living a separate life. We hardly ever see him. He works all day, and even in the evenings, too.'

'Tell me a little about him.'

'What would you like to know?'

'You could start with your first impressions of him.'

'I didn't like him.'

'Why not?'

'He tried too hard. I mean, it was as if he was always kneeling to my level and reaching out to me. But I didn't want him like that – as a friend. It was so awkward!' She spoke desperately, as if needing me to confirm that her feelings were justified. 'I wanted something else. Does that make sense?'

'Yes, it does.'

'Rolf never had any children of his own,' Irene volunteered. 'I guess he didn't quite know how to approach me.'

'But he learned?'

'Yes.'

'And when did you begin to like him?'

'I think it was when he started reading to me. I'd be in my pyjamas, lying in bed, and he'd take a book down from my shelves and sit with me.' She smiled gratefully. 'I loved the sound of his voice, and how he'd look at me expectantly, waiting to see my reaction to the story. I could tell he was really listening.' Nodding at the rightness of her words, she added, 'Dr Cohen, when Rolf is with you, you know you have all his attention. Maybe that's why his patients like him so much.'

'How do you know they like him so much?'

'Because I go to his office sometimes, and I talk with them.'

'So he's your doctor?'

'He wasn't when I was little. Though he is now.' She looked down, as if she'd said something shameful.

As Irene told me more about her present relationship with her stepfather, I began to suspect that her continued talk of his *separate life* meant that she might have spotted him with another woman – maybe before or after a medical appointment with him. If so, then she was probably petrified that he would abandon her and her mother – would 'kill' their family, in other words. She was likely convinced that history would repeat itself – her stepfather would spread foul rumours about his wife, and she and her mother would become outcasts again. Her father's sudden appearance may have reinforced that fear. She may have also had good reason to worry that she wouldn't be believed – and might well be punished – if she informed her mother of her stepfather's infidelity, since Mrs Lanik undoubtedly shared her daughter's fears of renewed poverty and ostracism. To Irene, the only way out of her predicament had seemed suicide.

Of course, my theory could have been wrong, and I was about to probe further into her stepfather's daily routine when I realized why I'd experienced déjà vu: Irene had repeated what a young patient of Freud's named Katharina had told him about the face of a man she envisaged whenever she suffered an anxiety attack: *He has an awful face, and he looks at me in a dreadful way.*

If those weren't the exact words quoted by Freud, they were very close. They were contained in Freud and Brauer's *Studies on Hysteria*, a work I'd read several times.

Katharina had told Freud she'd overseen her uncle making love to the family cook. Could that be why I'd concluded so quickly that Irene might have seen her stepfather with a woman?

The important question now seemed: was Irene aware that she had quoted a patient of Freud's?

'Tell me, Irene,' I asked, 'have you ever read any works on psychiatry or psychoanalysis?'

'Yes, at my grandfather's house in Zurich. I think he owns nearly everything Freud ever wrote.'

Since she showed no sign of having been caught out, I concluded that she'd repeated Katharina's words unconsciously – had appropriated them because her predicament was so similar. Unsure as to how to proceed, I returned to what might have happened a couple of weeks earlier to start Irene believing that she was under threat.

'Maybe it was a dream I started having,' she told me. She shifted forward in her seat, as though to commit herself to making deeper revelations, though she put her cushion over her lap again.

'Tell me the dream,' I requested.

Gazing into herself, she said, 'I'm with some children on a meadow. In the green grass are lots of yellow flowers. Each of us is holding a bunch of flowers we've already picked, and we start to pick more.'

'How many children are with you?' I asked.

'At least two, though I think there may be more. It's hard to tell.' She looked at me for approval to continue, and I nodded.

'A short man wearing a hat comes up from the town below, and he takes the flowers from us – from me and the children. And then he walks up the hill to a cottage where a friend of his is waiting – a much bigger man who seems almost like a giant.'

'Go on.'

'The man in the hat hands the flowers to his friend, and he receives a loaf of bread in return. And then the man in the hat walks to me and tears off a piece of his bread for me, and I . . . I look around for the children who've been on the meadow with me, so that I can share my bread with them, but they're gone. And then the dream shifts.'

'Shifts how?'

'I'm standing with the man in the hat on the sidewalk of Krakowskie Przedmieście.' Irene closed her eyes and reached her hand out as if seeking to touch what she was seeing. 'In front of me is a curving staircase, and it leads up to the Holy Cross Church. The street is empty. I don't know where the other kids are, and I'm terrified. And . . . and that's when I wake up.'

Her eyes opened and she looked at me purposefully; she'd undoubtedly read that it was my job to offer an interpretation.

I looked away, however; I was sure now that Irene had read Freud very closely. The children picking yellow flowers in a meadow had appeared in a dream of his that he'd discussed in a well-known, semi-autobiographical article called 'Screen Memories'. She was placing her own experiences into the framework of her readings on psychiatry. Whether on purpose or unconsciously, I had no way of knowing, but in either case I suspected that she intended for me to return to Freud's discussion of Katharina and extrapolate that they faced the same problem. In a sense, she was telling me in coded language, where to look for the origins of her troubles, without directly revealing any of her family's secrets – and in a way she could be sure I would come to understand.

'Can you see the face of the man in the hat?' I asked her.

'No.'

'Would you close your eyes and try to picture him?'

'Of course.' She did as I asked, but after a few seconds she shook her head. 'I'm sorry, Dr Cohen, but I can't tell you who he might be. I want to, but I can't.'

She used the words *tell you* instead of *see* or *recognize*. A slip? Very possibly Irene knew who he was but would risk too much by revealing his identity.

I was convinced by now that she'd used Freud's dream because she'd read his interpretation that a girl handing flowers to a man was symbolic of her losing her virginity. I suspected she'd had sex for the first time recently, and possibly with her stepfather. In that case, her guilt – at betraying her mother and threatening to destroy her family's happiness – had brought on her self-destructive behaviour. She wanted to murder herself, but she'd transposed those violent feelings to an unidentified killer.

'Do you know the children with you in the meadow?' I asked, thinking they might have been other girls her stepfather had seduced.

'No,' she replied.

'How old are they?'

'They're young – maybe ten or twelve. Like me.'

'So you're only ten or twelve in the dream?'

She looked inside herself again. 'I think so,' she said hesitantly, 'but I'm not sure.'

Was it possible that her stepfather had violated her years earlier and had started again more recently?

'Are the children boys or girls?' I asked.

'Both, I think. I'm not sure. They're wearing yellow, so I don't know.'

'They're wearing yellow?' I asked, puzzled.

'No, I meant that the flowers are yellow. Now I'm confused. You're confusing me!'

'I'm sorry. Can you identify the bigger man at the cottage who receives the flowers?'

'No.'

'Are he and the man in the hat Poles or Germans? Or maybe from Switzerland?'

She frowned nastily at me. Was I coming too close to unmasking her tormentor?

'I think they're Germans,' she told me, 'but I don't know for sure. In any case, I don't see why it matters.'

'Maybe it doesn't. How many times have you had the dream?'

'A few times – I'm not sure.'

'And how do you feel now – remembering it, I mean?'

She shrugged.

'Well, are you glad you told it to me?'

'Am I supposed to be?' she snapped.

Her touchy replies made me realize that it would be best to stop now – I'd scared her with my probing and she'd tell me little more today. I downed my coffee and looked at my watch. It was eleven minutes past three.

'Irene, for now, I only have one last question.'

'But you'll come back and see me?' she asked in a tiptoeing voice. 'You're not angry with me?'

'No, I'm not at all angry. And I'll try to come back. I'll speak to your mother about that as soon as I leave your room. But listen, Irene, I need you to promise me something or we won't be able to talk again.'

'What?' she asked anxiously.

'You must not try to take your own life while we're working together. We must trust each other, and I won't be able to work with you if I'm worried you might kill yourself if I say the wrong thing.'

'Do you sometimes say the wrong thing?'

'Of course,' I told her, smiling at her naivety. 'Everyone does. Though I shall try my best not to.'

I'd never admitted my failings to a patient so readily before. It seemed a change for the better, and I realized – astonished – that if I survived the ghetto, I'd be a gentler and more effective psychiatrist. Was that reason enough to go on living?

'So do we have an agreement?' I asked her.

'Yes, I promise,' she replied, and she showed me a relieved smile that convinced me she'd been waiting for me to take away her worst option from the beginning.

I stood up. 'I'll need your pills – the ones you took to try to end your life.'

'Mama has them.'

'Good.'

'So what's your last question, Dr Cohen?'

'Imagine that you could tell the man in the hat something, what would it be?'

She gazed down. 'I think I'd ask him to give me back my flowers.'

As I was leaving her room, Irene called to me. 'Dr Cohen, I'm very sorry about what happened to your nephew. Forgive me for not saying so earlier.'

Stunned, I stammered a reply, 'But how . . . how did you . . . I mean, who told you what happened to my nephew?'

'Your former patient Jaśmin Makinska,' Irene replied.

'You know Jaśmin?' I asked.

'I don't know her personally,' Irene replied, 'but she has been holding clandestine meetings since December – telling anyone who will listen to her about the wretched conditions in the ghetto. She's been heroic, I think. A week ago, I went to a meeting for foreigners living here – Mama took me. Jaśmin held up a note she'd received from your niece after her son's death, and she told the audience what had happened to him – and how you were suffering. After her talk, I started thinking that you might agree to help me.'

A patient's last words are often what they've been waiting to tell you since the beginning – which meant that Irene needed to make it clear to me that she was aware that Adam had been murdered. And that she'd wanted to talk to me since learning that.

'There's one other thing I should have told you,' she added. 'In my dream, the big man who ends up with the yellow flowers we've picked . . . I know his name. I know it because the man in the hat calls out to him when he's walking towards the cottage. It's Jesion.'

'And do you think his name is important?' I asked.

'I have a feeling it is. Sometimes it seems the key to everything.'

Irene remained in her room, though she refrained from locking the door, which seemed a hopeful sign. I paused on the gallery to measure her closing words to me against my own interest in names, and to consider, too, what she'd told me about Jaśmin, but Mrs Lanik, rushing up the staircase, drew my attention. She carried her horn-rim glasses in one hand and a book in the other. In the yearning of her eyes, I saw she feared the worst.

'Is Irene all right?' she asked.

'Yes,' I told her, 'we had a good talk. And, most importantly, she has promised not to hurt herself while we work together.'

'Thank you for that, Dr Cohen. What else did she tell you?'

'She fears she is in danger.'

'What kind of danger?'

'As I'm sure you know, she has adjusted poorly to her new surroundings. She feels threatened. If I were you, I'd do everything in your power to make her feel loved and cared for. And protected. Even if it means going away with her for a time. Maybe even to France – to Nantes.'

Mrs Lanik looked puzzled. 'Why Nantes?'

'Because of your parents.'

'My parents? But they live in Bordeaux,' she corrected me.

'I must have misunderstood,' I replied, wondering why Irene would have lied to me.

I was also astonished by her capabilities as an actress. How much else had she told me that wasn't true?

'Yes, I've been thinking of taking a trip with Irene,' Mrs Lanik told me. 'Dr Cohen, thank you.' She grasped both my hands. 'I'm forever in your debt.'

'I only hope I've helped a little with whatever is troubling her,' I replied, and as I said that I realized the real reason I'd stayed with Irene: she had needed to be heard, and my willingness to listen to her – to allow even the silence between us to speak to me – was part of a world of solidarity the Nazis wanted to destroy. By staying, I was fighting for all I'd once believed in. And I was asserting my right to live as the man I wanted to be.

'I'd like for you to see her again as soon as possible,' Mrs Lanik told me, 'but my husband is coming back tomorrow. I'll get word to you when I know he's going away again. Is that all right?'

'Yes, of course.'

She escorted me down the stairs. She had two wicker baskets of food waiting for me on the antique wooden table by the front door.

'I managed to get you fourteen lemons,' she told me, smiling happily.

Dispersed among red apples, the lemons were beautiful – a composition worthy of Cézanne.

'You'll never know how grateful I am for your help,' I told her.

'I only hope I've chosen well for you,' she replied, and she handed me an envelope. 'Here is your two hundred złoty.'

'Thank you. And one last thing – I'd like to keep your daughter's pills. She says you have them. If they are in the house, she might somehow find them.'

'Yes, you're right.'

While Mrs Lanik was gone, I put my pipe tobacco and two lemons in my coat pocket for safekeeping and examined the eggs, butter, cheese and ham. She'd even put in tins of Russian caviar and French foie gras. She handed me the pills as soon as she returned. I was in luck – Veronal, my tranquillizer of choice.

As I stashed them in my pocket, my relief made me close my eyes with gratitude. *The Nazis have lost control of me*, I thought – being able to summon death at any time was a guarantee I'd needed since I first saw Adam in the Pinkiert's cart. Ten pills would be all I'd need, and the end would be painless.

'What about my German escorts?' I asked Mrs Lanik. I didn't see them anywhere.

'Already in their car, waiting for you.' Smiling broadly, as people do who've been crying and are thankful for the help they've received, she said in French, 'And I've told them in no uncertain terms to keep their mouths shut and their hands off your food!'

The Germans were in the front seat. I got in the back, next to my picnic baskets.

As we took off, the Nazi comedian turned and pointed his gun at my face, vibrating with rage. 'I might just make a bloody hole where that Jewish nose is!' he threatened. 'All I'd have to tell my superiors is that you tried to escape.'

His words sounded practised, which made them less believable. Still, I didn't dare reply. I looked out my window instead, fingering the coins in my pocket, and after a few seconds he turned away and we started off. He said nothing more to me on the drive back home.

In my mind, I went over what Irene had told me, and all her revelations – whether fictional or real – now seemed to point to the man in the hat who took flowers from Irene and two other children.

Though there may be more than two, the girl had told me.

The distant white blanket of winter sky, the crack of ice beneath the wheels of our car, the ticklish wool of my scarf . . . All that I saw and felt vanished suddenly, because it was at that moment I realized that Irene had created her dream to fit what she knew about the murders inside the ghetto!

She'd intended for me to find out she'd been lying about Nantes or some other small detail, because she was eager for me to understand that her testimony had been carefully scripted.

Two children had vanished from the meadow; she was talking about Adam and Anna!

Except that Irene could not have learned about Anna's murder from Jaśmin.

Was it possible that she had witnessed Jewish children being murdered? Maybe she had overheard the killer talking about them. Then, when Jaśmin spoke about me, Irene understood that my nephew was one of the kids who'd vanished.

She'd wanted to identify the killer to me, but couldn't, which probably meant she was afraid of being murdered herself. By whom? Her stepfather? Maybe the man named Jesion.

Or perhaps even by her real father.

Bina, her mother and her uncle Freddi were waiting for me at home. 'I've brought food,' I told the girl, handing her the basket I'd carried upstairs.

I sat down on my bed, exhausted. Bina looked between the fresh fruit and me, beaming as if I were a messenger from God. She kissed me on each cheek, and I hugged her back, but I was still deep inside all that Irene had told me. Bina's uncle – a short, dark, hairy man with a boxer's build, smelling pleasantly of talc – burst into tears when he told me how grateful he was to be able to move in. Bina's mother went down on her knees to recite a speech she'd memorized. I felt trapped by their fervent hopes for a better life, so when the girl went down to the courtyard to get my second basket of food from Professor Engal, I retreated into what had been Stefa's room and locked the door. I'd left my list of the dead on my pillow. I stared at the names for a long time, hoping they would lift off the page and show me more of what I needed to know, but they didn't.

CHAPTER 24

After putting some supplies for Izzy in one of the baskets that Bina had emptied, I went down to the street with the girl and she hailed me a rickshaw. She kissed me goodbye tenderly; she obviously liked having a benefactor, even if he played the Big Bad Wolf on his own small stage at times.

Izzy danced around when he saw what I'd brought him; unfortunately for me, he made the same rubbery-handed movements that he'd taught Adam as an Indian raindance.

'Where'd you get all this?' he asked, picking his excited fingers through the cheeses.

'A new friend,' I told him.

I handed him the two lemons I had in my coat pocket. He cupped them if they were the goose's golden eggs.

While he prepared lemonade, I told him about my session with Irene, ending with how I'd come to believe that she had learned that at least two ghetto children had been murdered. 'Izzy, I don't know how, but she knows who's doing this!' I exclaimed.

He questioned me at length about my conclusions – a good thing, as it turned out, because my repeating so many details helped us come up with new possibilities and dangers.

'Irene might even have faked her suicide attempt to convince her mother to send for you,' he speculated.

'I suppose it's possible,' I replied. 'She told me that we can each play our part in preventing worse things from happening in the ghetto, and sending for me was her way of helping – she wants me to use her clues to catch the killer.'

Izzy and I were on our second cup of lemonade by then.

'We've got to go to Krakowskie Przedmieście and look for someone with the name Jesion,' I told him. 'Irene implied that he holds the key to solving these murders.'

'But we don't have an address and—?'

'Tomorrow,' I interrupted, 'you and I are crossing to the Other Side – early.'

He was seated as his worktable. I was standing, too jittery to sit.

'It could be a trap,' he warned.

'No, I don't think so. Irene lied to me, but only because she's terrified – and so I'd come to realize that she'd scripted some of what she told me. Whatever she knows has put her in physical danger. She couldn't tell me any more than she did without risking not just her own life but also her mother's – without *killing* her family. So she's leaving it up to me to identify the murderer – and to do whatever has to be done.'

'If that's true, then you'll never hear from her again,' Izzy said authoritatively.

'Why?'

'Because she's already told you all she could.'

'Except that Mrs Lanik said she would wait for her husband's next absence and then send a car for me.'

'What if she lied, too? She might have helped her daughter plan everything. Maybe her parents aren't in Bordeaux, after all. She might have told you that to make sure you knew that some of what Irene told you had been made up. And if her husband or ex-husband are involved in the murders in some way, it's more likely that she's the one who overheard what they'd done – or maybe even saw the bodies.'

While I thought that over, he cut us squares of foie gras. He put mine on a slice of bread and ate his plain because of his rickety teeth.

'There's more I need to tell you before we leave the ghetto,' I told him. 'I think that Adam, Anna and Georg were killed for the defects on their skin.'

'Defects? What are you talking about?' he asked.

'Remember the birthmarks on the back of Adam's right ankle?'

'Of course, but what good could they be to anyone?'

I explained why I believed Rowy and a partner outside the ghetto might be responsible for identifying the children to be murdered – possibly with the help of Ziv.

'Sorry, Erik, I don't buy it,' he told me, licking some foie gras off his fingers. 'Rowy wouldn't tell you how frightened he was of being forced again into a labour gang if that was his motivation for turning three kids over to the Nazis.'

'He probably didn't believe I would be any good at detective work.'

'Pfffttt!' he scoffed, in that Gallic way he'd picked up aboard the *Bourdonnais*. 'As for Ziv, Ewa told me he runs away every time a mouse appears in the bakery.'

'But he can think ten moves ahead at chess! He could have planned everything.' Then a perverse possibility made me start. 'He was jealous of Adam. My God, he wanted to remove the boy from Stefa's life!'

'Even if that were true, which I don't believe, why would he kill Anna and Georg?'

'I don't know, but he *did* volunteer to help Rowy find more kids for the chorus. What if it was so he could identify children for murder?'

'I admit that sounds suspicious, but you saw how shattered he was after Stefa's death. Is that the kind of young man who would plan to murder children?'

'Look, Izzy,' I told him, irritated that he was right, 'all I know is that after we try to find Jesion, we need to take a good look through Rowy's apartment and Ziv's room at the bakery. We have to turn up something incriminating. And we've got to work fast. We've no guarantee that whoever is responsible won't have another Jewish boy or girl killed.'

Izzy gazed down into that terrible possibility, then started. 'Erik,' he told me, 'what would you say if I could bring the murderer's Jewish accomplice straight to us?'

Izzy and I moved my desk and my old Mała typewriter into Stefa's room. We settled on the following wording for our note:

Someone has learned of our activities, and we're in danger. I need to talk with you. We need to meet outside the ghetto as soon as possible. Introduce yourself to the guards at the corner of Leszno and Żelazna this evening, at exactly 7.30. Do not try to contact me. The guards at the gate will know to expect you. A car will be waiting outside to take you to my home.

We typed three copies and left them unsigned. We put them in envelopes but wrote no name on the outside.

Whoever had been responsible for Adam's death would be terrified of being exposed as a murderer and would take the note seriously even if he wasn't absolutely sure it was genuine. As for whoever was innocent, he'd likely believe that the note had been sent to him in error – since his name was not written either in the letter or on the envelope – and stay far away from the guards at Leszno and Żelazna.

I paid a boy selling armbands embroidered with the Star of David to take the letter to Ziv in the bakery, and Izzy paid an old woman selling tin cups on the sidewalk outside Mikael Tengmann's office to hand an envelope to him.

I wanted to take a quick look at Rowy's apartment before leaving our note. It was on the ground floor of a stately neoclassical building, with impressive columns flanking the doorway, but much of the roof had imploded and was patched with wooden planks and burlap.

Luckily, I found the young man at home, practising the slow movement of what sounded like a Mozart concerto. His warm, full tone seemed to give form to my sense of abandonment. I could not bear it for more than a moment and knocked.

Rowy welcomed me warmly and put his violin back in its velvet-lined case. I told him I'd had some good fortune and handed him the caviar Mrs Lanik had given me – the price of putting him at ease. He insisted on opening the can right away, and on toasting some *challah* to eat with it. I sat at his worktable, which was piled high with musical scores. Next to me a rusted bicycle was leaning against a wooden dresser – Izzy and I would start by searching there.

A pink sheet hung from the ceiling halfway back, hiding the only window from view.

'A young couple with a toddler moved in a few weeks ago,' Rowy explained.

It was cold in the apartment, so he put more sawdust in his oven. Over our snack, we got to talking about the cramped conditions in the ghetto, and Rowy warned me that the Jewish Council had begun forcing residents with spare rooms to accept Jews who had arrived recently from the provinces. Waving off his concern, I said, 'Izzy already told me. A girl I know named Bina just moved in with her mother and uncle.'

'Three extra people – it must be hell,' he said, and from the way he looked at me, I knew he meant more than sharing my home with strangers.

I couldn't discuss my inner life with a man I didn't trust, so I made believe I'd failed to understand his implication. 'I'll be fine living in Stefa's room,' I assured him.

On saying goodbye, he embraced me. I went stiff, but then kissed his cheek to throw off his suspicions. After leaving, I waited a half-hour, then slid our note under his door and fled.

*

By then, it was just after five in the afternoon. Izzy had suggested the Leszno Street gate because there was a small café run by an acquaintance of ours nearby, and from there we could see everyone entering or exiting the ghetto. We met there at 5.30. We took a table by the window. We kept the brims of our hats low on our foreheads to be less recognizable.

At seven, we went outside to make sure we didn't miss any passers-by. I turned up my collar and stood with my back to the street to keep my face hidden, blocking Izzy from view at the same time. Whenever anyone approached, he would glance around my shoulder to see who it was.

We stood that way until fifteen minutes to eight. The coming curfew had emptied the street by then. A Jewish policeman told us we'd better make our way home.

We dragged ourselves off; we'd failed to trap Rowy, Ziv or Mikael.

Could the murderer's accomplice inside the ghetto be someone we'd never even considered?

Izzy and I agreed to meet the next morning at his workshop to settle on another plan. In my brief conversation with Rowy, he'd mentioned that he'd given a copy of his apartment key to Ewa, and I intended to make up a reason for her to lend it to me.

At home, Bina handed me my dinner: a silvery perch lying on a bed of leeks sautéed in *schmaltz*. I hadn't seen so beautiful a meal since the Before Time and told her so. The girl took off her apron and sat with me at the kitchen table, watching me eat with the pleased smile of a chef who's appreciated. After a time, she moved her hands to her lap, wishing to speak her heart but afraid that I'd yell at her. Caressing her cheek, I said, 'Listen, Bina, you're a wonderful girl, but don't grow attached to me.'

'But why, Dr Cohen?'

'Because one way or another I'm getting out of here as soon as I can, and I can't take you with me.'

Guilt for so many bad choices I'd made throughout my life chased me to Stefa's window that night to look up at the few stars that succeeded in penetrating the hazy gloom over the city. I puffed away at my pipe until long after midnight, grateful for the darkness and the quiet – and the comfort of good tobacco.

A first gunshot woke me from my half-sleep. I thought the bang had exploded out of a dream. Then a second shot thudded against the wall. Bina and her mother began screaming. I jumped up from my chair and pulled open my door. Uncle Freddi was slumped on the ground, a dark rose blossoming on his chest.

CHAPTER 25

I pressed both my hands over Freddi's wound, hard, but the blood sluiced out and ran down his bare chest on to the floor. Bina's mother was staring at her brother and shrieking his name.

'Turn on the light!' I shouted at her, but she didn't move.

Bina was next to me, on her knees, her hands clamped over her mouth. When I pleaded with her for more light, she jumped up and pulled the cord of the lamp by the bed.

Freddi's wound was deep. The killer must have hit an artery, because his blood was spilling out like wine from a spigot. The warmth of his life pulsing erratically below my hands made me shudder. His eyes were open, but they weren't watching anything in our world.

'Hold on, we'll get help,' I told him, but I knew it was too late.

I looked at Bina. Her eyes – darkly lit with terror – had just grasped the imminence of her uncle's death.

'Did you get a look at whoever shot him?' I asked the girl, but as I spoke she turned towards the doorway; neighbours had just appeared.

When I felt a slackening in Freddi's chest, I moved my hands to his wrist and felt for a pulse, but it was already gone.

While Professor Engal examined Freddi's body, Ida Tarnowski tried to calm Bina's mother, but she kept pushing the kindly old woman away. I fled the mayhem for the bathroom and scrubbed my hands over and over, but I couldn't get the blood out from under my fingernails, since the ghetto soap melted to a useless mush when mixed with water. My legs were shaking, so I leaned back against the wall, staring at the gnarled backs of my hands, wondering if I would ever stop feeling Freddi's life inside their grip. Then I summoned Bina into the bathroom and cleaned her face, which was splattered with blood. She went limp as soon as I touched her, like a small child, so I sat her on the rim of the bathtub.

'Did you see who did this?' I asked her.

She looked up at me as if unable to fit what had happened into her mind.

'Take your time,' I told her.

'It was a man,' she replied. 'But it was too dark to see his face.'

She was shivering, so I fetched my coat and draped it over her shoulders.

'How old was he – this man?' I asked.

'I couldn't tell.'

'What do you remember about him?'

'He was small. Maybe only a little taller than me.'

Bina was about five foot two, by my estimation. 'And did you see him shoot Uncle Freddi?' I asked.

'Only the second shot. The first . . . it woke me up. Maybe the man shot the lock. I'm not sure.' Her eyes focused inside. 'Then I saw him, and I knew I was awake but I didn't understand – I thought maybe you'd come into the room.' She showed me an inquisitive look, as if waiting for me to confirm that I hadn't been there.

'I was in my niece's room, asleep,' I told her gently.

'Yes, I know that now. Uncle Freddi . . . I saw him standing next to the chair where he'd been sleeping. He spoke to the man. I think he said, 'What do you want?' Maybe he also thought the intruder was you. Then I heard a second shot, and Uncle Freddi fell. And then the man ran out and you were holding my uncle, and Mama was screaming . . .'

I held Bina close to me while she sobbed. When she could talk again, I asked, 'Was Freddi involved in smuggling?'

'I don't see how he could have been. The Germans transferred him to the ghetto just two weeks ago. The only people he knew here were my mother and me.'

Professor Engal and another man carried Freddi's body to the courtyard. Bina's mother went with them to watch over her brother. The girl had wanted to accompany her, but her mother had said, 'There are some things I need to tell your uncle alone.'

I saw such disappointment in Bina's eyes that I steered her back to bed and covered her with a blanket. 'Lie there, and I'll make us some nettle tea,' I told her.

First, however, I went to the front door. The lock was intact, which meant that both shots I'd heard had been fired at Freddi. Yet I'd only seen one wound; the killer must have missed on his first attempt, which meant he probably wasn't a professional.

More importantly, he must have used a key to get in. Only Ewa and Izzy – and now Bina – had copies.

When we were seated together with our tea, Bina promised me that she had kept the key in her pocket since receiving it from Izzy and had not lent it to anyone. After I assured her that I believed her, she began to talk about her uncle in a frail, unsteady voice, as though pulling back details from out of the distant past. She told me that he had written a script for Conrad Veidt and had met with the actor at the Adlon Hotel in Berlin in the spring of 1939 to discuss changes.

She needed me to understand that her uncle had been on his way to becoming a famous screenwriter – and that he was irreplaceable.

We owe uniqueness to our dead at the very least, of course.

'Uncle Freddi had promised to write a part for me when I was older,' she told me.

'So you want to be an actress?' I asked.

'No,' she said, 'I wanted to be a dancer before we came here. But it made Uncle Freddi so happy to think of us together in Berlin that I didn't want to spoil his fun.'

I could see from the way Bina gazed off that she would write an entire future for her uncle over the next weeks and months. Another movie never to be made.

While I went to the window to see what was happening in the courtyard, Bina walked purposefully into to the kitchen and came back with a pot full of soapy water and a brush.

'Oh no you don't!' I told her. 'You have to rest!'

'No, I have to clean up,' she replied, and she got on her knees to begin scrubbing the bloodstains off the floor. Soon she was in tears again, so I lifted her to her feet, led her back to bed and instructed her to sleep. Now and then she would open her eyes to make sure I was still sitting with her. 'I'm right here,' I'd whisper.

When she drifted off, I began lightly caressing her hair. I learned the smoothness of her neck and the shadowed curves of her cheeks. I learned the way her chest would rise once, then once again before easing back down, as though she were overcoming her own resistance to life.

And once I'd learned these things, I walked away.

I took a rickshaw to Izzy's workshop just after eight in the morning. He came to the door in his winter coat, but with his pyjamas on underneath. Reading in my face that I'd had a bad night, he reached out for my arm. 'What's happened?' he asked, leading me inside.

When I explained about Freddi, he went pale. I sat him down at his worktable, where he'd been drinking coffee out of a bowl. 'And no one else was hurt?' he asked.

'No. Listen, did you ever give Stefa's apartment key to anyone?'

'Of course not,' he replied defensively. 'I just made the one copy for Bina.'

'Then Ewa must have given out our key. Or Stefa did.'

'How do you know that?'

I sat down next to him and took a quick sip of his coffee, but it was too weak to do me any good. 'The lock on the door wasn't shot. Freddi's killer let himself in.'

'Someone might have taken it from Ewa just long enough to have a copy made,' Izzy speculated. 'Ziv works with her and could have easily done that. So maybe you were right about him. Maybe he fled Łódź to get away from the police or something.'

'Except that Mikael could also have gotten it from Ewa. Though he let me see Adam's medical file, which I don't think he'd have done if he were involved in the murders.'

'Poor Freddi,' Izzy sighed. 'He must have made some bad enemies really quickly.'

'Freddi? This has nothing to do with him! The bullet in his chest was meant for me.'

'How can you be so sure?'

'Only you and I knew that Bina's family moved in yesterday. Though . . .' Remembering the talk I'd had with Rowy the previous afternoon, I cut my sentence short.

'What is it?' Izzy questioned.

'Listen to my thinking and tell me if I'm right. The murderer outside the ghetto and his Jewish accomplice must have thought I was still living alone. One of them came to put a bullet in me, or, more likely, sent someone else. Whoever it was panicked when he saw two women and a man in the room. It was dark, and he assumed the man was me. His first shot missed, which may mean he wasn't a trained killer. We'll probably find the bullet lodged in the wall somewhere. In any case, his trying to get me out of the way means that our note convinced Mikael, Rowy or Ziv that we were on to him.'

'So you think that whoever sent a killer knew that what we wrote was made up – and that it hadn't been sent by his accomplice outside the ghetto?'

'Yes, though I have no idea how. In any case, since he knew the note wasn't genuine, he also knew that I had to have sent it.'

'I don't follow you.'

'Because I'm the only one who's been investigating Adam's murder! It could only have been me. But listen, Izzy, this also means that Rowy can't be guilty.'

'Why?'

'Because while I was with him yesterday afternoon, he warned me that the Jewish Council would make me take on tenants, and I told him Bina and her family had already moved in – and that I was living in Stefa's room. If he sent a killer, he would have told him to walk through the main room into the bedroom – that I'd be sleeping there.'

'Unless the killer panicked and didn't follow Rowy's instructions. You said yourself he might not be a professional.'

'True, but after he took down Freddi, he'd have come for me in the bedroom.'

'Which makes Ziv our main suspect. We have to figure out how he could have known our note was a trap.'

Izzy and I tossed unlikely speculations between us, dissatisfied and irritable, until there was a knock at the door. He retrieved his gun from his tool chest. When he motioned for me to hide, I slipped behind the curtain that concealed his lavatory.

'Who is it?' Izzy called through the door.

I didn't catch the reply, but I heard the creak of the door opening.

'Put your hands over your head and take off your overcoat!' Izzy ordered our visitor.

'I'm afraid I can't take off anything with my hands in the air,' the man retorted in an amused tone.

I recognized his voice immediately and came out of hiding. Izzy had his gun pointed at Mikael, who rolled his eyes as if this were a badly written scene in a Yiddish farce.

'How about telling your zealous friend to put his weapon down before someone gets hurt?' he asked me.

'He might have a gun,' Izzy reminded me.

'Are you crazy?' said Mikael, shaking his head, and he lowered his arms with a sigh.

'Just take off your overcoat and toss it down,' I told him. 'I need to search your pockets.'

'Erik, I'm here to help you!' he declared.

'Just humour me.'

He let his shoulders slump as if we were exhausting him, but he had realized by now we were serious and did as I requested. Finding no knife or gun, I laid his overcoat on Izzy's worktable. Then I went to Mikael and confirmed that he had no weapon on him.

'I hope you feel ridiculous!' he told me in an offended voice as I was patting his trousers.

'Feeling ridiculous is a sign of life,' I replied.

'Talmud, Torah or Groucho Marx?' he asked – and it was his absurd humour that won him to me again.

'Sorry,' I told him, and I motioned for Izzy to put away his gun.

Izzy and I sat opposite Mikael, who looked at me with troubled eyes. 'Ewa sent word to me about what happened to your new tenant,' he began. 'She said a girl named Bina let her know that you'd come here. I need to show you something.' Grimacing, he added, 'I think maybe I should have showed it to you before.'

He took a folded sheet of paper out of his pocket. 'I want you to know I'm risking everything by letting you see this.' He handed it to me.

The note was typewritten: *If you should tell Erik Cohen anything that casts suspicion on me, you will never see your granddaughter alive again.*

There was no signature. But many of the letters were faded – as if they'd been made with a badly functioning typewriter.

'Who is this from?' I asked Mikael.

'I can't be sure,' he replied, 'but it must be from whoever is responsible for Adam's death. Maybe from Rowy. As you and I discussed, Adam and Anna had him in common.'

'When did you get it?'

'Three days ago. I'm only showing it to you because I'm worried that another child will be killed. Though, if I'm going to be completely honest, I'd never have gone to your home to show it to you.'

'But why?'

'I think Rowy is having me followed. I've spotted a man tracking me twice.'

'What did he look like?' Izzy asked, undoubtedly thinking – like me – that he might have been the same man who had killed Freddi.

'Young – maybe thirty. Small, wiry . . .'

'How small?'

'I don't know – maybe only a little over five feet.'

Izzy and I shared a knowing look.

'What else?' I asked.

'Nothing – it was after dark both times I noticed him. I didn't see his face. Anyway, this time I took a rickshaw here, and I made the driver take a circuitous route. I don't think anyone could have managed to follow me.'

'But why would Rowy be scared of what you could tell Erik?' Izzy asked.

'I don't know. He must think I know something about him that would prove he's guilty.' Mikael reached across the table for my hand and gave it a squeeze. 'Which is why you can never tell anyone about the note or that I came to see you.'

'No one will ever know,' I assured him.

'And you?' Mikael asked Izzy, who nodded his agreement.

I handed the note back to him.

'Now that I've shown it to you, I want to destroy it,' Mikael told us, moving Izzy's glass ashtray closer to him. 'It feels like a bomb in my pocket.' Crunching the paper into a ball, he set his lighter to it and dropped it into the ashtray.

I watched flames rising from the paper as if participating in a ritual linking the three of us into a conspiracy.

'There's a problem,' I told Mikael. 'The person responsible for identifying Adam and Anna to a German or Pole outside the ghetto may not be Rowy. It could be Ziv.'

'Ziv?' he scoffed. 'No, that's impossible. He's so . . . so inoffensive. And Ewa adores him. They're like brother and sister.'

'Ziv volunteered to help Rowy identify children for his chorus. And he's clever enough to have planned the murders. In fact, he once told me he can think a dozen moves ahead.'

'But what could he possibly gain from killing Jewish children?'

'I don't know.'

'Imagine the note you received is from Ziv, not Rowy,' Izzy suggested to Mikael. 'Is there something he wouldn't want you to tell us – or the police?'

He gazed off for a time, considering possibilities, then shook his head. 'I can't think of anything.'

Izzy and I questioned Mikael at length about Ziv, but nothing he told us seemed incriminating until he mentioned that when the young man had gone to him for a medical exam he had confessed that his mother was still alive and living in Łódź.

'So he's not an orphan?' I asked, stupefied.

'No, Ziv told me that he sends money to his mother every month. He made me swear not to tell anyone, because she disobeyed the Germans and never moved into the ghetto. She's in hiding in Christian Łódź, with a family she's paying, and when I talked to him about her, he said she was running out of money. The situation was getting desperate.'

'When was this?' Izzy asked.

'Some time in early January. I'd have to check my files to know for sure – to see when he came for his medical exam.'

'How does he get the money to her?' I questioned.

Mikael shrugged. 'Is that important?'

When I looked to Izzy, he told Mikael just what I was thinking. 'He'd need the help of a Pole or German outside the ghetto to make sure the money reached her!'

We instructed Mikael to return to his office and said we would be in touch with him later that day. He left the workshop by the back exit.

Ewa and Ziv were both working when we stepped inside in the bakery. We took Ewa out to the courtyard. She swore that she'd never lent Stefa's key to anyone, which meant that Ziv took it from her handbag and made a copy.

'Stay here,' I told her.

'But why?'

'I don't want to risk you getting hurt.'

We went back inside. Ziv was kneading dough on a counter, a paper bag on his head, white with flour from head to toe. I asked him to come into his bedroom with us.

'What is it you want, Dr Cohen?' he asked, backing up, fearful, undoubtedly sensing that he might have to dash past me to make his escape.

'Indulge me,' I told him, enjoying my power over him. 'I need to ask you something.'

Tears flooded his eyes. 'What . . . what have I done?' he stammered.

'That's what we're going to find out,' I answered.

By now, all the bakery workers except Ewa had gathered around us. Ziv still didn't move, but he glanced away for a moment, which was enough time for a skilled chess player like him to plan a strategy.

'Get into your room!' I told him harshly, determined to interrupt his thinking.

Taking the paper bag from his head, the boy turned and shuffled ahead of Izzy and me. Sacks of flour lined the back wall of the store-room he lived in, and the wooden shelves were stacked with tins and jars. I shut the door behind us and turned the bolt to lock it.

Ziv's cot was topped by a bright yellow blanket. His alabaster chessboard rested on top of his pillow. A photo of a dashing young man in a tuxedo was tacked to the left wall, and it was signed in blue ink by the chess champion Emmanuel Lasker. Below it was an old wooden chest. I started looking there.

'What are you searching for?' Ziv asked in a thin, apprehensive voice.

I made no reply. I began looking through his underwear.

'If you tell me,' he continued, 'I'll give it to you. Do you want the money I've saved up? I'll give you everything I have.'

I continued hunting for evidence, tossing the clothing I'd already examined to the floor.

'I . . . I think I understand now,' the boy told me, but in so unsteady a voice that I looked at him. He sat down on the edge of his bed, gently, as if afraid to make any noise. 'God, what an idiot I've been, Dr Cohen.'

That comment surprised me. Fixing my gaze, he said, 'I should have known. I've played this all wrong.'

'What should you have known?'

'What you're looking for is behind there,' he said gloomily, pointing to his photograph of Lasker.

Ziv was crying again – and silently. He was an excellent actor, but I already knew that.

One of the bakery workers must have summoned Ewa. She began pounding at the door and yelling my name.

'Go away!' I shouted back. Turning to Izzy, I said, 'Hold the gun on him.'

Taped to the back of the photograph was a white envelope. I ripped it away. Out of it spilled a slender gold chain holding a small enamel medallion of the Virgin Mary.

I would have expected a surge of righteousness or rage on finding the man who had betrayed Adam; instead, holding Georg's pendant gave me a sense of having been moved around Warsaw by a will that was not my own.

I leaned back against the wall and took a deep breath. My mouth was metallic tasting, as if I'd swallowed rust.

Ewa was still banging at the door and calling out to me. The noise and heat pressed down on me. I hated Ziv for making me kill him.

'It's not mine, I swear,' the young man told me, shaking his hands wildly. 'You have to believe me!'

'I know whose it is!' I hollered. 'It belongs to a boy named Georg – a street juggler. You remember him, I'm sure.'

'I don't,' he replied, moaning. 'I discovered the pendant in my room two days ago.'

'Who left it here?' Izzy demanded.

Ziv faced him and joined his hands together. 'I don't know. I asked everyone in the bakery about the pendant, but no one had lost it. You can ask them. Ask Ewa! I decided to keep it until someone claimed it.'

'Is that the best story you can come up with?' Izzy demanded.

'What did you get in return for Adam?' I asked.

Ziv looked helplessly between me and Izzy. Finding no sympathy in our faces, he gazed down and squeezed his head between his hands as if to hold his thoughts inside. His skilful performance only enraged me further.

'What did you get for my nephew?' I demanded again.

'I didn't hurt Adam! Oh God, I'd never have hurt him! Stefa loved him more than anything.'

'Give me the gun,' I told Izzy. He handed it to me. I pointed it at Ziv's head. 'Tell me the truth!' I ordered.

'Let me think!' the young man pleaded. 'Dr Cohen, now that I know I've been set up, I can figure this out. I'm good at figuring things out. You know I am!'

I put the barrel of the gun up to his temple. 'This is no game, you little bastard! Who have you been working with outside the ghetto?'

'I don't know anyone outside the ghetto,' he insisted, and he reached for my arm to implore me, but I batted it away.

A key turned in the door. Ewa opened it and faced me. 'If you hurt Ziv, you'll regret it for the rest of your life.'

'I have no rest of my life,' I replied.

'Still, you should be pointing that gun at me, not him.'

CHAPTER 26

'After Papa and I moved into the ghetto, we had difficulties getting insulin for Helena,' Ewa told me and Izzy. Seated next to Ziv, she was rubbing his hand to calm him – and to give herself the strength to tell me what she knew. Her lips were trembling, and she couldn't look at me. She kept gazing off; she would have preferred to be anywhere but where she was.

'And it became more expensive, too,' she continued. 'We were getting desperate, but in early January Papa told me that his German supplier had promised to get him insulin for almost nothing. All we had to do was find him Jewish children to photograph. Papa's friend was a medical researcher who'd just moved to Warsaw – a German doctor my father had known in Zurich. He told Papa he had theories about the Jews involving their skin, but I never found out exactly what he meant.'

Ewa – the quietest among us – was opening the final door of this mystery.

'Did your father mention this man's name?' I asked.

'I've tried to remember. I think I must have heard it.'

'It has to be either Rolf Lanik or Werner Koch. Think, Ewa.'

'Those names, they seem close, but . . . Could it have been Kalin . . . or maybe Klein?'

Ewa gazed at me questioningly, but I closed my eyes – out of gratitude, because I suddenly realized why a string had been put in Adam's mouth and a piece of gauze in Georg's hand. And how they identified the murderer. Though I still didn't know who had given me those clues. Might Irene or her mother have been brilliant enough to leave them behind?

Knowing who the murderer was also made me understand why his helper inside the ghetto hadn't been persuaded by our note to go to the Leszno Street gate.

Yet it was then that a first regret pierced my excitement: if only I'd figured out earlier that the *Rolf* who'd signed the photographs of the Alps hanging on Mikael's office walls had been Rolf Lanik, a talented little boy who'd juggled socks to earn his supper would still be alive.

'Are you all right, Dr Cohen?' Ewa asked me, and Izzy reached for my shoulder.

'Yes, I'm fine. Go on.'

'The researcher friend of my father's wanted to photograph skin defects, particularly on children,' Ewa continued. 'We were both so relieved to have his help! So when Papa examined Anna and noticed a blemish on her hand, he told her to go to an address outside the ghetto, where she'd receive a hundred and fifty złoty for letting a doctor there photograph her. Papa didn't know that she'd be killed.' Ewa held my gaze. 'He didn't know. He swore to me he didn't.'

'I believe you,' I told her, but I didn't believe her father.

'Anna told Papa she was going to sneak out of the ghetto anyway, so it seemed all right,' Ewa continued. 'He only began to think that something bad might have happened to her when she didn't show up for her abortion. Later, he learned from her parents that she'd been murdered.'

I faced Izzy. 'After Anna was turned away by Mrs Sawicki, she must have gone to the address Mikael had given her.'

'She risked everything because she needed money to pay back her friends,' he observed regretfully.

'Papa confronted his photographer friend,' Ewa continued, 'but he swore that he hadn't hurt Anna – that she must have been murdered after being photographed at his office and receiving her payment. Papa was sure he was telling the truth. Then Rowy chose Adam for the chorus, and my father noticed his birthmarks at his check-up – though I didn't know that then. Apparently, Papa visited backstage at a rehearsal one afternoon, and he told Adam that if he ever left the ghetto he should go to have his leg photographed because he'd get a hundred and fifty złoty.'

That made sense; Adam would have trusted Mikael because of the horseradish the physician had given him.

'With all that money,' I told Ewa, 'Adam must have thought he'd be able to buy enough coal to keep Gloria warm till spring.'

'I'm so sorry,' she told me, and she began to cry.

I felt nothing for her; her tears were too late to do any good. 'What was the address?' I asked her impatiently.

She wiped her eyes. 'I'm not sure. Somewhere on Krakowskie Przedmieście.'

Izzy looked at me knowingly. 'We have to find Jesion,' he told me.

Ziv put his arm over Ewa's shoulder, which only made her tear up again.

'Please go on, Ewa,' I pleaded. 'Every moment we wait puts another life at risk.'

'After I found out what happened to Adam,' she resumed, 'I remembered seeing his birthmarks once, when Stefa was getting him dressed for school. To think that my father might have been responsible . . . A black terror took hold of me.'

Ewa gazed down into her guilt. 'On the morning of Stefa's funeral, I finally confronted my father. At first he lied and said he hadn't spoken to your nephew, but then, when I threatened that he'd never see Helena again if he didn't tell me the truth, he admitted that he'd suggested to Adam that he go visit the photographer on Krakowskie Przedmieście – but only when he was still under the belief that his friend was innocent. Papa promised me he'd never tell another child about the photographs – and that he'd never speak to his friend again. That's why I didn't go to you or the police. I should have. I know that now. I'm sorry, Dr Cohen.' She turned to Ziv and squeezed his hand. 'And I'm sorry for risking your life,' she told him. 'It's my fault that you were almost killed.'

'It's all right,' Ziv told her. 'I'm fine now. And you were just trying to protect Helena and your father.'

Ewa shook her head as if he was too kind to her. Turning back to me, she said, 'After Stefa died, I couldn't face you. I'm sorry. And Papa . . . I couldn't entirely trust him, so I told him I no longer wanted his help in getting insulin. But it was hard to find another regular supplier, and Helena went into shock and nearly died. So Papa began helping me again – though he promised he wouldn't get insulin from his friend any more. He has another source now – a good, reliable source.'

'No, that can't be true,' I told her. 'And I think your father has lied to you all along.'

'What makes you say that?'

'Another boy was murdered more recently,' I told her coldly, wishing she'd come to me sooner. 'He was murdered after Stefa's death, and skin around his hip was sliced away.'

She shook her head disbelievingly. 'Which boy was killed?'

I held up the Virgin Mary pendant. 'The owner of this,' I told her. 'His name was Georg – Rowy or Ziv must have recruited him for the chorus. He juggled socks and sang old Yiddish songs.'

'It wasn't me,' Ziv told me urgently. 'Dr Cohen, you have to believe me. Rowy must have found him.'

'I believe you,' I replied. 'I'm sorry for ever doubting you. And I should never have put you through this.'

'It's all right, I understand,' he said, smiling sweetly.

I'd nearly killed him, and he smiled at me as if our friendship was stronger than ever.

'Ewa, your father must have decided that he couldn't risk Helena going into diabetic shock again. He's still sending kids to his photographer friend.'

'No, he swore to me he wouldn't do that!' she replied, moaning.

'There are other things you should know about your father,' I told her bitterly. 'He must have realized I was close to learning what he'd done, so he paid someone to shoot me. But he didn't know that new tenants were sleeping in my room. So the killer shot the wrong man.'

'It doesn't seem—'

'Possible?' I cut in harshly. 'Don't you see? He'll do anything to keep Helena and you alive – and to keep from being caught. He's even tried to frame Rowy and Ziv – he didn't care which one. He left Georg's pendant here, and I'll bet he left Anna's pearl earrings with Rowy. Ziv says he noticed the Virgin Mary pendant two days ago, which means your father has known for at least that long who my main suspects were. Though I don't know how.'

'Maybe I let something slip at Stefa's funeral,' Izzy observed apologetically.

'It could just as easily have been me,' I told him. 'And just before we came here, your father brought me a note – a threat that he said he'd received. The note said that if he ever revealed anything about the murderer, he'd never see Helena again. That was part of his plan to shift the blame. He even implied that he was being followed by the same man who had tried to shoot me.'

'I don't understand,' she replied. 'Who was the note from?'

'He led us to believe that it was from Rowy, but it wasn't. Your father wrote it himself.' I turned to Ziv. 'Once he realized I suspected you as well as Rowy, he cleverly revealed that you'd told him you needed extra money to send to your mother outside the Łodź ghetto. He let that slip as though he didn't understand the implication. The perfect touch was letting Izzy and me jump to the obvious conclusion about you.'

'So you thought I needed a lot of extra cash,' Ziv observed.

'Yes, and that you had a contact outside the ghetto helping you get it to your mother.'

'Which is why we came here,' Izzy told him. 'To search for evidence of who you were working with outside the ghetto.'

'But my mother died a month before I came to Warsaw,' the boy insisted, as if righting an injustice. 'I never told Dr Tengmann that she was alive. I promise.'

'So she's not hiding in Łódź?'

'If she had found a place to hide, why wouldn't I be with her? Or at least be hiding elsewhere in Łódź, where I could be nearer to her.'

'But can you prove she's dead?' I challenged him.

'Why would I have to?'

'Because if Ewa hadn't told me the truth, it would have been your word against her father's. I would have believed him, and you, Ziv . . . you'd be dead.'

The boy gazed down and smiled fleetingly, as if in admiration of Mikael's strategy. Looking up, he said excitedly, 'You sent me that note, didn't you, Dr Cohen? You wanted me to go to the Leszno Street gate!'

'Yes, we were trying to trap the killer, but no one showed up.'

'So Ewa's father must have known that your note was a trick, but how?'

'Because he knew that the German he was working with wasn't in Warsaw and couldn't have sent him that note.' I turned to Izzy. 'He knew that Lanik was out of town. They must have found a way to communicate with each other fairly regularly. Maybe Mikael has access to a working phone.' To Ewa, I said, 'Your father must have had someone leave Georg's pendant here secretly. He knew that when Izzy and I came here, we'd be sure to find the evidence we were looking for. He improvises well.'

'If that's true, then who left it here?' the young woman asked.

'Your father must have had a copy made of the key to the bakery and could have paid a streetkid to leave the pendant under Ziv's door.'

'But it wasn't left under my door,' Ziv told me. 'I found it under my pillow. It had to be someone with the key to my bedroom, or a person I let in.' His eyes opened wide with astonishment. 'It must have been one of my chess students.'

'Are you teaching anyone who knows Ewa's father?'

'That woman who came for her first lesson two days ago – Karina.'

'Who's Karina?' I asked.

Ewa replied for Ziv. 'She and my father . . . They've been seeing each other since late November.'

Izzy understood before me. 'Describe Karina,' he requested of Ewa.

'Pretty, in her fifties, with silver hair and . . .'

'Enough!' I said, angry at myself; I didn't need to hear more; Melka – whose real name I now knew – had told Mikael who my suspects were. I had to give her credit; she'd convinced me that she was hardly paying attention to all that I'd revealed to her after we'd shared her bed.

Mikael had used my vanity against me. He must have even told her to offer me a sugar crystal for my tea. He was a coldly observant and resourceful man.

'We've got to go,' I told Izzy.

Ewa jumped up and reached for my arm. 'What'll you do to my father?' she asked, terrified.

CHAPTER 27

Could I kill Mikael? I wasn't sure. So Izzy and I spoke instead of how we'd murder Lanik. He sat on Stefa's bed, curled over his angry ideas, and I stood by the window, cooler, but also more perverse – Mr Hyde creeping through the underbrush of his mind.

We decided we'd go to Lanik's office and shoot him there if he was unprotected. If he had soldiers or guards with him, we'd wait until he left for lunch.

I wanted to strip him, as he'd stripped Adam, and make him beg for his life while kneeling in the filth of a Warsaw backstreet, have him weep for all the springtimes of Germany he'd never see. I wanted a hungry-for-vengeance crowd of Poles to learn what a wrinkled, shivering coward he was minus his uniform, gun and guards, and without his beloved, dog-eared copy of *Mein Kampf* in his hands, justifying his murder of the most defenceless among us.

And once he was dead?

Izzy and I would flee across the river for the suburb of Praga; Jaśmin Makinska lived near the tram depot on Kawęczyńska Street. We would either stay with her or, if she could, she would drive us to Lwów, where we'd hide out in a rooming house or small hotel for as long as it took to sell my remaining jewellery. We didn't have Christian identity papers, but a couple of hundred złoty stuffed in an innkeeper's pocket would win us his grudging silence for a few days.

Our goal: the Soviet Ukraine. We'd bribe our way over the border and head to Odessa, where we'd catch a freighter across the

Black Sea to Istanbul. From there, it would be easy to get to Izmir. After our reunion with Liesel, Izzy would catch a boat to the south of France, where he'd buy forged papers. Then he'd sneak into the German-occupied territory in the north, for a rendezvous with Louis and his sons in Boulogne-Billancourt.

I wanted to be there to see my old friend's victory over all that had stood between himself and his dreams, but I knew by then I'd never leave Liesel again.

I felt strong knowing we had a plan, but Izzy started to cry.

'What's wrong?' I asked.

'Nothing . . . and everything. The relief of knowing I'll either be dead or free – it's too much right now.'

I began gathering together all of the small valuables that I could sell, including the letter opener I'd stolen. Izzy sat at my desk to read through Adam's medical file, and when he was done, he asked, 'So why do you think Mikael let you have this?'

I was sitting on the ground by my dresser and had just taken Hannah's ruby earrings out of the toe of one of my socks. 'He must have thought that his openness would convince me he had nothing to hide,' I replied. 'And he was right. Since Adam's death, he has been trying to outthink me.'

'And he nearly did,' Izzy observed.

'Convincing Melka to sleep with me was his master stroke. She must be deeply in love with him to have gone along with a compromising plan like that.'

I got to my knees and slipped my hand under the mattress to take out the record book of Adam's illnesses that Stefa had entrusted to me.

Turning round, Izzy said, 'While you finish getting together what you'll need, I'll be writing something.'

He'd already slipped a sheet of paper in my typewriter and was obviously hatching a plot, but I didn't question him; I had Hannah's earrings to hide in case we needed to make an emergency bribe. I cut a small square at the centre of fifty pages of Freud's *The Interpretation of Dreams*, dropped the jewellery inside the resulting cubbyhole and slid the slender volume back into its place on my bookshelves.

I put all the valuables I'd sell inside my old leather briefcase.

When Izzy was finished hunting and pecking, I led him into the kitchen, where Bina was scouring the oven. She was wearing her coat and her black beret.

'Give me your hand,' I told the girl, reaching out for her.

I put five hundred złoty in her palm. 'Make sure you stay alive!' I ordered her. She replied that it was too great a sum, so I shook her hard. 'Do anything you need to do, but promise me you'll make it out of here!'

'I swear,' she replied, starting to cry, because I was bullying her.

Apologizing, I hugged her to me, then counted out another 500 złoty and handed them to her. 'Give half of this to a little acrobat named Zachariah Manberg who performs outside the Femina Theatre every day at noon. But only give it to him a little at a time. Otherwise he'll just squander it – or have it stolen by the older boys.'

'And the other half, Dr Cohen?'

'There's a young woman who works in the bakery in the courtyard – Ewa. I want her to have it.'

'I've met her. I'll make sure she gets it.'

'Good girl. Also, if you run out of funds, there are some reasonably good paintings in Stefa's wardrobe, and first editions of psychiatry books on my shelves. Sell them on the Other Side if you can, but don't take stupid risks. You can sell everything but Freud's *The Interpretation of Dreams*. Leave that for me, in case I need to come back.'

Bina nodded.

I was left with a little more than a thousand złoty for myself, and Izzy had nearly six hundred at his workshop.

'All right, let's get going,' I told him.

'Where will you go?' the girl asked.

'We've one errand to run inside the ghetto, then we'll head for the Soviet Ukraine. I don't think I'll be back.'

She brought her hands over her mouth and moaned. 'You're . . . you're leaving for good?'

'Yes, it's time.'

'But we'll see each other when we're free, won't we?' she asked in a petrified voice.

'Yes,' I replied, smiling. 'I'll come back and find you. We'll have a reunion, right here in Stefa's apartment. So take good care of it.'

'I will. Now bend your head down, Dr Cohen,' she requested.

'What?'

'Bend down.'

I did. And then that astonishing girl gripped my shoulders and kissed me on my brow as if I were her child setting out for his first day of school.

I'd put on my good suit so that I'd look like an elderly gentleman out for a leisurely stroll. At Izzy's workshop, he, too, changed into his best clothes and put on his Borsalino. Then he counted his stash of złoty and grabbed his gold watch. I reminded him to take a lemon along. He took two. He slid his photographs from the *Bourdonnais* under his coat.

'I need to say goodbye to Róźa,' he told me.

I waited outside his apartment. When he returned to me, his face was flushed.

I hailed a rickshaw. I had to decide now where to go: Mikael's office or the Jewish Council.

'Where to?' the driver asked.

'Just a minute,' I told him. 'I still don't think I can kill Mikael,' I confessed to Izzy.

'Then let me do it,' he requested.

'It's not your war,' I told him.

'Erik, I loved Adam too!'

'Still, you should go to Louis guiltless.'

'Me, guiltless?' He grabbed my arm hard. 'Have you heard anything I've told you about my life?'

I took his free hand and kissed it. A strange gesture, but this was not a day like any other, and a quarrel with him could have ruined all our plans.

Izzy understood. 'Sorry,' he told me.

I turned round to face the driver. 'Take us to the Jewish Council's headquarters,' I told him.

Benjamin Schrei was in an office he shared with two other men. He rushed to greet us, smiling his million-dollar Gablewitz smile, and introduced us to his colleagues, who brought us desk chairs.

We sat down opposite our host. Four wilted, fire-coloured tulips sat in a turquoise vase on his desk between us.

'You might try watering them,' Izzy told him in his bantering way.

Schrei slicked back his gleaming hair and sighed. 'They were doing great till this morning. You should have come yesterday. It's your timing that's bad.'

'Yesterday, we didn't know what we know now,' I replied, and I told him what we'd learned about Mikael. When I was done, I handed him Georg's pendant and suggested that he question Ewa if he had any doubts about our conclusions. Izzy added that he'd probably find Anna's earrings with Rowy.

'You boys have done good work,' he told us. 'And the council is grateful.' He lit the cigarette that he'd dangled between his lips, then leaned towards us. 'So what do you have in mind for Dr Tengmann?'

He squinted at me through his smoke.

'Does it make any difference what I tell you?' I asked.

'No,' he replied, 'I'll take care of him whatever you say.'

'And *take care of* means exactly what?' Izzy questioned.

'He shall cease to cast a shadow on this earth,' Schrei answered in a dramatic voice. Catching my glance, he added, 'Nothing you can say will prevent that. Still, I'd like to know what you'd do in my position.'

'Why?'

'I'm a curious man. And I want your opinion. I don't think I've ever met anyone like you, Dr Cohen. You interest me.'

'Even though I'm an assimilated Jew?' I asked to provoke him.

'You're hardly assimilated now.' Eyeing me cagily, he said, 'Face it, Dr Cohen, you stink like a ragpicker from the most backward *shtetl* in Poland. And you'll never voluntarily speak German or Polish again to anyone who isn't Jewish. Am I right?'

'Probably,' I admitted.

'You know,' he added, an amused smile twisting his lips, 'if you learned a little Hebrew, you could be a pretty good Yid.'

'He *is* a pretty good Yid!' countered Izzy, ready for a fight.

'You're right,' Schrei replied. 'I'm sorry. It was a bad joke.'

'I think Stefa would want him dead,' I told him.

'Fine, but what do *you* want?' our host insisted.

'I want a cigarette,' I requested, stalling.

I knew that Schrei wanted me to give him the biblical answer: *an eye for an eye . . .* That would have proved I accepted the rules of the God of the Torah. But what he didn't understand is that I wanted to take responsibility for my revenge. I wanted that sceptre of red fire for myself.

'Mikael Tengmann being killed won't bring back Adam,' I told him after he'd lit my cigarette. 'And my sending him straight to hell wouldn't make me happy.'

'It won't make me happy either,' he confessed. 'But I'll still do it.'

'You've a hard job,' I told him.

'Ah, now you're beginning to understand,' he replied, showing me a gratified smile.

'You take care of Mikael, and I'll take care of the Nazi working with him,' I said as if we were trading stocks.

He shook my hand to complete the deal. 'All right, but do you know who the German is?'

'Yes.'

'How are you going to get him?'

Izzy answered for us. 'That depends on how well he's guarded.'

'Maybe you should take a few days to plan this,' Schrei suggested. 'If the Germans find you outside the ghetto, they'll shoot you on the spot. And that's if you're lucky.'

'I can't wait. If I wait, I may lose my nerve,' I told him.

'You have money for bribes?'

'Yes.'

'A gun?'

Izzy patted his pocket. 'It's German,' he replied, grinning at the irony.

'Then I'll let you boys get on your way.' He handed me his tin of cigarettes. 'Take this for good luck,' he told me, standing up.

He accompanied us to the door. We shook hands again, and then he leaned in and embraced me, whispering in my ear, '*Shoot quickly and don't ask him why he killed Adam. No answer he gives you will give you peace, and the delay will just increase the likelihood of your being caught. When you get back out to the street, don't run. It'll attract attention.*'

Good advice – one murderer to another – and it was flattering that he presumed that Izzy and I could still run. But I still had to know why Adam's leg had been worth stealing.

The border crossing at the back of the rickshaw workshop had been bricked up by the Jewish Council, which was under increasing pressure from the German authorities to curb smuggling. So we went to the women's clothing factory that led to Maciej's garage. We paid our toll to the head seamstress and crawled again through that tunnel of pressured darkness into the next world. Happily, Maciej heard our banging and let us out.

'You again – the angry Jew!' he said to Izzy, beaming, and they shook hands like cousins. 'Take off your armbands,' he reminded us.

We handed them to him, and Maciej added them to the collection in his office.

Maciej escorted us to the door, looked both ways to make sure the street was free of policemen, then summoned us out.

Krakowskie Przedmiescie was crowded with workers and shoppers. Owing to the freezing rain that had just begun to fall, it was a confusion of umbrellas battling for airspace. We bought a big blue one that would rule the street.

In front of the Bristol Hotel was a group of German soldiers standing around a tank, but we didn't detour around them or decay into our miserable ghetto shuffle; the murder drawing us forward had freed us from any fear of misfortune.

Can it be that criminals walk easier through their days and nights than the rest of us?

After passing Warsaw University, we spotted what we were looking for on the east side of the street: 'E. Jesion – Butcher.'

A little way back, guarding the west, were the twin pinnacles of the Church of the Holy Cross.

We looked in the shop window from twenty paces away. A red-faced butcher in a white apron, with wire-rimmed spectacles circling his puffy eyes, was working at a marble counter, cutting thick ribbons of fat off a side of pork and tossing them into a tin pail. He was big and broad. His flat-topped haircut – and the moustache hyphening his thick top lip – made him look as though he'd stepped off a Grosz etching.

Was this the brute who had taken Adam from us?

The anger that rose inside me was like a strangling wind – leaving no room for anything but the need to have Jesion's future in my hands.

He looked up and noticed us, then cut away more fat. When he glanced back at me again, I knew he was wondering why a stranger would gaze at him so intently. Guilt had made him observant – and quick to fear the worst.

Izzy sensed what was on my mind. 'Erik, he'll know where Lanik's office is,' he said. 'We can't kill him before we find out where it is.'

'I know. I was just thinking that the perfect crime is one you wouldn't mind being arrested for.'

'No one's going to capture us,' he assured me, and he told me what he had in mind for Jesion. It seemed like a good plan.

As we stepped inside, the butcher looked up with a forced smile. In Polish he asked, 'What can I get for you gentlemen this morning?'

I put my briefcase and folded umbrella down in the corner and looked around quickly. There was a door at the back. It must have led to his storage room.

'Is something wrong?' the man asked us, sensing trouble.

'Are you Mr Jesion?' Izzy questioned.

'That's me all right,' he replied, doing his best to sound jovial.

I locked the door with a firm click. 'We've got a gun,' I told the butcher. 'So drop your knife.'

'What? I don't understand.'

Izzy took out his pistol. 'Drop your knife to the floor,' he ordered, 'or I'll put a bullet in your head.'

I stepped around the counter to watch Jesion's movements. When he tossed away the blade, it made a metallic clang on the tile floor.

'I'm going to step through the door at the back to make sure no one is there,' I told the butcher, 'and then you're going to follow me in. You understand?'

'If it's money you want,' he replied, 'just take it.'

I pushed open the door and entered a dark, chilly room, nearly bumping into a goat's carcass hanging bug-eyed from an iron hook in the ceiling. I recoiled in horror. The smell of blood packed my nostrils.

I tugged on a cord attached to a bare bulb behind me. At the back, on a square marble table, were two other goats, not yet skinned. A vision of Adam lying beside them and stripped of his clothes made me avert my eyes.

'All right, send him in,' I called through the door.

Jesion stepped inside, followed by Izzy, who kept his gun pointed at the butcher's chest.

'Are you . . . are you one of the kids' grandfathers?' Jesion asked fearfully.

'So you've guessed,' I told him.

He cleaned his fingers on his apron. 'Well, you hardly look like robbers.'

'He was my grandnephew,' I explained.

'Which one?'

'The boy with the birthmarks on his ankle.'

Jesion raised a hand to his face and took off his glasses, wiping his eyes. He showed me a desolate look. 'What was his name?'

'Adam,' I told him.

'Adam,' he repeated to himself, listening keenly to the sound it made. 'Did you get his body back?'

'Yes.'

'And you've given him a proper burial?'

'I'm not sure. We've been waiting for the ground to thaw. Listen, Jesion,' I said, 'you seem awfully calm for a man with a gun pointed at his heart.'

'In a way, I've been hoping you'd come. I can't stand any more of this. I think all the time about what I might have to cut from another kid. It's too much.'

'How do you kill them? There are no marks on . . .'

'Me, kill them? It's not like that!' He shook his head. 'When the kids are brought to me, they're already dead – *brenen zol er*!'

His Yiddish was mis-pronounced. I wasn't sure I'd heard right. 'What did you say?' I asked.

Jesion cursed the murderer again.

'How in God's name do you know Yiddish?' Izzy questioned.

'My mother is Jewish, though she changed her name when she was a young woman to hide her background.' He started undoing the cord of his apron. 'I only ever spoke Yiddish when I stayed with my grandparents. I'm rusty.'

'Is it Lanik you want to burn in hell?' I asked.

His face brightened. 'You did it! You must have figured out the clues I left!'

'So you were the one who put the string in Adam's mouth and the gauze in Georg's fist?'

'Yes. I had to think of something to stop more children from being murdered. When did you understand what my clues meant?'

'Only today. You were incredibly clever.'

'I couldn't risk anything obvious,' Jesion replied, taking off his apron and folding it neatly, 'but I'd heard that the Jews inside the ghetto were working in anagrams these days, so I thought that someone in the Jewish police might just turn *linka* into Lanik and *Flor* into Rolf. And that they might be able to stop the bastard. Only a Jew would know both Polish and German well enough to understand that *linka* was string and *Flor* was gauze, so I felt that the right person would figure out Lanik's whole name.'

'But you left nothing on Anna,' Izzy interjected.

'She was the first. I was too shocked and upset to think of how I might leave a clue behind. Only when Adam was left with me did it occur to me how I could do it without risking too much.'

'If Lanik had discovered the string or gauze, what would you have said?'

'That it was carelessness on my part. He wouldn't have guessed. The Germans aren't talking in code like the Jews.'

'That was a good and brave attempt to help me,' I told him. 'Thank you.'

'After what I've done, you're thanking me?'

'Under the circumstances, you did the best you could.'

Jesion grimaced, then raised a quivering hand to his head, dizzy. We sat him down at his table, and he leaned over and cried as if life were spilling out of him.

At length, I asked him, 'How many children have been murdered so far?'

'Four – three boys and a girl.'

'Then there's one I don't know about,' I told him.

'Probably the first of the boys – he came in just after Anna. He wasn't from the ghetto. Lanik told me he and his family had been in hiding.'

'How did Lanik find him?'

'Christians denounce Jews in hiding all the time. It's become the national sport.'

'The body of this boy . . . Where was it left?' I asked.

'I don't know. I don't ask.' Jesion sneered. 'The son-of-a-bitch has his chauffeur bring the dead children here at night, and he tells me what I'm to do. When I'm done, he takes the body away. That's all I know.'

'And how does Lanik kill them?'

'My guess is that he offers them poisoned food. He once told me they come to him famished.'

'Have you ever heard of Mikael Tengmann?' I asked.

'No, who's he?'

'A doctor in the ghetto – an old friend of Lanik's. He's the one who identifies children who have birthmarks or blemishes.'

'I see. So how did you find me?'

'A courageous girl helped me figure out who the murderer was.'

'Was it Lanik's stepdaughter Irene?' he questioned.

'You know her?' I asked in astonishment.

'She and her mother often come into town to buy their meat from me.'

'So did you tell Irene that her stepfather was ordering you to cut up the children?'

'No, it wasn't me. I couldn't risk that. I was careful not to let on.'

'Then one of them must have overheard Lanik discussing the murders or seen the skin you've taken from the children. Or Irene figured things out from other clues we'll never know about.'

'Does Lanik photograph the skin?' Izzy questioned.

'I'm not sure. All I really know is that it has something to do with a transfer he wants to a more important job. When the first boy was brought to me, he told me that he needed the skin around his birthmark for a present he would be carrying with him to a camp – to Buchenwald. As best I can figure out, he's eager to work there so that he can perform experiments on the prisoners – medical experiments involving how to cure burns. That's his speciality, as I understand it. I think he left a couple of days ago for there. I'm betting he took the children's skins with him, though he talked of bringing them to a craftsman in leather before going and I'm not sure he's had time to do that yet.'

'Who's the gift for?'

'Someone at Buchenwald, but I don't know who. Whether he hopes to prove some racial theory with the Jewish skin or simply ingratiate himself to some madman there, I haven't any idea.'

'Why did he pick you to desecrate the children for him?' I asked.

'Lanik found out that my mother was Jewish. He threatened to have her and the rest of our family sent to the ghetto. Mama is seventy-seven years old. She wouldn't survive a week in there. I didn't have any choice.'

'Do you know where Lanik's office is?' Izzy asked.

'Yes, it's across the street – the second door to the left of the church. He's on the first floor, but getting to him will be risky for you. His patients are all collaborators and Germans – soldiers, Gestapo officers . . . I go there to make deliveries on occasion, and he keeps a heavily armed guard by the door.'

'Where does he eat lunch?' I questioned.

'I've seen him at a German restaurant nearby – a kind of beer garden.'

'Is it crowded?'

'Sometimes.'

I wasn't sure what to do, but Izzy saved the day; he took out the note he'd typed at home and handed it to me. It read:

Rolf, please come to the Cathedral in Praga at 1 p.m. I'm in trouble with the Jewish Council and need your help. Don't fail me, I beg of you. My life is in your hands.

At the bottom, Izzy had forged Mikael's signature beautifully, having found it at the end of Adam's medical file.

'You make a better detective than I do,' I told him gratefully.

'Those who lead a double life learn the ways of stealth,' he replied. A one-line poem he'd wanted to tell me for decades, I guessed.

I handed the note to Jesion. 'Go ahead, read it,' I told him.

When he was finished, Izzy said, 'Lanik doesn't yet know that we've identified Mikael Tengmann as his accomplice, and he'll believe the appeal for help is real. They're old friends, so he'll go to Praga.'

'Do you know if there are Germans patrolling the bridges over the river?' I asked the butcher.

'Sometimes, but you should be safe at lunch time. With so many people going back and forth, they don't usually make trouble. But do you intend to kill him in the Praga Cathedral?' he asked in a horrified voice.

'If you can tell me how to lure him to a synagogue,' Izzy told him with a crafty smile, 'I'll happily shoot him there.'

Jesion put our note in an envelope and took it across the street to Lanik; he planned to say it had been dropped at his shop by a ghetto courier. Ten minutes later, he was back, out of breath.

'I gave the note to him, but he didn't read it in front of me,' he told us worriedly.

'But you *did* tell him that the courier had said it was urgent?'

'Of course.' The butcher grimaced. 'He asked me what the man looked like, and I couldn't think of how to reply, so I described Jan Kiliński on his statue in Krasinskich Square – with that peasant hat and heroic moustache. It was all I could think of.'

Izzy had a good laugh, which made Jesion smile. 'I didn't foul things up?' he asked us.

'No, you did good,' I told him.

'What's Lanik look like?' Izzy asked.

'He's tall, over six feet, and he has dark brown hair that he wears very short, parted on the left.'

'That's it then,' Izzy said cheerfully. 'We're off!'

Jesion reached for him. 'Listen, I've been thinking,' he said. 'A gun makes a lot of noise, but a knife . . .'

The steel blade was four inches long, slightly curved, the handle polished ebony. It fitted into my hand as if it had always been mine. I kept it in its leather sheath, concealed in the inside pocket of my overcoat.

Jesion's last words to me were, 'If you free me from that son-of-a-bitch, I'll bless you in my prayers for ever!'

We encountered no difficulties on the bridge to Praga and headed straight to Jaśmin's apartment, but she wasn't home. The caretaker of her building told us she sometimes returned for lunch, usually just after noon.

To kill time, we sat at a café sipping weak coffee that had the unlikely aftertaste of smoked fish, then waited for Jaśmin down her street. Izzy and I hardly spoke; the murder we'd planned was too greedy for our attention.

Jaśmin never showed up. At 12.35 we couldn't wait any longer and made our way to Floriańska Street, and from there to the cathedral. We found it nearly empty. Two elderly women sat in the first pew – sisters, I guessed, since they had the same tight bun of grey hair and finchlike compactness. A balding middle-aged man with a bandage over his left ear sat in the third-to-last row, his sullen lips sculpting prayers, his eyes closed. We spotted no priests.

Izzy sat in the last pew. I stood just to the side of the main door. I put down my briefcase and held my knife behind my back.

At a quarter past one, Lanik stepped inside. I hadn't expected him to be in uniform. That troubled me – it was as if he now had an unfair advantage.

He took off his cap and brushed his hair off his forehead with abrupt, irritated flicks. He obviously thought it a burden to have had to travel so far from his office.

He had an intelligent face and large dark eyes. Stepping to the end of the centre aisle, he surveyed the pews.

Izzy turned to face him and stood up, just as we'd agreed. I crept left, towards the entrance, so that the German's back was to me. The dark moistness of the cathedral seemed to enter me, as if I were becoming a shadow – and as if my change of form was meant to protect me.

I was squeezing the handle of my knife so hard that my hand ached.

'Are you Dr Lanik?' Izzy asked.

I remember his eager tone of voice – as if he had pleasant business with the Nazi. Izzy proved himself an extraordinary human being that day.

'Yes, did Mikael Tengmann send you?' Lanik replied.

I rushed forward in what I remember as a mad charge, but in truth, I must have been too slow; before I reached the German, he turned to face me. I'd intended to lunge at him and thrust the blade into his back while Izzy spoke to him, but that was impossible now. Instead, I jabbed the knife into his throat, so hard and deep that my fist pounded against the taut firmness of his neck.

Blood sprayed on to my face. I tasted the salty wetness of him on my lips.

He fell back on to the floor, hard, his head knocking into a pew. His cap went flying. I heard myself gasp.

Did the sisters in the front pew turn towards us? Did the balding man stop praying? I'll never know; I never took my eyes from Lanik.

With desperate hands, he reached up and yanked the knife out of his flesh. If he was able to think at all, he must have been puzzled as to why Mikael Tengmann would send a killer after him.

Blood seeped from his wound. I'd been unlucky; I'd failed to hit an artery. He'd die slowly. Or if help came, he might even outlive Izzy and me.

Lanik looked at me imploringly as he tried to speak, making gurgling noises – as if a knot were lodged in his throat. He fought to sit up, pulling on the back of the last pew, and after he'd managed this feat, his eyes pleaded for mercy. '*Hilfe!*' he mouthed in desperate German. *Help me!*

Was he thinking he might never see Irene and his wife again?

I was stunned by how much life we have inside our bodies.

I knew it was now I should speak Adam's name, but I couldn't talk – proof that you can never predict how you will behave when you stand before the tower of vengeance you have erected.

Izzy retrieved my knife, which was streaked with blood.

'He might not die,' I whispered to him. Hearing my own voice made me shiver, and my hand clutching his arm was my request for help.

'Don't worry, Erik,' he replied.

How could he speak so calmly? I never asked him, though once he told me he had never felt more alive than when he stood over Lanik and realized what he had to do.

Sometimes I think that Izzy was the strongest person I ever met.

Kneeling down, he told the German, 'There was a beautiful boy named Adam, and he had birthmarks behind his ankle.'

He spoke sweetly and slowly – as if his words were the beginning of a children's story that Lanik still had time to read.

The Nazi shook his head as if he knew nothing about my nephew.

Was it his denial that incensed Izzy? He grabbed Lanik by the hair and smashed his head against the floor.

I cringed on hearing the cruel thud – like two billiard balls knocking together.

The German groaned, and blood spilled over his lips, as though he were vomiting his last chance for life.

Leaning down, Izzy spoke into Lanik's ear: 'Adam and Anna say hello.'

And then, using both hands, he planted the blade as deeply as he could in the Nazi's chest.

In the weeks to come, I would often wonder how I could have known Izzy nearly all my life and never suspected how good he would be at murder.

CHAPTER 28

A black Mercedes was parked outside the church, obviously waiting for Lanik to return. A dark-uniformed chauffeur was inside, reading a newspaper spread into wings. Remembering Schrei's advice, we didn't run. We walked east. I never looked back.

Izzy carried my briefcase; I'd left it behind and he'd gone back for it.

Rain splattered around us but didn't feel wet against my skin. Its relentless pounding seemed the world's way of insisting on a justification from me for my very life.

Izzy opened our umbrella and summoned me to him, but I needed to be by myself. I was listening for a policeman's voice to call out to us in Polish or German and demand we stop. I would have turned round and begged to be shot on the spot.

The voice never came.

I remember passing railroad lines. Did we zigzag along sidestreets to keep from being seen? What happened to my bloodstained overcoat? I can't recall, but I must have left it inside the church; I remember being chilled and noticing at some point that I no longer felt the protection of my muffler around my neck.

I was lost inside the labyrinth of ending a man's life. When we passed a bus stop, I considered waiting there for the Germans to find me, not out of guilt, but because I couldn't see how I'd ever find my way back to the person I'd been. Or why I'd want to.

Then, my heart seemed to leap in my chest, and the rain became wet, and I saw Izzy looking back at me with worried eyes, and I began walking purposefully behind him, towards the horizon, which was where freedom was waiting for us. It was as if a hand had tugged me back to my own hopes -- my daughter's hand, as it turned out; I realized I still had a chance to live out the rest of my life with her.

I don't know how far we walked. I next remember Izzy pointing to a brick building on the left. It was a grimy hotel, with dead geraniums in ceramic windowboxes.

'We'll call Jaśmin from in there,' he told me.

Izzy left our umbrella at the door. I took Jaśmin's phone number from my wallet. The owner of the hotel was standing behind the counter of a wooden bar, polishing glasses with a tea towel. When I explained what I needed, he lifted out a black phone and put it on the counter.

'Where are you boys from?' he asked us as I sat down on a bar stool.

'Muranów,' answered Izzy, drying his hands on his trousers. 'We're on our way to a wedding, but we got a little lost.' Izzy smiled and shrugged as people do to excuse their frailties. 'I rarely come to this side of the river.'

'How 'bout a little drop of something to take the bite out of the cold weather?' the man asked, slapping his cloth over his left shoulder.

'Two vodkas,' Izzy replied.

I picked up the receiver and began to dial. Our host was pouring our drinks when Jaśmin answered. Thank God she'd returned home.

'It's me,' I told her, unwilling to let the hotel owner overhear my name.

'You who?' she asked.

That had me stumped. 'Stefa's uncle,' I finally told her.

'Dr Cohen? Oh, my God! I thought I'd never hear your voice again.'

'We're lost,' I told her. 'We're outside Praga, but I'm not sure where.'

Izzy took the phone and described our location. 'Listen, baby,' he added casually, 'can you pick us up in your car and drive us to the wedding?'

After a moment, he nodded towards me to let me know that Jaśmin had agreed.

'Meet us down the street,' Izzy told her. 'We'll be waiting under a blue umbrella.'

The vodka didn't scorch my throat, as it usually did. Or more likely I was too far away from myself to feel it.

Izzy paid for our drinks and our phone call. Outside, he began walking away, towards the countryside. I stayed put.

'Erik, come on!' he exhorted me, summoning me with whirling hands to follow him. 'I don't want that hotel owner to see the car that picks us up.'

I obeyed. We both knew I was useless now and he'd have to take charge.

We waited in an empty lot strewn with refuse, out of sight of the hotel. Izzy held our umbrella over our heads, hiding our faces from the occasional cars that drove by. He hooked his arm in mine and held me close.

The rain had subsided a bit, but I was still freezing.

Irene would be grief-stricken on hearing of her stepfather's murder. Unless her keen affection for him had been part of her performance.

If she didn't intend for me to kill him, then why did she send for me? Maybe she feared that she, too, would end up on a butcher's table unless her stepfather was stopped. Perhaps she had been marked at birth, like Adam, Anna and Georg.

There were so many things I'd never get to ask her. Though perhaps Izzy was right and she'd told me all she could.

He put his arm around my waist because I was shivering. 'Look, Erik,' he observed cheerily, 'the worst that can happen is that the Nazis will find us and shoot us.'

Black humour under other circumstances, but in this case he meant: *We've done what we needed to do and, if we have to die, then at least we'll go together.*

A big black car with wooden doors pulled up a few minutes later. Jaśmin rolled down her window. She was wearing a peaked green hat topped by a golden feather – the kind of cap Robin Hood might wear in a theatrical production. On her slender hands were white kidskin gloves. 'Get in!' she urged us.

I sat in front and Izzy got in the back.

'You've saved our lives,' he told her right away.

I started to introduce them, but Jaśmin reminded me they'd met at my birthday parties.

She took off slowly, concentrating on the road. Her lips were pressed tightly together. She knew she might lose her nerve if she faced me, so she didn't.

Izzy began explaining what we'd done. Jaśmin said nothing, though when he told her how he'd stood up to address Lanik, she began hiccupping – an old sign of failing nerve I recognized from our sessions.

'You can drop us any time you want and get on your way,' I told her when Izzy had finished. 'We'll still be grateful for the help you've given us.'

She took her eyes off the road for just an instant and brushed my cheek. 'You once told me, "Terror traps us all from time to time, but the important thing is not to let it build walls around us."'

'I remember,' I told her, but in truth I'd said that to most of my patients.

'Do you recall what you did then?' she asked, showing me an eager look.

'No, I'm sorry. It was a long time ago.'

'You stood up from your chair and came to me on the couch. You'd never done that before. You were probably breaking all the rules. In any case, you reached out your hand to me, as though you were inviting me to dance. That terrified me more than anything. I closed my eyes and turned away. But you didn't move. You were showing me I could count on you. After maybe twenty seconds, I opened my eyes and took your hand. You'll find this hard to believe, but I think that was the first time I'd really touched anyone – the first time I was sure that another person was real. That moment changed everything. And you . . . You kissed my cheek – to acknowledge my bravery, I think. And then you went back to your seat. After lighting your pipe, you said in that professional voice of yours, "Now, where were we . . .?" '

Tears dripped down Jaśmin's cheeks and she gripped the steering wheel tightly.

Jaśmin waved away my effort to find adequate words of reply and smiled. 'I've already figured this out, Dr Cohen. We'll go to my sister's farm. No one will be able to find you there. We'll have some time to think of what to do next.'

'Thank you,' I told her, astonished that the small *mitzvah* I'd done for her twenty years before could change the direction of my life at this very moment.

'So where's your sister's farm?' Izzy asked.

'Between Warsaw and Lublin, just east of Puławy.'

'Puławy, great!' exclaimed Izzy like a boy eager for adventure, leaning over the front seat. 'I wonder if anything is left of the art collection in Czartoryski Palace.'

From the wild exuberance in his eyes, I realized he was running on nervous energy.

'I'm afraid we won't be able to visit the palace,' Jaśmin told him. 'The Nazis have sent most of the Jews of Puławy to labour camps, but there's still a small ghetto, and the Germans are everywhere. We'll have to avoid the city.' She put her hat down on the seat. 'I don't suppose you two have any false identity papers.'

'No.'

'Then we'd better steer clear of the main route.'

We drove on wretched backroads over the next hour and a half and twice had to push and curse our way out of mud – all to no avail it soon seemed, because after detouring around Żelachów, we came around a sharp turn only to meet up with two German soldiers conversing by their motorcycles at a railroad crossing. They were less than a hundred yards away and spotted us immediately, so it was too late to turn round. One of them flagged us down.

'Be a dear,' Jaśmin said to me as she eased the car towards them, 'and give me my hat.'

I handed it to her and she put it on.

'Eccentricity tends to startle our Aryan rulers,' she explained.

As soon as we'd come to a halt, Jaśmin rolled down her window. The soldier who'd signalled for us to stop opened his eyes wide with curiosity on seeing such a grand lady behind the wheel.

In faulty but charming German, Jaśmin told him, 'I don't suppose you know if we're on the right road to Puławy, dear boy?'

'I'm not sure. Wait a minute.'

He conferred with his colleague and then gave her directions to the main road.

'Thank you – you're a sweetheart,' she told him, waving coquettishly, and then, giving him no time to reply, she started off.

I counted the seconds before the soldiers would begin firing, but they never did. Had they intended to ask for our papers? On reaching a count of thirty, I turned around, but the Germans were already facing away from us and talking together – probably about what a peculiar people they'd conquered.

Jaśmin was glancing in the rear-view mirror to confirm we weren't being followed.

'Who knew Sarah Bernhardt was driving us to safety!' Izzy told her.

'Brilliant!' I seconded.

'Thank you both, but I seem to have peed in my knickers,' she confessed.

We pulled over after a mile and gave her a chance to dry herself and regain her composure. 'Was I really good?' she asked hesitantly, hidden behind the car, and when we nodded, she began to laugh, so that we did too.

The sun was peeking through a cavern of dark clouds. On both sides of the road were apple orchards. This valley would be a sea of pink blossoms in a month.

'Poland is a beautiful country,' I remarked to Izzy.

'Yeah, just don't get attached to it,' he replied. 'We're not staying long.'

It was four in the afternoon by the time we entered the gravel driveway of Liza's farm. I was asleep in the back.

I awoke to a woman with friendly brown eyes peering at me. She was so close that I could smell the wet wool in her blue and red tartan tam.

Had I died and gone to Scotland?

'Dr Cohen – time to get up,' the woman told me in a sing-song voice.

I sat up, still half asleep. Behind my Scottish fairy godmother stood Izzy and Jaśmin, talking together. A big black dog was jumping between them and barking.

'I'm Liza, Jaśmin's sister,' the woman told me sweetly. 'Welcome to my home.'

Liza's farm rose up a small slope from the grassy bank of the River Wieprz, across a thick wood from the village of Niecierz. An eighteenth-century stone house with two tiny upstairs bedrooms, it had originally been a second barn for a large manor house that lay a half-mile east and which wasn't visible because of a low hill topped by a copse of spruce trees. Liza lived alone; her husband had died a few years earlier and her son and daughter, now adults, lived in Kraków.

The floors were hexagonal terracotta tiles – darkly lustrous with age – and the furniture was all heavy wood. The whitewash on the walls shone with grey-blue tonalities in the slanting afternoon light. The ceiling upstairs was so low that I could touch it by standing on my toes.

There was no electricity and no phone. We were in the Poland of our ancestors.

Izzy and I moved our things into the spare bedroom. It was freezing, but Liza soon got a coal fire going in the iron parlour stove, then opened her husband's wardrobe and said, 'Take whatever you want.'

We found thick woollen coats and scarves.

Liza was a potter. Her workshop was in the apple cellar, which was empty at this time of year but still smelled like cider. We drank good coffee for the first time in months and gorged on her *gołąbki* while sitting around a stone table in her kitchen. I kept anxious thoughts away by watching the two sisters closely – Jaśmin so stylish and regal, and Liza in men's trousers and a moth-eaten yellow sweater. I could see they adored each other in the way they laughed over nothing and gave each other complicitous, sideways glances. Over the next few months, they would often seem telepathic. In the end, I came to the conclusion that each one was living out the life the other might have had.

Liza told us that first afternoon that she would teach us how to use a potter's wheel. We would be her assistants for as long as we lived with her. She assured us she was happy to have company.

When I pointed out that we were putting her life in danger, she shrugged as if the risk were of no importance.

Jaśmin told us she would stay the night, but would have to leave at dawn.

'I have to get back to Warsaw. Tomorrow's Friday, and if I'm not at the gallery on time, the owner will think it's suspicious. I'll come back on Saturday afternoon.'

That evening, over our early supper, I told the sisters about Irene and how she had heard Jaśmin speak about the ghetto, though I omitted that the girl had led me to Jesion and Lanik. I believed then that I held that information back because I didn't dare speak of Adam's murder in my fragile state. Now, I realize I was also protecting Irene; if Liza or Jaśmin were ever arrested, the less they could reveal about the girl the better.

CHAPTER 29

The very next day, Izzy and I diagrammed our plans for making it to Lwów, and from there to Kiev, but Jaśmin soon made contact with an arms smuggler in the Warsaw Underground, and he told her that he had information that the Germans were building labour camps and military bases all across eastern Poland; in consequence, we ought not to risk our escape just yet. Her smuggler friend would let her know when it was safer to leave.

We stayed with Liza from March all the way to early July. After a few weeks, we were glad not to have to leave, though we knew we would set off as soon as Jaśmin gave us the go-ahead – if for no other reason than to stop putting Liza at risk.

Izzy and I stayed close to the farmhouse at all times; we dared not go near the nearest village for fear of being spotted and denounced. Still, sometimes at dawn, before anyone was up, we'd take her dog, Noc, for walks through the fields.

Noc had an extensive Polish vocabulary, and Izzy and I taught him Yiddish, as well.

Hak mir nisht ken tshaynik! Izzy would yell at the beautiful mongrel when he was barking too heartily at some rabbit or squirrel he'd chased into the underbrush. Amazingly, the dog would go all quiet and sit on his haunches, looking back and forth between us with his deep brown eyes full of remorse. Given his luxurious black coat, we joked that he was the reincarnation of a Jewish furrier and had been waiting all this time to learn his true language.

★

A few days after our arrival, Liza purchased insecticide at a local apothecary, and Izzy and I dusted ourselves with the white powder from top to bottom, turning ourselves into foul-smelling snowmen.

Izzy submerged in our bathtub first. When he was done, I stepped into the scalding water, sat down and closed my eyes. And entered paradise. I could not have been happier had I been five years old and embraced by my mother.

I hadn't been aware of how tense and constrained my body had been – as if I'd been tangled in vines. Away with the lice went months of grime.

Still, I sobbed alone that night, hidden in Liza's cellar.

Izzy and I wrote just a single letter to our children, fearing that our correspondence might cause trouble for Liza. I told Liesel I'd contact her again when we reached the Soviet Ukraine.

I'd get up every morning to watch the sunrise, grateful for the boundless pink and russet sky, for all that blessed light falling over the earth, for the warm breezes of spring and the butterflies fluttering over the flowers, for eagles and hawks and magpies and all that could fly beyond the control of the Nazis. Grateful, too, for a red fox that I saw late one afternoon, and who stopped to watch me as if I had descended to the earth from out of *his* sunrise.

The sound of my whispering with Izzy as we fell asleep was like protective netting. We covered ourselves with our voices every night.

He and I fired a few of our lopsided cups and vases in the kiln over those first weeks of refuge. One day, however, Liza decided she would teach me to centre a pot or die trying. She put her hands over mine and moved them through the luxurious wet clay, while that wheel of creation spun round and round between us like a *dreidl* that would never stop proclaiming the miracle of our escape. If she and I had been younger, maybe we'd have had a chance at another life. But one passes a gate without knowing it, and then

288

there is no point in turning round and starting over. We both knew that and ended up laughing.

Still, it was good to be able to learn a new trade at my age.

Izzy and I were occasionally at each other's throats over the most meaningless trifles, but we never forgot we were riding on the same raft at the centre of an angry sea, and that made all the difference. We were careful to give Liza enough time for herself and often stayed in our room – teaching Noc the subtleties of Yiddish grammar or tossing him his leather ball – when we would have preferred to be with her.

Imagine having to care for two elderly good-for-nothings. God, what we put that woman through!

It was a small life we had, but anything bigger would have put us at risk. Besides, we were exhausted. We hadn't realized how depleted we were till we were off our island.

I slept twelve hours a night over those first weeks. And once my stomach adapted to wholesome food again, I made Liza's dinner plates shine at every opportunity.

My hunger may have been obsessive at times, but Izzy's nose hadn't been dulled – like mine – by fifty years of pipe-smoking, and once his sensitive sniffer picked up the scent of good food again, it turned him into a slavering wolf; for a month or so he was unable to hold a conversation if there were even just a few grains of kasha or a smidgen of creamed sorrel still available. He would eye any crumbs Liza and I left over as if they had been stolen from him while he was reaching for the butter or pepper, and you could hear him counting the seconds he regarded as requisite – given our turn-of-the-century notions of etiquette – before he could make a headfirst dive for our plates.

When he was on one of his binges, cannibalism seemed a real possibility. Liza and I kept our distance and advised Noc to do the same.

His scurvy proved no match for his boundless appetite.

In the silence of the forest protecting our farm, I began to believe that as long as there were women like Liza in the world, Jewish history could never come to an end – not here or anywhere else. And that sooner or later, the world would come to its senses.

Liza sold her bowls, mugs and vases at two shops in Puławy. The owners came once a month to pick out the merchandise they wanted. Jerzy, one of them, selected a Japanese-looking bowl of Izzy's one day – blue, with calligraphic black strokes near the rim. His first sale. We celebrated with wine that evening.

At night, in bed, Izzy and I would talk about the friends we'd left back in Warsaw. It always seemed strange to us how geography can determine everything during a war. I wondered if I would ever see the city again. And if I'd want to.

In the early hours of the morning, I'd sometimes hear my name being called, as though from downstairs, and I'd try to get out of bed, certain that Liza was in trouble, but I'd find – to my horror – that I was unable to move. My arms and legs were paralysed. Never had I known such helplessness. And then I'd see Izzy's face lit with crescents of light and dark by the white candle in his hand, and hear him whisper my name, and I'd realize he was waking me again from the nightmare that was being sent to me by all that I'd failed to do.

Twice a week, a stocky labourer and his teenaged son came from Niecierz to work Liza's land; she had an agreement with them that allowed her to keep half of her fruit and grain. Izzy and I would hide in the cellar whenever we heard their donkey cart rambling down the potholed dirt road that skirted our farmhouse, reading by candlelight until Liza sounded the all-clear, which was a high whistle that would make Noc race up the staircase and bound into her arms.

I started fishing in the early evening in late May, on a quiet bend in the River Wisłoka guarded by dense, leafy woodland – mostly paper-barked birches and tall, broad oaks, but also curlicuebranched hazel bushes near the water. Noc would tag along, his tail twirling. He'd try in vain to catch dragonflies in his snapping jaws and watch the dark water around my line as if expecting a river sprite to surface at any moment.

On two occasions, I caught trout big enough to eat.

Izzy and Liza planted a kitchen garden, so that by early June we were able to begin harvesting fresh vegetables. The sweet, earthy smell of our beets carried me back to the days of my childhood when I'd go marketing with my mother. Liza, on sniffing at our perfumed trellis of pink and blue sweet-pea blossoms, would always fake a swoon, like the heroine of a nineteenth-century novel overcome by love.

Food had never tasted so good as the meals we ate on Liza's small patio, listening to the Polish trees and fields speaking in the language of wind from the Ukraine. But no matter how much I ate, crabs of hunger would still sometimes scuttle through my belly during the night. I'd light a candle and creak down the stairs into the kitchen. Often, Izzy would accompany me. We'd sit in our underwear at the kitchen table – little kids gorging on cheese and pastry while their parents lay sleeping.

One warm dawn in late June, I took off all my clothes and lay next to Noc in a potato field. The ground seemed solid below me – incapable of giving way – for the first time in a year.

Izzy and I were in the cellar on 7 July, helping Liza stack her freshly fired pottery on her shelves, when we heard two cars approaching. By now, we knew the routine. We crept behind the kiln, out of view. She rushed upstairs and closed the cellar door behind her. Two men soon entered through the front door, and Liza began talking German, but we couldn't make out her words.

After a few seconds, she shouted, 'Get out of my house!'

I listened for a gunshot. Instead, a German yelled, 'Where are you hiding him?'

Him . . . I understood the significance of that right away; whoever had denounced us to the Nazis had only spotted one of us.

When Liza screamed, I jumped up.

'Stay here!' I whispered to Izzy.

'Where are you going?' he demanded, gripping my arm.

There was no time to explain. I leaned down. 'Go to Louis when you get out of here.'

When I kissed him on the lips, he held me for a startled moment, then kissed me back.

'Erik, no!' he whispered desperately as I stepped away.

I meant to say with my eyes that our time was over, and I meant my smile to mean that I had no other choice. Did he understand?

When the cellar door opened, I started up the stairs with my hands extended high over my head.

'I'm coming up!' I called out in German. I didn't dare glance at Izzy, because I was sure that his darkly shadowed eyes – and everything in them that I wanted to live for – might steal my courage, though I wished I could have reassured him that I'd be all right.

Three SS officers had come to the farm. Though I put up no resistance, the two younger ones knocked me down and kicked me. Liza stood by, shouting curses at them, until the one in command – forty-ish, with greying hair around his temples and black eyebrows – grabbed her and threw her to the ground.

'I didn't tell them!' she shouted to me as I was dragged away. 'I swear!'

The Germans shoved me into the back seat of their car.

Before I was able to holler out the window that I knew she could never betray us, the older Nazi raised his gun and fired. Liza fell over with a guttural cry, clutching her arm.

I shoved open my door and got out. 'Stop!' I shouted at him. 'She only hid me to make money!'

He never even turned to me. He put the barrel of the gun up to Liza's ear.

She showed him a bewildered look.

I can still hear the explosion of the bullet; it's the sound of all the best people I ever knew being murdered.

The German in command got in the back seat beside me, demanding to know my name and where I was from. He slapped me across the face when I made no reply. Struggling for breath, I told him my name was Izydor Nowak and that I was a clockmaker from Warsaw; I appropriated my old friend's identity because he'd be able to disappear more completely if the Nazis believed that they had captured him already.

I also told him that he had murdered a wonderful woman who had not deserved to die.

I next remember entering Puławy, where my captors made me stand in a town square with a group of about fifty other Jewish men for the rest of that day and all through the night. The Christian residents – thousands of them, it seemed to me – passed us on their way home from work, but none of them offered us a crust of bread or a cup of water. The Germans wanted to prove to us, I think, that we were nothing – less important to our Polish neighbours than dogshit on the sidewalk. And it was true.

By the time morning came, I was unable to escape my misery even for a moment. My throat felt as though it had been blasted with sand, and I was having trouble breathing. I had no more tears left.

Polish and German soldiers soon marched us off. To where, we had no idea. My good fortune was that exhaustion and dehydration made me delirious. Puławy was substituted by Warsaw, and I was rushing down Leszno Street. The dome of the Great Synagogue was rising into a sunlit sky just ahead, imposing, but like a grandfather only pretending to be stern, and summer rain had begun to fall, and its hammering against the dome was a good sound, the sound of life being born . . .

I stayed in Warsaw until a gunshot tugged me back to myself. A man in front of me had collapsed and been executed. Flies were already feeding at the wound in his head. We were walking down the platform of a small train station.

'Keep going!' someone yelled at me in German.

Stepping over the man, I knew that our blood would never be completely erased from the streets of every Polish city and town – not even if it rained every day for a thousand years. And I was thinking: *The Poles who survive this war will hate us for ever, because the bloodstained cobblestones of their cities and towns will remind them of their guilt.*

On the train, inside an oven-hot cattle car, I dropped down and curled into a ball to keep from being crushed. I wanted water so badly that I'd have opened a vein had I carried anything sharp on me.

I must have passed out. When I awoke, soldiers were jabbing us with their rifle butts, their Alsatians straining for a chance to taste Jewish flesh. They marched us forward. My head was heavy and cumbersome, as though it might fall off from its own weight, and my dry, useless tongue was a dead lizard inside my mouth.

We arrived at a large camp of wooden barracks and were marched through the front gate up to a desk where two prisoners were ladling water into tin cups. The liquid tasted of metal, but I gulped it down as fast as I could. I didn't have enough saliva yet to eat, or even an appetite, but I grabbed my crust of bread as if it were Hannah's hand.

I slept that night on a wooden floor surrounded by other recent arrivals.

The next morning, after roll call, one of the head prisoners called out Izzy's name, and when I answered, he led me into a barracks that had become a workshop for tailors and escorted me to the back, where three skeletal men were seated tightly together, hunched over a table piled with hundreds of watches. 'Enjoy your new office,' he told me, and just like that he walked away.

A tall, anxious-eyed young man with a shaved head stood up and shook my hand. I told him my legs were still unsteady and asked if I could sit.

'Of course,' he replied, standing aside and gesturing towards his chair.

He told me his name was Chaim Peczerski. He introduced me to his two co-workers, Jan Głowacz and Jakub Weinberg.

Jakub had a torn ear and spectacles missing a lens. I thought that maybe one of the Alsatians had attacked him. Later, when I got to know what he was capable of, I asked some other prisoners, and I was told he'd started a vicious fight with a tailor from Turobin who'd bitten him to keep from being strangled to death.

Chaim explained that the watches on their desks had been stolen from Jews, as well as from Polish and Russian prisoners of war. We were in a labour camp run by the SS.

I was so disoriented I asked him if we were anywhere near Lublin.

'You're in Lublin, you idiot!' Chaim replied, laughing.

'You're a Hebrew slave working for Pharaoh now,' Jan added, sticking a homemade cigarette in his lips and grinning.

He had a waxy, sweaty face that I found frightening – as if it were a mask.

'You'll work with me,' said Jakub, and his tiny brown eyes darted falcon-like from my face to my hands and then my feet, as if he was on a stimulant. Only a week later did I realize why.

'We've a lot of work,' Chaim told me. 'We have a quota to meet each day or we don't get any bread.'

'The problem is, I know nothing about fixing watches,' I confessed. 'I lied to the Germans.'

'You what?' Jakub demanded indignantly.

'I lied.'

'You old bastard!' he spat out, and he looked over at Chaim as though to demand my execution. The youngest among us was apparently in charge.

'I had to protect a friend,' I explained.

'That's fine, but you're not working with me!' Jakub snarled.

I stood up to go, but Chaim pushed me back down roughly. 'What do you really do?' he asked.

'I'm a failed novelist,' I replied, since it seemed safer to keep pretending I was someone other than myself.

Jakub laughed at the absurdity, and Jan sneered, 'You're useless!'

'Get up!' Chaim ordered. He pointed to the door. 'Wait outside while we talk.'

When he called me back in, he told me that Jakub and Jan had voted against letting me work with them, but that he had overruled them.

'You've got three days to learn enough to hold your own,' he told me in a voice of warning.

I worked hard, but after three days I was still pretty much useless with the tiny screwdrivers and pliers. Chaim came up with a solution, however; I would polish all the watches that he and his colleagues fixed, thereby doing a quarter of our total work. Jan found that acceptable, but Jakub cursed me. He also began referring to me as *Dostoevsky's Jewish Idiot*, which he regarded as witty.

One night, about a week later, I awakened to find Jakub leaning over me, whispering Hebrew words I didn't understand. When I tried to sit up, he pushed me back down. Then he tugged my shoes off my feet.

'What'll I wear?' I asked, moaning.

'That's your problem!'

As he crawled back in his bunk, I realized that when we'd first met, he'd studied me for what I had that might be worth stealing.

The camp had an active black market, and in exchange for five days' worth of the rancid broth that passed for our soup, I was soon able to obtain flimsy leather shoes – three sizes too big – that I stuffed with newspaper.

Jakub then started taking my bread right out of my hands, mocking me when I refused to fight him for it and only stopping when a bigger prisoner put a homemade knife to his neck.

Jakub wanted to punish me as much as he wanted life. Maybe they were even the same thing for him.

Sometimes I think he uttered a magical curse over me on the night he stole my shoes, or on another occasion when I didn't wake up in time to know he was with me, and that's why I'm still here.

Before the ghetto, I'd have thought that was impossible, Heniek, but listen . . .

Jakub's brother-in-law was a rabbi from Chelm named Kolmosin – a sturdy little red-nosed man, maybe fifty years old. He and Jakub used to pray together on Friday evenings behind a burlap curtain they hung over their adjoining bunks. The rumour I heard was that the rabbi was a descendant of Shabbetai Tzvi, and that he knew powerful incantations that had been passed down from branch to branch in their family tree for twenty generations – incantations that governed life and death. He had bribed the guards to be able to keep a Torah the size of a deck of cards with him, and we often caught glimpses of him huddled over it, making rapid annotations with a tiny pencil. Chaim told me that if he wrote down your name, your destiny would change, and it would be good or bad depending on the nature of the verse in which he had inserted it. In consequence, prisoners would try to win Kolmosin's good graces by polishing his shoes or darning his socks, or by giving him smuggled cigarettes, sugar or other small gifts. He was the only prisoner I ever saw in a clean white shirt. He lived like a pasha.

Once, in August, I saw the would-be holy man sitting naked on his red velvet cushion and singing to himself. He carried that ridiculous velvet cushion with him everywhere because of his haemorrhoids – which were apparently beyond the control of his magical annotations. Later, he taught the oriental-sounding tune to Jakub and some of the other prisoners. He claimed that he'd learned it in a vision and that it would keep us safe.

I was of the opinion that singing '*Deutschland, Deutschland über alles*' would produce better results, but maybe Kolmosin had the last laugh; the more I think about it, the more I wonder if he might not have helped Jakub tether me to the earth by writing me into a verse of Torah that would make me return after death. Perhaps I represented an opportunity for him as well, but for what I cannot guess.

Grudgingly, I have to admit that I have come to believe in magic, though I remain an atheist. A paradox? Probably, but what could be more common than that?

On waking and going to sleep, I'd picture Liesel sitting with Petrina on a beach near Izmir. I wrote long letters to her in my head, and while I was polishing watches, I'd often daydream about her, though my favourite fantasy was of Izzy surprising Louis – appearing at his door one day, unannounced. In my mind, the two men embraced for a long time, and then went for an arm-in-arm promenade along the Seine. Sometimes I joined them for tea and cake at Les Deux Magots.

I lived inside my head. For hours at a time, I'd walk through the Warsaw of my childhood and the London of my honeymoon, and the tours I took by myself – and sometimes with Hannah – kept a small pale flame alive inside me.

Come September, I was nearly always freezing, and often sapped of strength by a cold or diarrhoea. My body had become a cumbersome nuisance, and – like most of the men – I longed to be able to discard it.

★

There were a thousand of us in the camp – a thousand moths caught in a black and red lamp, fluttering against the glass of our Jewish identities.

But one of us found a way out, and his escape soon became mine as well.

On the morning of 7 December, our German guards noticed that a prisoner from Lublin named Maurice Pilch was missing. He had been a tannery worker. It was later discovered that he had concealed himself inside a shipment of hide bound for Austria. In effect, he'd mailed himself to Graz for Hanukkah!

The camp inmates were cheered by Maurice's witty escape, but only briefly; the commandant, Wolfgang Mohwinkel, decided to execute ten men to compensate for Pilch's effrontery.

An hour or so after this news spread through the camp, Chaim, Jan, Jakub and I heard screaming outside the barracks where we worked and rushed outside. Two guards had caught a teenaged prisoner and pinned him to the ground. One of them had his right knee pressing hard into the young man's chest. We called this particular guard Caligula, because he enjoyed murder and was good at it. So far, he'd shot seven men for sport as they sat on the latrine.

Caligula told us gleefully that the boy was one of the ten Jews to be hanged. 'The commandant likes 'em young!' he gloated, as though he were talking about rape.

The trapped teenager had freckles and stiff blond hair like a brush. Chaim knew his name – Albert – and that he worked in the printing shop with his father. They were from Radom.

Caligula soon took away his knee and pressed his club over Albert's neck so that he'd stop screaming.

I learned that day that a boy will punch and kick like a demon to see his seventeenth birthday, even if his windpipe is being crushed and he is unable to draw any breath.

'He looks like a beetle on his back,' Jakub whispered in a sneering tone.

After what seemed an excruciatingly long struggle, though it may have been only half a minute, Albert stopped gagging and flailing. His arms relaxed and his head sagged to the side. His eyes closed.

I thought he was dead, but the guard knew differently. Sensing a good time to be had, he eased off on the boy's neck. After a second or two, Albert's eyes fluttered open and he gulped for breath. He tried to sit up, but Caligula pushed him back down.

The Nazi brute called me over. 'Stand on the ends of my club!' he ordered.

Albert's brown eyes shifted urgently to me, pleading for mercy. He tried to speak, but the German pressed down harder.

The weight of even my flimsy body would have broken the young man's neck, so I shook my head.

'Stand on the club or I'll shoot him!' Caligula yelled at me.

'I can't,' I replied, though I knew he would carry out his threat.

'Do it, you Jewish pig!' he shouted.

'Take me instead,' I told him; it was all I could think of saying that would end this stalemate, though I admit I wanted to retract my offer a moment later.

But Caligula didn't give me time for that.

'You? Why should we waste our time killing an old man like you?' he demanded contemptuously.

I felt cornered, and all I had with me was the truth. 'Because I'm more dangerous to you than the boy,' I replied.

'And why is that?' he asked, amused.

'Because he's young and may forget you if he goes on to lead a happy life, but I won't. I'll write about what you did to us and then dance on your grave.'

The malevolent guard smiled at me and lifted his club from Albert's neck, as if my courage to speak my mind had purchased both of us our lives, but by now I was aware that the Nazis adored playing a game called Fool the Jew. I sensed the worst and raised my hand for mercy. And to cut a deal. 'If you let us both live, I'll tell you where to find some ruby earrings that I've . . .'

Rearing back with his club, Caligula ended my plea by giving Albert so brutal a blow to his head that the crack of his skull sounded like a branch being snapped.

The young man groaned. His head sagged, and his arms went limp.

The German kept hitting Albert until blood was flowing down his face on to the ground.

When he was done, he stood over the boy like a prizefighter posing for cameras. It was his theatricality that made me realize how vain our Nazi guards were, all of them eager to be stars in their very own Leni Riefenstahl film.

When the flashbulbs in his head stopped going off, he pointed his club at me. 'You!' he snarled. 'You're number ten now!'

The body has a life of its own; when the noose was placed around my neck, the constriction that had gripped my gut for the last few days burst open. Several hundred men were watching, but none laughed at the moist sag I'd made in the seat of my rumpled trousers. I wished I could have recited a verse of poetry equal to all the damned and shipwrecked faces around me, but my mind was dim, as if a sack had been placed over my thoughts, which were all jumbled together.

I remember looking for Izzy, thinking that seeing his face would help me to leave this world. When I recalled that he wasn't with me any longer, my heart dived towards a panic so wide and deep that I felt as if I would never hit bottom.

I wanted one of Kolmosin's incantations now – one that would make me land on the solid ground I'd known at Liza's farm, even if it meant my back would be broken.

And I wanted a phrase of wisdom that would sum up what I'd learned over the course of my life.

I wanted more time. And more words.

I spotted Jakub. *Hate is eternal*, he was telling me with his ugly frown.

That was when I realized he'd needed a mortal enemy to keep himself alive.

A man in front – I'll never know his name – diverted my attention with a small wave. He was bent and twisted, like a bonsai plant. He was crying.

His tortured form had made him understand what I couldn't say. I was sure of it.

He held me through his jade-coloured eyes, and he assured me with all he was that I didn't need to find any wisdom. All I had ever done and thought added up to Erik Cohen and that was enough.

I thanked him silently for his tears.

I made believe that Hannah, Stefa and Adam would welcome me beyond death.

Near the end, I heard a melody from out of my childhood, a folk song called '*Hänschen Klein*' that my mother always sang in a mixture of Yiddish and German – and that I'd taught to Adam when he was tiny. Had I started to sing or had the man in front? I didn't know. My senses were clouded by too great a wish for life.

When the hangman pulled the chair out from under my feet, I tried to hold my breath, but the taut heaviness of my own weight squeezed the air from me. Choking, I pulled at the ropes binding my hands, but the pressure drawing me down was too greedy.

And then the pain was gone. I found myself standing at the front of the crowd, next to the bent-backed man who had held me with his eyes. I watched my body swinging. And yet, looking down, I saw my own legs. I stepped my fingers across my cheeks and nose and lips, like a blind man reading a face.

I wasn't who I'd been. And I was in two places at once. And no one could see me.

But I wasn't scared. I felt as though all of the forward motion of the earth had ceased; that I'd stopped hurtling through my life.

But, of course, it was *life* that had stopped hurtling through *me*.

When I understood what had happened, I took a first step towards the front gate of the camp. And fell on my face. My nose and mouth pushed half a foot through the ground, into what felt like cold clay.

And yet when I picked myself up, I saw that I'd left no imprint in the earth.

Imagine a landscape continually sliding away from you – men and barracks slipping away into the distance, as though tugged by the horizon.

My first steps left me dizzy, lurching, groping along walls that weren't there. I fell several more times, and on each occasion my hands penetrated several inches into the ground.

After an hour, I'd learned to focus only on objects close to me. What was in the distance I just let slip away. It took my feet and eyes a full two days to adjust to death. Then, I strode out of the camp.

While crossing Lublin, I looked up at a handsome woman leaning out her third-floor window, beating a sisal mat with a broom, and for a moment it seemed as if she could see me. My heart leapt towards hope, but then I realized she was glaring at a skinny white cat pawing some garbage behind me.

When I closed my eyes, each dry thud of the woman's broom took form as a bluish square – one that quickly faded to pale green inside my inner darkness.

That was my first experience of a confusion of sight and sound, but later that day I'd notice that my heartbeat pulsed reddish-orange at the fringes of my vision, and that my breathing – particularly at night – appeared as a white-grey mist.

I headed out of town, northwest, towards Liza's farm.

Sometimes, I believed I could feel the turning of the earth below my feet. And when I grew tired, the cold December air began to shimmer around me, as though made from pearls. It was beautiful – and it made me understand that something of the world's exuberance had remained far beyond the reach of the Nazis all the time I was in the ghetto and the labour camp.

I trudged on for two days and nights by my count. I often felt the urge to lie down, and on occasion I did, but I learned I no longer needed sleep.

I discovered Liza's house empty and abandoned; Izzy was long gone.

On the floor by the potter's wheel was the intricately designed skeleton of a dead mouse – the scaffolding of a life so perfect and unlike our own. Sitting by it, I began to think of Liza and of how quickly everything can be lost.

I realized I had to make the journey back to Warsaw, to where I'd started life.

Perhaps all the dead must go home before they can leave for ever.

CHAPTER 30

As I dictate these words to you, Heniek, I can see a group of twenty-seven Jews from the Łaskarzew ghetto digging a pit in a forest just outside town.

As I was walking back to Warsaw from the labour camp, I'd heard the clanging of their shovels and left the road. They'd already dug a couple of feet down into the hard earth when I reached them.

It was very early in the morning. Birds were arrowing through the trees, and once the fog burned off, we'd probably have a day of sun. Five German soldiers and one German SS commander stood outside the pit, their guns drawn.

After the Jews had excavated another foot of earth, the SS Officer ordered them to go down into the pit. The men, women and children helped one another. A few of them dared to whisper, though they'd been warned not to talk.

A father jumped in before his daughter and raised his arms to summon her forward.

She hesitated. 'Where's Rudy?' she asked; perhaps he was her older brother, or maybe even the family dog.

'Come here, Katarzyna,' her father whispered.

She knelt down, reaching out to him, and he lifted her into his arms.

He kissed her on the cheek, then again on her lips. He never told her where Rudy was. Instead, he pressed her head gently into his chest so that she could no longer see the soldiers.

Katarzyna was the youngest among them. She looked seven or

eight. She was calm, but twenty-six other hearts were racing, including her father's. I knew that from the way they looked up at the soldiers.

The SS Officer's order came as a surprise. As did the hail of bullets.

The Jews in the pit weren't yet ready. And I wasn't either. But whoever is?

The German soldiers used automatic rifles. Katarzyna's father fell right away. The girl spilled out of his arms.

Several people screamed and kept screaming. But not for long.

Katarzyna's father died immediately, as best I could tell.

The girl didn't. I stood at the rim of the pit and looked down at her. One bullet had hit her in the shoulder, another in the leg.

For several more minutes she continued breathing, though her eyes were closed. *She'll bleed to death*, I thought. But I was wrong.

By the time the Germans picked up their shovels all but two of the Jews were dead, though most of the twenty-seven bodies had become tangled and I can't swear that they were the only ones left alive.

Besides Katarzyna, the only other person who showed signs of life was a young man with a shaved head and bright blue eyes, in his twenties I'd guess. He was groaning and trying to sit up.

The German soldiers shovelled soil on top of him and Katarzyna, and kept shovelling until I could see nothing more of either of them.

Why am I telling you a story you'd prefer not to hear, Heniek? Because one of the things it proves is an essential truth that you may not yet have understood: we can never return to the Before Time.

We must create a new calendar, one that begins in 1939, when we were walled inside.

It is now Year Two in our struggle to keep our shadows from vanishing.

I lost what I loved most, and with it, my second chance. Not unusual, of course; before this struggle is over, the best among us will have been killed, imprisoned or exiled. Those left alive will be the cowards and collaborators – the tiny, fearful men who worship darkness and call it the sun. They will live to a ripe old age. Their faces will pucker and their hair will fall out, and they won't even remember their own birthdate, and yet they will recall the days when they fought for the Fatherland in fine-edged detail and with proud fondness, as if a rousing Wagner fanfare were always playing in the background. Because they were young and ruled the world for a few brief years.

They will tell their children and grandchildren – and anyone else who dares to ask – that they had no choice but to work for the Nazis, though they were never Party members . . .

Caligula will even tell little Martin and Angela – his beloved grandchildren – that he worked hard to save the Jews in his care.

And little Martin and Angela will believe him.

But you and I, Heniek, we know how it was. And our understanding means everything to me now, because it means I can stop telling my story. And I can let you put down your pen.

We all want to be listened to – to feel we matter. We want to be able to tell the story of our life without being interrupted or judged, or asked to get to the point.

Freud and Chekhov, Jung and Dickens would all agree with me. I know it. And that is why they would understand why I've told you about my life the way I have.

'The worst that can happen is that the Nazis will shoot us,' Izzy once told me.

How many of us are able to live our lives knowing that there are far more terrible things than dying with a German bullet in your chest or a noose around your neck?

Those who can't will always hate those of us who can. We know that now, you and I.

If you make it out of here, Heniek, then remember this: beware of men who see no mystery when they look in the mirror.

CHAPTER 31

'What'll you do now that we've finished your story?' Heniek asked me.

We had spent the last two days editing the manuscript and were seated on his couch. He was putting a slice of boiled onion onto a wedge of black bread.

'I'll wait around Warsaw,' I replied.

'For what?'

'For Adam and Stefa. I made it back home, so maybe they will too.'

'Listen, Erik, don't get your hopes up,' Heniek told me. 'If they haven't come back by now . . .'

'Still, where would I go? And I can't bear the thought of Adam not finding me here if he makes it home. Though there is one thing you can do for me.'

Heniek grinned; he'd known this was coming since I first started dictating to him.

'All right, what is it you want?' he asked, amused – but also eager to help.

'Go to my apartment across the street and get Freud's *The Interpretation of Dreams* from the bookshelves. It should still be there. Then bring it here.'

'What if the apartment is locked?' Heniek asked.

'Get the building supervisor to open it for you. Tell him you need to return a book to the previous owner.'

Heniek returned a few minutes later with the book in his hand.

'Open it,' I told him, excited by the chance to help him.

'What do we have here?' Heniek asked with merry surprise on spotting Hannah's ruby earrings.

He lifted them out and held one up to his ear. 'What do you think?' he questioned. He was grinning with delight.

'I've seen worse,' I told him dryly.

He sat down beside me again. 'So what do you want me to do with them?' he asked.

'I want you to sell them and get money for bribes. I want you to leave the ghetto.'

He shook his head. 'I don't know if I—'

'Listen,' I interrupted harshly, 'if you don't make it out soon, then you won't survive.'

'So, our neighbourhood *ibbur* can see the future now?' he asked, trying to use humour to mollify me.

'Heniek, the kids that Lanik murdered . . . I no longer think that it's mad to regard Adam's death and the fate of all the Jews as linked. The Nazis want our children dead because they want to take our future away from us. I see that now – as clearly as I see you. So I don't need a crystal ball to know that when the Germans run out of patience, everyone here will be packed into cattle cars and deposited at a labour camp – or marched out of town to dig their own graves in a nearby forest.'

'But if I left, where would I go?' he questioned.

'I don't know. But surely you've got an old friend or two on the outside.'

'Maybe,' Heniek said, but I could see he meant *no*.

'Look, you think I've come for a reason. Maybe it's to save you.'

'But maybe not.'

'If you need a better reason than your own life, then go and find Izzy and Liesel for me. Tell them how I died. Say that you were in the camp when I was hanged. Tell them I was ready to go. Kiss them for me and assure them that I met death with my hands in my pockets, that I wasn't scared.★

★ *Erik asked me to put down my pen here, but we continued to converse for another minute at my kitchen table, and I include what we said to each other, this time, from my point of view:*

'But what you've just said isn't true,' I insisted. 'You wanted to live. You told me so!' I spoke desperately because I didn't want him to send me away.

'Yes, you're right,' Erik agreed. 'Despite everything, I wanted a chance to go on. It was silly.'

'Don't you dare be ashamed of wanting to stay alive!' I yelled.

Erik was quiet for a long time after that, but then, breathing deeply – as though summoning all his resolve – he reached slowly across to me and took my hand.

I could feel him – the roughness of his skin and warmth of his life. And it wasn't painful.

Both of us were shocked. And reduced by gratitude to what was essential – two men acknowledging that nothing now could hold them apart. Not even their bodies.

I stood up and embraced him hard, and he hugged me back.

When we sat down again, Erik looked at me for a long time, and deeply, and I knew he was thinking that I understood him, and even more importantly, that I loved him, which was why, I think, he was able to stop telling me his story. And maybe it was why, too, I was able to leave the ghetto.

POSTSCRIPT

by Heniek Corben

I took Erik's advice and fled our island.

His parting words to me were, 'Say a kaddish for me if you ever make it to the labour camp where I died.'

'But you don't believe in God!' I exclaimed.

'True, but you do!' he replied, flashing a mischievous smile. Then he fixed me with a grave look. 'And one more thing, Heniek. After the Germans lose, they'll want us to forget all that has happened. One person – just remember one! – and you will have foiled their plans.'

My last memory of Erik: he is standing on the rooftop of Stefa's building, raising a hand to hail me and smiling. Was he aware that he had those bamboo arms he used to notice on all of us?

It was a blessing that he didn't realize how far he'd fallen. And that he didn't know that the stench of decay he often smelled was his own.

I thought he'd soon leave the roof and let me get on my way alone, but every time I turned, he was still waving to me.

Two weeks later, I reached a boyhood friend's house in Vilnius, but it was too risky to go any further. I'll call my friend Johann, though that's not his real name; I wouldn't want anyone to be able to identify his children or grandchildren, since they might one day suffer reprisals for his having hidden a Jew.

Johann owned a small grocery and lived alone in big old draughty house on the outskirts of town; his children were already grown and his wife was dead. I stayed for nearly two years with him. I never went outside. During

312

the day, I mostly read novels and listened to the news on the radio. In the evenings, the two of us played backgammon, listened to symphonies on his Victrola and discussed how the war was going.

Johann buried Erik Cohen's manuscript in his back garden, underneath a rosebush. I'd begun calling it The Warsaw Anagrams *by then, because Erik had told me that that was his working title.*

The Nazis discovered my hiding place on 7 October 1943, while Johann was at his grocery. They took me to a local prison. A week later, they sent me to the Stutthof labour camp.

Eighty-three pounds.

When the Soviets liberated the camp in late May 1945, that's what I weighed. My arms weren't bamboo; they were fishing rods!

Dysentery had turned me inside out by then and I was in the infirmary.

By the time I saw my first Soviet soldier, Stutthof was nearly empty, since the Germans had evacuated most of the internees weeks before, marching them towards more secure territory and leaving only the sick behind.

In a way, I came back from the dead, too — as a ghost haunting his own life.

I've always believed I survived because of meeting Erik and taking down his story. It's the only answer I have for why I am here and six million others are not. I'm aware that my explanation doesn't make logical sense, but we all know by now that logic is not God's strong point.

As soon as I had the strength, I made my way back to Johann's house and dug up The Warsaw Anagrams. *I learned from neighbours that he'd been executed the evening I'd been captured.*

Lately, I've begun to cling to my memories of Johann when I begin to believe what the Nazis tried to prove to us all — that anyone can be made to betray those they love.

I moved back to Warsaw and opened a printing house again. Occasionally, I'd show The Warsaw Anagrams *to the people I trusted, but Christian friends didn't want to read about what the Nazis and their Polish helpers* had done to their one-time neighbours, and the handful of Jews who'd returned were too fragile to revisit the past.

Erik and I wrote his story and it helps me pass my days easier knowing that we did it together. And I think the very act of reading is important – it means we have a chance to participate in a culture that the Nazis couldn't kill.

Knowing you have done one good thing – no matter how small – is a comfort that no one can take away.

I like the tingling in my fingertips when I choose the type for the books I print. I like to have ink stains all over my hands. I like to invent words for the new language Erik wanted us to have.

Herzsterben – the death one feels in one's chest on pushing away a starving beggar.

I try to live without expectations. I try to accept people as they are. I try to celebrate waking up every morning.

Zunfargangmeyvn – a connoisseur of sunsets; someone who has learned to savour what others take for granted.

And I try to live in a world where the most soft-spoken people win all the arguments.

Noc die Zweite.

The name of my dog. He's a wiry dachshund who sleeps in my bed, his snout next to mine, and his snoring eases me into my dreams.

I try never to go to sleep without him. Too many memories await me if I enter the darkness alone.

Like almost everything else in the Warsaw ghetto, Stefa's apartment house was blown up by the Nazis during the Ghetto Uprising of April 1943, then levelled by the Russians when they took control of the city. All those rutted old streets – and all we had suffered – were gone. Except inside our heads.

Some day, weeds and trees will have covered up all the rubble. And after that, when the developers have enough złoty, buildings will go up – even steel and glass hotels with fountains in the lobby. Tourists will spread their *gaze over an urban landscape being born again, and they will whisper to their children,* Hundreds of thousands of Jews were imprisoned here for years, *but the kids will see only the maze of construction in front of their eyes and an army of helmet workers scurrying back and forth. They'll ask if they can go swimming now in their hotel pool.*

And why shouldn't they?

Those who feel guiltiest will try to make us doubt the existence of all the bones that lie buried under the Polish topsoil and all the ash scattered through the Polish forests.

A walnut tree that was two feet high. Starting again like the rest of us.

An old man passing in the street spotted me staring at the spindly trunk and identified it. I'd thought it was a hazel. 'No, it's definitely a walnut,' he told me, and he smiled at me as if it was a good omen.

I guess we'll know if he's right when we see the kind of nuts it gives us, five or ten years from now. Sometimes we need to wait a long time to know the meaning of what's happening right at this very second.

I found the walnut tree growing out of the earthen pit where the courtyard of Stefa's building had been.

I looked for Erik all over the city, but I never found him. How long must ibburs *wander the earth? I've asked learned rabbis from Paris, Marseille and Istanbul, but none could tell me. 'Their time may not be like ours,' one of them explained to me, but I already knew that.*

I like to think that Erik found Adam and Stefa, and during the easy days of summer, when the high, midday sun turns the rooftops to gold, I can almost convince myself that he must have. At night, however, when I'm listening to the rise and fall of Noc's breathing, and beyond him to the loose web of silence that means that he and I are alone in a city that was once mine and no longer is, I trust only loneliness. I'm not much good at happy endings, just as Erik sensed.

While reading about the death camps a few years ago, I stumbled upon the identity of the official at Buchenwald to whom Rolf Lanik must have given his 'gift' of skin taken from Adam, Anna and Georg: Ilse Koch, wife of the commandant of the Buchenwald camp, Karl Otto Koch. In her trial for murder in 1951, German prosecutors revealed that she had made keepsakes – including lampshades – out of the skin of prisoners. Apparently, she was particularly fascinated by distinctive tattoos and often had men killed and their skin tanned so that she could display them in her home.

Lanik's effort to win Ilse Koch's gratitude does not seem to have won him the transfer to Buchenwald that he coveted, however; there is no record of his ever having served at that camp, which was overseen by Karl Otto Koch from July 1937 to September of 1941, when he and his notorious wife moved to the Majdanek camp.

Was it really Rabbi Kolmosin – the much-feared mystic Erik met in the Lipowa Street Labour Camp – who caused him to return as an ibbur? That is indeed what he led me to believe, though he was never sure. And yet I sometimes think that Erik may not have been entirely honest with me – that he may have had more to do with his unusual destiny than he was prepared to admit. After all, there were times when he seemed to let it slip that he was not the confirmed atheist he claimed, and that, at the very least, he knew about some traditional Jewish mystical practices. For instance, just after Stefa's suicide, he chanted the names of everyone he'd ever loved until he lost his voice. Would a secular Jew really have made that effort? Additionally, Erik made it clear to me that he came to believe in the magical efficacy of names – a central tenet of kabbalah. After re-reading The Warsaw Anagrams *on numerous occasions over the last few years, I have been forced to consider – though this remains just a speculation – whether Erik worked with Rabbi Kolmosin or some other unnamed sage in the labour camp in order to bring about his own return from the dead. As to why he wouldn't have admitted this to me, there is a strong Jewish tradition that forbids such arcane and dangerous practices, and I suspect that he may have feared my judgement – or the judgement of any god he might have begun to believe in.*

I mention this because I desperately want to do justice to Erik as the complex human being that I came to know, especially because it was he who gave me back a reason to live. But I must admit that the how of his reappearance among the living is no longer very important to me. Now that we know the full scope of the Nazi genocide — that the Germans almost succeeded in annihilating us — it's only the why of his return that I still speculate about.

And, of course, I still wonder about the people whom he describes in The Warsaw Anagrams.

It was Dawid Engal, the superintendent of the building where Erik lived in the ghetto, who was able to tell me what happened to several of them. In the Before Time, he had been a professor of Polish literature at the University of Warsaw, and a colleague of his there was able to tell me that he emigrated to Brooklyn just after the war and found employment as a German teacher at Lafayette High School. We began corresponding during the summer of 1949.

Engal confirmed to me that Mikael Tengmann had indeed been killed shortly after Erik and Izzy's escape from the ghetto. He told me that the physician's body had been discarded one evening outside the front door of the Nozyk Synagogue. The rumour that Engal had heard was that bruises on Tengmann's neck indicated that he had been strangled.

In response to my questions about Erik's friends and neighbours, the professor added that the bakery in the courtyard where Ewa worked was shut down by the Nazis in July 1942. Shortly after that, Ziv purchased a pistol on the black market and joined the Jewish Combat Organization, telling everyone he would never permit the Germans to catch him alive. I have since discovered that, along with most of the members of that fighting force, he very likely died in the Ghetto Uprising, which began in January of 1943.

Ewa and Helena disappeared around the time the bakery was closed, and Professor Engal lost contact with them. In February 1952, however, the American Joint Distribution Committee was able to supply me with more information. Writing to me in Yiddish from New York, a researcher for that relief organization informed me that Ewa and Helena had been on the *transport that left for Treblinka on 3 August 1942. They were gassed on arrival. My correspondent added that Rowy Klaus was transported to Treblinka several days later. From a camp survivor I later met while visiting Łódź, I learned that the young musician played violin in the camp orchestra that summer, but in the autumn he became ill with tuberculosis and was sent to the gas chamber.*

Through my research, I have also learned that Zachariah Manberg – the little acrobat whom Erik hoped to save – managed to go into hiding with his mother and sister in Christian Warsaw in December 1942. Shortly after liberation, they moved to Canada. Zachariah is currently enrolled as a law student at the University of Toronto and we have established a correspondence.

I never learned whether Bina Minchenberg or Benjamin Schrei survived. They have vanished, like so many others.

Izzy was the person I most wanted to find out about, but I was unable to discover anything about his whereabouts – even if he had survived. Times were hard in Poland and it was impossible for me to travel to France to pursue my investigations. It took me years to accumulate enough savings and obtain the necessary papers from our Communist government. Finally, in the summer of 1953, I received authorization. Realizing that my wallet was as full as it was ever likely to get, I packed a bag and left.

Unfortunately, I didn't find his sons at the address in Boulogne-Billancourt that Erik had given me. By then, I had learned that Erik had made an anagram of Izzy's surname, which was not Nowak but Kowan. I located two Kowan families in Paris, but they weren't Polish Jews and they had no relatives who were watchmakers from Warsaw.

To protect his old friend, Erik must have lied to me about Boulogne-Billancourt. Izzy's sons were probably living in some other Paris suburb or elsewhere in France. I wished I had asked him to give me Louis' full name – and made him swear to me that it wasn't an anagram.

Shortly after my hunt through Paris for Izzy, I was able to locate Irene's mother, Sylvie Lanik, in Bordeaux. When we met, however, she refused to tell me anything about her daughter except to say that she was alive and well, and living in Switzerland. Irene bore some responsibility for her stepfather's death, of course, and though more than a decade had passed since his murder, Mrs Lanik may have still feared her daughter's arrest.

In August 1953, after my travels around France, I caught a boat to Cyprus and went on to Izmir by freighter. By then, I had learned that Erik's wife Hannah had had Sephardic cousins named Zarco. I questioned three members of the family about Erik's daughter Liesel, and I talked to about a dozen other Izmir Jews, but no one admitted knowing her. On one occasion, while speaking with her second cousin Abraham Zarco, I had the feeling that his denial wasn't entirely genuine, but all my attempts to win his confidence proved useless. Maybe Liesel didn't wish to be found. Or perhaps the family wanted nothing to do with her because of her relationship with Petrina.

My most recent find is Jaśmin Makinska. Only three months ago, I learned that she was living in England, where she had emigrated shortly after the war. To my great joy, I received a reply to my letter to her about a month ago. She told me that she was living near Weymouth, in a two-room cottage by the sea.

Jaśmin confirmed that she drove Erik and Izzy to Liza's farm in March 1941, and that her sister was murdered by the SS when Erik was captured on 7 July.

Izzy fled on foot late that same afternoon, she told me. He managed to telephone her from a nearby town and give her the terrible news about Liza.

Jaśmin received one letter from Izzy, mailed three months later from Istanbul. He had made it there by freighter from Odessa, just as he and Erik had planned, and he would soon be on his way to Marseille. He was in excellent spirits and had already received a friendly letter from his old friend Louis, though he was full of remorse over Liza's death and without much hope for Erik.

'Izzy told me that he would write again when he was settled in the south of France, but I never received another word from him. The war had spread by then, and I suspect that his letters simply never made it to Warsaw.

After I moved to England, he had no way of finding me — and there was no way I could locate him either.'

I expect that Izzy, his sons and Louis may be living in or around Marseille. I shall do my best to find them.

Jaśmin promises not to give up searching for him, as well, though she also says that she'll never set foot in Continental Europe again.

*

On the way home from Izmir, I stopped in Lublin and said a kaddish for Erik outside the Lipowa Street camp. And for all the other heroic friends of ours who were long gone, especially Johann, who had given up his life for me.

Seeing the muddy clearing where Erik had been hanged and hearing my trembling voice undid me, however. I felt as if I were pulling my existence out of an emptiness so great that everything I saw and felt was only an illusion.

I stayed just long enough to intone an 'El Male Rachamim' for Erik's soul and then fled, though turning away from where he'd been murdered made me feel as though I was leaving behind the best part of myself.

I think of Erik every day of my life. I try to remember the dead in all their uniqueness, as he would have wanted.

The autobiography of the Jews is still being written. That is our victory. And I believe now that Erik's deepest hope was for The Warsaw Anagrams to serve as his contribution to it. I am convinced, in fact, that that was why he returned as an ibbur.

Heniek Corben
Warsaw, 3 Kislev, 5715 (28 November 1954)

GLOSSARY

(all words are in Yiddish except where otherwise indicated)

Alter kacker – Literally, 'old shitter', but with the meaning of 'old fart'.

Brenen zol er! – 'May he burn in hell'; a common curse.

Challah – A yeast-leavened egg bread, usually braided, traditionally eaten on the Sabbath.

Der shoyte ben pikholtz – 'The idiot son of a woodpecker'; a traditional epithet.

Dreidl – a four-sided top inscribed with the Hebrew letters נ ג ה and ש, which together form the acronym for נס גדול היה שם (a great miracle happened there).

Ech – A groan or exclamation of displeasure or disparagement.

'El Male Rachamim' – Hebrew prayer for the repose of the soul of the departed.

Festina lente – Latin for 'hurry slowly'.

Flor – German word for the gauze or crepe used in women's clothing and in veils.

Gehenna – Hebrew word for hell, used commonly in Jewish folktales and kabbalistic literature.

Gołąbki – Polish for stuffed cabbage leaves; part of the country's traditional cuisine.

Golem – Hebrew: גלום. In Jewish folklore and mystical traditions, a golem is an animated being created entirely from inanimate matter. The most famous story of such a creature involves Rabbi

Judah Loew of Prague, who was said to have created a golem to
defend the Jewish ghetto from anti-Semitic attacks.

Gottenyu – My God!

Goy – Non-Jewish person, gentile.

Goyim – The plural of Goy.

Hak mir nisht ken tshaynik! – Literally, 'Don't knock me a teakettle,'
but with the meaning, 'Stop rattling on and on with that endless
chatter!'

Hänschen klein – Little Hans in German.

Hatikvah – An anthem written by Naphtali Herz Imber, a Galician
Jew, who moved to Palestine in the 1880s. The Hebrew title
means 'The Hope'.

Hilfe – 'Help' in German.

Ibbur – Hebrew word for ghost, spirit or spectre.

Kaddish – The Jewish prayer of mourning.

Katshkele – Little duck.

Levone – Moon.

Linka – 'String' in Polish.

Macher – Important person or big shot.

Mazel tov – Of Hebrew origin, an expression that means 'I'm
thrilled for your good fortune', 'Good for you' or simply
'Congratulations!'

Meshugene – Crazy.

Meiskeit – Very ugly person, sometimes used with affection, as when
applied to a child so ugly only its mother could love it.

Mitzvah – Hebrew word for commandment. It generally refers any
one to the 613 duties of each and every Jew, as enumerated in the
Torah. By extension, any good deed.

Noc – 'Night' in Polish.

Noc die Zweite – Night the Second (as the name of a dog in the
text).

Payot – The sidelocks of hair (often ringlets by the temple) worn by
Hasidic Jews and others.

Petzl – pee-pee, as in a young boy's penis. From *putz*, a vulgar term for penis.

Piskorz – 'Small fish' or 'minnow' in Polish.

Reb Yid – A traditional and polite form of address.

Schmaltz – Chicken fat used in cooking.

Schul – School and, by extension, synagogue services.

Sheygets – An elongated pastry stuffed with poppy seeds and glazed with honey. From its resemblance to the uncircumcised member of a *sheygets* – a gentile boy.

Sheyn Vi Di Levone – 'Beautiful is the Moon' (the name of a Yiddish lullaby).

Shiva – The week of mourning for the dead prescribed by Jewish law.

Shmekele – Little penis.

Shtetl – A small Jewish town or village.

Sitra Ahra – The Other Side (from the Aramaic term used in kabbalistic literature to designate the demonic sphere or domain of evil).

Tsibele – Onion.

Tzitzit – Hebrew word for the tassels or fringes at the corners of a prayer shawl. They are to remind us of the commandments of Deuteronomy 22:12 and Numbers 15:37–41.

Ver mir di kapore – Literally, 'become my sacrificial hen' and by extension, 'drop dead!' An expression taken from the religious practice in which a sacrificial chicken (*kapore-hun*) is waved around the head of a Jew on the eve of *Yom Kippur* (the Day of Atonement) and then slaughtered as a 'scapegoat' for the sins of the chicken's owner.

Żydóweczka – Little Jew-girl in Polish.

ILHA TERESA

RICHARD ZIMLER was born in Roslyn Heights, New York, and studied journalism at Stanford University. He has published eight novels over the last fifteen years, including the famous *The Last Kabbalist of Lisbon*. They have been translated into twenty-two languages and have been bestsellers in twelve countries. He has won numerous prizes for his work, and is a regular contributor to the *Los Angeles Times Book Review*.

WWW.ZIMLER.COM

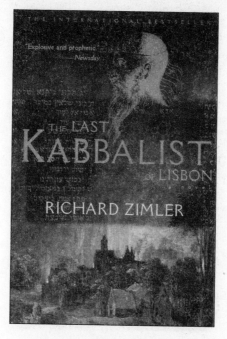

The Last Kabbalist of Lisbon
RICHARD ZIMLER
PAPERBACK
978-1-58567-022-7

PRAISE FOR *THE LAST KABBALIST OF LISBON*

"You won't regret spending a few hours with this book ... a
moody, tightly constructed historical thriller that is both
entertaining and instructive."
—Richard Bernstein, *The New York Times*

"Drenched in atmosphere and period detail ... [Zimler]
does succeed in conveying the surrealistic nightmare of being
a Jew in the age of the Inquisition"
—*The Wall Street Journal*

"Zimler's central thesis is explosive and prophetic. It ought
to be read as the reverse of Philip Roth's diasporism as
explained in *Operation Shylock*."—*Newsday*

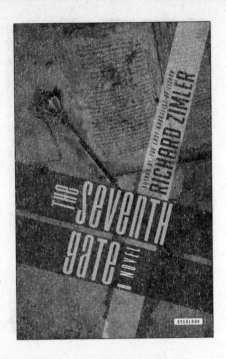

The Seventh Gate
RICHARD ZIMLER
HARDCOVER
978-1-59020-713-0

PRAISE FOR THE WORK OF RICHARD ZIMLER

"A gripping, heartbreaking, and beautiful thriller…unforgettable,
poetic, and original."
—Simon Sebag Montefiore, author of *Young Stalin*

"Brilliantly written, moving and disturbing. . . . Packs
a powerful emotional punch."
—*The Guardian*

"Equal parts riveting, heartbreaking, inspiring, and intelligent."
—*San Francisco Chronicle*

W9-CQT-410

x   Colman, Hila   c.1
                 Sometimes I don't
                 love my mother

DISCARDED LIBRARY
CAL POLY HUMBOLDT

DATE			
JUL 7 '78	FEB 11 '91	OT 9 OKT	
AUG 11 '78		OCT 14 '11	
DEC 22 '78	APR 17 '91		
	May 8, 91		
APR 27 '79	JAN 24 '92		
OCT 17 '80	MAR 23 '92		
NOV 28 '80			
JUN 3 '80	MAR 06 '92		
MAR 12 '82	JAN 7 '94		
APR 2 '82	MAY 28 '93		
DEC 22 '86	APR 10 '96		
OCT 12 '88	AUG 27 2001		
DEC 18 '88			

SUBJECT TO LATE FINE

THE LIBRARY
CHILDREN'S LITERATURE COLLECTION
HUMBOLDT STATE UNIVERSITY
ARCATA, CALIFORNIA 95521

© THE BAKER & TAYLOR CO.

Sometimes I Don't Love My Mother

By the Same Author

After the Wedding
The Amazing Miss Laura
Bride at Eighteen
Chicano Girl
Classmates by Request
Claudia, Where Are You?
Daughter of Discontent
The Family and the Fugitive
Friends and Strangers on Location
The Girl from Puerto Rico
The Happenings at North End School
Mixed-Marriage Daughter

Sometimes I Don't Love My Mother

Hila Colman

William Morrow and Company
New York   1977

Copyright © 1977 by Hila Colman

All rights reserved. No part of this book may be reproduced or utilized in any form or by any means, electronic or mechanical, including photocopying, recording or by any information storage and retrieval system, without permission in writing from the Publisher. Inquiries should be addressed to William Morrow and Company, Inc., 105 Madison Ave., New York, N. Y. 10016.

Printed in the United States of America.

2   3   4   5   6   7   8   9   10

Library of Congress Cataloging in Publication Data

Colman, Hila.
  Sometimes I don't love my mother.

  SUMMARY: When her father dies, seventeen-year-old Dallas must cope not only with her grief, but also with her mother's sudden and total dependence upon her.
  [1. Death—Fiction. 2. Mothers and Daughters—Fiction]
I. Title.
PZ7.C7Sr   [Fic]   77-23445
ISBN 0-688-22121-1
ISBN 0-688-32121-6 lib. bdg.

X
C. 1
                    THE LIBRARY
        CHILDREN'S LITERATURE COLLECTION
            HUMBOLDT STATE UNIVERSITY
              ARCATA, CALIFORNIA 95521

Sometimes I Don't Love My Mother

1

The kitchen was hot and bright from the western sun streaming through the wide windows. Dallas threw her library books on the table and, without thinking, quickly lowered the bamboo blinds. Then she stopped and stood still. Funny that her mother had left them up. "Mom, Mom, are you home?" Dallas's voice echoed through the house, and instinctively she knew that it was empty.

Then she noticed the melting butter on the

kitchen counter, the half-eaten sandwich, and the cup of cold coffee. She must have been in the kitchen at least five minutes before she saw the note. The sun had probably blinded her eyes, but there it was, a piece of yellow paper partly hidden by the sugar bowl on the kitchen table. In her mother's round, almost childish handwriting she read:

Dearest,

I'm at the hospital. Dad taken sick.

Come over if you want to.

Mom

Dallas read the note several times. "Come over if you want to." It took a few minutes for it to sink in. "Dad taken sick." "Dad taken sick." She grabbed her handbag and ran out the door.

The hospital was an easy walk from Dallas's house along a pretty, tree-lined suburban street. Despite the heat of the August afternoon she ran. It was a long, uphill climb to where the hospital sprawled on the summit, overlooking the village. Halfway up Dallas had to slow down to catch her breath. "Dad taken sick." The words made a nagging rhythm in her head. Why hadn't he come home? Why was he in the hospital? Sick didn't sound like an accident. In all her life her father had never been sick except for one bout with the flu several winters before. Just this past Sunday, the day before yesterday, he had beaten her in two sets of tennis, and she had thought, as she did so often, how lucky she was to have a father who was so much fun. He wasn't like some of the fathers she knew, someone who came home from work and settled down to watch the news without paying any attention to his teen-age kids, except to complain about their playing their music too loud, or taking the car, or spending too much money.

Last evening, after supper, he had taken her and her mother to a special place to look for blackberries. He had known exactly where to find them. They had picked a large basketful, and Dallas suddenly remembered that she and her mother had planned to make jam that afternoon. The basket of blackberries had been sitting on the kitchen floor, and she wondered if her mother had had time to buy the sugar.

Outside the hospital, Dallas hesitated. She didn't know whether to go up the steps to the main entrance or to go around to the side where the sign pointed to *Emergency*. She decided on the main entrance, and she went directly to the information desk.

"My father, Mr. Henry Davis, is in the hospital, but I don't know where. He may be in Emergency. I think he came in a few hours ago."

"I'll call Emergency and see if he's there." The woman behind the desk looked at her with sympathetic eyes. "Was there an accident?"

11

"I don't know. I don't think so. My mother's note at home said 'sick.' "

After speaking on the phone for a minute or two, the woman nodded her head. "Yes, he is in Emergency. Go down the first corridor, then take a left, and keep walking. You'll see the desk there."

"Did they say what it is?" Dallas asked.

"No. You'll find out," the woman said kindly.

Dallas walked swiftly down the long corridor. She averted her head when she saw a figure, wrapped in blankets, wheeled out of an elevator on a stretcher.

She hadn't gotten as far as the desk when her mother came running up to her. "Dallas . . . Dallas. . . ." Her mother threw her arms around her and held her close. "It's awful, it's just awful. . . ."

Dallas held on to her mother and tried to quiet her sobs.

"I'm all right. I've really been all right. I'm so glad you're here," her mother sobbed. "I was just going to call the house. . . ."

"I was at the library. Tell me, what happened?" Dallas led her mother to a bench where they could both sit down.

"They called me from his office." Mrs. Davis finally spoke in a quiet voice and looked at her daughter. "He had a heart attack, darling. I almost can't believe it. He's so young. Only forty-one. . . . But that should be in his favor, shouldn't it?" She looked at Dallas pleadingly, asking for reassurance.

12

"I—I guess so." Dallas felt stunned. "How could he have a heart attack? Just like that, out of the blue? He's always been so healthy—"

"I know. And he's done all the right things. . . . I mean he took care of himself, and I took care of him. I thought he'd live to be a hundred. . . ."

"But Mom, he's not going to *die!* Lots of men have heart attacks and go on living. He's strong, and young, and healthy. Mom, he can't die."

"People die, Dallas." Mrs. Davis spoke softly. Her face was stricken with pain, and she closed her eyes.

"What did the doctor say? Where is he now? What are they doing for him? Can I see him?" Dallas asked one question after another, not waiting for answers.

"He's still in the Emergency Room. I think they're going to take him to Intensive Care. The doctor doesn't say anything. He says they're doing everything they can. He's in an oxygen tent. He's unconscious, darling." Her mother gripped her hand hard. "I'm afraid he's in a coma."

"Mom, he's going to be all right. He has to be. He just has to be." Dallas held her mother's hand between her own two, and they sat there, waiting.

They waited throughout the night. At various times the doctor came out to speak to them. Once Dallas persuaded her mother to go out for sandwiches and coffee. Another time Dallas brought up more coffee and sandwiches to the waiting room. Once her mother was allowed to go into the Intensive Care Unit to see her husband and came out looking like death herself. In the early hours of the morning, Dallas begged to be able to see her father.

A nurse led Dallas through long corridors and then into a deadly quiet room. Her father was on a bed flat on his back, enclosed in a transparent tent, with a tube attached to his arm and a machine making a frightening, erratic ticking as it monitored his heartbeat. "Dad, Daddy. . . ." Dallas whispered softly, but the figure on the bed made no response. His eyes were closed and his breathing was hard. Dallas stood as close as she could get, looking at him. She was aching to bend down to kiss him, but she knew she could not. She felt that if she concentrated hard enough he would know that she was there.

In a few minutes the nurse tapped her on the shoulder and said her time was up. Dallas didn't want to go back to her mother. She was afraid that her father was dying, and she wanted to be alone to try to digest the thought. How could a person be alive and well one day, and the next be dying? It was too frightening to grasp. Her father's parents, her grandparents, were healthy and active. How could their son be dying? Old people died, not someone young and strong like her father. . . .

But he did. At twenty minutes past seven in the morning the doctor came into the waiting room. Dallas knew the minute she saw his face what he had come to tell them.

He nodded his head at their questioning faces. "I'm sorry. We did everything we could for him. He wasn't in pain. He died quietly. Do you want to see him?"

Mrs. Davis nodded her head. They followed the doctor down the corridors again. He didn't look any different in death, except that there was no tent or tube or machines. Dallas had never seen a dead person before, and she was almost afraid to look at her father. But he looked exactly the same. His face was still suntanned—she remembered how he had taken off his hat on the tennis court on Sunday, saying he wanted to get more sun—and when she timidly bent down to kiss him, his forehead was warm. Her mother whispered to her, "Darling, do you mind? I'd like to be alone with him for a few minutes."

Dallas squeezed her mother's hand and left her. She felt peculiar that she wasn't crying. She ought to be crying. Instead her throat felt dry and choked up. She sat in the waiting room, wondering what was wrong with her. It was as if she were trying to figure out *what* to feel instead of experiencing the feeling itself. The only thing she felt was stunned.

After a while her mother came to her. Her

mother, all of a sudden, looked very young. She had no makeup on, and her face was pale and drained, but with her bare legs and sandals, short skirt, and hair bleached by the sun and falling to her shoulders, she looked like a kid. She looks like me, Dallas thought, even her figure's almost as good as mine. The only difference is her eyes are brown and mine are blue. . . .

"Dallas!" Then her mother burst into tears, and Dallas felt the tightness in her own throat break, and she was sobbing with her mother. They clung to each other and wept.

Viola Waters, her mother's closest friend, was pouring coffee for the three of them. It was late in the afternoon, and the kitchen counters and refrigerator were filled with casseroles and cakes, tinned hams, fruit, cookies, cheeses, and wine, all food that friends and neighbors had been bringing during the day. "There's enough food here to feed an army," Vi said, sitting down at the kitchen table with Dallas and her mother. She was a round-faced, energetic woman, mother of two sons, one, Victor, who had graduated from high school with Dallas in June, and the other Andy, who was a junior in college.

"I suppose we'll need it," Mrs. Davis murmured. She had sat back and seemed relieved to let her friend and Dallas take care of what had to be done.

Even when the undertaker had arrived and the time came to select a casket, Mrs. Davis had said, "You decide, Dallas. You and Vi. Something very good but simple. I can't even think about it." Dallas had let Vi talk to the undertaker. She didn't want any part of it either and had quietly gone up to her room until he left.

Everyone had been extremely solicitous of Mrs. Davis. Dallas admired the way her mother had held up during the day, keeping herself under control, and breaking down only when her father's partner in their architectural firm had arrived. Then she had clung to him and wept unconsolably. Dallas kept herself busy pouring coffee, serving cake, answering the phone, and a few times she had thought, My mother lost her husband, but no one seems to remember that I've lost my father. She had gone into the bathroom and cried softly to herself, ashamed of her horrid thought. Maybe the loss was worse for her mother, but her father hadn't been just an ordinary father, and no one in the world, not even her mother, knew of the special relationship they had had. She wanted to scream when one neighbor, someone she had never liked anyway, said, "You'll have to take care of your mother now, Dallas. She'll be all alone." She hadn't one word of sympathy for Dallas's loss.

"Is there anyone else that should be called?" Vi asked, consulting the list of names in front of her.

"Bob will meet Hank's parents at the airport," she said, Bob being her husband. "And are you sure you don't want to call your mother?" she asked Mrs. Davis.

Ellen Davis shook her head. "No, I'll call her in a few days. I don't think I can cope with my mother right now."

"You two never did get along, did you? Well, you do what's best for you, Ellen. Your mother'll probably be furious, but don't worry about that now."

"I don't intend to," Mrs. Davis said. "Dallas, is Jennifer going to spend the night here?"

"I'll be glad to stay if you want me to," Vi said before Dallas had a chance to answer.

"No, thank you. You have your family at home. Jennie is such a dear girl, and it will be nice for Dallas."

"I don't need anyone. I'd just as soon be alone, but if you'll feel better. . . ." Jennifer Kinney was Dallas's best friend, but she did want to be alone.

"I think it will be nice to have her here."

Dallas took one sip of her coffee and put it aside. She didn't want another cup of coffee. Abruptly she stood up. "Mom, do you mind if I go out for a little while? I just want a little air. You're not leaving right away, are you, Vi?"

"No, you go ahead. It will do you good. Go for a walk. I'll be here."

Mrs. Davis reached out her hand to Dallas. "Don't be too long, love. I'll worry about you."

Dallas bent down to kiss her mother. "I'll just be a short while."

Dallas was glad that there was no one around when she went outside. It had been a hot day, but now the sky had clouded over and there was a slight breeze. Dallas walked past the carefully kept lawns, the neat clapboard houses, and the gardens blooming with marigolds, petunias, roses, and phlox to the end of the street. There she turned into a narrow dirt path that led through a patch of woods. In these woods her father had shown her, years ago, how to look for mushrooms, had taught her the names of the wild flowers, and, one summer, had helped her build a tree house. She wished the tree house was still there and she could sit in it forever.

She found a clearing and sat on the trunk of a fallen, dead tree, her head cupped in her hands. Her feelings were still too deep and entwined within her to dig out and examine. What she felt was a heavy weight; she had never known that "a heavy heart" was an actual physical feeling. She couldn't imagine life at home without her father. He was the one who had brought vitality into the house. He liked to have people around. He was always suggesting that they ask someone over or go on an outing somewhere. Her mother was more withdrawn, moodier. She didn't like to give parties—she said they made her nervous—and when her parents did have them, her father was the one who did most of the work, with Dallas helping.

But I'm not going to be home this year, Dallas thought. She had been accepted at Dartmouth in New Hampshire and was supposed to leave their Connecticut home in early September. Her heart dropped. She couldn't go away now. The thought struck her like a blow. But I don't want to stay home, I don't want to stay home! When she had gone to visit Dartmouth with her parents, her father had fallen in love with the place. "It's just right for you," he said. "I hope you get in." He had been as excited as she when her acceptance letter arrived.

Dallas started to cry, softly at first and then in loud, body-wrenching sobs. "I'm selfish, thinking of myself. I'm a terrible person, but Daddy, Daddy, what am I going to do?" She felt that her father was close to her here in their woods, and she knew that this clearing was going to be her place. It was where she would come to grieve and to find some comfort in being alone with her thoughts and her feelings, where she could think of her father and herself apart from the rest of the world.

Dallas cried until she felt worn out. She would have liked to stretch out on the moss beside the tree trunk and go to sleep, but wearily she pulled herself up. The sun had come out again from behind the clouds and was lighting up the horizon.

It was low, seeming to touch the treetops in the distance, and Dallas hurried down the path. She had stayed away too long. Her mother would be upset. When Dallas got to the street, she ran the long block to her house.

2

The house was filled with people, as if a party were going on. A long table was laden with food, and some of her mother's and father's friends were drinking cocktails and highballs. Dallas didn't like the sight.

The church ceremony had been right. Their minister knew her father, and he had spoken of him in simple words of affection; he had not delivered an impersonal eulogy the way the minister had at Jennifer's grandfather's funeral, the only other one Dallas had ever attended. Going to the cemetery had been awful. Dallas hated the funeral limousine. "I don't see why we can't go in our own car," she had said. "We just can't," her mother told her. And standing by the graveside had been the worst. The sun was too bright, the day too beautiful. How could they be lowering her father in a box into the ground?

Many people were there, standing around silently, her mother wept hysterically, and Dallas felt alienated from everyone, as if no one knew what was going on, no one knew that they were burying *her* lively, energetic, beautiful father under the earth. Dallas kept thinking, Are they sure he's dead? What if he came out of the coma? What if he woke up and couldn't get out? For a few wild moments she wanted to scream and tell them to stop. Instead, she bit her lips and held a handkerchief up to her face, because she didn't want to watch what they were doing.

Now people were acting as if there hadn't been a funeral at all. The gathering was like one of the big cocktail parties her father liked to give, except that he wasn't there. He wasn't there to mix the drinks, to move among the guests, to ask Dallas to pass around trays of food, to give her his wide grin and say, "Just two glases of wine for you, sweetie. And I saved a plate of shrimp for you in the kitchen. Get it before someone steals it."

Dallas watched Victor Waters, Vi's son, pass a plate of small sandwiches around, handling the larger platter as if he were a professional waiter. Dad would get a kick out of him, Dallas thought. He always said Victor was much better mannered than his older brother Andy. But Dad was dead. He would never see Victor again. Dallas turned away, her eyes flooded with tears.

Her mother looked in a daze, as if she didn't quite know what was going on. She was sitting on the sofa, pretending to listen to what someone next to her was saying, her face white and strained against her black dress. But her eyes kept following Dallas as if she were afraid to lose sight of her for a moment. At one point she asked Dallas to come and sit beside her and gripped her hand tightly. "What are we going to do? What are we going to do without him?" she kept saying. Dallas had no answer for her.

At last the people were leaving. They kissed Dallas and her mother good-bye, there were more tears, and finally the house was quiet, the way Dallas felt it should be. Only her father's parents were left, and they were staying on for a few days. Vi and Jennifer stayed behind too, and they were already busy clearing the rooms of glasses and dishes.

"I'm going to make a fresh pot of coffee," Grandmother Davis said. "You haven't eaten anything all day, Ellen," she said to her daughter-in-law.

"I'm not hungry." But her grandparents and her mother and Vi sat around the kitchen table drinking coffee. Dallas could hear her grandfather ask her mother about money—had her father carried life insurance, were they going to have enough to live on. . . . Dallas didn't want to listen. That kind of talk made her father's death seem too real. She and her mother might have to go on living without him, but she wasn't ready to accept the fact.

"Do you want to go for a walk?" Jennifer asked.

"Yes," Dallas agreed quickly.

"Don't be gone too long," her mother said, and there was a pleading note in her voice that frightened Dallas, but she pushed the unpleasant thought out of her head.

The two girls walked in silence for a few blocks. They had been friends since elementary school, and Dallas, an only child, felt that Jen was as close to her as a sister. In fact, she was closer, because a sister wouldn't have been only a week older than she. They had celebrated their seventeenth birthday together earlier that summer. There was nothing that they didn't tell each other. They could, and often did, talk for hours about themselves, their friends, their parents, about Jen's younger sister and two brothers; they had examined their bodies together when they were first developing, they had gotten sick together when they had eaten two pounds of cherries between them, they had gone out on their first dates together, they had taken a week's bicycling trip together when they were sixteen.

Dallas felt closer to Jen than perhaps anyone else in the world. She thought Jen was beautiful, the better looking of the two of them, but she wasn't jealous. Dallas didn't believe Jen when she told her she was the prettier one. Jen's black hair was thick and curly and she wore it long, her eyes were very dark, and her skin seemed to be tan all year around. She was taller than Dallas and had a full figure. "You're Mother Earth," Dallas teased her, and in a way she was, with her sturdy body and large, capable hands that could make things grow, cook and sew, take out a splinter or handle a hurt kitten.

In contrast, Dallas was smaller, slimmer, more delicate in her looks, her hair light and soft and silky, her feet and hands long and narrow, her skin, even with her tan, more honey-colored than brown. But in her own way she was as strong and capable as Jen. She could outrun her, climb a tree faster, and beat her at tennis consistently. They gave to each other without counting, their friendship cemented by honesty and an ability for each to be herself and to laugh away disagreements whenever they arose.

"Have you thought at all about going away?" Jen asked, when they turned at the end of their street into another road.

"You mean going to college? I've been thinking about it as much as I can think about *anything* now. I just can't believe it happened. It was all so fast. I can't get it through my head that he's dead."

"I know. It's awful. It seems so unfair. Your family always seemed so close. I mean your father was different. You—I—could talk to him, not like he was a parent. I don't see how your mother can bear it. She seemed so dependent on him. You know, we've talked about it, the way she always let him decide everything, as if she wanted to stay a kid."

"I know. Jen, I'm scared. My father would want me to go to Dartmouth, I'm certain he would. He was so happy when I was accepted, right? But how can I leave her? She looks at me now as if I'm all she has in the world, and I guess I am. I can't go, but—I wouldn't say this to another soul—I'm scared stiff of staying home. I don't think I can bear living alone in that house with my mother. Not that I don't love her, I do, but I have an awful feeling I'll be with her for the rest of my life. I'll be like that Miss Jackson. She must be around sixty now, and what's her life been? Just living in that house taking care of her mother, who will live to be a hundred and fifty. She must be nearly ninety now, and she still calls Miss Jackson her dear little girl."

Jen's dark eyes looked directly into Dallas's blue ones. "You've got to go. You just have to. You can't replace your father for your mother. You have to live your own life, and so does she. Your mother has a lot of friends here in Millstone, and maybe she's not as helpless as she seems. I mean, when she could depend on your father, she did, but I think she's stronger than you think she is. You've got to go."

"I knew that's what you'd say, and I guess I wanted to hear you say it. But I don't think I can leave. I feel awful even worrying about myself now. Oh, God, why did this have to happen? I can't bear it, I can't. . . ." Dallas broke into sobs and cried with her friend's arms around her.

When they returned to Dallas's house, Mrs. Davis was lying down in her bedroom. "I don't know if she's sleeping, but go in and see," her grandmother told her. "She'll want to know that you're back. She kept wondering where you were for so long."

"I didn't think we were gone long. We didn't go far."

"I know. But she's upset now. Come back here afterward." Her grandmother patted the sofa seat beside her. "Dad and I want to talk to you."

Dallas tiptoed into her mother's room, but her mother opened her eyes immediately. "Is that you? I was worried. Stay close, darling. I need you so much now."

"I know." Dallas bent down and kissed her mother's forehead. "I'm not going anywhere. Don't worry. Try and go to sleep. You need it."

"I'll try." She spoke like an obedient little child.

Back in the living room Dallas sat down beside her grandmother. Her grandfather sat opposite, in the big rocking chair, her father's favorite chair. He was the only one she didn't mind having sit in that chair.

"We've been talking about you, Dad and I," her grandmother said. "It's early to make plans, but we have to leave tomorrow, so this is the only time. Have you thought about what you're going to do?"

"Not really. You mean about college? I don't know. Daddy really wanted me to go to Dartmouth, but I don't even know if there's money for that."

"Thank God, I don't think you'll have to worry too much about money right now. Your father carried a lot of life insurance. You're not going to be rich, but you and your mother should manage all right," her grandfather said. "The mortgage on the house is covered by insurance, and after a while your mother should find a job. There is money put aside for your education, and your mother will get a social-security allowance for a dependent child. That's not the immediate problem."

Dallas looked from one to the other. "I know. I know what you want to tell me. I shouldn't go away."

"We thought that if you waited a year. You're still very young. You could stay home this year and go away next fall. By time time your mother will be much better than she is now. It's been a terrible shock for her . . . for you too, but you're young and still have your own life ahead of you." Her grandmother was looking at her sympathetically, dabbing her eyes now wet with tears. "It's awful for all of us. I never thought we'd outlive our son. . . ."

"You're right. I know you're right." Dallas could not tell them of the misgivings and fears she had. "I'll stay home. I had pretty much decided that myself."

"You're a lovely girl," her grandmother said. "You're especially precious to all of us now."

"Don't burden the girl," her grandfather said, with some of her father's wry humor and his same crinkly smile. "She doesn't need three doting parents hovering over her. Let the kid breathe."

Dallas gave her grandfather a grateful hug.

3

Dallas turned on her record player as loud as she could. She couldn't stand the quiet of the house. But after a few minutes she turned it off. Music didn't suit her mood. She didn't know what would. Dallas felt as though she were living in a morgue. The word *morgue* made her think of death and brought everything flooding back again. No matter how hard she tried to think of other things, she kept coming back to death, because the house was so quiet, so very still.

Vi Waters had warned her. "A few weeks from now," she said, during the busy first week after Dallas's father had died, when people kept filling the house with food and visits, "a few weeks from now it's going to be worse. When things quiet down will be the hardest part."

But Vi hadn't told her when the depression would let up, when the heaviness and the quiet were going to slacken. Dallas didn't think it ever would. For the first time in her life, she realized, she had nothing to do. Summer vacations had been different. Sometimes she had worked, and there were always some friends free to swim or play tennis. But now everyone was busy doing something. Jennifer was going to secretarial school, the boys and girls who hadn't gone away to college were working or looking for jobs, and Vic Waters and some of the others were going to a nearby community college. Staying home was all right for a while, sleeping late and being lazy, but the thought of the long winter ahead frightened Dallas. There had been times when she longed to have time to herself, but now she felt as if her life had been put into a deep freeze.

Her mother sat silently in the house not wanting to do anything or to see anyone. Dallas wondered if her being there was really any help, and yet she felt that discussing her own problem with her mother would be an intrusion.

Dallas went into the kitchen where her mother was having a cup of coffee. It was ten o'clock in the morning, and her mother had been sitting there since breakfast. She'd probably drunk five or six cups of coffee by now. No wonder she didn't sleep at night, drinking all that coffee all day long.

"Why don't you call up someone?" Dallas suggested. "Call up Vi. I'm sure she'd love to have you come over there for dinner tonight."

"I don't feel like it," Mrs. Davis said. "I couldn't bear it. To see her and Bob together, with their kids. They're such a mushy family. No matter who's around, Bob kisses Vi as if they were still on their honeymoon. I just can't bear to see our old friends, to see everyone in couples. The whole world goes two by two."

"But Mom, you need your friends now, more than ever. They can help you. That's what friends are for."

"I know. That's what everyone says. I guess I'm peculiar. I'd rather be alone. But you don't have to be. I feel awful having you stay home with me this way. You should have gone away. It's not fair to you. . . ."

"I'm okay, Mom. I stayed home because I wanted to. But maybe I will go out tonight, if you don't mind. I'll call up Jen and see what's going on."

"Dallas. . . ." Her mother spoke hesitatingly. "Dallas, why don't you ask some of your friends over here? I'd like that. Your friends would be cheerful."

Dallas was going to say, but I wanted to get out

of the house, and then she realized that her mother didn't want to stay alone. Her mother needed her physical presence. That was what made Dallas feel a prisoner in her own house. If she were doing something useful, she would feel different, but her mother seemed anxious to know that she was there all the time. She didn't dare suggest that she look for a job or even take some courses. Each time she looked at her mother's strained, taut face, she knew that she couldn't say a word. After all, if her mother wanted her close by, that was where she'd have to be.

"You're sure you wouldn't mind? I mean they'll play records and make a lot of noise, and you may want to rest."

"I do nothing but rest. No, I'd like it. You call them up, and then we can go out and buy some food and soda and beer, I suppose. The boys drink beer, don't they?"

"I wasn't thinking of a party, Mom. I was just going to ask a couple of kids over."

"It doesn't have to be a party. But you'll need some snacks and something to drink. We could get some frozen pizzas too." Her mother's face was more animated than Dallas had seen it in the month since her father had died.

"I'll see who's around," Dallas said, glad to see her mother take some interest in something.

Jennifer and Vic came, and Ted Bateman and

Nancy Edwards and Sue Prince with her boyfriend, Joel. Dallas and Jen wore long denim skirts, and all the others were in jeans. Mrs. Davis had dressed up for the occasion in a long, purple caftan and eye shadow to match.

Dallas hadn't expected her mother to spend the whole evening with them, but she did. Apparently she was enjoying herself, and Dallas was glad. Everyone had been very considerate of her, and she had talked and even laughed, but now Dallas found herself looking at the big clock over the mantel, thinking it was time that her mother went up to bed. Dallas had brought her record player down from her room, everyone had consumed quantities of potato chips, pretzels, soda, and beer, but somehow the party, if that's what it was, hadn't got off the ground. Her friends acted differently with her mother there. The atmosphere was different, although Dallas couldn't put her finger on why.

Now her mother was sitting on the floor talking animatedly to Victor, whom she always had liked—after all he was her best friend's son—and tonight Dallas was especially glad. In the past month something had sprung up between Dallas and Vic that had not been there before. He had always been one of her crowd, but since her father died he'd been around the house a great deal more than usual.

Without any words between them, Vic had suddenly become more than just a good friend. Somehow when Dallas needed anything done, Vic was around to do it. He had rewired a lamp for her and helped her clean out the garage. Then one gloomy, chilly day she was raking leaves, furious that they kept blowing back across the lawn, when Victor came by. She was close to tears, thinking how her father had always done this job. Then Victor made some remark about her father too, and she burst out crying. Victor simply held her in his arms until she cried herself out. He didn't say anything, but when she lifted her head from against his wooly sweater, she caught an expression on his face that startled her and made her suddenly aware of new feelings. He was no longer just attractive Victor, a dark-eyed boy who was a friend; he was someone who set her heart racing, someone who looked at her with an emotion that held both tenderness and wonder. She quickly disentangled herself from his arms and chattered inconsequentially. Victor stayed to help her with the leaves, and more than once their eyes met with that same quick recognition that their feelings for each other were turning into more than friendship.

"Do you really want me to get it?" Mrs. Davis was saying to Victor.

"Yes, come on. I'll help you find it." He pulled Mrs. Davis to her feet.

"I hope I can. It's way up in the attic someplace. I haven't played it in years."

"Then tonight's the time to start. It just so happens I have some extra guitar strings in case yours are no good."

"You are the handiest young man to have around I ever did know," Mrs. Davis said laughingly.

"You bet."

"Where are you going, Mom?" Dallas called out.

"Victor has persuaded me to get out my guitar. I've probably forgotten how to use it, but someone else can play it if I can't."

"No one forgets how to play a guitar," Ted Bateman said. "You'll remember. It's like riding a bike. You never forget."

"Do you want me to go up and get it?" Dallas asked.

"No, Victor will help me find it."

Dallas thought that her mother and Victor were gone for a long time. She turned on the oven and put in the frozen pizzas. They were sizzling hot, and still her mother hadn't come back down. What am I worrying about? Dallas thought. It's my mother and an eighteen-year-old kid! I only hope she's not showing him all those old baby pictures of me that are up in the attic someplace. In fact, Dallas half hoped that her mother *was* showing him the pictures. When they came down Victor was carrying her mother's guitar, and her mother looked flushed and bright-eyed. "What took you so long? The pizzas are going to get dried up."

"I found an old box of letters up there that I'd forgotten all about. They're from boyfriends of mine when I was around your age, Dallas. I was reading some of them to Victor."

"Pretty hot stuff," Victor said. "Your mother was quite a dame. I don't mean was," he added hastily, "still is."

"Thanks for those kind words," Mrs. Davis said, giving Victor an affectionate pat. Her face clouded over. "I guess one of the things I miss is some male attention. Hank was great about paying compliments. Even if I looked terrible, he made me *feel* attractive."

"Giving you compliments is easy," Victor said.

"Just give me what you have left over from Dallas," Mrs. Davis said, her smile returning.

She sat down and started strumming on the guitar.

"You see, you do remember," Ted said.

"Play something," the others urged.

"I'm no Joan Baez, but I'll try." Mrs. Davis strummed on the guitar for a few minutes, and then in a soft, sweet voice she played and sang an old English folk song.

"That's neat. That's really neat." Dallas and her friends applauded enthusiastically. "Give us some more," they demanded.

Mrs. Davis kept on playing while Dallas and Jen were in the kitchen. "Your mother's pretty good," Jen said to Dallas.

"Yes, she is." Dallas kept her eyes on the pizza she was slicing.

"You having a rough time?" Jen asked.

Dallas looked up for a second and then spoke while she went on cutting. "It hasn't been easy," she mumbled. "Damn." She put the knife down and sucked her finger where she had nicked it. Dallas took a Band-Aid from the kitchen shelf and wound a small strip around her finger. When she looked at Jen, her eyes were brimming with tears. "It's awful. I feel terribly sorry for her, but I feel like a prisoner too. I can't step out of the house without her. And now tonight, spending the *whole* night with us— Jen, do you ever not love your mother?"

Jen's face was serious. "I don't know. I've never thought about it. Sometimes I get mad at her, but I don't think I really stop loving her. . . ."

"Well, that's what worries me. Sometimes I don't love my mother, I think. Wouldn't it be awful to live with her and get to hate her? I never felt that way before, but then I always was closer to my father. Now my mother and I are stuck with each other." Dallas shook her head impatiently. "Forget what I've been saying. I'm just in a bad mood. Forget it."

"Do you have a thing for Victor?" Jen asked.

Dallas gave her a sharp look. "What made you ask?"

"I don't know. You've been talking about him a

lot this past month. Are you upset because—well, because he doesn't feel the same way?"

"No," Dallas blurted out. Then she laughed. "I wasn't going to talk about it, not even to you, because there's nothing really to talk about."

"You two would be great together," Jen said shrewdly.

"Come on, let's bring these pizzas in before they get cold." Dallas picked up one tray and left the other for Jen.

Everyone had left except Jen and Victor. "I'll help you clean up," Jen said.

"I was going to do that," Victor said with a grin. "My mother's been telling me about men washing dishes."

"You picked the right time. There are only a few," Jen told him. Then she whispered to Dallas, "I can take the hint. He wants to be alone with you."

"Fat chance of that around here," Dallas whispered back, eyeing her mother handing glasses to Victor to carry into the kitchen.

"She'll go to bed," Jen answered, and then said good-bye and left.

Dallas thought her mother never would go upstairs. She seemed to find a million excuses to stay downstairs, but Victor cheerfully stayed on too. When Mrs. Davis started yawning, Victor said, "You go on. We'll finish up."

"There's not much to finish," Mrs. Davis said, putting the last glass away on the shelf. "But I guess I *am* tired. I hope I can sleep. It was a nice evening, Dallas. Thank you. We'll have to do this more often. I hope having your mother around isn't a drag, but being with you kids is marvelous for me. You can't imagine what it does. . . ."

"It's our pleasure," Victor said gallantly. "Your guitar and singing made the evening, honest. It isn't as if you were an old lady."

Mrs. Davis kissed Dallas good-night and pulled Victor, who was a full head taller than she, down to give him a kiss too. "Don't stay up too late, kids. Tomorrow's another day."

When they were alone, Victor suggested that they go outside. It was a warm, starlit night, and they went out back to sit in the Davis's wide hammock.

Dallas lay on her back, looking up at the sky. Victor sat beside her, swinging the hammock gently with his foot.

"How are you doing?" he asked her after a while.

"I guess I'm okay. I go up and down. It's not easy."

"Your mother's pretty terrific. She seems to be doing very okay."

"She was tonight. This was a good evening for her."

"Anyway, I'm glad that you're home this year. I mean I'm not glad for the reason that you are," he added hastily, "but just that you are. I'd been thinking about you a lot this summer, but you were going away to college and there didn't seem to be any point to, well, getting involved. I mean I was involved, but I didn't want to do anything about it. Now it's different."

Dallas sat up alongside of him so that the length of their legs stretched out, side by side. "I've been thinking about you too," she said softly. "This last month, since my father died, I've been feeling raw and exposed, but when you were around I was okay. It's funny, isn't it, the way we've known each other for so long, and then all of a sudden something happens?"

"It's not funny, it's good. It's terrific," Victor said.

"I know. But I keep thinking it has something to do with Dad's dying. Losing him has made me take notice, feel things more deeply. He liked you. He'd be glad if he knew; maybe he does someplace. I wish I understood—"

"You don't have to understand," he said, putting his arm around her. "So long as you feel what I feel, that's all that counts. Turn around." Dallas turned her face to him, and he kissed her on her lips, gently at first and then hard, holding her close to him. They sat in the hammock swinging and talking quietly.

"I never expected to fall in love this way," Dallas said after a while. "I thought it would be more thunder and lightning, but I feel so—I don't know

—so right with you. I feel as if I've known all along that this would happen sooner or later."

"I'm glad it happened sooner rather than later," Victor said.

"Hold me close." She clung to him feeling the pain of her loss diminished by the swell of her love for him.

They were still talking when they were startled by a shadowy figure in the kitchen doorway and a voice calling, "Dallas, are you out there?"

Dallas sat up abruptly. "Yes, Mom. Are you okay? Anything the matter?"

"No, not really." She came forward, her bathrobe wrapped around her. "I couldn't sleep, as usual, and you weren't in the house, so I panicked. Oh, it's beautiful out here, isn't it?"

Dallas and Victor stood up. "Yes, it is," Dallas said.

"I guess I'd better be going home," Victor said.

"Don't let me chase you away."

It was a bright night, and Dallas was sure she saw tears in the mother's eyes. "Do you want to sit out here for a while? Maybe you'll get sleepy," Dallas said. She started to follow Victor along the walk to the front of the house and the street.

"I don't think I want to stay here alone," Mrs. Davis said.

"I'll be right back," Dallas called out. She kissed Victor good-night hurriedly.

"I guess she's not as okay as I thought. It must be

pretty rough for her," Victor said sympathetically.
"It is."

Dallas went back to the hammock and sat down beside her mother. "Maybe the hammock will make you sleepy." She swung the hammock back and forth, feeling very sleepy herself and aching to be alone in her bed. She wanted to think about Victor, to think about the evening, to go over their conversation in her mind. . . .

"I don't know what I'd do without you," her mother said, gripping her hand. "I'm afraid I'm being a terrible burden, but I can't stand being alone—not yet. . . . I get this awful panicky feeling. Maybe I'm still in a state of shock, I don't know. Dallas, I'm so sorry. . . ." Her mother started to cry softly. "It was such a nice evening. . . . I enjoy seeing you kids together, but then I feel my own loneliness so much I can't bear it."

"You ought to see more of your own friends. You should invite them over. Honestly Mom, it would do you good."

"Maybe, maybe. . . ."

When Dallas finally did get upstairs to her own bed, after seeing her mother into hers, she wanted to think about Victor and herself, but one sentence she had said to Jen kept coming into her mind: "Sometimes I don't love my mother, I think." The words kept persisting, and she couldn't shake them off. She fell asleep thinking how frail and ghostlike

her mother had looked standing in the back doorway, and yet how strong and firm her grip had been
on Dallas's hand.

4

Ellen Davis leaned over, bending her flat stomach almost in half, to apply soft-pink nail polish to her toenails. Doing so made her think of Hank, who in the early days of their marriage had said, "Never stop taking care of yourself, honey. I like that." She recalled how he had loved her femininity, how he liked to see her wear soft, silky robes in the house, and how he liked to buy her gifts of jewelry and lacey nightgowns.

What in God's name am I doing this for now? she thought to herself. Yet she felt that if she didn't she would be betraying Hank.

"Mom!" Dallas was calling her. "Victor's here for his lesson."

"I'll be down in a couple of minutes. As soon as my nail polish dries." And I brush my hair and put on some makeup, she added to herself. She liked to look pretty for the lessons. The guitar lessons had been Victor's idea and he was her first pupil, although two more of Dallas's friends were due to start later in the week. Victor had suggested that she give the guitar lessons, and Ellen had grabbed hold of the idea enthusiastically. He didn't have to convince her that working with young people would be fun, that it would give her something to do, and that the few extra dollars wouldn't hurt.

Victor was waiting for her in Hank's study. This was his third lesson, and he was a good pupil.

"Did you do your practicing?" she asked him.

"You bet. You'll see." He strummed on the guitar and played a simple tune, hesitating only a few times and hitting one or two wrong notes.

"Pretty good," Ellen commented, "but you're not watching what you're doing."

"I want to get that dreamy, faraway look in my eyes you guitar players get," Victor said. "Like you."

"You'll have to do a lot more practicing for that."

The lesson lasted for around forty minutes, and

Ellen was sorry when it was over. A few forty minutes out of a whole week to forget herself, to forget everything, and feel almost that life could be enjoyable again. "You can't imagine what this does for me," she said to Victor. "It was such a good idea of yours."

"I did it for myself. You're doing me a big favor giving me these lessons." He was looking at her admiringly. "You're a terrific woman, Ellen. You don't seem like, well, like someone's mother. I feel I can talk to you."

"I'm glad. I certainly do hope you talk to me anytime you want."

Victor looked at her with his dark, long-lashed eyes. He had his mother's Italian looks, was tall and sturdily built, his black hair worn just long enough to give him a soft look without detracting from his masculinity. "I think I'm in love," he said abruptly. "I'm not going to tell you who she is and please don't ask me. But I keep thinking about her all the time when I should be doing something else. I make up all kinds of excuses to see her. . . ."

"Does she know how you feel?"

Victor nodded. And then he surprised Ellen with a blush. "I shouldn't be talking about her to you. It's all crazy. I gotta go, or I'll be late for class. Can I leave my guitar here and pick it up later?"

"Sure, of course."

Victor left, and Ellen watched him run down

the street and jump into his car. He was taking courses at the community college and also working part-time at a local garage.

"Where did Victor go in such a hurry?" Dallas asked.

"He was late for class. He'll stop by later to pick up his guitar."

"You must have given him an extra-long lesson." Dallas sounded cross.

"We got to talking."

"Oh. I don't know why he's taking guitar lessons all of a sudden. He never even used to like folk music. He was hipped on jazz."

"I guess he changed his mind," Ellen said. She studied her daughter's scowling face. "Don't you like Victor?"

"What makes you say that? He's one of my oldest friends."

"That's what I thought. But you've been acting queerly whenever he comes over for his lessons, as if you didn't want him to."

"Forget it. I don't want to discuss Victor with you."

"You brought him up, I didn't." But Dallas was gone before she finished her sentence, gone out of the house. Ellen poured herself a cup of coffee and sat down at the kitchen table. She felt as if she'd been slapped. Her first thought was, Dallas wouldn't talk to me like that if Hank were here, and then her eyes filled with tears. How awful for them to be quarreling, although it wasn't a real quarrel. Yet she had felt such a wave of hostility from Dallas. I can't bear it, she kept thinking, I can't bear to go on living without Hank. It's all too much. I can't handle Dallas alone. Perhaps she shouldn't be staying home, but I couldn't bear to be alone either. . . .

And yet she felt that she wasn't being entirely selfish in accepting Dallas's offer to stay home with her this year. She knew how much Dallas missed her father. To be absolutely honest with herself, she had to admit that she had at times been jealous of the closeness between them, but now she thought their loss, hers and Dallas's, would bring them closer together. They would have this year to get to know each other better, to comfort each other. She had always hoped that as Dallas grew older they would become the close, intimate friends she imagined a mother and daughter should be. In so many ways Dallas was like her father, strong and outgoing, so different from Ellen herself, but Dallas often seemed a stranger. Ellen thought of Dallas as someone sure of herself in a way that she had never been, and certainly not when she was Dallas's age.

She did not think that depending on Dallas's strength was wrong. The one thing she had tried hard never to do was to put Dallas down, the way her mother had always been critical of her. She had never been able to please her mother. Even a few weeks ago, when she had called her mother in Florida to tell her of Hank's death, her mother had criticized her for not sending for her immediately. The scolding had left her with the same childish tears she had had in the past, and she had thought, I hope I never do that to Dallas. I hope Dallas will be my friend, my best friend.

Ellen stared out the window thinking, and her thoughts turned to Victor and Dallas. His quick, embarrassed confession of being in love made her smile, and then she realized, of course, Dallas had to be the one he was in love with. The thought gave her a stab of pain and made her feel old and terribly lonely. She mustn't be jealous of Dallas, her own daughter, and yet Dallas had everything ahead of her, while for her love was now all in the past. Still, she wasn't sure how Dallas felt. Was Dallas in love too, and was she jealous of the guitar lessons? Perhaps she should stop the lessons, but they gave her so much pleasure. . . .

Ellen buried her face in her hands, wanting to stop all thoughts, afraid of her own helplessness, aware as she was a hundred times a day of her inability to cope. She wanted to be a good mother to Dallas. She needed Dallas's love desperately. And yet she felt at this one time in her life she was entitled to indulge herself, not to have to please anyone, not her mother, not her daughter, and yes, not even Hank. She had had a miserable childhood and girlhood, hardly knowing her own father because he had traveled most of the time and always meeting criticism from her mother. And even with Hank, whom she had loved dearly, there had been adjustments to make: he wanted her to be social, to entertain, to share his passion for active sports, none of which she had ever been good at.

She had cared about his work. Her greatest pleasure had been when Hank turned to her for what he called her sharp eye for color. "You are better at that than I am," he had been fond of saying, and she would fill with pride. The thought gave her an idea.

She ran up to her bedroom and rummaged through a bureau drawer until she pulled out a bunch of fabric swatches. Before Hank had died she had planned to redo their bedroom, and now spread out on the bed before her were the samples of materials she had painstakingly gathered. She looked at them all and wondered what she'd had in mind. Carefully she examined them one by one, along with the color samples of paint and squares of wallpaper. They were a confused jumble. She tried to concentrate and remember why she had picked any of them, what colors were supposed to go with what, but the only result was that she felt dizzy and sick to her stomach. Feeling a compulsion to make a choice, she picked up a floral pattern for a bedspread and then put one solid wall color after another next to it, or perhaps a matching wallpaper for one wall and the others solid. But she could not make up her mind. What difference did any of it make? What was the use of a sparkling, new bedroom without Hank in it? And what frightened her the most was that she could not decide. She had lost her sureness, lost that confident, sharp eye Hank had admired so much.

Ellen dumped all the colorful samples into the wastebasket and sat down on the edge of the bed. She was afraid, afraid of herself, afraid to be alone. She wished Dallas would come home. At last she went downstairs and made herself a fresh cup of coffee, trying to steady her nerves. She forced herself to go to the phone, and she called up Hank's partner, a young man who had joined him only a year before.

Ellen got past the secretary and finally had Sam on the phone. "Sam, are you by any chance free for lunch?" she asked.

"I'm afraid not. I'm awfully sorry. I'm up to my neck. We sure miss Hank around here. Sorry, Ellen, I guess I shouldn't say that to you. How are you doing? You must come over and have dinner with us. I'll ask Jane to give you a ring and make a date. Take care."

He sounded busy, in a hurry, and she hardly knew Jane, his wife, and had not warmed to her when they'd met. Ellen hung up the phone with the tears streaming uncontrollably down her face, feeling absolute and utter rejection. She knew the reaction was foolish, illogical—there was no reason why he shouldn't be busy for lunch, be busy altogether—yet the rushed telephone conversation was the last straw in a day whose only remotely bright spot had been the guitar lesson with Victor. She didn't want to have dinner with Sam and Jane; she had wanted to see Sam, to talk about his work, to have that small connection with Hank. She wanted to be reminded that she'd been the wife of a fine architect, a woman who had been loved, not someone floundering alone, unable to pick out a color for a bedspread, who didn't even care whether she had a bedspread or not.

Ellen couldn't bear being alone in the house another minute, and she got up, put on her coat, and went out to the car. Without stopping to think, she knew where she wanted to go: the cemetery. She wanted to be close to Hank, to sit by his grave and hope to get some comfort from the simple, physical act of being there. She was there for a long while. At one point she pulled out some weeds, and then she went across the street to a nursery where she bought some plants and put them into the ground. Mostly she just sat. Her thoughts roamed over the years of her marriage, back to the time when she first went out with Hank, their excitement when she learned that she was pregnant, the vacation trips they had taken together. She kept trying to pull her mind back to the present, to think some positive thoughts about a future, but all she kept drawing was a dull blank—except for the guitar lessons. They seemed the one, tiny light on her horizon. Yet she made a resolution before she left the cemetery: she was going to try to see their old friends. She was not going to be thrown by one rejection. Ellen comforted herself with the thought that, no matter what, she had Dallas and her young friends. That companionship was more than some widows had.

Ellen stopped at her friend Vi's house on the way home. She got a warm welcome. "I'm glad to see you!" Vi greeted her with a hug and a kiss. "Where've you been hiding? I hear about you, of course, from Vic. He goes around strumming that guitar, and he thinks you're terrific. Have a cup of coffee. . . ."

"Victor's very good. He was a dear to suggest those lessons. They've been wonderful for me. I have two new pupils coming this week, Nancy and a friend of hers."

Later, as both women sat drinking their coffee, Vi asked, "How's it been going for you, Ellen? I worry about you. No one sees you; no one hears from you. You shouldn't be alone so much."

"I'm not alone. I have Dallas, and her friends are around a lot. It's nice to have the house filled with kids."

"I know, but. . . ." Vi was looking at her with a worried expression on her face. "I'm going to talk to you straight. We're old friends so why not? Having kids around is great, but they're not your life. You can't depend on kids, on Dallas and her friends. You've got to make your own life."

Ellen thought of Sam's impatient voice on the phone, but she didn't want to act the complaining widow to Vi. "I'm not depending on them; I simply feel more comfortable with the kids. You can't understand—no one can—until it happens. You're all couples, and I'm not part of your life anymore. I don't have the same problems as the rest of you. You and I can't talk about the things we used to, about our husbands, their careers, our marriage."

Vi stretched out her hand to Ellen. "I know it's hard, believe me I do. But we all care about you. You're still you, an attractive woman with lots to talk about, a lot to offer. This is when you need your friends, what friends are for. Why don't you invite a few people over for dinner, the way you and Hank used to? I'll help you. Maybe in your own home it will be better than going to someone else's. Hank would like it, Ellen."

Ellen didn't want to cry, but the tears were choking her throat. "Hank's dead, and I have to go on living. It isn't fair . . . it just isn't fair. . . ." Vi put her arms around her until she stopped sobbing. ". . . I'm sorry. I feel okay one minute, and the next I burst into tears. I'll try. I'll give a little dinner party. . . ." But she knew that her heart wasn't in it. She felt like a child obediently doing what her mother tells her to do as she sat making plans with Vi for a small dinner party.

She was just about to leave when Victor came home.

"Hey, I'll walk back with you and get my guitar," he said.

"Good." Ellen had to walk quickly to keep up with Victor's long stride, and her full skirt was blowing up high around her legs. A laundry truck went by, and the driver let out a loud whistle. Ellen looked around to see who was his target.

Victor laughed. "He was whistling at you. Doesn't that make you feel good?"

"It's ridiculous. I'm not a kid."

"You look like one."

Ellen saw that he wasn't teasing her. "Sometimes I feel like one. Say, when you were little, did you ever play that you couldn't walk on the lines on the sidewalk? We used to do that. Like this." Ellen started to walk carefully, avoiding the lines and the cracks. In a few seconds Victor was following her. They were both giggling as they progressed. Once Ellen had to take a wide jump and almost fell, but Victor caught her in time.

When they reached the Davis house, Ellen sighed. "That was fun. I didn't think I would ever laugh again. Thanks, Victor."

"Anytime. At your service."

Dallas was in the kitchen when they came into the house. Her hello was cool, and Ellen's sudden burst of good spirits left her. What was she laughing about? Nothing had changed. For her the house was still empty, and Dallas's coolness was too much for her to cope with. She craved warmth and affection, longed physically for Hank, for his comforting arms, his warm smile. She wanted to cry with angry, bitter tears because the tiny bit of warmth that a mere kid like Victor gave her could mean so much. Being so dependent on such tiny crumbs was frightening.

"Victor, why don't you stay for supper?" she asked, thinking he would cheer Dallas up.

"There's not much to eat," Dallas said. "I was just going to fry an egg for myself."

"Well, don't. Vic, call up Vi and tell her you'll have supper here. I'll take a steak out of the freezer, and we can have a bottle of wine. We'll have a party, just the three of us." Ellen felt desperate. The whole house suddenly seemed hostile to her, and she was afraid that if she was alone with Dallas she would start crying hysterically.

"Sounds good," Victor said, and made for the phone in the hall.

Ellen went over to Dallas and put her arms around her. "Are you all right? You'd like Victor to stay, wouldn't you?" She could feel Dallas stand rigid and still in her arms. "Dallas, please, Dallas, don't turn against me. What am I doing that's wrong? I need you now so much. Maybe that's wrong, but bear with me, just for a while, please. . . ."

Then Dallas was sobbing wildly and pushing herself free. "Don't you ever think that I miss my father too? You're not the only one who's had a loss. I'm not some rock for you to lean on. I have moods and feelings too. I loved my father more than anyone in the world. . . ." And she ran out of the room.

In her mind Ellen finished the sentence for her, ". . . more than I ever loved you." Ellen felt numb. She was still standing there, not even thinking, in a state of shock when Victor came back into the room.

"What's the matter? Where's Dallas?"

"I think she's gone up to her room." Ellen was surprised by the calmness of her voice. "Why don't you go up to her? I'll get dinner started."

Victor looked puzzled, but she could hear him leaping the stairs, calling, "Dallas, you up there?"

Mechanically Ellen started preparations for dinner. She took the steak out and set the table. Only when she got out the bottle of wine from the leather wine holder on the wall did she burst into tears. She and Hank had bought the leather holder together on one of their vacations. It had been handmade in a little shop in a Maine waterfront town where they had climbed rocks together and gone fishing and had a glorious time.

Ellen had lost her appetite for food, but she still

wanted terribly for dinner to be a party. If her mother had ever invited a boyfriend of hers for dinner, she'd have thought the millenium had come. Her mother had always criticized her friends; they had never been welcome in her house. Ellen wanted desperately to make life different for Dallas. Before, Hank had brought gaiety into the house, and now she didn't want Dallas to be stuck home alone with a mournful, silent mother. The most important thing she could do now, she believed, was to keep the house filled with cheerful young people, to keep both their lives as full of fun as possible.

"Dallas, Victor, are you coming down? I'm going to put the steak on. It'll take a while to cook because it's still frozen, but come down soon. Please," she called.

5

Dallas heard Victor loping up the stairs and call-ing her name, but she didn't answer him. At that moment she wished that both he and her mother would disappear and leave her alone. Her mother went around the house doing everything the way her father liked it—just the other day she had scolded Dallas for taking some books out of his study and not putting them back, as if it mattered—but Dallas was the one who had been made to betray him by not going to college. Dallas thought she'd never stop crying, and she didn't care. They were tears not only of grief, but of anger and bewilderment. How could you feel sorry for someone and almost hate her at the same time?

Sometimes I don't love my mother, I think. Sometimes I even hate her, Dallas thought, frightened by the vehemence she felt.

"I don't want any supper," she said to Victor, who was standing at her open door.

"What's the matter with you?"

"Nothing." Dallas spoke sullenly.

"Nuts." Victor came into the room and sat down on the bed beside her. He tried to put his arm around her, but she pushed him off. "Don't do that. Didn't you mean any of the things you said that night out in the hammock?"

Dallas spoke with her head muffled in a pillow. "I guess I meant them then."

Victor pulled her around so that she faced him. "You mean only then? What's happened to change you?" His face was deadly serious.

"I don't know. Nothing, I guess. Forget it."

"Forget what? That time in the hamomck or now?"

"I don't know. Please, leave me alone. Go downstairs and have supper with Mom. She's calling."

"Are you mad because she invited me to stay? But that doesn't make any sense."

"Nothing makes any sense. It didn't make sense that my father died, it didn't make sense for me to stay home, it doesn't make any sense for my mother to think I'm her best friend. I'm not. I'm not a good person, Victor, so just forget about me."

"Don't say that. You're terrific to have stayed home this year. Not that I'm sorry," he added with a little grin, "but I know it must be hard to have your mother breathing down your neck every minute. Remember what we said that night. We love each other, Dallas, just hang on to that. That's what I do. When I get depressed about my lousy garage job, and I feel I'm just marking time, I think of you. It gives me a goal. I'm saving money, and my father says that in another year, when Andy's finished college, he can help me. Then I can get started to be a lab technician. Come on down. We can't let that steak and wine go to waste."

He put his arms around her again, and this time she nestled against his chest. When she looked up at him she had a half smile on her face. "I do love you, Vic, but everything gets so complicated."

"Tell me. You can talk to me."

"I know I can, about almost everything. But I get so mixed up about my mother, I can't even think straight. One minute she says she's depending on me too much, and I think, hurrah, she's going to stop. Then the next minute she doesn't want me out of her sight. The fact that she realizes what she's doing almost makes it worse. She doesn't seem to have any control."

Victor was sympathetic. "Maybe she hasn't. Maybe that's the trouble."

"I know. But that's pretty awful, isn't it?"

Victor took her in his arms, and she let him hold her close. "She'll get better," Victor said. "My mother said it takes time."

When Dallas came downstairs, she resolved not to let herself feel angry with her mother. Her mother's face looked particularly strained, and Dallas started to talk gaily. Soon the three of them were laughing. Dallas and her mother vied with each other in remembering funny things that had happened. "And how about the time I dropped the platter of spaghetti, smothered in meat sauce, right on the patio?" Dallas said, giggling.

"Not once, but twice, Victor. I couldn't believe it. She was about nine years old and insisted she could carry out the platter. But plop, down it went a second time."

"Anyway it wasn't as bad as when you spilled the chocolate milk all over your new white rug. You were crying and laughing at the same time," Dallas said.

"The funniest of all was when Dad and I were going to some big architects' shindig. Hank got all dressed up in his tuxedo and discovered the cleaner had sent him the wrong suit. The pants were about six inches above his ankles, and the sleeves were almost up to his elbows. He looked so funny, I laughed so hard, and he was so mad at the cleaner. Hank was furious with me for laughing until he saw himself in the mirror, and then he couldn't stop laughing himself." Mrs. Davis was giggling now too.

"What did you do?" Victor asked.

"We had a terrible time. The cleaner was closed, and we had to find out where he lived. We finally did, I don't remember how, and it turned out that the mayor had Hank's suit. What a night that was! Fortunately the mayor was home and the cleaner got the suit from him and brought it over to us. We got where we were going just in time for salad and dessert, which Dad said was probably the only decent part of the meal anyway."

"I don't remember any of that," Dallas said.

"I guess you were too little," her mother said, wiping tears of laughter from her eyes. "I haven't laughed this much in a long time."

"I'm glad you can," Dallas said, feeling close to her mother and thinking that she had been imagining a lot of nonsense. It was a happy evening, and by the end of it Dallas was sure that her own emotional state had been the cause of her resentment of her mother.

* * *

"Wow, you're going to have some party," Dallas said to her mother and Vi Waters, sniffing the cooking smells in the kitchen. "Save some of that food for me."

Her mother looked up from the cutting board, where she was chopping vegetables. "Why? Where will you be? You'll be home, won't you?"

"No, thanks. I don't want to be around for a dinner party. There's a group playing we all want to hear."

Her mother's face was distressed. "I took for granted you'd be home. I thought we'd be doing this together."

"I don't know where you got that idea. Vi's here to help you, and you'll have your friends." Dallas was on the run, half out the door, but her mother was still talking.

"Don't go off in such a rush," her mother said. "I thought you'd be a hostess with me. I suppose it sounds silly to you, but it's my first attempt at a dinner party without Hank, and I guess I'm nervous about it."

"It never occurred to me you'd want me home. You'll be okay. You've got to start sometime, Mom." Dallas knew her voice was getting impatient.

"Maybe I'm not ready yet. Oh dear. . . ." Her mother's voice trailed off, and she looked to Vi for help.

"You don't really need her," Vi said hesitantly. "We're in good shape."

Her mother's disappointment was written on her face. "It isn't a question of needing her. I guess I thought she'd want to be here, that she'd understand it was going to be a painful night for me."

"I'm sorry, Mom. I thought this party was supposed to be fun for you. Anyway I've arranged to go hear the group. They're playing only this one night. Besides what would I do with all your friends? I thought the whole idea was to—" she stopped short.

"Was to what?" her mother asked sharply.

Dallas felt embarrassed. "Was to get you together with your friends again. You know what I mean."

"It wasn't my idea. You and Vi persuaded me to do it. Now you won't even be here. I don't think it's very considerate."

"It's going to be fine," Vi said soothingly. "Everyone who's coming is an old friend. You don't have to be nervous."

"I don't have to be, but I am. I never was the one to give parties. Hank was the one. He made them work. I'm no good at it; I don't like being a hostess. I really counted on Dallas."

"Then you counted wrong." The minute the harsh words were out, Dallas felt guilty, but she stood her ground. The idea had truly never occurred to her to stay home for her mother's party, and she had thought it lucky that the group was playing that same night, so she could get out without leaving her mother alone. She said as much to her mother. "It's the first time I've gone out since Dad died, and you won't be alone, so you should be glad," she ended up.

"I can't force you to stay home, but it would be nice," her mother said lamely.

Dallas walked out of the house. She had been headed for the library, but instead she took the path up into the woods. She walked up to her fallen tree and sat down. The last time she'd been here was the day her father died, and all her feelings of loss came flooding back. What would her mother do if she just packed up and left? she wondered. But she couldn't do that; she knew she couldn't. Leaving would be a betrayal of her father. But what *was* she to do? Was a seventeen-year-old girl supposed to take care of her mother? To be a companion to her constantly? Dallas had read enough books to know that in the Victorian age many unmarried spinsters (and a woman was a spinster then if she wasn't married in her early twenties) had been stuck at home taking care of aging parents, and there was sixty-year-old Miss Jackson and her ninety-year-old mother right in Millstone. But not me, Dallas vowed to herself fervently. Not me.

Yet what was she to do? Dallas's sense of loss was turning to anger and resentment. She wanted to stand up and shout, "Get off my back, Mom, get off my back!"

While Dallas knew that her mother had depended heavily on her father, she didn't believe that her mother had to be as helpless as she now was. She's not even trying—she's depending on me for everything, for her life—and I can't bear it, I can't bear it. . . . Dallas choked back her sobs. She didn't want to cry; she wanted to think. She wanted to figure a way out of her dilemma, but she could find no answer. It's going to go on and on, she thought, until I'm an old lady and it'll be too late for anything. Sometimes I hate my mother, I hate her, I hate her. . . .

At last Dallas got up and went on to the library. She met Jennifer there, and after the girls had picked out their books they stopped for a soda.

"I'm glad you're getting out tonight," Jen said.

"Me too. You'd better believe it."

"It must be awful having to stay home all the time." Jennifer was sipping her soda thoughtfully.

"At least the kids come over. That's a help."

Jennifer gave her a sidelong glance. "Don't count on it forever."

Dallas could tell that Jennifer had something on her mind. "What's the matter? Tell me."

Jennifer looked uneasy. "Well, it's not much fun with your mother around. I mean, we really want to help, but why does she sit there all the time?"

"She likes young people," Dallas said flatly. Then she turned to her friend. "I don't blame the kids if they stop coming around, but then I'd never see anyone. I don't know what to do."

"Don't worry about it. I shouldn't have said anything. At least you're going out tonight. We'll still come over as much as we can. Sooner or later your mother will feel better, and she won't need you so much."

"I sure hope so."

When Dallas left Jennifer she was feeling more depressed than ever, but the thought of the evening cheered her up somewhat.

"You look beautiful." Dallas had come into her mother's room to say good-bye, and she was taken aback by her mother's good looks. Mrs. Davis was wearing a long, clingy dress that showed off her figure. Her long hair was brushed so that it was shiny and silky, its gold color accentuated by long, gold earrings. "It's nice to see you all dressed up."

"I don't know what for. They say it's good for morale, but sometimes I think it can be more depressing when there's no one you care about dressing up for."

"Oh, Mother! There are lots of people. I care."

Her mother gave her a halfhearted smile. "You're a dear, but it's not the same. You look very pretty yourself," she added.

Dallas had felt she looked okay in a long, denim skirt and a sheer, white Indian blouse, but looking at herself in the mirror she felt that she couldn't touch her mother in looks. Her mother seemed to be reading her mind. "You're a very pretty girl,

Dallas. More than pretty, you're beautiful. You have such vitality in your face, and your skin glows. You'll still be glowing when I'm old and wrinkled. Don't forget that."

"You'll never get old. I can't imagine you old."

"I will, though. We're a mutual admiration society," her mother added with a laugh. Then she said casually, "When will you be home?"

"I don't know. Probably late. Don't wait up for me."

"I never go to sleep until you're home—if I get to sleep at all."

"Maybe you should take a sleeping pill."

"I hate sleeping pills. Don't get home too late." An anxious note was creeping into her voice.

"Don't pin me down. Listen, Mom, I'm seventeen, going on eighteen, and I haven't been out in over two months now. Maybe your party will be late, and you'll be tired enough to sleep."

"I'm never sleepy after a party. The nicest part is always sitting in the kitchen afterward and talking about it. I'm disappointed you won't be here, but I thought when you came home you could tell me about your evening and I'd tell you about mine. It's awful not to have anyone to share something with. . . ."

Dallas was speechless. How could you tell your mother that you didn't want to share your life with her? Her mother was looking at her so appealingly, and even though she smiled she gave the impression that her tears were near the surface.

"You can tell me about it in the morning," Dallas said in a gentler voice. "Please don't wait up for me. It will make me nervous. I'm looking forward to tonight."

"I wish I were," her mother said glumly. "I'll be nervous worrying about you. You know it is a responsibility to bring up a teen-age daughter without a father."

"Mom, you don't have to bring me up. I'm brought up. I'm not a little kid anymore. What do you think's going to happen to me? I'm not about to get pregnant or anything like that. Stop worrying."

"Don't talk that way. I don't like it. I worry about everything now more than I used to. I can't help it. The smallest thing throws me into a panic—paying the bills, making sure the oil gets delivered, having the furnace cleaned, so many things Hank automatically took care of. I don't want to have to sit up and worry about you too."

"You don't have to sit up and worry about me," Dallas yelled. She didn't mean to shout, but she did. "Dad's dying was terrible enough, but you're making it a tragedy every minute of the day. I miss Dad as much as you do, but he loved life and he would want us to. I don't think you want me to go out tonight because you don't *want* me to enjoy myself. That's the crux of it. You're ruining my life."

Her mother looked shocked. She stood still and stared at Dallas. When she spoke her words were slow and distinct as if each one was said with a great effort. "That's the worst thing anyone ever said to me."

"I'm sorry." Dallas felt guilty, but she also believed what she had said. "I don't want to fight with you. That's the last thing in the world I want. But you don't need to feel so responsible for me. I'm old enough to be responsible for myself."

"You think you are, but you're still very young."

Dallas shook her head impatiently. "I don't understand you. You want to be young and with kids, but you're the most old-fashioned mother I ever heard of. You think you're modern, but you're not. You're worse than a Victorian grandmother! You may look young, but you sure aren't."

"I think that's about enough," her mother said angrily. "I didn't want this party in the first place, and now you've about ruined it for me."

"I didn't mean to. You know I didn't. But you didn't have to tell me when to come home either. I hope your party is good, I really do." Dallas went over to kiss her mother good-bye, and her mother gave her a cool kiss on the cheek.

Dallas felt terrible when she walked down the street to Jennifer's. Victor and Ted were going to pick the girls up there. She was angry with her mother, and at the same time upset about quarreling with her. Yet she had meant every word of what she had said. She felt that her mother *was* making their tragedy such a living part of their everyday lives that she was causing them to suffer much more than they had to.

The pub was crowded with Dallas's friends and many of the young people from the area, but Victor found a table for the four of them not too far from where the musicians would be playing. Dallas was anxious for the music to start. She didn't feel like talking and wanted only to sit back and listen to the music.

The music was good, and it suited Dallas's mood. She wanted to empty her mind, and the music did so for her. She let the sounds seep through her, so that she wasn't thinking at all, just listening. Sometimes she could feel Victor looking at her, studying her face, but he had the sense not to talk, which she appreciated. The music stopped at one o'clock, and then they went to an all-night diner, where they stuffed themselves with grinders.

It was around two thirty in the morning when Victor drove her home. Dallas was alarmed to see her house lit up like a Christmas tree. She ran inside, with Victor close behind her, and found her mother, wrapped in a robe, pacing the floor. "Thank God you're home. Where have you been?"

"At the pub, and then we stopped for something to eat. What's the matter? What happened?" Dallas was frightened by her mother's pale, strained face.

"What's the matter!" her mother shrieked. "What do you think's the matter? It's half past two. I've been waiting for you since midnight. I've been worried sick."

"I told you not to wait up for me," Dallas said. "How was your party?"

"Terrible. I couldn't wait for them to go home. I knew it wouldn't work, and it didn't."

"You didn't want it to work. You made up your mind before that it wouldn't. What went wrong?"

"Everything. I couldn't stand it. Everyone feeling sorry for me, having them here without Hank. It was ghastly. I felt like an outcast, listening to their plans for vacation trips over the holidays, everyone in couples, no one who *really* cared about me. It's no use. . . ."

"Mom, they do care. You just think they don't. It's all in your mind."

"Wherever it is, it's there. I can't help it. It's the way I feel. I'm sorry, Victor, to talk this way in front of you, but I think you understand better than my own daughter does."

That remark made Dallas boil with anger. "That's a terrible thing to say."

"I think you're just upset, Ellen," Victor said. "Why don't you put on a coat, and we'll all go for a little ride and cool off? It'll make you sleepy," he added.

Mrs. Davis's face brightened. "That's a great idea." She went to get her coat.

"You can go for a ride," Dallas said to Victor. "I'm going to bed."

"Come on, please. It will calm your mother down."

"Right now I don't care whether she calms down or not. She's not the only one who's missing my father, and I can't take much more of this."

"Dallas, please come." Victor's face was pleading. "I don't want to go for a ride with your mother. I was just trying to be helpful."

Dallas shook her head. "No. I'm afraid you're stuck with her. I'm sorry, Vic, but I just don't want to go."

"Damn, I guess I *am* stuck. Damn. It was a nutty suggestion."

"Okay, kids, I'm ready. Let's go." Her mother sounded more cheerful.

"I'm going to bed. Good night," Dallas said.

"Dallas, please come," her mother asked.

"I don't feel like it. Good night."

Up in her room Dallas could hear Victor start up the motor and the car take off. Then the situation of her mother off riding with her boyfriend at three o'clock in the morning struck her as funny, but in a hurtful, angry way. What would her father have made of it? But none of this would be happening if he were alive, Dallas thought. The whole world wouldn't be turning upside down; her mother wouldn't be going crazy. She banged her fist against her pillow in anger, and then, exhausted, buried her head in the pillow and fell asleep.

She was awakened by a sound and realized it was the car coming into their driveway. Then she heard her mother opening and closing the front door. Dallas peered at her night clock and saw that it was after four o'clock. I hope they had a good time, she thought ruefully, and turned her face back into the pillow. This time, however, she didn't fall asleep for a long time. She was adding figures in her head: Victor was eighteen and a half, and her mother was thirty-seven. She had heard and read about young men falling in love with older women, but she wondered if older women also fell in love with young men. The thought made her sick, and she tried to think of something else so that she could get to sleep.

6

The next morning Dallas and her mother had a late breakfast. Mrs. Davis seemed in a good mood. "I guess going to bed late is the trick," she said. "At least last night when I got to bed I fell asleep."

"That's good. Maybe you should go out riding every night," Dallas suggested.

Her mother gave her a sharp look. "Victor's a very nice boy. Vi and I used to talk about you two when you were little. We always thought how nice it would be if you and he got together. Vi would be a good mother-in-law."

"If you don't mind, I'll pick my own mother-in-law. Or perhaps I should say my own husband—if I ever do."

"Of course." Dallas could tell that her mother was determined to keep things smooth. "But you can't blame me for noticing, and for hoping too."

"You can hope all you want, but it won't do you any good. I told you before I don't want to discuss Victor with you."

"You don't want to discuss anything with me." The determination was rapidly weakening.

"That's right. I don't. I don't want to discuss my friends." And I don't want to share them either, Dallas added to herself. She had a strong feeling that her mother was ruining everything between Victor and herself. She didn't know exactly why, but her mother's approval of Victor irked Dallas to the point of making her want to turn against him. Her mother treated Victor as if he were already one of the family, as if he somehow belonged to her as much as to Dallas. Dallas couldn't stand the way her mother overreacted to Victor's attentions. She should realize that Victor was trying to be helpful mainly because of Dallas. But Dallas felt impatient with Victor too, because he played up to her mother and did dumb things like suggesting the ride the night before.

Dallas felt out of sorts with everyone. She was sick of staying home, tired of hanging around. She didn't often indulge in self-pity, but today she felt that her life was truly a mess. Victor was the one good thing in it, and she felt that her mother was nibbling away at the relationship. Logically or not she was annoyed with Victor too. Some part of her wanted Victor to be the one to get her mother off her back since she seemed incapable of doing so herself, although she knew that no one could make the break for her.

Dallas still had these thoughts on her mind when Victor came by later in the afternoon for his guitar lesson. He was there early, and her mother was out at the beauty parlor getting her hair done.

"Is your mother feeling better today?" Victor asked, after he had greeted Dallas and there had been a dead silence for several minutes.

"Of course. Riding with you last night was fantastic."

"You should have come with us."

Dallas glanced across the kitchen table, where they were having a soda, to look at Victor. She took a sip before answering. "Riding around with my mother at three o'clock in the morning is not my idea of fun."

"It's not mine either. I only suggested it because I thought you were coming along."

"Well, you thought wrong." Dallas spoke firmly,

and stood up to take her empty glass to the sink.

Victor got up too and tried to put his arms around her, but Dallas pushed him away. "What's eating you?" he demanded. "You're the one who changes every minute. Don't take your problems with your mother out on me. Dammit, I think you're jealous of her."

Dallas whirled around to face him. "Don't be stupid. What's there to be jealous of? I think she's acting ridiculously, and you're helping her make a fool of herself."

"What the hell have I done?" Victor looked truly surprised.

"If you don't know, I can't tell you. Forget it."

"You're always telling me to forget it. I don't want to. You can at least tell me what I do that's wrong." Victor was facing her with his hands on her arms.

"I feel sorry for my mother," Dallas said, speaking slowly, searching for the right words. "But I think she's relying too much on us, on you and me and the kids, instead of facing her own life. And I don't want to encourage her."

"And you think I have?"

Dallas nodded. "I don't really blame you. My mother's crazy about you, but—"

"But you don't like it," Victor finished for her.

"No, I don't," Dallas said vehemently.

"Well, I think you've got a pretty wild imagination. And I think you *are* jealous of your mother."

"If that's what you think, think it," Dallas said angrily.

"I've been trying to be nice to your mother because of what happened, but mainly because of you, you dumb idiot. I thought you'd like me to. And I think it's too damn bad that you don't."

"Well, bully for you. Here's my mother now," Dallas said, as the car pulled into the driveway. "You can have your guitar lesson."

"I certainly will."

Dallas slammed out of the kitchen and went up to her room.

She certainly made a mess of that, she decided, aware again that in some far-out fantasy she wanted Victor to solve her problem for her. She was furious with herself for feeling so helpless, unreasonably annoyed with Victor because he was absolutely right to be nice to her mother (though in her fantasy he told her off), and most of all angry with her mother. Her mother was at the bottom of all the trouble, behaving the way she did, as if she hadn't a friend of her own in the world, as if she were the only woman who had ever been widowed. Dallas felt a deep, anguished longing for her father. He would understand, but then, of course, if he were alive none of this would have happened.

She was sitting and brooding, half listening to the guitars playing downstairs and to her mother's and Victor's voices, when the phone rang. It was Jennifer, and Dallas agreed to go over to her house. "I suppose I can go out now. My mother has Victor here," she said.

In a few minutes she was at Jen's house, and Jen suggested that they go for a walk. Jen had no classes and had some shopping she wanted to do. "Have you heard the news?" Jen asked, when they were outside.

"No, what?"

"Andy Waters is coming home from college."

Dallas was surprised. "I just saw Victor, and he didn't say anything. I guess he didn't have a chance. We had a fight. Tell me about Andy first, and I'll tell you about Victor later."

"I saw Mrs. Waters this morning, and I think she's pretty upset. Andy is tired of school and decided to take a year off. She'll be furious if he doesn't get his tuition back, but he said he was sure he would because it's still early in the term."

"What's he going to do?"

"He wants to stay home and write, she said. I bet he'll never finish college. He waited a year to go, didn't he?"

"Yes, he did. He must be twenty-two or -three by now."

"What did you and Victor fight about?" Jennifer asked.

Dallas's mind was spinning ahead, wondering

what Andy's being home would mean for Victor. Would there be money for him to go to school sooner? But she answered Jennifer's question.

"It was stupid." Dallas told her about the night before and her mother's going out for a ride with Victor. "I certainly wasn't going to go with them," she ended up. "The whole thing was crazy."

"What are you going to do, Dallas? Maybe you ought to look for a job," Jennifer suggested.

"Doing what? I don't want to be a baby-sitter, and I hate housework. What's there to do around here for someone like me? Besides I bet my mother wouldn't let me."

"But what are you going to do?"

"Sweat out this year and go to college next year, I hope. If she lets me. Maybe I'll never get away. I keep thinking I'll figure out something, but so far I haven't had any brainstorms."

They had walked to a shopping plaza, and Jennifer said she wanted to buy some slacks. The girls discovered that a sale was on, and since Dallas knew her mother had a charge account at the store, she picked out a pair of slacks too. The girls were delighted with their purchases and wandered around looking at other shops.

They stopped at a jeweler's, and both girls became enchanted with the display of earrings. "Let's go in," Jennifer said.

There was a large assortment, and the girls peered

admiringly over display cases. The only trouble was that most of the earrings, and particularly those that they liked, were made for pierced ears. "Why don't you girls get your ears pierced?" the woman behind the counter suggested. "It takes only a few minutes, and it doesn't hurt, I promise you. It's just a little pinprick."

"Maybe I'll buy some earrings and get my ears pierced later," Jennifer said.

The saleswoman shook her head. "That's not the way to do it. You couldn't try them on, and earrings look different when they're on. I wouldn't like to sell them to you that way."

"Let's do it," Dallas said. "Let's get them pierced."

The girls looked at each other and giggled. "Why not?"

The price that the saleswoman quoted them didn't seem too much, and it included the tiny gold earrings the girls would have to wear after their ears were pierced.

"But I don't have any money with me now," Dallas said.

"Neither do I," Jennifer added.

"Actually my partner, who does the piercing, isn't here right now. She'll be back in an hour or so. Why don't you girls go home, get your money, and come back in around an hour and a half? And don't get cold feet," she added, as the girls agreed

85

and were leaving. "You'll be glad to have it done."

Dallas was enthusiastic as they walked across the plaza toward home. "I adore earrings, but I keep losing the screw-on ones. I've been wanting to do this for ages, but I never had the courage. Victor will be happy. He says my earrings are always falling off. Aren't you excited?"

Jennifer nodded. "Sure, but I hope it doesn't hurt."

"She said it wouldn't. Let's get a slice of pizza. You want to?"

"Yes, I'm starving."

They got their slices and ate them as they continued their walk slowly. The day, which had been cloudy earlier, had cleared up into beautiful fall sunshine. Dallas gave a contented sigh. "This has been the best couple of hours I've had in a long time." She put her arm through Jennifer's. "Not that we've done anything spectacular, but I was able to get away from home, and . . . ." She hesitated, and didn't finish her sentence.

"And get away from your mother," Jennifer finished for her.

Dallas smiled wryly. "I didn't want to say so, but it's true. She makes me feel so heavy. She's around all the time, trying to live her life in mine. Now she's taken over Victor, and she's kind of killing everything between us. I should be glad that she likes him, but she's so possessive. You know, I wish she'd meet a man and get married again."

"It's much too soon. But maybe she will one day. She's still young, and she's pretty."

"She'll never meet anyone hanging out with us. And I can't imagine having a stepfather either. That might be worse." Dallas stopped to throw her pizza-stained paper napkin into a trash bin. "I shouldn't talk this way."

"It's okay," Jennifer said. "It's only me."

Victor had left by the time the girls got to Dallas's house. The minute Dallas walked inside, she knew, before her mother said a word, that her mother had been waiting for her and wondering where she was. Dallas didn't give her mother a chance to say anything but immediately opened her package to show the slacks. "They were on sale. Aren't they terrific? They fit just right. I knew you'd be glad I bought them. And Mom, Jen and I are going back to have our ears pierced. We saw the most adorable earrings, so many I hardly know which to pick, and they're not expensive. They have loads of them for two and three dollars."

Jennifer showed Mrs. Davis her purchases too. "You girls sound excited. You really had a good time," Mrs. Davis said. "Why didn't you wait for me? I would have loved to have gone with you. Anyway I'll go back with you and get my ears done too. I've always wanted to. What fun! We can go to the pub for supper too. Wouldn't that be nice, just the three of us?"

Dallas could feel her chest tightening, and her

mind searched wildly for an excuse not to go. "We may not have time to get our ears done now. Jen and I were planning to go to a movie." She knew the minute she'd spoken that she had said the wrong thing, and she looked at Jennifer hopefully.

Jennifer looked surprised, but before she could answer, Mrs. Davis spoke up. "We can do everything. We can get our ears done, have supper, and go to the eight o'clock show. What movie were you going to?"

"I forget the name of it," Dallas said helplessly. She knew she was licked.

Mrs. Davis shrugged. "I don't care what we see, whatever you girls want. Oh, this will be fun. I was dreading another empty evening at home. There's not even anything to watch on TV tonight." She hugged Dallas. "I don't know what I'd do without you. I'll go upstairs and get out of these old slacks and be down in a minute."

Dallas looked at Jennifer helplessly. "You see what I mean?"

Jennifer was laughing. "I know I shouldn't laugh —it *is* pretty awful—but your face when your mother said she was coming with us was really funny. You never should have said we were going to a movie."

"I know. But I couldn't think of a darn thing we could do that she wouldn't do with us. There isn't anything," she added gloomily. "And when she hugs me and says she couldn't get along without me, it's worse. I should write a song, 'Sometimes I Don't Love My Mother, I Think.' It keeps running through my head."

"I guess we all don't love our mothers sometimes. Maybe mothers don't love us either."

"I wish my mother didn't love me so much," Dallas said.

Her mother came downstairs in a short while, looking very chic in a camel-colored pants suit. "You're all dressed up," Dallas said.

"Why not? It's a treat for me to go out with you two."

Dallas had no answer. She no longer wanted to get her ears pierced, she didn't want to go to the movies, she didn't want to have supper out with her mother. She and Jennifer had been having a good time together, but now everything had gone flat. She wanted to be a good sport, and her mother's enthusiasm was sad and touching, but going out with Jennifer and going out with her mother and Jennifer were two different things.

Dallas tried hard. They all had their ears pierced —it *was* like a pinprick and took only a few seconds— and they all got mimeographed sheets of instructions on how to take care of their ears until they were healed. After they selected earrings, though, there was little to talk about. Alone, Dallas and Jennifer never ran out of conversation, but during supper there were long silences that her mother tried to fill with a lecture about nutrition. Since her husband's death, Mrs. Davis had become very concerned about food and diet, and she tried hard to persuade the girls not to order pizzas. Dallas didn't dare tell her that they each had already had a slice in the afternoon. "Did you ever read the list of ingredients that go into these things?" Mrs. Davis demanded.

"Those are frozen. These aren't," Dallas said patiently.

"I don't think there's much difference," her mother said. "There's no nutritional value in them, just a lot of unhealthy fat."

"Mom, you're the one who wanted to go out for supper. You eat what you want and let me eat what I want."

"After what happened to your father, Dallas. . . ."

"Please, Mom. Let's not talk about it now."

Her mother's hurt look made Dallas feel both guilty and terribly depressed. Her mother could never seem to let go of her pain for a moment. She not only had to carry it with her constantly, she had to take it out and examine it for others to see. Dallas kept telling herself that not quite three months had gone by since her father had died, and she was being impatient with her mother, but when, when was she going to start to face her new life?

After the movie, when they had taken Jennifer home and were back in their own house, Dallas could see that her mother wanted to sit up and talk. Dallas wanted to go to bed, but, trying to be as nice as she could, she sat down at the kitchen table with her and drank a glass of milk she didn't want.

"Jennifer is such a nice girl," her mother said. "You do have nice friends, Dallas. You're very lucky, and I'm happy for you."

"You have nice friends too. Vi would do anything for you. And what about the people you and Dad saw all the time, the Burnses and the Dugans and the Bernsteins?"

Mrs. Davis wrinkled her nose. "I know. They're all very nice people. I have nothing against them. But I just don't feel right with them anymore."

"But what will you do if I go away to college next year? I probably shouldn't talk about it now, but you know how much Dad wanted me to go to college, and I want to go too. You'd be alone so much . . . ."

"I've been considering next year, darling. Don't think I don't appreciate what you're doing, staying home this year with me. You should go to college, and I'd like to see you with a profession of your own. But perhaps a school in a city would be better for you. I know you fell in love with New Hampshire, but outside of the school there's nothing there, no cultural life. I thought if you went to a school, say, in Boston, I wouldn't mind getting out of here for a change too. We could take a little apartment together. It would be no more expensive than a dorm, probably cheaper, and being in a city could be fun. We could go to concerts and the theater. I might even take some courses myself."

Dallas listened to her mother with her heart dropping as she talked. Oh, no, Dallas's mind was screaming, *no, no, no!* This suggestion was too much. The one gate ahead that she had seen open, the only gate in a solid, thick wall, was being gently, firmly closed in her face. Her mother was so logical, so enthusiastic, so buoyed up by her idea that Dallas could only look at her in amazement and keep her dismay to herself. If her mother were mean to her, if she picked on her the way some mothers did, if she openly tried to undermine her, she could get angry and fight back. Yet her mother didn't do any of those things. She just clung. She had always taken for granted that she loved her mother, but she had never felt her mother's dependency before. Naturally not. Her father had been there for her mother to hold on to, and Dallas hadn't paid much attention to their relationship. It had seemed okay that her father had made her parents' social life, that he had brought people and liveliness into the house, and that her mother had been content to let him do so.

"I don't know, Mom, I really did like New Hampshire, and so did Dad. We don't have to decide now, do we? There's lots of time."

"I like to think ahead, to have something to look forward to," her mother said wistfully. "My life seems so empty now, and when I think of the years stretching ahead, alone . . . ."

"Don't think that way," Dallas said. "You may not be alone."

"Widows are alone," her mother said dolefully.

They were still sitting in the kitchen when the telephone rang. It was after ten o'clock, and Dallas wondered who could be calling. She answered quickly. "It's Grandma calling from Florida," she said in an aside to her mother, before turning the phone over to her.

Dallas could hear her mother's end of the conversation: "I'm doing all right. . . . No, I'm not by myself. I have Dallas here. I told you she stayed home with me. . . . No, this wouldn't be a good time for you to come to visit. . . . The weather's not good now. . . . Maybe in the spring. . . . No, Mom, I don't think you should come now. . . . No, I don't want to come to Florida. I have a lot of things to take care of, about the estate and all . . . . Thank you for calling, take care."

Her mother gave a long sigh when she hung up. "The last thing in the world I want now is my mother."

"Maybe a trip to Florida would be good for you," Dallas said.

Her mother scowled. "Not to visit my mother.

She's not what I need right now. Too depressing. I'd be with a bunch of old ladies down there, and she upsets me."

Dallas stared moodily into her empty milk glass. How could she tell her mother that she felt the same way about her?

7

Dallas had been dreading Thanksgiving. She knew that her mother dreaded it too, and she could be honestly sympathetic with her. There was no use in asking any of her friends over, since they all would want to be home with their own families. And the idea of the two of them going to a restaurant alone was too depressing. Then Vi Waters invited them to dinner, and Dallas was greatly relieved when her mother accepted.

But in spite of the fact that they were going out to dinner later in the day, Dallas could see immediately at breakfast that her mother was feeling very low. "I would like to go to the cemetery today," her mother said. "Would you come with me?"

Dallas had not gone to the cemetery since the funeral. She had simply said, "I can't," to her mother's repeated request, and her mother had gone without her. But today she felt different. She felt that she had to help her mother in every way that she could, so, keeping her apprehensions to herself, she agreed. The day was raw and cold, and when Dallas got into the car with her mother, she thought she had never felt more depressed in her life. In a way the return was worse than the funeral itself. The shock had worn off, and now she felt only the pain of their loss, both her own and her mother's, plus the heavy burden of the last months of living with her mother.

Dallas had never walked through a cemetery before. At the funeral she hadn't looked at anything, but today she went slowly, stopping to read the tombstones. She recognized family names from the town, and a few times she was shocked to read of six-month-old infants and two- and three-year-old babies who had died.

Her mother was silent, obviously wrapped in her own thoughts as she walked beside her. When they got to her father's grave, Dallas helped her mother pull out some weeds, pick off dead flowers, and the two of them sat on a narrow stone bench. Neither of them spoke, and Dallas, for the first time, understood why her mother kept coming back here. There was a certain quiet and peacefulness, a sense of closeness to her father. There was no logical explanation for her feelings, yet Dallas was sure that her mother felt the same way. The sense of closeness extended to and included her mother. Dallas felt ashamed of the bad thoughts she had been thinking about her and vowed not to let them take over again.

In a burst of tenderness she did something that she had thought she would never do. "When we leave here," she said, speaking softly, "I want to take you someplace."

Her mother looked at her inquiringly. "I'll show you where Dad used to take me all the time," Dallas said. "You remember when Dad and I made a tree house one summer, ages ago? You got mad because we spent so much time there. Dad said that it was my private place, and he was only there to help me build it."

"Yes, I remember. I wasn't mad. I guess I was hurt at being excluded."

"I thought you might like to see it."

"Now? After all these years?" Her mother's face did not brighten as Dallas had hoped. But she said, "That's dear of you. Yes, I'd like to go."

* * *

Dallas felt stupid sitting on the dead tree branch with her mother. What crazy impulse had made her bring her mother up here? she wondered. What had she expected? She didn't know, but whatever it was, her mother was not responding. She couldn't blame her. After all, it was only a patch of woods, and her mother had none of the memories that Dallas connected with it. Perhaps her mother was remembering her own hurt. Dallas had never thought of her mother being excluded; she had only been happy to be there with her father.

"It's pretty here," her mother said politely, the way a person says thank you without meaning it. "It's nice that you had this with your father."

"He didn't come up here with me that much," Dallas said, wanting to comfort her mother. "I was here a lot alone."

They didn't sit there very long. "We should be going home to get dressed to go over to Vi's. I'm not sure I wouldn't be better off staying home," her mother said.

"No, you wouldn't be. That would be awful. It will be okay at the Waters'."

"I hope so." Her mother did not sound convinced.

"It's wonderful to have you here." Vi Waters greeted them warmly. The house was filled with the good smells of a traditional Thanksgiving dinner: turkey and sweet potatoes, apple and pumpkin pies.

Through the open living-room door Dallas could see the large dining-room table set with Vi's best linen and silver. Mr. Waters' parents, an aunt of Vi's, and another couple, the Dugans, who were friends of her parents, were also there. After saying hello to everyone, Dallas gravitated to Victor and Andy, who had been home for several weeks by now. The three young people sat together, Dallas and Victor each with a glass of white wine, while Andy sipped a cocktail like the others.

"What are you going to do here all year?" Dallas asked Andy.

"I don't know. Think, I guess. I got sick of school."

"Someone said you wanted to write."

Andy looked defensive. "I'm not broadcasting that. I may turn out nothing. I have some ideas."

Dallas's mother was not far away, and she came over to them. "Did I hear you say you wanted to write, Andy?" she asked.

Andy's restless eyes stopped for a few seconds on Mrs. Davis's face and then wandered off again. He was a bigger, stronger-looking version of his younger brother, with a thrust to his chin that indicated an aggressiveness, even an arrogance, that Victor did not have.

"No, you didn't," he said bluntly. "Your daughter said she heard a rumor."

Mrs. Davis laughed. "It's not a crime, you know.

I've often thought about writing myself. I have lots of ideas for stories."

"Why don't you?" Victor asked.

"I guess I haven't the confidence. I need someone to push me. Isn't that the way you feel?" she turned to Andy.

"No." He looked bored and turned away to get himself another drink.

Mrs. Davis handed him her glass. "I'll have one too, please. Another of the same."

Dallas had often heard her mother say that one drink made her feel dizzy. She had already had two, and Dallas worried what a third would do to her. Her mother's face was flushed, and her eyes bright, but Dallas did not think she should say anything to her.

When Andy handed her glass back to her, Mrs. Davis herself said, "This will really get me cock-eyed, but I don't care. It's the only way I can get through this day."

"Why not?" Victor said sympathetically. "It must be rough for her," he added in a low tone to Dallas.

"I don't think getting drunk is going to help," Dallas said to him.

Dallas watched her mother down her third drink and center all her attention on Andy. Mrs. Davis was leaning over talking to him without stopping. Andy was lolling back in his chair, listening to her, sipping his own drink, with an expression on his fact that Dallas could not fathom. She couldn't make out whether he was amused, bored, or leading her on with some devious plan to shut her up when it suited him. At first Dallas was apprehensive for her mother. Andy always had been an enigma to her. Victor jokingly called him a schizo, because he could be friendly and nice one time and then act as if you weren't there the next. Then she began to get angry. Still, she was not her mother's keeper, and she tried to talk to Victor and to pay no attention to the conversation going on in the corner between her mother and Andy.

But she wasn't doing a good job of ignoring them. "What did you say?" she asked Victor, when she realized he had said something she had not been listening to.

"I said don't worry so much about your mother. She can take care of herself."

"I'm not so sure. I hope Andy doesn't give her another drink."

"I'll tell him not to," Victor said.

"No, you'd better not. My mother might get mad."

Dallas didn't know what to do. Her mother's voice was getting louder, and she felt that something embarrassing and terrible was going to happen. She looked around the room and caught Mrs. Waters' eye, who obviously also was aware of Andy and Mrs. Davis in their corner. Vi stood up and

101

said that dinner was almost ready, and why didn't they all go in and sit down at the table?

Dallas got up quickly with relief. However, in the dining room she saw her mother hastily change places with Vi's aunt so that she could sit next to Andy. And then Mr. Waters began to serve the wine.

That morning Dallas had really been looking forward to going to the Waters' for dinner with her mother. She had felt close to her, had decided that she had been unfair, and resolved that from now on she was going to be sympathetic and warm, not resentful. But now, watching her mother center all her attention on Andy, not even bothering to talk to anyone else, Dallas was becoming resentful all over again. She started to do some figuring in her head. Andy had lost time in high school with hepatitis, and he had waited a year after high school before going to college. He had to be twenty-three years old now; her mother was thirty-seven.

Dallas remembered that this was the second time she had done such figuring. Andy was closer in age to her mother than Victor, yet the idea of her mother falling for Andy was as repugnant as thinking of her and Victor. Andy, of all people. He was attractive, very attractive. Lots of girls she knew had had crushes on him, but Andy had always gone his own way. Maybe that was his charm. No one ever knew what Andy really thought about anyone, and while he was not rude he kept a certain distance that people wanted to get through. To get a compliment from Andy was worth a million from anyone else.

But her mother couldn't seriously be interested in Andy. Dallas decided she was nuts even to be thinking such thoughts. As hungry as she had been before, however, her taste for the marvelous food set before her was gone. She just nibbled at it.

"What's the matter, Dallas? You're not eating." Mrs. Waters was looking at her sympathetically. "Are you all right?"

"I'm fine, and the food is delicious. I guess I ate too many crackers before we sat down."

"She's mad at me." Her mother's voice shot across the table. "I can tell. She's been keeping an eye on me all day." Her mother was obviously drunk. "My daughter doesn't approve of me. My mother never approved of me, and now my daughter doesn't. That's pretty funny, isn't it? She thinks I'm ancient, old-fashioned. Don't you, Dallas? Don't you?" Her mother's voice was high and bordered on the hysterical.

Dallas knew her face must be a fiery red, and tears were smarting in her eyes. She didn't know what to do or say and was grateful to Vi Waters for taking over.

"All our kids think we're ancient, the same way we thought our parents were. I remember I thought my science teacher in high school was an old man, and then later I discovered he was only fifteen years older than I. It made a big difference when I was fifteen, but then one of my classmates married him when she was thirty and he was forty-five, and the difference didn't seem much at all."

But there was no stopping Ellen Davis. "Dallas, you didn't answer me. When I ask you a question, you should answer. We taught you manners, your father and I. Your dear, darling father—" Her voice broke. "He wouldn't like you to be rude to me, but he's not here, is he? You would be nice to me if he were here. . . . Answer my question, Dallas!" Her voice turned sharp.

"I don't remember it," Dallas mumbled, wanting to die.

"She doesn't remember it." Her mother laughed hysterically. "She doesn't remember it. . . ."

Dallas could feel Victor's hand on her arm. She didn't dare look around the table, but she could feel the weight of everyone's silence and embarrassment.

"Oh, God, she doesn't remember it. . . ." Her mother started to weep with loud, racking sobs, and in a second Mrs. Waters was by her side and taking her out of the room. Dallas got up quickly and followed them.

Her mother was in the bathroom being sick. Vi was holding her head, and Dallas stood by, feeling helpless. She was both sorry for her mother and embarrassed.

When the sickness was over, her mother sat on the edge of the bathtub with a peaked, wan face. "I'll take you home," Dallas said.

Mrs. Davis shook her head. "No, I don't want to spoil your dinner. I can take myself home."

As if she hasn't spoiled it already, Dallas thought. "I don't mind. I don't think you should drive."

"I'm perfectly capable of driving," Mrs. Davis said, pulling up her hunched shoulders. "But I'll walk anyway. I'll leave the car for you."

"If you want to go home, Andy can take you. But why don't you lie down here until you feel better?" Vi suggested.

"No. I'm sorry I've been such a nuisance. I shouldn't have wine on top of a cocktail. Hank always said I was a cheap date when it came to drinking. If Andy doesn't mind taking me home, that will be fine."

"He'll be glad to," his mother said.

Dallas thought that arrangement was about the worst she could think of. Vi did persuade her mother to lie down until Andy finished his dinner. Dallas hated to go back to the table, but she had no choice. Everyone asked after her mother, and after Dallas and Vi assured them that she was all right, the whole unpleasant episode was dropped. But not for Dallas.

She had resented her mother before, but now she was frightened. She felt that her mother was living on such a shaky emotional level that she might do anything. Dallas wished that her grandmother had come up from Florida, but she was afraid her mother would be furious if she called her. And consulting her grandparents, who called regularly from Oregon, didn't make such sense to her. What could they do? She couldn't see any point to getting them alarmed.

Andy finished his turkey, said that he would have his dessert later, and went off to take her mother home. Dallas longed to leave too, but her mother had made it clear that she didn't want her daughter to go with her. She was glad that Victor gave up trying to make any conversation with her. They finished their meal in silence, with Dallas half listening to the general conversation, and at last they all got up from the table.

"What do you want to do?" Victor asked.

"I don't know. Nothing. Go home I guess. Maybe Andy's waiting for me to get there." She was wondering why he had been gone so long.

"I doubt it. Andy doesn't wait around for anyone. Do you want to go to a movie?"

Dallas really wanted to go home, but she thought that if she went to a movie her mother might be asleep by the time she returned. She dreaded another scene with her.

"Okay, let's go to a movie. It's better than sitting around."

"Anything's better," Victor agreed.

When Dallas said good-bye to Vi, she was grateful for her breezy voice saying, "Don't worry about your

mother. That can happen to the best of us." Still
Dallas was glad to get out into the fresh air. Victor
took her arm and tucked her hand into his coat
pocket with his own as they walked to the movie
house. "Don't take it so hard," he said. "You're not
responsible for your mother."

"I know. But I never thought she would be this
way. She didn't use to be. Do you think she'll ever
get better?"

"I don't know. But you can't wait around to see.
I haven't had a chance to talk to my father yet, but
I'm hoping now that Andy's left school, maybe I can
go next fall. Not wait another year. If Andy does
want to go back, I don't think my father will pay
for it. Andy will have to make it on his own. You
know what that means?"

"No, what?"

Victor squeezed her hand. "It means you and I
could get married in a year or so."

Dallas was stunned. She was sure she loved Victor,
but marriage was something to think about for the
remote future. The thought gave her a scary but
warm feeling. "How do you figure that?" She held
on tightly to Victor's hand.

"If our parents pay for our tuition at school,
which they'd do anyhow, we could both work and
handle the rest. Lots of other couples do."

"Wouldn't that be terrific." Then she let out a
long sigh. "You know what my mother said the

other day? She wants me to go to school in Boston and take an apartment with me. Maybe I'll never be able to get married. Maybe you'd have to marry my mother too."

"Fat chance of that. You're going to have to get out from under. We'll work something out," he said, but Dallas thought his voice sounded less certain than his words.

Later, when they left the movie house, Dallas thought, If anyone ever asks me about this picture, I won't be able to tell them a thing. She only hoped that Victor wasn't going to discuss it. Her mind had been elsewhere, wondering what she was going to find when she got home.

The house was in total darkness when they arrived. It was only around ten o'clock, but even if her mother was asleep, Dallas thought, she would have left a light on. She started to run up the walk to the front door. "Let me go in first," Victor called out and went ahead of her.

They both pushed through the door at almost the same moment. They could hear her mother's voice in the living room, crooning a ballad in a plaintive voice and strumming softly on her guitar. Dallas threw open the door and switched on the lights.

"Oh, don't do that." Her mother shielded her eyes. "Turn them off." Dallas turned off the overhead light and turned on a shaded lamp instead. In the few seconds of bright light she had seen that her mother's face was streaked with mascara and tears. She looked awful. Andy was stretched out on the floor, on his stomach, sound asleep.

"Are you all right?" Dallas asked.

"I don't know," her mother said in a dull voice. "You have beautiful pink cheeks, Dallas. You look pretty. It must be cold out."

Victor nudged his brother with his foot. "Hey, get up." Victor looked both amused and exasperated by his older brother. Dallas knew that he often felt that his brother got away with murder, and she had sensed earlier in the evening when he had talked about Andy, that Victor had been quite pleased that their father was getting tougher with him. Now he poked at Andy harder. "Get up."

"Lay off," Andy mumbled. Then he sat up and looked at them with sleepy eyes. "What's going on?"

"You tell us," Victor said.

Andy didn't answer, but he stood up. "Where the devil have you been?" he asked Dallas.

"We went to the movies."

"You've been gone a helluva long time. Your mother was afraid to stay alone."

"You didn't have to stay," Mrs. Davis said apologetically. "You could have gone."

"Yeah, and left you here bawling your eyes out." Andy sounded disgusted. "All right, Vic. You want to go."

Victor looked at Dallas. "Go on," she said. "We'll be okay."

After the boys had left, Mrs. Davis looked at her daughter meekly. "I'm sorry, Dallas. I've made an awful fool of myself today, I'm afraid."

"I guess you couldn't help what you did. Come on up to bed now. Do you want some hot milk?"

"That would be very nice." Her mother kept looking at her, as if she wanted something. Love? Approval? Forgiveness? Dallas didn't know what. She herself was so tired from the strain of the day that she was aching to get right into bed. But she took her mother upstairs, and then went down to the kitchen to fix the hot milk. While she was watching the pot so the milk wouldn't boil over, she wondered again if this was going to be her way of life. Was she going to spend it taking care of her mother? She would never get married if her mother was going to have to live with her. Would there ever be any way out?

Dallas watched her mother sit up in bed and sip the milk like a docile child, and she thought, My father must have loved her a great deal to have taken care of her so much. She had known that he had been the strong one, but she had never realized how much he must have done. But she did not want to be the one to carry on where he had left off. When her mother was finished, Dallas took the empty mug away and kissed her mother good-night.

Her mother squeezed her hand and said, "You're a very good daughter."

Dallas said nothing, but inside she cried, "No, I'm not. I'm not. You don't know, you just don't know how hard it is. You don't know how much I sometimes hate you."

8

"I wish I were dead." Ellen Davis wrote the words in her large, scrawling hand across the page. She sat and stared at the paper for several minutes before she crumpled it up and dropped it in the wastebasket.

The whole Thanksgiving weekend had come and gone, but she was still feeling the effects of it. The fact that Christmas was looming ahead did not help. She had said to Dallas that morning, "Let's ignore

Christmas. Let's just pretend it doesn't exist. I'd like to go to bed and wake up when it's over. I don't think I can bear it."

But Dallas wouldn't agree. She had said that she wanted a tree. It didn't have to be a big one like those they used to have, but she wanted a tree and presents, and she wanted to invite friends in for Christmas Eve the way they always had. They had gotten into rather an argument about it, the way they did so often lately about everything. "I can't stand it," Ellen said aloud, although there was no one there to hear. She had told Dallas that she was being childish, she was too old for Christmas, and Dallas had accused her of being a child. "You can't crawl into bed and pull the covers over your head," Dallas had shouted at her at one point. "You have to face life. Maybe if you thought of someone else beside yourself for a change. . . ."

That had hurt. Dallas didn't understand; no one understood. Yes, Dallas had lost her father, but that was different, even though their relationship had been close. No one knew how much that closeness had hurt her as Dallas grew older—the way Hank and Dallas had gone off on their jaunts together, had their secrets, as if she didn't count, wasn't part of the family. Ellen had always known that Dallas loved her father more than she did her, and Ellen was still paying for it now. Dallas must wish that she was the one who had died.

So. She was feeling sorry for herself. What was wrong with that? Didn't she have a right?

Ellen got up from the kitchen table and walked around the house restlessly: from the kitchen to the living room, to the dining room, to the sun porch, and back to the kitchen.

The kitchen needed to be painted. The living-room sofa could use a new slipcover. But she didn't have the energy for any such projects. What was the use of fixing up the house without Hank? Ellen felt a pang of guilt. There was Dallas. The house should be kept up for Dallas, for Dallas and her friends. They came to the house. She shouldn't let it get shabby. If her mother were here, she would scold her, would say that she was lazy, that she was behaving badly. She probably was, but it wasn't laziness. It was the awful feeling that nothing mattered, that nothing made any difference anymore. Thinking that way was not fair to Dallas; Dallas mattered. There her mother would have some reason to criticize her. She wasn't doing a good job with Dallas. She was trying every way; she wanted desperately to be close to Dallas, to be her friend as well as her mother, but Dallas kept pushing her away, and she was vulnerable. An angry word or look from Dallas sent her into a panic, made her feel lost. She felt like someone going backwards; for every forward step she thought she made, she was pushed two steps back.

She poured herself another cup of coffee, glancing

at the clock on the kitchen wall. It was beginning to get dark already, and Dallas should be home. She had gone to the library and to do some Christmas shopping with her friend Jennifer. Ellen could feel her awful loneliness, with its ensuing sense of panic, start to creep in as the darkness enveloped the house. She could turn on the lights, but she chose not to. Not yet. It was as if plumbing the depth of her loneliness was some kind of comfort; she had first to go to the limits of her pain in order to find any relief anywhere.

She didn't have to turn on the light. Dallas came in with an armful of bundles, dumped them on the table, and turned the switch. "Why are you standing here in the dark?"

"I don't know. I guess I felt like it. What did you buy?"

"Not to be opened till Christmas."

"Do you need any money?"

"No, I saved out of my allowance. Thank you anyway."

Slowly Ellen felt herself relax. Strangely, she thought, although the tensions between Dallas and herself were irritating, she felt much better when Dallas was home. Tension, she supposed, was better than emptiness.

Dallas hurriedly took her packages out of the room, probably to hide them in her closet. But she soon was downstairs again. "What's for supper?"

"Nothing exciting. I was going to make some hamburgers and salad. Do you want potatoes?"

"I'll fix them if you want me to," Dallas offered.

Ellen could tell that Dallas had something on her mind, and she was right. As soon as they sat down to eat, Dallas started to speak. "Mom, I want to talk to you about something, and please don't get excited or upset until you hear me out, and really think about it. It's important to me."

"All right. Go ahead." Ellen kept her voice calm, but she had a foreboding of something definitely unpleasant.

"Okay. I'll give it to you straight. Jen said that a bunch of the kids are planning to go up to Vermont the day after Christmas to go skiing. And I want to go with them."

Ellen breathed a sigh of relief. "Well, that's not so terrible. Who all is going?"

"Victor, Jen, and I think Nancy and Sue and a couple of the boys. Andy may come too, I don't know."

"No chaperone?"

"Mom, we don't need a chaperone."

"I think you do. I wouldn't mind—"

Dallas didn't let her finish the sentence. "Now, Mom, please don't misunderstand. This is a kids' party. I don't think anyone wants someone's mother around."

Of course. She should have known. She was always falling into these traps, leaving herself wide open

116

for rejection, when any rejection these days was a deep wound, opening up all the pain of her aloneness. "I didn't think of myself as just someone's mother. I thought your friends liked me, accepted me as a person without hanging a label on me."

"But you're still a mother. Of course they like you, except that. . . ."

"Except what?" Oh, God, why couldn't she shut up and say she didn't care. But she did care. She didn't have the strength to put up a front the way some women did and pretend that life alone, without her Hank, was okay. She couldn't pretend, and she didn't see any sense in doing so anyway. "Have they said anything?"

"Well, no. . . ." Dallas was squirming, and all Ellen's senses were crying out, drop it, drop it, but she couldn't. She had to poke at her own wound.

"Tell me. Have your friends said that they don't like to have me around?" She was looking straight at Dallas, waiting for her answer.

"Not in so many words. They like you, I'm sure they do. But they wouldn't like anyone's mother around all the time, no matter how great she was."

"Maybe you're the one who doesn't want me around," Ellen said, knowing she was opening herself to another hurt.

Dallas gave her a swift glance and then looked away. "That's beside the point. I'm your daughter—"

"And you have to put up with it."

"Mom, let's not go into that. I stayed home because I thought you needed me, and I wanted to help. But going away for a few days is different."

"But I can't let you go away for a few days with a bunch of kids, because I don't think it's right. I feel a double responsibility. When a girl your age is without a father, it *is* different. I have no one to discuss the plans with, so I do have to be stricter. For my sake as well as yours. This is our loss, Dallas. I don't have a husband and you don't have a father, so we are not like all the other families. You are not like all the other kids."

"It doesn't seem fair." Dallas looked so woebegone that Ellen wished that she could say yes. But she felt that she was right. And also she thought of the long days and nights alone in the house without Dallas, and she knew that her own fears were part of her thinking. She didn't like herself for those secret thoughts, but she felt justified in indulging her own need. Sometime, in some hazy future, she would be able to face being alone, but not yet, not yet.

"I won't spoil your fun," Ellen said, trying to smile. "I'll make myself inconspicuous."

"Maybe I'll stay home," Dallas said glumly.

"That's not fair. That would really make me feel terrible. It will be good for you to go, even with me along. I'm serious about insisting on a chaperone anyway."

"Nuts! You just don't want to stay home alone. Why can't you be honest about it?"

"That's not fair. I do think there should be a chaperone, but what if I don't want to stay home alone? Going off to Vermont would be a nice change for me. Is that a crime?"

"You'll never understand!" Dallas cried, and she got up from the table and went upstairs to her room.

Ellen pushed her own unfinished meal away from her and sat at the table drinking her coffee. She could feel her heart pounding and wondered if she was having a heart attack.

The pounding subsided after a few minutes, but there was no relief from her sense of abandonment.

Ever since Hank had died, her life had been a series of rejections, one after another. She didn't feel as if she belonged anywhere. She loved her house, the rooms that she and Hank had filled over the years, but even here among her own things she felt alone and couldn't sit still for long. She was not a stupid woman, and she knew that she should not cling to Dallas as she was doing, but she also knew that intelligence had little to do with the state of her emotions. Her loss cut through all else, like a bulldozer doggedly making its way through a forest with no thought for any tender shoots in its path. She could not think of herself as a hard or selfish woman, only that she had been so hurt that even as she wished to die, she was fighting for survival at any cost.

It was still very early, just after seven, and Ellen felt that she could not bear another evening in the house. Ellen was sure that she could feel Dallas's resentment creeping down the stairs, pervading the house. Vi often said to stop by whenever she wanted. "If you don't feel like being alone, just come right over," Vi had said many times. Ellen had not done so, but now she put on her coat, called up to Dallas that she was going over to Vi's for a while, and without stopping to phone first went out.

The Waters' house was only a few blocks away, and since it was a bright, moonlit night, Ellen decided to walk rather than get out the car. She enjoyed the walk although she was thinking that she had never walked alone in the dark. before.

The house was lit up, but Ellen quickly noticed that the garage doors were open, and one car was gone, the one Vi and Bob used. The other one was there. Her heart gave a little jump of excitement that made her wonder for a minute whether she should turn around and go home. I'm being ridiculous, she told herself. These boys are the sons of my best friend, and besides maybe they have the big car and Vi and Bob are home. Dismissing her wave of excitement as nonsense, she rang the bell.

Andy answered the door. He had on jeans, an old sweat shirt, and was in bare feet. His curly hair was tousled, and he looked utterly surprised to see Ellen. They stared at each other for a second or two. "Come on in," Andy said.

"I just thought I'd drop in for a few minutes to

see your folks." Ellen spoke hurriedly to cover her unease. "Are they home?"

Andy shook his head. "No one's home but me. They went to an early movie and then out for dinner. Vic's working tonight."

"Then I guess I should go."

Andy didn't say anything, but she still stood there facing him. She had not seen Andy since Thanksgiving when he had taken her home, and she wanted an opportunity to talk to him. "But maybe I'll warm up for a few minutes first," Ellen said, giving Andy a smile. "That is, if you don't mind."

"I don't mind."

She followed him into the living room and took off her coat. The hi-fi was playing a jazz record. "That music sounds familiar."

"It's an old Dizzy Gillespie record."

There was no use trying to make conversation with Andy. She had already discovered that was a lost cause. Better to say what she had on her mind and then leave. "I guess I owe you an apology for Thanksgiving. My recollection is that I made a fool of myself."

Andy smiled. "You were very seductive."

Ellen blushed. "I was still drunk. And I really was afraid to stay alone. Was I pretty awful?"

"I would not use that word," Andy drawled. "You were kind of funny. I could have taken advantage of you."

Ellen felt her face flaming, but she tried to be dignified. "I don't think so. I wasn't that drunk."

Andy laughed. "You mean you knew what you were doing?"

"No," Ellen said indignantly. "Don't try to trip me up. I mean I would have come to my senses."

"Possibly." Andy still had that smile on his face. "Want to hear another record? How about some Benny Goodman?"

Ellen looked at him defiantly. "You don't have to put on an old record for me."

"I'm not doing it for you. I've been listening to old records all evening. Can I get you a drink?"

"No, thank you."

They sat in silence listening to the music. Andy got a beer for himself and persuaded Ellen to take a glass of wine. Slowly she found herself relaxing, sipping her wine and losing herself in the music, her foot tapping in rhythm to the sound.

"Would you like to dance?"

Ellen was startled by the suggestion. She had been thinking that Andy was being polite and probably feeling sorry for her, which was why he had asked her to stay. She loved dancing, but Hank had not. Although he had liked music and had a good sense of rhythm, he had never danced, and she had missed it. "I don't know if I remember how," she said.

"There's nothing like finding out."

Andy was a beautiful dancer, and after a little bit of uncertainty, while Ellen was getting used to his steps, she was delighted to find how easily she could follow him. She felt as if the clock had been turned back and she was in her teens again dancing with a college boy. For a few golden minutes she could forget her pain, forget the bleakness of her life, and simply lose herself in the physical exuberance of the dance.

"That was wonderful," she said, when the music stopped. "You're a dear to dance with an old lady like me."

"You don't dance like an old lady," Andy said. "Let's try another."

"I think I should go," she said primly. Her mind was hazy about that Thanksgiving night. She remembered feeling dizzy and clinging to Andy, asking him not to leave her alone. She did not want again to be accused of being seductive. Not by this handsome young man—boy—a boy who looked and acted older than his years and who had a provocative, self-contained air that put her on the defensive, but also reminded her that she used to be considered a very attractive woman. She was uneasy with Andy; whether because of her own emotional state or because she suspected he could be blunt at times, she wasn't sure.

He did not give her a chance to think. He put on another record, and they danced again.

They were still dancing when the door opened and Vi and Bob Waters came in. Vi showed her surprise at finding Ellen there, but she quickly covered it and said warmly, "How nice to find you here. I'm glad Andy was home."

"I felt lonesome and I just stopped by. Andy kept me here dancing." Ellen was embarrassed. Both Vi and Bob were pretending that it was quite natural to find Ellen in their house dancing with their son, but she could feel the strain. "I really have to go now."

Bob Waters gave her a sidelong glance and tried to make a joke. "I hope we haven't interrupted anything."

"Oh, Bob, don't be silly," his wife said.

"I'll walk you home," Andy offered.

"No, thank you. I'll be all right." Ellen wanted to leave and leave in a hurry. She did not want Andy to walk her home, and while he looked all innocence, she had a feeling that he was deliberately trying to give his parents the wrong impression.

"No, it's late. I'll take you."

Ellen said good-bye hurriedly and went out. Furious with Andy, she walked quickly and in silence.

"What's the matter?" Andy asked.

"I really didn't need anyone to walk me home."

Andy took her arm. "Is there anything wrong with my taking you home? It's late and it's dark."

"No, there isn't anything wrong."

When they got to her door, Ellen turned around to say good-night. "Aren't you going to ask me in?" Andy asked. His hand was still on her arm.

"No, Andy, I'm not," she said, but there he was, with that mischievous grin on his face and the moonlight giving a glow to his dark hair. They stood there looking at each other, and Ellen wondered if he could hear her heart hammering. How she missed just the simple touch of a man's hand, of an arm. For weeks after Hank had died she walked with her fist tight in her pocket because she had longed so for his hand in hers, the way they had so often walked together. Her whole body was aching to let Andy put his arms around her, to let her longing take over. . . .

"I'm not such a kid," Andy said. "I've got feelings too, you know."

"Of course I know." Ellen moved away from him and risked a laugh. "I've got to go in. I enjoyed dancing with you, and you were nice to suggest it."

"If that's the way you want it," Andy said, but he was still looking at her knowingly, as if he realized exactly what was going through her mind.

"I guess it is," she mumbled, confused, and went into the house. She felt stirred up and wondered what she would have done if Andy had persisted. But Andy wouldn't do that. He would never coax, and she knew that if there were to be any move it would be up to her. The whole idea was repugnant and frightening and tantalizing: another phase of being a widow. She was not even thinking of sex. That was something she did not want to consider at all. Just dealing with her need for some physical contact with a man was enough to try to sort out for now. But the answer couldn't be Andy. She'd have to be sick to think of Andy in any other role than as the son of her good friends. She was like a beggar, picking up tiny crumbs of affection anywhere she could.

Wearily she went upstairs to bed, grateful that Dallas's light was out. She wasn't up to facing Dallas now. How awful, Ellen thought, that for a few moments of pleasure she had to pay such a high price emotionally. It was as if she were an adolescent again, trying to find her place, trying to learn where she belonged, and to whom. She felt like a wandering soul. And all she could see ahead was more desolation.

9

The first snow fell a few days before Christmas. Dallas jumped out of bed when she saw the white flakes dashing against her window and ran to look out. She always felt excited by the beauty of the first snowfall. Nothing looked ordinary anymore. The commonplace houses, the familiar street became transformed, like a girl dressed up for a party. Dallas opened her window, gathered up a handful of the lovely white stuff, and washed her face in it.

"Mom, it's snowing." Dallas put on a robe and ran down the stairs to the kitchen where her mother was already having her morning coffee.

"I can see it," her mother said drily.

"Isn't it beautiful!"

"I'm thinking about who's going to shovel it."

Dallas's face fell. Of course. Her father was the one who previously would have been out there with a shovel, clearing a path to the garage, clearing the walk from the house. But Christmas was only a few days away, the first snow was coming down, and Dallas was not going to let her mother dampen her spirits. "I'll shovel it. I can do it."

"I should help you," her mother said halfheartedly.

"You don't have to. I'll be okay."

"What would I do without you?" Her mother's arms were around her in a tight hug, until Dallas wriggled herself free. "You're a beautiful girl."

"I'm not," Dallas murmured, uncomfortable under her mother's wistful affection.

They sat down to breakfast, and Dallas's mother broke a slice of toast into small pieces, as if eating were too much of an effort. She said, "I'd like to go to bed and wake up when Christmas is over."

"Do you want to get the tree today?" Dallas asked, determinedly cheerful.

"All right if you insist. I could do without it."

"You said we could have one."

"I guess I hoped you would change your mind," her mother said heavily.

"I haven't."

After breakfast Dallas put on warm slacks and a heavy sweater, and she got the snow shovel out of the garage. She felt good in the brisk air, and she quite liked the idea that she was carrying out a job that had been her father's. The doing of it made her feel close to him without the depression that had come to accompany her thoughts of him. And it was satisfying to see a smooth path slowly emerge, with the snow neatly piled on each side. But the work was tiring. Soon her arms began to ache, and the walk to the house seemed much longer than she thought it to be. She should have cleared the driveway first.

"Hello." Dallas turned, and there was Victor, pink cheeked, his red woolen cap bright against the snow. With a snow shovel in his hand, he was a welcome sight indeed. "I thought you might need some help."

Dallas threw her arms around him. "You *are* an angel. If you want to do the driveway, I'll finish the walk."

"Okay." But first he leaned his shovel against the house and tackled her in the snow.

"Angel my eye, you devil. . . ." They were both rolling in the snow, laughing, getting wet, until finally Dallas shook herself free and put a handful of snow down Victor's neck.

"Oh, boy, I'll get you for that!" He had her down again, burying her face in the snow until she cried for help.

They were laughing and floundering in the snow when her mother came to the door. Her face was stained with tears. "Oh, Dallas, Dallas. . . ."

Dallas jumped up and shook the snow from her clothes. "What's the matter? What happened?" She ran up to the door, and Victor followed.

"Nothing happened, but I feel terrible. I'm so ashamed. Today's our wedding anniversary, and to think I almost forgot. I've lost track of dates, and I just happened to look at the calendar. We would have been married nineteen years today."

Dallas put her arms around her mother and went inside with her. "Don't feel so bad. It's good that you almost forgot. I mean—"

Her mother pulled away from her. "It's not good. It's awful. I can't forget. I'm not built that way."

"I don't want you to forget him. I never will either," Dallas said. "I just think you shouldn't make a big thing out of dates. You shouldn't add to your mourning with dates."

"How can I not?" Her mother heaved a long sigh. "Everyone says time will help, but it just seems to make things worse."

"You're not giving yourself a chance. Come on and get dressed, and we'll go for the tree. It's so beautiful out."

"It's too beautiful." Her mother turned to Victor. "Forgive me for making a scene. I can't help it."

"Don't mind me. I'll go with you for the tree if you want. I'm good at picking one out."

"That will be nice." Mrs. Davis gave him a weak smile.

Her mother went upstairs to get dressed, and when she came down she was brighter. The thought struck Dallas that her mother could brighten up for about everyone except her daughter. While she was grateful that Victor was there, she resented the fact that she seemed to be the main recipient of her mother's grieving. Maybe her mother's behavior was only natural, but the burden was too much.

Although Mrs. Davis had said she didn't want a Christmas tree, she was fussy about buying one. It had to be exactly the right shape and the right height. Finally they picked one out, and Victor put it in the trunk of the car and tied the lid down over it.

They brought it home and set it up in the living room. Dallas immediately brought out the lights and ornaments that had been boxed away the year before. Victor stayed to help, and he and Dallas decorated the tree. In the afternoon Jennifer and Nancy and some of the boys came over, and they made a fire in the fireplace and popped corn. Dallas was glad to see that her mother's gloom had disappeared and she seemed to be having a good time.

Before Victor left he took Dallas aside to talk

about the ski trip. "You shouldn't stay home because of your mother," he said. "I won't go if you don't, and I want to go."

"I don't want you to stay home because of me." Dallas felt caught in a dilemma. "I'm afraid she may spoil the trip for everybody."

"She won't. Don't worry. Maybe Andy will be her date," Victor said mischievously.

Dallas made a grimace. "Is he definitely coming?"

"He says so. All his friends are at college. I guess he's pretty bored at home, and he's mad for skiing. Anyway we're going, you and me and your ma. That's definite."

"Whatever you say, Mr. Macho." Dallas made a deep bow and then kissed him on the nose.

When everyone had gone, Dallas said, "It really feels like Christmas, doesn't it?"

"It did for a little while," her mother said.

"Let's have our supper by the fire. It will be cozy," Dallas suggested.

"That sounds pleasant," her mother agreed, visibly trying to stay cheerful. "I'll fix something special. Would you like a quiche?"

"Super." Dallas set a small table for them in front of the fire, but by the time they sat down to eat she saw that her mother had to make a conscious effort to keep up her spirits. More than once she caught her mother staring moodily into the fire, and she

132

knew where her thoughts were. She seemed genuinely pleased, though, when Dallas told her she had decided to go on the ski trip and that Ellen could come along.

How can you sympathize with someone, love her, and yet sometimes not love her at all? Dallas sat in front of the tree on Christmas morning, feeling as full of despair as her mother looked. Her heart went out to her, and yet she kept thinking, Sometimes I don't love my mother. . . . Time is supposed to help, but how long will it take? When will she let me go? When will she let us both start living again? She wanted to help her, but there was nothing more that she could do. A short while before Christmas Dallas had suggested timidly that perhaps her mother could go to see a psychologist or psychiatrist. But her mother had rejected that idea quickly. "What can a psychiatrist do? No one can bring Hank back to life for me. There's nothing the matter with me; the problem is what life has done."

Dallas could tell by her mother's face that there was no use arguing the point. She had wanted to say that perhaps her mother could be helped in her attitude, but she didn't dare.

Their friends had been generous, and there were plenty of presents to open, but after everything was admired, clothes tried on, and the torn paper thrown into the fireplace, the day dragged. Mrs. Davis had refused to accept any of the invitations they'd received for Christmas dinner. "Thanksgiving was enough," she said. "I couldn't bear being the fifth wheel at a family Christmas dinner." Then she added, "But you can go out if you want to." Dallas knew that was a ridiculous offer. Her mother would have a fit if she said yes, and she wouldn't dream of leaving her.

Dallas could see, however, that her mother was making a real effort to give her a good Christmas. Instead of the usual Christmas dinner, her mother fixed a special shrimp dish that was Dallas's favorite. She also opened a bottle of wine, and in a poignant way she tried to make the meal festive without being pointedly Christmasy. When they sat down to eat, her mother talked about some of the Christmas dinners she had eaten alone with her mother when she was a child and her father was on the road. "They were awful Christmases," her mother said. "My mother would be furious that he didn't get home and took out her feelings on me. My father always sent me fabulous presents, huge dolls and once there was a beautiful dollhouse. I think my mother was jealous. I think I vowed even then," her mother said with a wistful smile, "that if I ever had a daughter she would be my friend. You are my friend, aren't you, Dallas?"

Dallas thought a minute before she answered. "I am your friend, but I think I'm your daughter first. It's different."

134

A hurt look crossed her mother's face, but she covered it quickly. "I suppose it is," she said lightly. Dallas wished she knew how to tell her that she wanted a mother, not a girl friend, and wondered if a too loving mother could be as bad as an unloving one.

She was relieved when after dinner her mother suggested a movie and was glad that when they came home it was ten o'clock and a reasonable time to go to bed. The next day they would be going away skiing. Dallas was happy that she had decided to go, even though her mother was coming along.

The next day was a perfect winter's day. The snow was still on the ground and had a hard crust on it; the air was dry and brisk. Dallas was taking their car and picking up first Andy and Victor and then Jen on the way. The others were going in another car.

At the Waters' house, Andy greeted her mother with a sardonic grin. "Do you ski as well as you dance?" he asked. Dallas was surprised to see her mother blush.

"No, I don't," Mrs. Davis said vehemently.

"You sure you want to go with these kids?" Vi asked.

"I'll be their chaperone," Mrs. Davis said.

"Some chaperone. We'll have to watch you so you don't get loaded," Andy remarked, still grinning. Her mother gave him a dirty look.

"Andy!" Vi remonstrated. "Don't pay any attention to him," she said to Ellen. "He's a terrible tease."

"I think I can take care of myself," Ellen said with some dignity.

They met the other car, with Nancy Edwards, Sue Prince, Ted Bateman, and Joel Kirkman in it, and they followed it to the highway. It was a four-hour drive up to the ski area in Vermont. Dallas and Jen had agreed before that they wanted to room together, but when they got to the motel, Mrs. Davis objected. Nancy and Sue were taking one room, which left her in a room alone.

"That's what I assumed you would want," Dallas said to her mother.

"I don't like to be in this big double room by myself, and there's no such thing as a single, which I wouldn't want anyway. If they put up a cot, the three girls can share one room and you can come in with me. It'll be cheaper that way anyway."

"We're not worried about the money," Jen said mildly.

"You women make up your minds," Andy said. "We're going to dump our stuff and get out on the slope." The four boys went off to their two double rooms.

"We just need two rooms," Mrs. Davis said to the man at the desk, "and you can put a cot in one of them."

The girls looked at each other as Mrs. Davis took the keys and got directions to find their rooms. "It doesn't matter," Nancy whispered to Dallas. "We're only going to sleep in the rooms anyway."

But Dallas was furious. Once in the room with her mother, she said, "I don't think you should be the one to tell everyone where to sleep. Jen and I wanted to be together."

Her mother didn't look up from the bag she was unpacking. "The girls didn't seem to mind." Then she swung around and faced Dallas. "You're the one who's bothered. You're critical of everything I do. You're worse than my mother! Let's try to have a good time these few days, Dallas."

"I want to. But I didn't expect to share a room with my mother."

Her mother looked at her with hurt eyes. "You make me sound like a monster. Is it so terrible to be with your mother?"

"Oh, Mom, we've gone over this before. You're a great person, but think of your mother. You don't want her to come to visit you. Why don't you want her around?"

"Because she always puts me down," Ellen said. "I try so hard with you, but nothing I seem to do is right."

"Maybe you're trying too hard."

"See, there you go again. I try too hard, or I don't try enough. Why can't you be as nice to me as you are to Jennifer, to your friends? What's so awful about wanting to share a room with my own daughter? If my mother had ever treated me like a friend, like someone she loved and admired, I would have been deliriously happy. We should be close now, Dallas. We need each other."

Her mother's eyes were fastened on her pleadingly. Dallas looked away before she answered. "I wish I knew how to say it right."

"Say it. Tell me, what am I doing wrong?"

Dallas was groping for the right words. "There's a difference between loving and needing. Of course we need each other, but not in the way you think. You need your own life, and I need mine, and they're different."

"But I have no life. You are my only life now. Don't take it away from me. That would be too cruel."

Dallas felt hopeless. She couldn't come out and tell her mother that she was a burden, that what her mother thought was close was pushing Dallas farther and farther from her. She didn't say anything, but went on with her unpacking.

Out on the slope Dallas forgot her troubles. She loved to ski, and gliding down the crusty snow she felt marvelous, like a bird flying. Her mother was on the beginner's slope, and after several runs, Dallas felt obligated to go over to see how she was doing.

"I'm having a terrible time," Mrs. Davis said crossly. "I'm glad you came over. Maybe you can help me. I'm falling all over the place."

Good-naturedly, Dallas stayed with her mother and tried to teach her how to manage her skis. "Dad would have loved being here. He was a beautiful skier," Dallas remarked.

Her mother gave her a sharp look. "You mean you wouldn't have had to help him."

"You misunderstand everything I say." Oh Lord, Dallas thought, I have to watch every word. How nice getting away from her for a few days would have been. But, damn it, I'm not going to let her spoil my skiing.

They stayed out until it got dark and then gathered at the Ski Shack to warm up by the fire. That evening everyone was tired and went to bed early.

The next day Dallas and her friends stayed out on the slopes the whole morning. Dallas spent some time with her mother, but Mrs. Davis gave up and said she'd go into the Shack and read. Dallas and Victor decided to try cross-country skiing in the afternoon.

"Do you know your way around up here?" Mrs. Davis asked at lunch, when Dallas mentioned their plan. "Won't you get lost?"

"No, of course not. Don't worry about us. We'll be fine."

"Maybe you'd like to spend the afternoon in a

bar with me," Andy said to Mrs. Davis. "That'll take your mind off Dallas."

"And what is that remark supposed to mean?" Mrs. Davis's eyes flashed at Andy, but he kept looking at her innocently.

"It means it would be good for you to forget about Dallas once in a while. Have some fun on your own." Andy spoke as if he meant what he said, and Mrs. Davis was obviously taken aback.

"I don't think I need your advice about what I should do," Mrs. Davis said coldly.

"Can't blame me for trying," Andy said good-naturedly. "Just thought someone ought to tell you you're too wrapped up in your daughter, and there's a big world out there to enjoy."

"He's got a point," Dallas murmured.

Her mother turned to her. "I'm glad everyone's so concerned about me." She was furious. Dallas thought that Andy's remark had hit home, and she was glad he had said what he did.

After lunch Dallas and Victor rented the skis they needed for going cross-country. When Dallas told her mother that she and Victor were leaving, she said, "Why don't you go and have a drink with Andy later? It might be fun."

Her mother surprised her by saying, "Sometimes I think you kids are making fun of me. At times you make me feel so good, and at other times when I'm with all of you I feel a million years old. No, I don't want to have a drink with Andy. I'll stay in and read."

Dallas didn't know whether she was feeling sorry for herself or if she preferred to be alone. She bent down and gave her a kiss before she left.

10

There wasn't much chance for talking as Dallas and Victor skied across the open fields. The snow-covered countryside glistened under a brilliant sun. They went through some patches of woods, and when they came out into the sunshine again, Dallas was so warm she stripped off her top sweater and tied it around her waist.

They must have gone miles, Dallas thought, when Victor suggested they sit down on some rocks and rest. They both took off their skis and turned their faces up to the sun.

"This is heavenly," Dallas murmured. "The best I've felt for months."

"I've been worrying about you. You've been awfully distant." Victor was examining her face.

"I suppose I have." She sat up from her reclining position. "I wish I could talk about my father. Everything seems to be bottled up inside of me. I can't talk about him at home. My mother keeps misunderstanding. It sounds crazy, but I don't feel as if it's right for me—well, to love anyone, to be involved so soon after he died."

"That's crazy," Victor agreed.

"It's as if I have to get my feelings straightened out first."

"You need to get straightened out with your mother."

"Don't I know it! But how do you go about doing that?"

"By doing something absolutely independent, taking some step on your own. You've got to break away."

"You mean go away?"

"That could be one way. But even while you're home, you've got to have something private, something that's yours alone."

"Easier said than done. I'll think about it."

"Thinking's not going to help." Suddenly Victor's

arms were around her, and he was kissing her and holding her tenderly. Dallas felt a great surge of warmth for him, and with the sun on her face she responded to him happily.

When they pulled apart, Victor was gazing at her seriously. "You remember what I said to you about going to school in the fall. I'm going to do it. And if you went to school too, and we both worked, we could get married. Nothing would hurt you then. I would be your protection. . . ."

Dallas looked at him in wonder. "You make everything sound so simple. I couldn't get married. I'm not eighteen yet."

"I don't mean we have to set a date now, but let's plan to get married. I love you, Dallas."

"I love you too." Her arms were around him, and she was clinging to him. She could feel the strength of his body against hers, and she thought, This is ours, ours alone. No one can touch it; no one can spoil this. Standing close, with their arms around each other, in the wide expanse of the snow-covered fields, Dallas knew that she would remember this time always: the snow and the sun, and Victor's cold cheeks against hers.

When she finally pulled away from him, she stretched out her arms. "We'll talk about it. We have lots of time."

"I'm very serious," Victor said.

They put on their skis and turned back to the

beginning of the trail. Dallas felt lighthearted and happy.

"You see, we came back in one piece," Dallas said to her mother gaily.

"I'm glad of that." They were in their room, and Dallas was about to take a shower and get dressed for the evening. She felt elated. Maybe Victor was right. Even the knowledge of their private conversation gave her the feeling of a protective wall, a comforting defense against her own irritability with her mother. How wonderful if all the little annoyances of living with her mother did not bother her because she had her own secret life! Sometimes I don't love my mother, I think. . . . But if she let herself love someone else, if she was secretly engaged to Victor, perhaps her feelings for her mother would not be so erratic. They wouldn't matter so much.

Spontaneously she gave her mother a hug. "You see, you mustn't worry about me so much."

"I worried all afternoon. Are you wearings slacks tonight or your long skirt?"

"I'll wear my denim skirt. I think there's a discotheque down the road where we're going dancing."

"Then I'll put on a long skirt too."

Of course her mother would be coming along, but she didn't care. She wasn't going to argue or fight anymore.

When they arrived at the discotheque, the place was jammed with teen-agers. "Oh, it's so crowded," Mrs. Davis said. "Do we have to stay here?"

"I'll run you back to the motel if you'd rather," Andy offered, but Ellen shook her head. "If all of you want to stay, I will too."

The group managed to squeeze in at two small tables off in a corner, and as soon as the music started, everyone got up to dance. That left Mrs. Davis sitting alone, trying, not too successfully, to look at ease. The floor was crowded, but Dallas and Victor danced well together, and she was having a good time. But before the music stopped, Dallas said, "We'd better go back and sit with my mother a bit."

"You are a darling," Mrs. Davis said to Victor, as if returning to sit with her had been Victor's idea.

"I love dancing," Mrs. Davis remarked.

"Do you want to try the next one with me?" Victor asked.

"I'd be delighted," Mrs. Davis said brightly.

When the others came back to the table, Andy sat down next to Mrs. Davis, and Dallas heard him order a drink for her. "Drink it slowly," he said in his teasing voice, "and it won't hit you. It's all in knowing how."

He was not letting up on her mother, but Dallas was rather pleased to see that her mother, rather than being annoyed, was getting back at him. "You're obviously very experienced," her mother said, sipping her drink, "but I think I'll give *you* a little advice for a change."

"And what's that?" Andy said.

"How about making up your mind where you fit in? You don't seem to be able to decide whether you're a kid or an adult." She smiled at him smoothly.

"That's some advice coming from you. People in glass houses . . . ."

Her mother flushed. Andy was hitting home again. "I know very well who I am," Mrs. Davis said. "I'm a mother."

"We all know that," Andy said, in a voice that implied he didn't think much of her motherhood.

The music started then, and Victor said to Mrs. Davis, "Let's have our dance."

Dallas shook her head when Andy asked her to dance. "I'll watch this one," she said, and he went off with Jen. Alone at the table, Dallas watched her mother trying her best to follow Victor's steps on the crowded floor. She felt both sorry and embarrassed for her. Her young-looking mother looked old and rather foolish amidst all the teen-agers. Dallas's throat felt choked, and she wasn't sure whether her sadness came from affection or annoyance.

Her thoughts were interrupted by a tall, bearded man who was suddenly standing by her table. He was much older than she, probably older than her mother, and Dallas's first thought was to wonder what was he doing there. When he spoke he had a slight foreign accent. "Would you care to dance?" he asked Dallas. "I saw you here alone, and it seemed a pity for you to sit and for me to sit with such music playing."

He stood tall and straight and was distinguished looking. Dallas thought he might be a professor from the college nearby. She was intrigued and said that she would be delighted. He danced well, although remarking that he could only dance to slow music like the number that had just began. Dallas was amused by the looks her friends gave her when they saw her on the floor with him. He said he was a visiting professor in Russian studies at the college and that he came to the discotheque because he was very interested in what young Americans did. He asked if he might come to see her at her home and was disappointed when she told him that she was only visiting in the area.

Her mother and Victor had stopped and gone back to their table. Across the floor Dallas caught her mother staring at her with a worried frown on her face. When the music stopped, her escort led her back to her table, bowed from the waist, and thanked her for the dance.

"Who was that?" her mother demanded.

"I don't know his name. He's a professor at the

college. A visiting professor in Russian studies, and he's interested in American young people."

"You mean that's what he told you," her mother fairly shrieked. "I'll say he's interested, coming here to pick up some young girl. That man is older than your father. Haven't you got more sense than to fall for that? An old man like that comes to a place like this for only one reason—to find some foolish girl like you!"

"You're a fine one to talk!" Dallas was furious. "Andy was right. People in glass houses . . . . What are you doing here with a bunch of kids? You have no business bawling me out. How do you think you look, sitting here with us, dancing with kids, flirting with boys half your age? You'd better not tell me what to do. I don't have to stand it anymore. I'm leaving." Dallas marched toward the door, and Victor quickly followed her.

Jen ran after them. "Don't go. Please stay."

"I can't. I'm sorry. I hope the evening hasn't been spoiled for everyone."

"Don't worry about that," Jen said. "Are you okay?"

"I suppose so," Dallas said morosely.

Victor drove her home in silence. When they got to the motel, he said, "Come to my room. We can watch some television."

"Okay." She certainly didn't feel like going into the room she shared with her mother.

Victor switched on the TV, and Dallas sat on the bed to watch. But she wasn't seeing anything. Her eyes blurred, and then she burst into tears. Victor's arms were around her. "Cry it out," he said.

She leaned against him, sobbing. "I don't know what to do. There's no end to it. Every time I try to be friends with her, she starts something all over again. . . . I can't stand it anymore. . . ."

"Just relax. Cry. You'll feel better." Victor was holding her close, patting the hair away from her face.

The warmth of his arms was comforting, and soon she stopped her hard sobbing. "She lets all her hurt and angry feelings out on me. I wish I knew what to do."

"Remember what I said this afternoon. You have to make a break." He jumped up and went to the door and locked it.

"Dallas, remember what I said this afternoon? Let's make a real commitment to each other. I love you, and you love me. We need each other. Let's make love, really. You'll—we'll—have something that no one can touch, not even your mother. It will be just yours and mine."

"Do you really think so?" she asked, nervously aware of her own strong desire to forget all else in Victor's arms.

"I know so." Victor stood over her, smiling, and pulled her to her feet. "I love you, Dallas. We love each other, we're going to be married sometime, we belong to each other."

Dallas stood facing him, holding both his hands tightly in each of her own. "I love you, too, Victor," she said seriously. He pulled her to him and kissed her, tenderly first, then harder, and Dallas felt a delicious warmth spread through her. Why not? she thought, and tried to ignore the nagging little question at the back of her mind. Maybe Victor was right; maybe they should just let go and enjoy what they had with each other.

"Dallas, let's get into bed where it's warm," whispered Victor. They turned, and suddenly the bed looked huge to Dallas. It seemed to take up the entire room. All at once she pulled away and sat down on a chair.

"I can't do it. I can't," she whispered.

Victor knelt in front of her. "Don't be scared. If we love each other, it's all right. We're not strangers, and we're not kids anymore. It's going to be all right. Dallas, I love you so much."

Dallas shook her head. "I can't." She sat silent for a few minutes, running her fingers through Victor's hair. "No. You see, Victor, I'd be doing it for the wrong reason: to get back at my mother. I don't want that. She would be part of this, the way she is everything else in my life. It's no good, Victor. I feel as if she's right in this room with us now. It won't work."

Victor groaned and stood up. He sat down on the bed with his head in his hands. "But I love you, Dallas," he mumbled.

"It has nothing to do with you, don't you see? When we get together, it's got to be just you and me, without my mother mixed up in it. God, I don't want to make *love* because of her. It's too important. You said it's very private, but if I'm doing it because I'm mad at my mother, it's not private anymore. And she'd always be part of it. You've got to understand."

"I suppose I do," Victor said reluctantly. "I suppose you know your own feelings."

"I think I may be beginning to. Let's go out for a walk."

"Okay."

Outside, arm in arm with Victor, the cold night air hit Dallas with a refreshing briskness. She felt that she had accomplished something tremendous that night. She didn't at all know what she was going to do, but she felt that she had acquired a nugget of understanding, of self-awareness that was valuable. She seemed to have stepped out of a fog, and now with luck perhaps she could find the right direction in which to go.

When she got back to her room, she got into bed quickly and pretended to be asleep when her mother came in a short while later. Dallas didn't want anything to touch the good feeling that she had, although she didn't think that her mother would talk about the evening. Her mother had a knack of backing away from arguments and behaving as if they had not happened. She would withdraw into silence until ordinary, daily communication filled in the gap.

11

Dallas still felt confident when she came home. They managed to get through New Year's Eve by paying no attention to it. "It's just another night, Mom. I hate New Year's celebrations." Dallas honestly felt that way, and her only acknowledgment of the occasion was to invite Victor over for dinner and agree to the opening of a bottle of champagne. When her mother wept at midnight, Dallas tried to comfort her. Soon after she sent Victor home and went to bed herself. Her one big New Year's resolution was not to let her mother's tears ruin her life.

She was beginning to see that she had to plan for the future. Until then she felt that she had been marking time and getting lost in the maze of her mother's unhappiness. In the long run her mother was going to have to face her own life; Dallas could not solve her mother's problems for her.

Easier said than done. For all her fine resolutions, Dallas found herself getting caught up again in the daily irritations of her life with her mother. The guitar lessons had petered out over the holidays, and no one seemed to want to start them again. Her mother made no effort to fill her days. In the past few months Dallas had mentioned that she was thinking of going out to look for a job, but her mother had discouraged her. Now she decided that was the first thing she had to do: find a temporary job, since she was still hoping to go away to school in the fall.

Her mother again was not encouraging. "What will I do here all day alone?" Mrs. Davis asked.

"I guess what you do when I'm home. I may not even get a job, but I'm going to try. I'd like to have some money of my own."

"I thought I was very generous with you."

"That's not the point, Mom. You *are* generous, but I want to make some money myself. I need to get out of the house. I'm sick of doing nothing."

"But you're doing a lot, being here with me. Don't you think that's important?"

Dallas faced her mother. "I shouldn't be with you twenty-four hours a day. You don't want to let me out of your sight. I feel as if I can't breathe anymore. It's not good for you; I know it's not. Can't you see what you've been doing?"

Her mother looked stunned. "I thought you understood." She spoke in a low voice. "I thought you knew you were the only one I had left, that you were my only reason to get out of bed each morning. . . ."

"But I *can't* be," Dallas said vehemently. "You're asking the impossible. You're asking me to exist only for you. Dad had his own life, but you want to own me completely."

Her mother didn't say anything. She just sat staring off into space. Finally she said, "What kind of a job are you going to look for?" Her voice sounded tired.

"I don't know. Whatever I can get." Dallas didn't know whether to approach her mother or not. She was afraid that if she made a gesture, her mother would push her away. Their emotions lay between them like a heavy fog in the room until, wordlessly, Dallas went out.

Dallas scanned the newspapers every day, but there were no jobs for someone with no experience. Too many people were out of work.

Then one day she ran into a piece of luck. On one of her frequent trips to the library, the head librarian asked if she knew any young person who might want a part-time job doing clerical work. "We need someone to make out the cards for the new books, catalogue them, and put them in the stacks."

Dallas jumped at the opportunity. "What about me? I think I could do that. I'd love to work here."

"I'd like that fine." The librarian was enthusiastic. "I have to take it up with the library board, and I'll let you know. There's not much pay, and there won't be more than probably twenty hours a week."

"I don't care. It would suit me perfectly."

Dallas went home feeling ecstatic, but she was not surprised that her mother had little to say. Ever since she had expressed herself so strongly, Mrs. Davis had seemed withdrawn. When she got a call about a week later that the job was hers, her mother still didn't react. The next Saturday morning Dallas started to work.

Dallas wondered why she hadn't taken this step before. The hours that she spent working in the library seemed to her the happiest she had had since her father died. It was such a relief to be out of the house, away from her mother, and not to feel guilty, as she would if she were out having a good time someplace. She was working, earning money, and that made a difference. A big difference. As she thought about the last months, however, she came to the conclusion that she hadn't been ready to get out before. She couldn't have left her mother alone any sooner.

Not that she was gone that much. As the librarian had said, she worked only twenty hours a week, five hours on Saturday and five hours three afternoons a week. Yet Dallas soon discovered that her mother would make her pay for this small step toward independence. Dallas didn't know whether her mother was consciously punishing her, but either way her behavior was just as painful.

Litttle as her mother had done before, she did almost nothing now. She seemed to have completely given up any interest in living. Each afternoon that Dallas came home from work, she found her mother sitting in front of the television set, watching a soap opera, usually with a cup of cold coffee nearby. She didn't do any shopping; she had nothing in the house for their supper.

"You're the wage earner," she said to Dallas with a weak smile. "You can decide what to eat."

Dallas went out as cheerfully as she could to market, and by the time she had their supper ready her mother cheered up some. But the next day was the same all over again.

"I guess I have to learn to be alone," her mother said wearily one evening, "but so far I don't seem to be able to."

"But you were alone during the day when Dad was alive," Dallas pointed out.

158

"That was different. I knew he was coming home in the evening. I had a reason to market, to cook. I had a reason to live."

"I thought I was your reason to live now," Dallas said. "I'm here. I come home. For heaven's sake, Mom, get with it."

"I'm sorry I'm such a drag," her mother said. But nothing changed.

Sometimes Dallas thought that if her mother drank, if she were an alcoholic, the problem might be easier. There might be a cure for alcoholism; but this listlessness, her total immersion in her own sorrow seemed to have no solution. She refused to see a psychiatrist, insisting that there was nothing wrong with her. She seemed truly to believe that she was behaving naturally for someone recently widowed.

Dallas had been working at the library for a few weeks when Jennifer came in one afternoon all excited. "Have you talked to Victor today?"

Dallas shook her head. "No, he's coming over later."

"He'll tell you about it then. But I met Andy. He's buying a van he wants to take to California, and he wants passengers to help pay expenses. The trip won't cost much, if he gets enough people, except for the fare back. He wants to stay out West. I want to go. It would be terrific to see Yosemite and the Grand Canyon. You've got to come."

"I'd love nothing better, and I have some Christmas money my grandparents sent me." Then Dallas's face fell. "My mother would never let me go. Don't count on me."

"You've got to go. Forget your mother, Dallas. Andy said Victor wants to come, but he won't without you. By the summer your mother will be okay."

"Not the way she's going now. She's worse, if anything."

"We'll probably only be gone about four weeks. I want to see something of California once we get there. Let's talk about it. Andy wants to get together tonight. I suppose your house as usual?"

"As usual," Dallas said glumly. "I wonder where Andy's getting the money for a van," she mused.

"You know Andy. He has a way of getting what he wants. Maybe he borrowed it. I don't know and I don't care, so long as he has it. It's a fantastic opportunity, Dallas, and you and Victor have to come."

That evening Victor and Andy came over, armed with road maps, tourist's books, and large bags of potato chips and pretzels. Soon Jennifer, Nancy, and her boyfriend Ted joined the group.

Nancy counted noses, "Andy, Victor and Dallas, Jen, Ted and me. Six of us. That's just about right, isn't it, Andy?"

"We could squeeze in one more, I think, but six would be okay."

They were discussing whether to go to New Orleans and across the South through the desert or to keep to the North, when Mrs. Davis appeared. Dallas had purposely not told her about the proposed trip.

"What's going on?" she asked.

Andy explained to her. "Are all of you going?" she asked. "You didn't say a word to me," she said to Dallas.

"It all just came up today. I have the money Grandpa sent me, and we'll only be gone three or four weeks." Dallas spoke quickly. "We're only driving with Andy one way, and then I'd fly back and be home in no time."

"That's not the point. You know how I feel about a chaperone, Dallas. Just you kids alone. . . ." Mrs. Davis looked from one to the other. "And don't tell me about other parents. I don't care what other parents do. I'm in a different position."

"I'm not a kid," Andy stated flatly. "And, if you don't mind my saying so, I think you're being ridiculous."

"I do mind your saying so, very much. I think this is between Dallas and me, and we do not need a public discussion."

"Maybe we do," Victor said. "Don't you trust me? What do you think is going to happen anyway?"

"The matter has nothing to do with trust. I do not want my daughter, not yet eighteen, traipsing across the country in a van with a bunch of kids. You may not think yourself a kid, Andy, but that's a matter of opinion."

"What do you suggest?" Victor demanded, looking as if he wanted to strangle her.

"I will discuss this with Dallas alone," Mrs. Davis said.

"I know what you're going to suggest. You'll say that you want to come along," Victor said.

"And would that be so terrible?"

Dallas could see that her mother was close to tears by this time, and she had that defenseless, hurt look Dallas had come to know so well. Dallas didn't think she could bear a tearful scene with her mother in front of her friends.

"We'll talk about it later, Vic. We're only in a planning stage now anyway, Mom." Dallas stood up. "I'm going in to make a pot of coffee."

Victor followed her into the kitchen. "You can't let her get away with this, honey. It's too much. She's not going to push herself into this trip."

"I don't want to talk about it now." She put her arms around Victor and leaned her head against his chest. "I can't even think straight anymore."

"You're going to come to California with me. That's all there is to it," Victor said. "And without your mother."

Dallas shook her head sadly. "We'll see."

When they went back to join the others, her

162

mother had gone upstairs. Dallas only halfheartedly listened as the group discussed their plans. She knew that when everyone had left, she would have to deal with her mother.

She was almost relieved when the meeting broke up early. Before he left, Victor said, "Remember, you're coming with me. Just stick to that."

"We'll see," she said again, realizing that not even Victor could fully understand how she could hate her mother and sympathize with her at the same time. Once again her mother would play on her sympathy, making her feel guilty and sorry.

When she went upstairs, Dallas was not surprised to find her mother's light on and to hear a call from her room. Her mother was in bed with a book in her hand. "Come and sit down," Mrs. Davis said, patting the side of the bed and putting her book aside. "I think we have to have a talk."

"What's there to talk about?" Dallas sat on the edge of the bed.

"Don't start off that way. Why are you so hostile to me? Okay, that's a dumb question. I suppose all daughters sometimes feel that way about their mothers. I just wish you weren't going through that phase now, so soon after we lost Dad."

"Maybe you're the one going through a phase, not me," Dallas said.

Mrs. Davis sighed deeply. "If only it were a phase. I see my whole life stretching ahead, empty years—"

"Is that all you want to talk about?" Dallas asked, standing up.

"No. I want to talk about this trip to California. Is there any reason why we can't both go?"

"Yes. Lots of reasons. If you don't know them, I'm not going to spell them out. Let's forget it. I'm not going."

"You're being very unfair. You're not trying to understand my side of it."

"I do understand it. You don't want to be alone. You want to be with me every minute, and it's terrible." Dallas wanted to rush out of the room, but her mother reached over and took her hand.

"Don't be so harsh with me. Think about it, Dallas, think about my side of it. Think what a good time we could have on such a trip. Don't deprive us both."

"I'm not going," Dallas said. "Good night."

Alone in her room, Dallas sank down on her bed and tried to clear her thoughts. One thing she was sure of: she would not change her mind. She would not go on the trip if her mother insisted on coming along.

The next day was a work day for Dallas, and Jen came to the library to pick her up at five o'clock. As soon as they were alone outdoors, Jen said, "What are you going to do? About the trip, I mean."

"Nothing. I'm not going. I told my mother last

night I wasn't going. She thinks I'm being unfair."

"That's the dumbest thing I ever heard. You've got to do something, Dallas."

Dallas felt her newly found strength ebbing. "I'm trapped. I've told you that before."

"No one has to be trapped who doesn't want to be. You've got to get out."

The girls parted at Dallas's corner, but Dallas kept on thinking about what Jen had said. On the spur of the moment she decided to stop in to see Vi Waters. She felt that maybe talking to her mother's friend would help.

Vi was very glad to see her and sat her down with a cup of hot tea. "I think of you a lot, and of course Victor tells me about you," Mrs. Waters said. "How are you doing?"

"I'm doing okay. It's my mother. She doesn't seem to get any better. If anything, she's in a worse state now than right after my father died."

"I know. I try to get her to go out, but she won't. The boys told me she wants to go to California with all of you in the summer."

"I'm not going," Dallas said.

"Dallas, you know the kids don't want your mother along. I can see their point. But you should go. Why don't you?"

Dallas shook her head. "I can't."

"We'll see. Your mother has a birthday coming up in a few weeks. Why don't we give a party for her? I'll give it here. We'll surprise her. I'll invite all her old friends. Maybe if she sees that we all do care for her, she won't feel so alone. It can't hurt anyway."

"That's a good idea!" Dallas felt some hope. Perhaps Vi was the one who could really help.

In the next few weeks Dallas spent a lot of time with Vi Waters planning the party, sending out invitations, and helping with preparing her mother's favorite dishes that would be kept in the Waters' freezer until her mother's birthday.

A few days before the party, Dallas was home and her mother was at the beauty parlor when a call came from her grandmother in Florida. "I'm coming up," she told Dallas. "I won't take no this time. I'll surprise your mother for her birthday. Don't tell her. It will be a happy surprise."

Dallas didn't know what to say. She didn't think it would be a happy surprise for her mother, but she didn't say so. Suddenly the idea sounded good to her, and she said, "Fine, Grandma. I'll meet you at the airport. Give me your flight and arrival time."

Dallas wrote down the information and wondered what excuse she would give her mother to take the car for an afternoon. She'd figure out something.

12

Ellen stood at the window and watched Dallas drive off in the car. She had been mysterious about where she was going, but Ellen hadn't pushed her to tell. She was quite sure something was going on about her birthday the next day. Dallas had been spending a lot of time at the Waters' house, and there had been much low-voiced telephoning. Ellen liked the idea that that nice bunch of kids was planning something for her. Although her own daughter got annoyed with her, the young people accepted her, even at the coming age of thirty-eight.

Thirty-eight. In two years she'd be forty. She might live until her seventies or eighties. The thought of all those years extending ahead made her spirits sink with despair. One day was as empty as the next, one empty afternoon like another. Mechanically she turned to the television set and flicked it on. She poured herself another cup of coffee and sat down to watch the troubles of a fictional family.

She had fallen asleep on the sofa when the car coming into the driveway woke her up. Miraculously the afternoon had passed; she had gotten through another day. Already it was dark outside. She stood up, straightened her crumpled skirt, and turned off the TV. Dallas disapproved of her watching television, but Dallas didn't know how slowly the time passed, how agonizing each new day was. Dallas disapproved of her altogether, which seemed so unfair. She should be pleased that she had a young mother —comparatively young anyway—who wanted to be her friend. But Dallas didn't want her friendship; she never confided in her. She never allowed the nice, cozy, heart-to-heart talks a mother should have with her daughter. All her daughter's friends treated her like one of their own crowd, but not Dallas.

"Mom, where are you?" Dallas had come in the back door and was calling from the kitchen. Someone was with her.

Ellen went to the kitchen and then stopped dead still. She couldn't believe her eyes. "Mother! Good heavens, where did you come from?" It took her a few minutes to get over the shock.

"From the airport. I wanted to surprise you for your birthday." Her mother was kissing her, and Ellen could smell her mother's sweet scent that she had never liked.

"You certainly did surprise me. My goodness, it's a shock."

"I hope a pleasant one," her mother said. "Let me look at you." Eva Hendrix stood off at arm's length to examine her daughter. "You're too thin and you're pale. You're not eating enough."

"I eat plenty," Ellen said. She was examining her mother too. Mrs. Hendrix was a tall woman who still retained some of the prettiness her daughter and granddaughter had inherited. She had a full figure, which she had not let run to fat, and the same fine skin as the two younger women. Her imposing appearance made Ellen feel the same old mixture of pride in her mother's strength and the sense of inadequacy that it generated in her. If she lived to be a hundred, she thought, she would still feel overshadowed by her mother.

"This house is drafty," Mrs. Hendrix commented, taking off her coat. "I'm not used to this cold weather. Can you turn up the heat?"

"Oil is expensive," Ellen said.

"You're not so poor that we have to freeze. Dallas, turn up the thermostat. I'll take my things up to your room, Ellen. I can sleep in the other twin bed."

That she would not have, Ellen decided. "I don't think you'll be comfortable there, Mother. I get up a lot at night, and I sit up and read."

"I don't mind. I sleep very well. You won't disturb me."

"All right. You take my room, and I'll fix up a bed for myself on the sofa."

"I wouldn't hear of it. You just stay in your own bed, and you won't even know I'm there."

Small chance of that, Ellen thought.

Dallas spoke up. "Grandma, you take my room. I don't mind the sofa, I really don't. I like it."

"If you insist. I suppose you're young enough to sleep anyplace."

Ellen gave Dallas a quick squeeze of her hand and a murmured "Thank you," as she followed her mother up the stairs to her daughter's room.

It was a trying evening for Ellen. Her mind was flooded with memories of the times that her mother had come to visit when Hank was alive. He had been a protective shield for her. He had always been very kind to her mother, and her mother had adored him. Ellen had been grateful to him for being so considerate of his mother-in-law, catering to her in a way that Ellen never could. At the same time, however, she resented the way her mother had imposed on his good nature and at times wanted to shout at her, "He's doing it for me, not for you, you vain old woman."

Hank had laughed when she had admonished him not to let her mother take advantage of him. "I don't mind. She's not my mother—I don't have your old hang-ups—and she doesn't come that often."

Now, as the evening progressed, Ellen was amazed at how patient Dallas was with her grandmother. She was behaving very much like her father. Ellen was touched and a little amused, although her amusement was tinged with a streak of envy: Why was Dallas so gentle with her grandmother and so abrupt with her?

Ellen noticed the difference in Dallas's attitude right at the start when she and Dallas were preparing dinner. "Don't you have a cutting board?" her mother had demanded, watching Dallas cut vegetables on the counter.

"Yes, of course," Dallas said agreeably. "I forgot."

When she had brought out the board, Mrs. Hendrix then proceeded to show her how to use a knife to chop the vegetables finely.

"Dallas knows how to do it," Ellen said. "You'll make her so nervous she'll cut herself."

"I'm showing her how to do it right," her mother said.

"You make me nervous," Ellen mumbled.

"It's okay, Mom," said Dallas. "Why don't you and Grandma sit down and have a glass of wine. I'll fix dinner." She gave them a smile.

"That's a good idea." Mrs. Hendrix put two glasses on a tray. "Let's go into the living room."

Ellen followed her mother, carrying the wine.

"You're a lucky woman to have such a daughter," her mother said with a sigh. "She's a wonderful girl."

"I know it," Ellen agreed, thinking immediately that her mother was implying she had a terrible daughter in Ellen. "She was very dear to stay home with me this year."

"You don't know what it means to be alone. Sometimes the loneliness gets so bad that you don't think you can live through another day."

Ellen ran her hand through her hair. She seemed to hear herself speaking. "I'm lonely even with Dallas here."

"But wait till she goes. Then you'll know what it's really like." Ellen almost laughed at the way her mother spoke: as if she *wanted* Ellen to know. "I was thinking, Ellen," her mother continued, "if I sold my condominium in Florida, I could add on a room and bath here for myself, and maybe we wouldn't have to be so lonely. Someday I may be too old to live alone."

"But you like Florida," Ellen said firmly, "and you don't like the cold weather."

"I could still go down for a couple of months in

the winter. Maybe you'd come with me." Her tall, imposing mother, sitting erect in her chair, looked at her wistfully, but Ellen shrank from being taken in by her mother's wiliness. No, she said determinedly to herself, I am not going to end up living with my mother. She is a remarkable woman, and there's a lot to admire, but not for me to live with.

"I don't think it would be a good idea for us to live together," Ellen said.

"Why not? Why shouldn't a mother and daughter live together? Your daughter is living with you." Mrs. Hendrix's questions sounded like statements.

"Dallas is still very young," Ellen said defensively.

Not until Dallas had called them into the kitchen to eat, and they were sitting at the table, did the thought forcibly strike Ellen: Dallas hates living with me! Ellen had been pushing the realization from her mind ever since Dallas's anguished, blunt words when she had spoken about getting a job. She had tried to put Dallas's outcry down to a bad mood, because to accept what she had said as true was to be destroyed. Ellen felt she was very different from her mother: she wasn't forever criticizing Dallas or trying to change her. All she wanted was love and friendship. Maybe that's what every mother wanted from her daughter, and there was no right way to seek it. Surely Dallas loved her, or did one just take for granted that a daughter loved her mother? Did she love her mother? She hadn't thought about loving anyone except her husband

and Dallas for a long time. Ellen felt that she had to stop and give the matter a lot of thought. Growing up, she had assumed that she loved her mother, and then, when she was adolescent and found her mother bossy and constantly critical, there had been a lot of arguments. But she wondered if she had stopped loving her. After she had married, her parents had moved to Florida, and her father had died, she hadn't thought much about her mother except for phone calls and visits—visits that Ellen had never looked forward to.

Sitting at the table between her daughter and her mother, Ellen thought, Here we are, three generations. Dallas doesn't get along with me well, and I don't get along with my mother well, and yet Dallas and her grandmother get along fine. She felt depressed by her thoughts and yet her mind kept worrying at them. She had read enough to know that the love between a mother and a daughter had a lot of ambiguities as she had said to Dallas when they were talking about the summer trip. Yet some daughters adored their mothers almost unconditionally. Perhaps she had never learned about love from her mother, had never learned that a parent's love had to be more giving than taking, and that one cannot take a child's love for granted. Maybe she had never really loved anyone but Hank. . . .

"You're very quiet, Ellen," her mother said.

"What's wrong with that?" was her sharp and automatic response. Oh, Lord, she thought, my mother is over sixty years old, and I am a married woman with a grown daughter. Will I ever get over reacting so strongly to her? "I was just thinking," she added more gently. "I'm sorry. What were you saying about your friends in Florida?"

Ellen listened patiently to a long tale her mother told about a luncheon she had been to, including a detailed explanation of what every woman had worn (people Ellen didn't know and never would know), what they had eaten, and what her mother thought of each dish. Ellen had to keep reminding herself, She has no one to talk to at home. Naturally she wants to talk to us. I must be kind to her.

By the time Ellen was ready to go to bed she was exhausted. Her evening had been torn between irritation with her mother's insistent chatter and preoccupation with her own feelings, as well as an honest desire to try to make her mother's stay as pleasant as possible. Once she was in bed, however, she tried to figure out how she could diplomatically send her mother back to Florida in a few days. By the looks of her luggage she had come for at least several weeks.

They were both very sweet to her on her birthday. Dallas brought her breakfast in bed, and her mother insisted on taking her out to lunch. She was with the two people in the world closest to her, and yet her longing for Hank colored her whole day gray. The awful thing was, she thought, that the times she had enjoyed most before, family holidays and festivities, now were the most painful.

Dallas said that she couldn't lunch with them; she had some other things to do. "I'll pick up something for dinner tonight," Ellen said.

"No, I'll take care of it. You're not supposed to do anything today."

Dallas wasn't very good at lying, and Ellen was positive that something was in the air for the evening. She wasn't surprised when later in the day Dallas said they'd go out to eat and that, since it was a celebration, they should all get dressed up.

Before getting dressed, Ellen stretched out on her bed to rest. At lunch her mother had spoken again of selling her apartment and coming up North to live with Ellen. Ellen had felt her defenses breaking down. After all, what difference would the change make? She didn't think she could be unhappier than she already was, so how she lived or with whom didn't matter. She was ready to give up. Hank was gone, and what happened to her was unimportant.

Ellen had never felt so depressed in her life, and in a way the attempts by her mother and Dallas to celebrate her birthday made things even worse. But she got up and took a shower and got dressed. Perhaps a party with those young friends of Dallas would cheer her up. At least, they made her feel that she wasn't ready to be put on the shelf quite yet.

"You look lovely, Mom," Dallas said to her, when she came downstairs.

But her mother had to spoil the compliment. "I don't think you ought to wear earrings and a gold chain. I'd take off the earrings if I were you."

"I like them," Ellen said. "I'm not you."

Her mother looked disapproving.

"We're going to stop at the Waters' for a few minutes. Vi called when you were out and invited us for a drink before we go to dinner," Dallas said in the car.

"That's nice," said Ellen.

Ellen knew before they went into the house that there was going to be a party. All the lights were on, and she could see the people. But when she stepped into the entrance hall, and everyone came out shouting "Surprise" and "Happy Birthday," she truly was surprised. She had simply assumed that the party was going to be given by Dallas and her young friends, but instead here were all the couples that she had been avoiding since Hank died. She was completely taken aback, but she tried to cover her dismay as well as possible. She hugged Vi, let everyone kiss her, and introduced her mother around.

In the living room there was a bar set up and there were beautiful canapes. Ellen hoped that she could shake her depression now compounded by her disappointment. But she wasn't doing a good job of it. She still felt alienated from her old friends; the women all had their husbands and she had her mother. Undoubtedly they were all feeling sorry for her, and too many of them said, "It's nice for you to have your mother visiting," as if to have her mother was some great treat for poor, little, lonely Ellen. Yucky, thought Ellen, borrowing one of the kids' words.

And, as Ellen was being reminded, her mother was the kind of woman who made her presence felt. Unabashedly she asked personal questions and made opinionated comments. Everyone was polite to her, but Ellen could see her mother fasten onto one person after another. No sooner did one make an excuse to get away than her mother, undaunted, would find another ear for her compulsive talking and carry on. I am not responsible for her, Ellen told herself, but yet she felt that she was. Between worrying about her mother boring everyone and her own discomfort, she wished that the evening would end. But there was still a buffet supper ahead.

While supper was being served, Andy and Victor joined them. Ellen watched them fill their plates and promptly get hold of Dallas, who had been helping with the serving. They maneuvered her to a small table, where the three of them sat down. Ellen was just about to get a plate for herself and join them when her mother beat her to them. She could hear her mother's loud, clear voice. "My, how you two boys—or I should say young men—have grown. Now you must tell me all about yourselves. I'm go-

ing to sit here with you. I don't have much opportunity to dine with two such handsome young men."

Andy and Vic looked embarrassed but made a
place for her, and the four of them sat at the small,
crowded table.

Ellen tried to shrug off her mother's appropria-
tion of the three young people. Let her have a good
time, she thought. But as the meal came to an end,
and her mother continued to monopolize the two
men—Dallas left the table and was helping Vi clear
the plates away—she grew annoyed and began to feel
that she should do something to rescue them. But,
she argued with herself, it was not her problem; it
was theirs. However, her eyes kept going back to
them.

"Your mother seems to be enjoying herself with
the boys," Vi said to her.

"She's probably boring them stiff," said Ellen.

"It won't hurt them. They're good-natured with
older people. I hate to see kids be rude, although I
don't believe in asking too much of them. I don't
like to see older people make fools of themselves—"
Her friend stopped suddenly, and Ellen could see
she had said more than she'd intended.

"Like who?" Ellen demanded. "Are you trying to
tell me something?"

"Tonight's your birthday. Let's talk about it some
other time." Vi was looking at her, and Ellen knew
that Vi would not lie to her.

"What's there to talk about? You think I've been

making a fool of myself with the kids?" Ellen followed Vi into the kitchen, where they were alone.

"I think you've been hurting yourself. The people here tonight are your friends; they care about you. You've been running away, and I think you should stop."

"I suppose the boys told you that I want to go on the trip to the coast with them this summer."

"Yes, they did." Vi, who had been busy at the sink, swung around to face her. "Don't push it, Ellen. You'll get hurt."

"You mean they don't want me?"

Vi nodded her head. "None of them will go if you go along. The trip will be called off."

Ellen stood still. Feeling shaky, she balanced herself against the kitchen counter. She was glad that Vi kept busy with the dishes and did not try to comfort her. The blow had been coming for a long time, like a tornado that one sees whirling in the distance, and now it had landed with all its force and hit her.

Of course it was true. She had known it was true, but she had kept on kidding herself. She was as bad as her mother, worse. Her mother was trying to hold on to her, and she had desperately been clinging to Dallas. And her clinging had been worse because she had used not only her daughter but her daughter's friends. How Dallas must hate her. The last thought choked her throat.

"Don't think about it now," Vi said. "Let's go back and join the others.

"I'll be along in a few minutes," Ellen said.

She went to the bathroom and washed her face and reapplied her makeup. Before she went out, she sat for a few moments on the edge of the tub and thought about her husband. She felt that he was close to her. She could almost hear him saying, "You've had a rough time, darling, but you're going to be on the right track now." She prayed to God that she would be.

Ellen had had only one cocktail before dinner, and now she took a liqueur and sat down to talk with the guests. Victor and Dallas had disappeared. She didn't know where and was not going to ask, and her mother was still bending Andy's ear. She had thought the liqueur would relax her, but the tensions of the evening were more than a small glass of cherry brandy could cure. She was trying to fight down a tremendous anger against her mother. Her mother's bossiness, her constant criticism had taught her nothing about love, nothing about how a relationship between a mother and a daughter should be.

But could anyone teach that to another human being?

"Are you all right?" Bob Waters came and sat beside her. "You look worried."

"Not worried. Just thinking. I'm not used to it,"

she added with a little laugh. "We take so many things for granted, don't we?"

"You mean like life just going on? Are you thinking about Hank?"

"No, strangely enough, I'm not. I was thinking about Dallas. About mothers and daughters. I haven't been very good to Dallas since Hank died."

"She's very devoted to you."

"Maybe. But that's what we take for granted: that our children love us. They don't have to, do they?" She was studying Bob's face.

"Most children love their parents. But parents have to be wise in knowing what to accept. A parent has to help a kid break loose when the time comes."

Ellen knew he was choosing his words carefully, and she did not say anything. What was the use of trying to defend herself?

When the party started to break up, Ellen looked around for Dallas, but neither she nor Victor were in sight. She went to gather her mother to go home.

"Where's Dallas?" Mrs. Hendrix asked.

"I don't know. I guess she's gone off somewhere with Victor."

"What do you mean you don't know? She's your daughter. You should know where she is."

"Mother, come on. It's time for us to go home."

"You're not going to leave without Dallas!"

"She knows how to get home. Please, Mother, everyone is leaving. I'm tired, and I'm sure the

Waters are." Ellen turned to say good-bye to her friends and to kiss both Vi and Bob warmly. "It was a beautiful party. And," she whispered to Vi, "an extraordinary evening for me. I'll never forget it."

"Would you like me to drive you home since Dallas isn't here?" Andy offered. "I don't mind walking back."

"No, thank you, Andy. I can drive. No problem."

Andy had warned her too. In his half-insolent, teasing way, he had been telling her she was on the wrong track. She felt mortified that she had been attracted to him, had flirted with him. Andy was the last person she wanted to be with that night.

Ellen practically had to pull her mother away, still insisting indignantly that she could not understand her daughter going home without Dallas.

13

"It's nice to be here alone with you," Dallas said, looking across the table at Victor. They had slipped out of the Waters' house to get some air, and then, on the spur of the moment, decided to go for a ride and ended up at a coffeehouse.

"It's nice to be with you." Victor grinned. "I'm hungry."

"After all that food at your mother's!"

"That was a long time ago." He ordered a cheeseburger for himself and sodas for them both. Dallas insisted she was still full.

Dallas felt herself unwinding. "I don't think my mother enjoyed her party very much," she said.

"Your mother doesn't enjoy anything very much, does she? Has she said anything more about the trip? You've got to go."

"I don't see how I can." Dallas shook her head. "She'd figure out a way to come along."

"No way. You've got to level with her. Tell her that no one wants a mother to come. Not any mother. This problem has got to be settled once and for all. I'm marrying you, not you and your mother. Don't you see, honey, if you don't tell her now, it's only going to get worse."

"You think it's easy. . . ."

"I don't. Believe me. I think you're fantastic to have put up with what you have. All right, I know why you have, but at some point you'll become plain self-destructive, and that point is now. You've got to take a stand."

"Jen says that too. . . . I kept hoping the situation would work itself out, that she would see what she was doing. But I guess nothing is going to happen by itself." Dallas had been leaning against the back of the booth, but now she sat up straight. "I'm going to do it. I'm going to make the break."

Victor picked up her hand. "Now you're talking. Promise?"

"I'm not promising you. I'm promising myself."
She felt a surge of confidence. "I'm really going to
do it. I'll tell her."

They talked about other things, but Dallas's mind
kept going back to her mother. She was thinking
aloud when she said, "I didn't mind staying home
this year. I think my mother really did need me.
But I didn't figure on her taking me over so totally,
me and my friends—" She looked up at Victor and
laughed. "I guess I'm rehearsing what to say."

"You're doing okay. What are you so nervous
about?"

"I want to say what I have to say, but I don't
want to hurt her. It's funny, when I'm away from
her, I feel that I love her. Then when I'm with her,
I feel I can't stand her. Do your feelings ever change
that way?"

"I don't think about the family the way you do.
I guess having your father die made you think about
a lot of things you didn't before."

"It sure did. Like feeling responsible for my
mother. I never felt that before. I suppose that's part
of loving, but it can be a terrible burden."

"Loving you is easy," Victor said with a grin.

When Dallas looked at her watch, she was startled
to find it was almost midnight. "We'd better go.
My mother will be having a fit wondering where I
am."

They drove past Victor's house and saw that all

the cars were gone and that the house was almost dark. "My mother will be furious that we didn't get back before everyone left," Dallas said nervously. "She'll tell me I spoiled her birthday party."

"Don't worry about what she tells you. It's what you have to tell her that's important," Victor said, and stretched his hand out to squeeze hers.

Dallas was not surprised that all the lights were on in her house and, after she kissed Victor good-night and went inside, that both her mother and grandmother were waiting up for her.

"I'm sorry, Mom. I didn't realize it was so late." Dallas looked apologetically from one to the other.

"I should think you would be sorry," her grandmother said tartly. "Where in the world were you? Disappearing like that, and staying out until midnight."

"Vi knew I went out with Victor. We just started to go for a little air, and then he got hungry and we stopped and got to talking." Dallas gave her explanation breathlessly.

"Did you have a nice time?" her mother asked quietly. "I'm glad you have Victor. He's a good person."

"I don't think it was very good of him to take her off like that," Mrs. Hendrix said crossly. "From your party, Ellen."

"It was my party, not hers. You and Vi did a beautiful job, Dallas, and it was a lovely surprise. I really thank you." Her mother seemed preoccupied, and Dallas wondered what she was thinking. Mrs. Davis turned to her mother. "Why don't you go up to bed, Mother? I want to talk to Dallas for a bit."

Now the reaction would come, Dallas thought. Her mother would do her scolding in private.

"Hmmph," was all her grandmother replied, but she said good-night and went up the stairs to her bedroom.

Dallas sat down and watched her mother take off her earrings and shake out her hair. She didn't want to get into an argument, and she decided she had better speak her mind first, before her mother started to scold her for leaving the party. "I want to talk to you," Dallas said firmly. "I've made up my mind to go to California with the kids, but not if you come. I'm not going to baby-sit for you anymore. You've used me, you've used my friends, you've taken over my life until it's unbearable. I've got to lead my own life, and I hope you can lead yours. I can't replace Dad, and I don't want to try. Maybe you're going to hate me, to think I'm a terrible daughter, but I can't help it. I've stuck it out as long as I can, and now I've got to take a stand. You talk about being friends—I hope we *can* be friends— but you want to own me, and that's not love or friendship."

She stopped, breathless, her heart hammering. Dallas was afraid to look at her mother. When she did, her mother was curled up on the sofa, her shoes kicked off and her feet tucked under her. She looked young and vulnerable, the way she had the day in the hospital when Dallas's father had died.

Her mother spoke slowly. "I suppose I have this coming to me. What can I say? I'm not surprised. You've been trying to tell me this right along, but I didn't want to hear it. I haven't faced anything, Dallas. I haven't faced that Hank is dead, I haven't faced being alone. I've been putting everything off. I couldn't even buy a new bedspread. I'm glad you had the courage to come out with what you think. I probably never could."

"I'm sorry it has to be this way," Dallas said.

"Don't be sorry," her mother said fiercely. "Be glad that you're young and have a strong sense of life. I've been feeding on your strength and that's wrong. I have to find my own."

"Why don't you have Grandma come up to live with you?" Dallas asked.

Her mother shook her head. "No, I need to be alone. Maybe someday when my mother is too old to live by herself, I'll be able to take her on, but first I have to find my own way." Her mother looked at her thoughtfully. "It's funny, isn't it? I seem more the adolescent than you. I guess growing up has little to do with age." She cupped her chin in her hand. "Sometimes you know you're doing something wrong, but you keep on doing it, unable to stop. Many times I could actually hear myself saying things I knew I shouldn't have. I hope I can stop, Dallas, but people don't change overnight. All I can do is try."

"That's doing a lot. And you won't really be alone. I mean you're not getting rid of me altogether. Even if I go away to school in the fall, or when I get married, we'll always be mother and daughter."

Her mother laughed. "I guess you're stuck with that. Your father would be proud of you, Dallas. You're solid and strong. But that's enough for now, I'll make up the sofa for your bed."

"I'll help you." But first Dallas stopped and looked at her mother searchingly. "You're going to be okay, Mom, you will. And thank you, thank you, very much. I hope you had a good birthday."

"It turned out better than I thought it would," Ellen said.

But there was a sad, lonely look on her mother's face that Dallas knew would be a long time in fading. Yet Dallas was certain that she could not be the one to erase it. She could only hope that eventually the pain would diminish and that her mother would find her own way.

About the Author

Hila Colman was born and grew up in New York City, where she went to Calhoun School. After graduation, she attended Radcliffe College. Before she started writing for herself, she wrote publicity material and ran a book club. Her first story was sold to the *Saturday Evening Post,* and since then her stories and articles have appeared in many periodicals. Some have been dramatized for television. In 1957 she turned to writing books for teen-age girls. One of them, *The Girl From Puerto Rico,* was given a special citation by the Child Study Association of America.

Mrs. Colman lives in Bridgewater, Connecticut, and has two sons.